THE COWBOY FROM THE WILD HORSE DESERT

A story of the King Ranch

Bobby Cavazos

LARKSDALE

The Cowboy from the Wild Horse Desert
A Story of the King Ranch
Copyright © 2000 by Bobby Cavazos

———

———

Senior Editor -- Mary Margaret Williamson

Copy Editor -- Charlotte St. John

Technical Advisor -- Becky McCracken

Cover Graphics -- Richard Noriega

———

All pictures are reprinted by permission
from the Corpus Christi Caller Times.

Library of Congress Cataloging-in-Publication Data:

Cavazos, Bobby.
    The cowboy from the Wild Horse Desert : a story of the King
Ranch / Bobby Cavazos.
        p.   cm.
    ISBN 0-89896-453-9
    1. Cavazos, Lauro, d. 1958 Fiction. 2. King Ranch (Tex.) -- History
Fiction. I. Title.
    PS3553.A9654C69 1999   99-31453
    813 ' ' .54--dc21   CIP

LARKSDALE
Printed in the United States of America

DEDICATION

This book is dedicated to my friends, the Kineños, who rode with me on the Wild Horse Desert.

And to my children Clay, Douglas, Cathleen, and my grandchildren Justin, Christopher, and Victoria with all my love. Never forget where you came from. Be as proud of yourself as I am of you.

ACKNOWLEDGEMENTS

My thanks to Gwen Miers Phillips, and Jack Tichacek, whose work, help, and encouragement made this book possible.

And to my true friends, Foss and Becky McCracken; Donnie and Frannie Stewart; my brother, Joe A. Cavazos; and Sam Brown of Bandera, Texas.

PREFACE

The Working of a One Million Acre Cattle Ranch

I was born in a little white house on a hill on the King Ranch, located at the Santa Gertrudis Division Headquarters. My father, Lauro, worked on the King Ranch until his death in 1958. That was the saddest day of my life, for I loved and respected him as no other man. He was the best judge of men, and the best judge of cattle and horses I have ever known.

I would like to thank the many people who have encouraged me to write this book. It seems when people find out I was born on the King Ranch they always say I should write a book about it and all the stories I've heard and lived. I have taken their advice.

This book is historical fiction. Although most of the stories are true, it must be fiction when I put words in the mouths of the characters to describe the scenes. The history of the King Ranch and my family is very complicated and has been told many times by many authors.

Tom Lea's *THE KING RANCH*, Volume One and Volume Two, published by the King Ranch in 1957 is a magnificent work. It comes closest to telling the full history of the ranch and the Wild Horse Desert than any the other I have read.

THE KING RANCH, 100 years of ranching, sponsored and published by the Corpus Christi Caller Times in 1953, was a fine special edition in honor of the King Ranch Centennial.

ECHOES OF THE RIO GRANDE, by John R. Peavy, published by Springman-King in 1963, also contained a good account of events of that period. As good as it was, it was biased to the Anglo side of the story as told to him by D. P. Gay, the Immigration Officer. Gay was there, and he fought bravely in the Norias raid, but I got the real story from my father and from the old timers I worked with at the Santa Gertrudis Division, and later at the Laureles Division where I became foreman in later years.

Most of the books about the King Ranch are written from the Anglo perspective. My story reflects the Tejano side of the history and operation of the ranch. The description of working the cattle is detailed from my own personal experience and may be used by historians, researchers, and reviewers interested in the operation of the largest cattle ranch in the world. It is also an insight for youngsters who want to ''grow up to be cowboys.''

The love affair illustrates the difficulties that often arise when people of different racial descent live and work together.

Some of the words and phrases are South Texas colloquialism, and they differ in some parts of Texas and Mexico.

I hope you enjoy the work.

Until next time — Adios.

Bobby Cavazos

Illustrations:

Pictures:

TABLE OF CONTENTS

A publication of:

TRES B'S
31 Cherry Lane
Kerrville, Texas 78208

The Cowboy from the Wild Horse Desert

A Story of the King Ranch

Bobby Cavazos

1

THE COWBOY FROM SAN PERLITA

Laurel Ranch

Willacy County, Texas

1912

His name was Lauro Cavazos. He had a touch with horses very few men had and it was natural to him. He came from down near San Perlita, about forty miles north of Brownsville, Texas, where his father owned a small ranch.

Lauro started training horses when he was very young. When his father recognized the boy's natural abilities with horses, he allowed him to have his own way training the outlaw horses. The other ranchers would sell the horses to him cheap when they were unable to break them. A cowboy had to have a mount he could rely on. Working cattle was dangerous, and a cowboy didn't need to be worrying about a mount bucking. So Lauro, at age fourteen, started breaking the horses.

First, he would get the horse to trust him and not be afraid. He was patient with his horses and worked with them every day. At first, he would get close enough for the horse to become familiar with his smell. Once a horse knew Lauro, he'd approach it, talking softly, while extending an ear of corn. "Hello amigo, we are going to be good friends, you and I. I'll treat you right and reward you when you do the things I ask. But if you don't do the things I ask, I'll start over again and you'll waste my time and yours. You will make me proud of you when the big Patróns finally ride you and you will be proud of yourself as well.''

Lauro would talk to them in this manner, while he gave them their corn. Sometimes he would pour running water over a colt to gentle him. Then he was able to work with him.

Many of the two and three-year-old colts and fillies already had been taught to lead by the ranchers. One man would grab the colt while the other rubbed him down with a blanket or a flour sack until the colt got used to being handled by humans. That was an easy job.

Next came the hard part, the lifting of the feet. One man held the colt by a rope halter, while another would lift one foot at a time by grabbing the hoof at the ankle, and holding on until the colt stopped kicking. This went on until one could work on the horse's feet and not be kicked. All this time, the other man worked with the colt, rubbing him down and talking to him, teaching him to respond to the halter rope, to make him go forward, turn right or left, to stop, or whatever the cowboy wanted. Pretty soon, the colt could be led anywhere, would stop, and would allow his feet to be picked up, one by one. These things were essential for a cowboy to take proper care of his mount.

After the cowboy got a colt to this point he'd introduce the saddle blanket. He'd let the colt smell the blanket first, and begin to rub him down with it, even slapping him with it, until the colt allowed him put the saddle blanket on and not flinch or shy away.

He would do the same thing with the saddle, until the colt got used to it and let the cowboy put it on his back. Soon, the colt would stand quietly while the saddle was put on. Then the cinch was tightened with just a little pressure around his belly until the colt got used to it. At the same time with his left hand the cowboy held the halter. While doing this he had to keep a close hand on the colt and keep talking to him. When he was saddled, the colt was led around the pen while the cowboy kept an eye on him. If he tried to run or buck, the man had control of him.

Finally, the halter was taken off and the colt was led by a snaffle bit. Through all of this the colt was never allowed to buck. If he ever learned to buck he would never forget, and the job would be much tougher.

Many of the colts that Lauro's father bought, however, had learned to buck, and that's why he got them cheap. Still, with patience, Lauro was able to make the colts forget their nasty habits. Soon he had them eating out of his hand.

Once the three year old colts were fully trained they were ready to be sold. Most were sold into Mexico under contracts with the army.

Usually Vallejo Garcia, a working hand on the ranch, went with Lauro or his father on the trip. The year Lauro was eighteen, Vallejo broke his leg while chasing a steer and was unable to go along. Lauro's father had to stay and take care of things on the ranch which left Lauro to go alone to take the horses.

Lauro was all ready to go bright and early on the morning he was to start the journey. The older Cavazos brought a sack full of canned peaches, beef jerky, *pan de campo*, and a little bit of change from the kitchen to the pens where Lauro was waiting. His father looked at his son sitting in the saddle like a conquistador.

Lauro looked at his father with love in his heart and smiled. "Father, don't look so sad, I've made this trip before and have always come back with the money. I know what to do in case I run into bandidos. Run like hell and let them take the horses."

"You laugh," his father said. "But your life is worth more than all the horses in Texas, or in the world. And that is exactly what I have told you to do. Do not disobey me. Come back safely to us. Please, my son."

Lauro looked toward the kitchen door to see if his mother was watching them, but she was not there. He knew she was angry and upset at him for going alone to Mexico to sell the horses to the Mexican Army. However, they needed horses all the time and paid a good price.

"Please, Father, take care of Mama and tell her I love her, but I must go. General de la Cruz is expecting these horses to fulfill our contract. I'll be careful and be back before you and Mama even start to miss me."

"Go with God, my son, keep your eyes open for those bandidos." His father handed him the sack with the food, reached up and embraced him, and sent him on his way to the land of his ancestors.

Lauro's father went to the gate and opened it, moving along the fence of the corrals, just far enough to let the leader of the remuda see that the gate was open. As they ran toward the gate his father positioned himself just inside, counting the heads just one more time as they passed through to be sure they had them all. There were thirty. As the last one went out, he closed the gate and waved to his son to move on.

Lauro turned the herd south down the *Camino de los Bueys* toward Mexico, a road he knew well. When he was a small child he had been sent to his grandmother's house in Brownsville, to go to the school at the Mission there, the only school for miles around. He would catch the stagecoach in front of the house on the Camino de los Bueys. It went from San Antonio to Brownsville, Texas, every Monday and returned on Friday.

Lauro loved to go to Brownsville. It was an exciting place, the largest city in South Texas with its bustling port and entry to Mexico. It was a wild place with cantinas, girls, and music. Gunfights were common, and the Anglos still ruled the town. The Kings, of the King Ranch, were the power, being the largest ranchers in Texas. The Texas Rangers were the peace officers, along with the sheriff and his two deputies. Still, they couldn't be everywhere at once, so the town had a rough reputation, but it was as exciting as a town could be in those days.

Lauro headed the herd of horses down the road. He would make better time going down a road than across country, at least until he got close to the border. Then he had to head across country to dodge the bandidos and sometimes the Indians.

This was the first time he was responsible for something so valuable and important to his family. The trip meant money to pay for the staples, to pay Vallejo and the rest of the hands, and the taxes the county required everyone to pay. Lauro wondered if the Kings paid the same taxes on the land that they owned. He still believed that much of that land belonged to his family. It was from a Spanish Land Grant that Texas hadn't recognized. His great grandfather was forced to sell it, bit by bit to the Kings at a very cheap price, or else lose it all to taxes. It made him angry when he thought about it.

His people fought for Texas, too, but when the war was over, the educated Anglos pulled the slickest deals to get whatever they wanted. They forged deeds and took cattle and property that the Mexican people had owned for years. In those days, to kill a Mexican was nothing. Hatred and distrust were rampant on both sides. To be sure, there were good men who made Brownsville their home, men who tried to be fair and have law and justice prevail in the United States and Texas for everyone.

Lauro kept an eye open for bandidos and other unworthy looking hombres who might try to take his horses away from him. Vallejo used to tell him, *"Pela el ojo, pela el ojo"* -- always looking, always looking. That was the way to stay alive in this country.

Even so, Lauro didn't hear the stage come up behind him, with four outriders on either side, and four riders, behind the stage, all watching him closely. Finally, when he took notice, he nearly fell off his horse and started to grab his Colt revolver, but stopped just in time when he realized who it was.

The outriders were fully armed with the 30-30's and sidearms that were the Kineños trademark, and rode the finest horses that Lauro had ever seen. They wore wide Mexican sombreros and had bandeleros of spare cartridges running across their chests, and big knives on their hips. They wore Mexican-style chivarras, so they could move or run fast if needed. These were fighting men armed to the teeth.

The coach itself was a work of pure beauty, although it was a bit dusty from being on the road from the Ranch Headquarters in Kingsville, about seventy miles farther north. The coach was trimmed in white and brown, the Kings' colors. It could carry six passengers and two drivers and was pulled by six beautiful sorrel horses, the best that Lauro had seen.

The Caporal of the fighting men raised his hand in a gesture to slow the stage down but not to stop. "Hey, Chico," said the Caporal. "Get those bags of bones out of the way, or we will run right over them and you, too."

Lauro turned in the saddle with his hand on the Colt. "You do and you will have to answer to me, Lauro Cavazos, son of Nicolas Cavazos, owner of the Laurel Ranch and the real owner of the San Juan de Carricitos Land Grant, you fat son of a toad."

All the vaqueros doubled over with laughter. The Caporal sat there and stared at the young man who talked with such courage. "Who is this young man who dares talk to a Caporal of the Kings' outfit with so much authority in his voice? Well, the eagle has claws, but no wings to get out of the way," the Caporal said.

He started for his whip when a voice rang out. "Javiel, que paso?"

Robert Kleberg, Sr. stuck his head out of the coach. He was the manager of the Kings' Ranch, as well as the ranch lawyer. Perhaps, he was the most powerful man in Texas.

"This ragweed is trying to take up all the road with that bunch of mustangs. They look like they couldn't outrun a jackass with a load on its back," the Caporal said. All the outriders laughed.

Kleberg looked and saw an impressive young man on a better than average sorrel horse with a herd of equally good looking horses. The young man was slim with long legs and a long waist, broad shoulders and thick muscles that came from hard work. The coloring of his skin said he was no Mexican, but one of Spanish blood. He had a sharp nose and his eyes were gray. That gave him the look of the eagle, one who looked you in the eye and would apologize to no one, yet was fair in all things. Someone you'd like to know and call friend.

A very handsome boy, thought Kleberg. Kleberg looked at the outfit he wore. Brush jacket, chaps, spurs, boots, and an old Stetson hat with a sweat band woven with white and brown horsehair. He wore a khaki shirt buttoned at the collar and a pair of khaki pants.

"Good afternoon, young man. Where are you taking those mustangs?" Kleberg said. He spoke in English.

"To Brownsville to sell," the boy replied. "I'm taking them . . ."

At that moment a mustang decided to split and to go back to the ranch. Lauro saw the bay take off and in one split second was after him. Side by side they ran, but Lauro's mustang overtook the bay in a few quick strides and turned it back to the herd. Kleberg was impressed.

"Who trained your *caballo*?" he said.

"I did," the young cowboy told him.

"A very nice job. Come see me when you get back. I might have a job for you," Kleberg said. He waved at the Caporal to get the stage moving again.

The Caporal signaled the men to move out and looked at the boy with new respect. "You come and see us, chico, when you get back. I can always use good hands." He waved good-bye at the boy and moved out with the coach and riders.

"I just might do that, jefe." The coach passed him and he looked inside. There were plush satin seats and cushions with curtains on the windows. One curtain was pulled back by a small hand. The most beautiful face he had ever seen was looking straight into his eyes. The girl nodded slightly, a small smile on her lips, her beautiful blonde hair blowing softly in the wind. She released the curtain and sat back as the stage went past. Lauro kept staring, waving at the outriders.

"A prettier face you'll never see, but that's all, vaquero," one man warned him. "That's the Patrón's seventeen year old daughter, and she is not for the likes of you. Adios."

Lauro drove his remuda toward Rancho Viejo, where as a boy, he visited his grandmother. However, she had been forced to sell Rancho Viejo because of her health and move to Brownsville, closer to the only doctor for eighty miles. They had moved into the old part of Brownsville where she owned some land and a house.

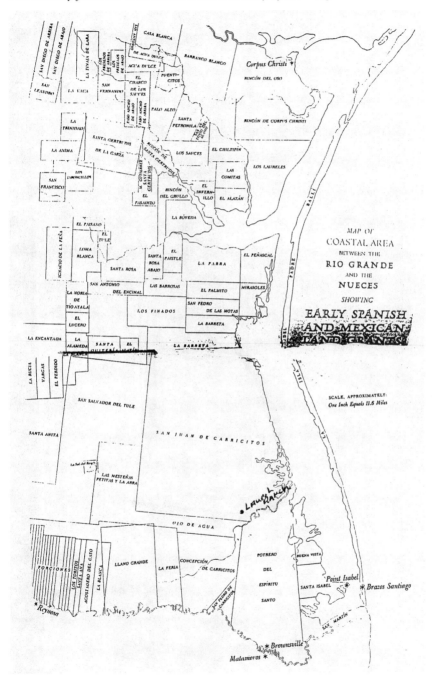

Map of COASTAL AREA between the RIO GRANDE and the NUECES
RIVERS showing EARLY SPANISH and MEXICAN LAND GRANTS.

Lauro loved to go visit his grandmother at Rancho Viejo. He would hunt there and had become an excellent shot with both the rifle and pistol, one of the best around. He remembered Vallejo's words, "Anyone can draw a pistol fast, but to hit your target takes a steady hand and eye. He remembered how he and Vallejo would set up a camp near the reseca when the Rio Grande overflowed. They would watch the thousands of birds that went there to drink late in the afternoon. All types of waterbirds made their permanent home at the reseca. The great blue heron, the many types of ibis, roseate spoonbill, ducks of all kinds, and geese by the thousands. He loved to watch the small water birds stick their long bills into the mud looking for food. It was a time of plenty.

Lauro learned many things on those trips. He learned to trap many animals such as bobcats, raccoons, and coyotes for their fur. But his favorite time was when they would sit around the campfire and talk about the old times. His father would tell about the times when he was a boy living on his grandfather's hacienda and about the servants and the fiestas and the food. He would talk about the hunts they used to make and how they could ride from sunrise to sunset and never get off the San Juan de Carricitos Land Grant. They would get up at dawn and ride again until sunset and still be on their land. It was a beautiful time, and he would see that far away look in his father's eyes, longing for those times again.

Lauro pushed the remuda across the dry creek that went into the reseca. He cursed the farmers who plowed the land and changed the flow of the water. That was why the resacas were drying up. Some of the birds were still there, but not like they had been at one time.

Lauro made it to Brownsville just as the sun was beginning to set. He pushed the herd around the outside of town, hoping not too many people would see him. He was driving a large bunch of horses that thieves would love to get their hands on. He headed toward the railroad tracks and the shipping pens. Moving ahead of the herd, he opened the gate to the pens and raced back into position to move the remuda in through the gate. Once they were in the pens, Lauro looked for Mr. Carter, the foreman for the railroad. He found him just leaving his office.

"Howdy, Mr. Carter, how are you?"

"Well, if it isn't my favorite horse trainer; how are you, Larry? What you got, another bunch of southbound horses?"

Lauro smiled. "That's for me to know and you to ponder on, Mr.

Carter. How's that kid's pony I gave you doing?'' Lauro had given Mr. Carter a pony for his young son.

"Say, Larry, let me tell you, that's the best pony I've ever seen. That kid just loves to ride Bogger. That's what Johnny named him, you know. I sure appreciate you giving him to me.''

"I'm glad he's enjoying him. The moment I saw it I thought of Johnny,'' Lauro said. "Say, Mr. Carter, is it all right if I leave my horses in the shipping pens?'' He knew it would be okay, but Lauro always asked first.

"Sure. You put this lock on the chain, and I'll watch them for you. And Larry, go into town and have a meal on me. Just tell them to put it on my account.''

"Thanks, Mr. Carter,'' Lauro said smiling. "You're a good friend.''

"Don't even mention it, I'll see you later,'' Carter said.

Lauro took the lock and went back to the pen where he had left the horses. He tied Lobo to the fence before he moved inside the pens to knock open a couple of bales of hay and spread them around for the horses, making sure they had plenty of water in the trough.

"Rest my beauties, for tomorrow we have many miles to travel.''

It had grown dark by then and Lauro was in the middle of the horses. The night carried voices very easily, and what he heard made the hair on his neck stand up.

"We'll wait till late and then get the girl from her room by the way of the upstairs balcony and slip out nice and easy. We'll take her across the river into Mexico. Then we'll tell those Kings if they want their granddaughter back they better come through with the money we ask for.''

"How much are we gonna ask for?'' another voice said.

"Yes, how much are we going to ask for?'' a third man said.

"Plenty,'' the first man said. "Kleberg will give any amount to save his daughter.''

Lauro couldn't see the men. They were in the alley by the tracks. They drifted away from the pens, and Lauro moved slowly under the boards. At that point, he began to run toward the hotel down Main Street.

Miller's Hotel was one of the most elegant hotels in the country, built to house important guests and dignitaries. Cowboys didn't stay there because it cost too much. They went further down the street to the barrio. Of course, the Kings stayed at Miller's because they owned part of the hotel along with their share of the railroad. The Kings kept a floor for their exclusive use whenever they were in town.

Lauro hurried into the hotel and looked around the spacious lobby with the big winding stairway and all the elaborate curtains and paintings and furniture. Lauro had never seen it before. He stood there wondering where to go next when he heard a voice he recognized. It was the Caporal from the Kings' outriders with the stagecoach.

"Well, chico, what are you doing here? You are in the wrong place. The Patrón told you to come to the ranch at Kingsville when you got through with your horse trading."

"I need to see the Patrón right away," Lauro said.

"Well, you cannot see him. The Patrón is having dinner and can't be bothered by the likes of you. Now move along before I toss you out on your head, *cabron.* Now, MOVE," the Caporal said.

As the Caporal moved toward him, Lauro pulled his gun. "I must see the Patrón. It's very urgent," he said.

The Caporal stood there with his mouth open. Never had he seen such speed with a gun. "Well, since you put it that way, he's in the dining room. Follow me, but put that thing away. I'll take you to him."

Lauro put the gun in his holster and followed into the dining room. He felt that everyone in the room was staring at his brush jacket, his chaps, and the gun on his hip.

Lauro saw the Patrón at the far table. Kleberg was sitting with about twelve people enjoying wine and food. Everyone was drinking, eating, and talking all at once, that is, everyone except the girl. She sat quietly next to her father and looked with lowered eyes at the handsome cowboy who had stormed into dining room with the Caporal.

"Well, what have we here?" Kleberg said. "Already looking for a job? See me at the ranch, chico."

"My name is not chico and I'm not looking for a job. But if you value your daughter's life, you better listen to me."

Kleberg choked on his wine and jumped to his feet. "What are you talking about?"

"He insisted on seeing you," the Caporal said. "I think we better listen to him."

"Very well, but not in front of my guests. Let's go into the lobby," Kleberg said. They stopped where Kleberg could still keep his eyes on his daughter, even though the Caporal had signaled two men to watch her closely.

"Now young man, this better be good. What is so urgent?"

Kleberg demanded.

Lauro looked him straight in the eyes. "I overhead three men talking about kidnapping your daughter, Mr. Kleberg."

"What did you say?" Kleberg said. "Three men were talking about my daughter?"

Just then Mr. Carter walked up. "I can vouch for this kid. He's a good boy, and I'd trust anything he told me and with anything I had."

"Well, that's one for your side, whatever your name is. Now, tell me from the beginning what you heard," Kleberg said.

"My name is Lauro Cavazos, and I heard three men talking down by the railroad pens. They were going to get your daughter and take her to Mexico and demand money from you. I couldn't see their faces, but they were gringos and cowboys, judging by the way their spurs rang," Lauro said.

"Javiel," Kleberg said to the Caporal. "Get the men together. Don't take your eyes off of Reina. Go to the room and wait there for me. Don't leave that room for a minute."

The Caporal gave a signal, and they brought Reina out of the dining room.

"What's the matter, Daddy?" she said. Never had Lauro seen eyes so blue or a face so like an angel's.

"Nothing, honey, but I want you to go with Javiel and the men to your room and stay there with Donna Maria till I get there," Kleberg said. "Go on now. And Javiel, tell Donna Maria that I will hold her and you personally responsible for Reina's safety. NOW GO!"

"Don't worry Patrón, I'll guard her with my life," the Caporal said.

Javiel followed the girl up the stairs without looking to see if his men were following. Kleberg's eyes followed Reina all the way. Then he turned to Lauro. "Young man, thank you, but I have just one more request to make. I don't want you to mention anything to anyone about what you heard. Promise me. I want to take care of this myself."

Lauro nodded. "Aren't you going to tell the Rangers?"

"No," Kleberg said. "I want to handle this."

"You're taking a big chance with your daughter's life, Mr. Kleberg. I'd never do that."

Kleberg was taken back a little by Lauro's boldness. "I want to teach this scum a lesson so no one will ever want to harm anyone from the King family again."

"Very well, sir," Lauro said. He started out the door.

"Lauro, wait." Kleberg started to reach into his pocket for his money. Lauro put up his hand.

"No, I didn't do it for the money. I did it because it was the right thing to do to protect a girl's life." He turned and walked out before Kleberg could say any more. Kleberg looked after the boy with his mouth open. After a moment, he turned toward the dining room and spoke to Carter. "That's quite a young man."

"Yes, he is," Mr. Carter agreed. They went into the dining room.

Kleberg addressed himself to his guests. "Sorry folks, but something came up. You'll have to carry on without me. I hope you'll forgive me. Just go ahead and enjoy yourselves. I'll see you tomorrow at the bank meeting." He waved at the guests and went upstairs, smoking a cigar. He began planning what he was going to do to the men who threatened his family's welfare.

Lauro went to Mother's Cafe, a restaurant down the street that made the best chili that side of the Rio Grande. Mama Garcia, the owner, was a friend of his family. When he came in, she let out a shriek and rushed around the counter and grabbed Lauro in a bear hug.

"O, lindo muchacho, where have you been? How are your mother and father, your brother and sisters?" She was a large, tall woman with abundant breasts and hair that was red and unruly. "Here, sit and tell me. How goes everything? What's new in San Perlita? Who was born and who died? Tell me all the news. Oh, but how thoughtless of me. You must be starved. I'll fix you a big steak while you talk to me."

Lauro spent the evening talking to Mama Garcia at Mother's Cafe. When he finally left, he had to loosen his belt. Mama Garcia had fed him too much, as she always tried to do.

Outside the cafe, Lauro stopped and looked up and down the street. It was deserted, although a few horses were tied in front of the saloon. The stores had long ago closed their doors. Most people had gone to bed. The cantinas were the only things left open. Since he was the last customer at Mother's Cafe, it also had closed. Lauro headed toward the hotel, stopped in a dark doorway where he could observe without being seen. He had a good view of the hotel, but didn't know which room the girl occupied. He sat and waited.

Lauro figured it must have been about two o'clock in the morning when he saw a shadow move toward the hotel. Then he saw another, and it looked like it was carrying something. It was a ladder, and there were four men instead of three, as he had thought. Slowly, Lauro rose from his position and followed them down the street, slipping from door to door until they got to the hotel. Lauro waited. He wanted to see what Kleberg was planning for the outlaws. And he wanted to be in position to help, if help was needed.

The bandits put the ladder against the hotel wall. It reached all the way to the balcony. Two of the men went up and over the balcony guard rail. The first man bent over as he headed toward an open window. When he got to the window, he straightened up and started to go in. He stopped and grabbed his throat. There was a slick *cuchillo* sticking out of his neck. The other man got to the ladder before a shot rang out, hitting him squarely in the back. He had no chance to cry out before he fell backward over the rail, landing at the feet of the two men below.

These two wasted no time heading for their horses. The leader of the band jumped on his mount, turned, and headed up the street. Lauro came out of the doorway, stepped off the porch, and tripped on the second step. The outlaw looked right at him and fired a quick shot. Lauro had rolled when he hit the ground and didn't get a chance to fire his weapon. The bandit had fled by the time he recovered. But Lauro had a good look at him before he got away.

Then he turned his attention to the other man, who was cut down by the Kings' men. He yelled at them, "Don't shoot. It's me, Lauro."

"Don't kill him, he's a friend," the Caporal said.

Lamps began to appear all over town, and people came out to see what was going on. The Rangers ran out half-clothed. Other people came out in their night shirts, the women with wraps on, looking frightened and bewildered. A crowd gathered quickly around the three bodies, staring as if they had never seen a dead person before.

Kleberg came out of the hotel just as the Rangers came toward it.

"Mr. Kleberg, are you okay? Why did you kill them?" said Captain Ransom. Captain Henry Ransom was the commanding officer of the Texas Rangers station in Brownsville.

"They were trying to kidnap my daughter, but thanks to this young man, we set a trap for them. One got away," Mr. Kleberg said.

Captain Ransom looked at Lauro with a shake of his head. "You were lucky, son. That bandit took a quick shot at you but missed. Who are they anyway, does anyone know?" The crowd was still gathered around looking at the bodies.

"I have seen this one around town, just a bum looking for a handout," Mr. Carter said.

No one knew the others. "I got a good look at the one that got away. He had a scar across his face from here to here," Lauro said, indicating with his finger from the forehead to the throat. "He wasn't a handsome man."

"Does anyone know the fellow this lad is describing?" the Ranger asked. When no one said anything, he continued. "We'll put wanted posters all over the country, but I'm afraid he'll be across the border by then. He'll head to the badlands of Mexico where he can live with the rest of the outlaws.

"You men get that wagon and help clear this trash out of here. Take them to the undertaker. I'm surprised he's not here yet." No sooner did he quit talking than they heard a wagon coming.

The undertaker had taken time to hitch his team to the wagon. He came to a stop right near the crowd. "Who we got this time? Rangers? Oh, Mr. Kleberg, I didn't see you there. Well, who's going to pay for the burial?"

"Give them the cheapest burial you can, and I'll pay," Kleberg said. "Though they don't deserve a decent burial. Now, where's that boy? I want to thank him again."

The boy was nowhere to be found. The sun was beginning to break over the horizon. Lauro was back at the pens, putting his saddle on Lobo, his pony, and tieing his bedroll and slicker on the back of the saddle. He led Lobo to the gate where the horses were. He opened it, mounted, and slowly let the horses out of the pens. He let them graze a while, then started them toward the Rio Grande and Mexico.

Lauro looked at the Rio Grande. It was bigger than the Nueces River which he had crossed many times with his father. He had also crossed the Rio Grande, but he always had a strange feeling before crossing any river. He never knew what might happen.

2

MEXICO

Lauro let the remuda graze while he took off his clothes, everything but his hat. He rolled them into a bundle and held them high above his head. He drove the herd of horses into the river and started toward the Mexican shore, holding to the saddle with one hand until his horse started swimming. Then he slipped out of the saddle, back over the rump of the horse to the tail and held on for dear life. The sun was shining off the horses' backs, manes, and tails, and the boy was hollering like a crazy man. "Vamanos, Brutos! Let's go to your new home. Vamanos."

The water was cool and felt good on Lauro's skin. He held on until the horses were almost across, then he slipped back into the saddle, grabbed the reins and pulled to a stop. He knew they were safely on the Mexican side. The horses started grazing, so Lauro let Lobo graze also, while he got out some soap. He then shaved, took a bath, and brushed his teeth with baking soda he kept in a can. Lauro had been taught like his brother and sisters that cleanliness was next to godliness.

Lauro took a can of peaches and a sack of coffee and a small coffee pot out of the sack that his father had given him. After building a small fire he made the coffee, felt in the sack and found some beef jerky, and put some in his mouth to soften. He stared into the fire and thought about the Klebergs and the girl. She was the most beautiful woman he had ever seen. He hoped that all the confusion had not scared her too much.

Maybe when he got back, he would take the job that Kleberg had proposed. Then he thought maybe they had forgotten all about the job offer. He knew he could make some money working for the King

Ranch, since his brother was getting old enough to take his place at home. It was time for him to see the rest of the world, maybe even join with the trail drives to Kansas, although those days were about over because of the railroad being built to Kansas and New Orleans. Maybe he would get to see the yellow-haired girl again.

Lauro put the fire out with the remaining coffee, packed his things, and caught Lobo. Mounting, he looked to see where the remuda was and began to drive the horses farther south through the city of Matamoros. He didn't want too many people to see him with the herd, so he tried to miss the main part of town. Matamoros was the biggest Mexican town on the border, a very old and beautiful city.

Lauro came to the frontera, the imaginary line that was the frontier of civilization, the beginning of the Llano Colorado, the most desolate wasteland on God's earth. It was the land of the Apache. Lauro knew that he had to keep a look-out at all times for Apache signs. He was just forty miles from the fort, and he didn't want to take any chances.

He would travel at night. His father taught him to choose the right star and follow it. He wouldn't travel during the day because of the heat. That many horses would make too much dust and could be seen by the Apache. They didn't miss any sign cut by a stranger.

He picked a shady spot of overhang rock and waited for the sunset. He let the horses browse, but kept the only water in a big canteen with him so the horses wouldn't stray too far. Lauro kept watch, smoking his Bull Durham and thinking. Finally, dusk came and the horses started looking for water and returned to his camp.

Lauro poured the water in a dished out rock he found, probably used by an Apache for the very same thing. With the remuda all watered, Lauro took a drink and ate a bit of the *carne seca*. He mounted, took one more look around, and started to Fort San Miguel. He kept moving with the stars. It was cooler than during the day, so he put on another shirt and his brush jacket.

Two days later, he came to Fort San Miguel. He hollered his name at the guard who let him enter the stockade. The soldados came out of their barracks to watch the horses being put in the corral.

"Buenos dias, chico," one of the men said.

"Buenos dias. *Como amancistes? Está el Coronel?*" Lauro said.

"Yes, the Coronel is in his office by now. No doubt he will be with you in a minute, he was expecting you. Oh, here he comes now," the soldier said.

The Coronel was a short, fat man with a round face and a short nose. "Buenos dias, Lauro. It's a good thing you showed up. I just about gave up on you. Where is Vallejo? I don't see him with you?"

"No, he's back at the ranch. He broke his leg roping a steer. It was a wreck, but he'll be all right. He was worried about my coming alone, but as we had made the trip many times, I convinced him that I'd be able to do the job, and here I am with the caballos."

Lauro looked around the fort. "Where are all your men? It looks empty."

"Oh, we had some trouble over by Helotes, and I sent half my men over with Captain Longoria to see what damage the Apaches had done," el Coronel said.

These raids were always happening, and the Apache were great tacticians. By raiding one village, then another, they confused the Army so that they had no way of knowing where the Indians were going to hit next. They usually hit where the village wasn't strong with soldiers, guns, and cannons. They stayed away from Fort San Miguel. It was too strong and the Army was very near. San Miguel prospered and grew.

By all standards, it was a growing town. There was a blacksmith shop, a mercantile, a doctor, a saddle shop, blanket weavers, five cantinas, and a church. The civilian population was over two hundred people, not counting the farmers who came to sell their produce to the Army. They sold chickens, eggs, corn, dried pinto beans, meal for tortillas, goat cheese, and goat milk. The peons also bartered with their produce. Lauro liked the busy little village.

"Well, let's see what you got my friend," the Coronel said. His practiced eye looked over the remuda. He climbed into the pen and started toward a canelo filly that caught his eye. It was very important that a soldier's mount had good manners. He didn't want his men to worry about their horses when they were trying to stay alive in battle.

Coronel Filipe Garza Garcia took care of his troops. Many officers didn't, and that was why they weren't so successful chasing the Apache or bandidos. His men knew it and did a better job than other troops. He walked around the canelo and stopped behind the horse's rump. He stepped forward, close to the horse, so the animal couldn't kick him. The canelo didn't flinch.

The Coronel reached up and grabbed the strawberry roan's tail and began feeling for knots. That was one way to tell if the roan had good manners and had been trained right. He turned loose of the tail, moved to the roan's shoulder and picked up it's foreleg, as a farrier would nail the horseshoes in place, or check the condition of the horses' hooves.

He did this with all four feet without even putting a rope on the roan. The animal just stood there the way a properly trained horse should. Garcia did this to several horses. "Well, chico, I see that these horses are going to cost me top price." He examined the teeth of several more horses. They were all in excellent shape. "If you can't sell a man as good a horse as you would ride, don't sell it to him," Lauro's father would always say.

The Coronel turned to his sergeant. "Put a saddle on that one," he said, pointing toward an Alazan horse. He turned to Lauro. "Okay, my friend, let's see what that one can do." Lauro took the reins from the sergeant, adjusted the stirrups and mounted the sorrel. He put the sorrel through the same paces the whole herd had been put through before.

Lauro looked outstanding in the saddle. The Coronel loved to watch him. Lauro would start with the figure eight, then ride down the fence and turn on a dime, going back in the opposite direction. He would come to a standstill, then all of a sudden take off again, coming to a halt and backing up in a perfectly straight line the full width of the corral. The troops watching erupted into cheers, clapping, waving hats, and slapping backs. Some of them had never seen such horsemanship by a boy.

Many tongues would wag over tequila that night and for days to come. The Coronel shook the sergeant's hand like he had ridden the alazan and slapped him on the back. "Did you see that boy? How I wish I had a son like that."

Lauro dismounted and handed the reins to the sergeant, pulling his hat down over his eyes and smiling. "Well, Coronel, do we have a deal?"

"Lauro, that was magnificent! What a show you put on for the troops. Magnificent!" He slapped Lauro on the back. "I'll give you top price for the whole bunch."

Lauro's smile got bigger. "In gold, Coronel, in gold!"

"In gold, my friend, in gold," the Coronel said.

After they settled up, Lauro asked the Coronel if he could leave the gold in the fort safe for the night. "Of course you can. Then we will go to the Las Palmas and drink a tequila or two to cement the deal."

"Just let me clean up a bit first," Lauro said.

"Of course, you can use my quarters. I have a tub you can use. I will tell the sergeant to bring some water from the well. Hurry now, it is almost supper time."

Lauro took his bath, changed clothes, and combed his black curly hair. Being a boy, he hardly noticed how handsome he was. He was pleased the Coronel had given him top price for the horses, sixty dollars a head, in gold. He was taking almost two thousand dollars back to the Laurel Ranch. His father would be very pleased.

He heard a knock on the door. He turned, and there was a very pretty young girl with a basket in her arms. She had raven black hair, big brown eyes and a face that would turn any man's head. "Pardón Señor, but the Coronel said for me to pick up any dirty clothes you had to wash."

"Oh, that's all right," Lauro said. "I'll wash them later."

"Oh no, señor. I will lose my job if the Coronel finds that I didn't do as he ordered."

Lauro went to his pack and got his dirty clothes and put them in the basket. "Thank you, señor. I will have them back in the morning."

"Please do. I'm leaving very early and thank you. What is your name? I have never seen you before," Lauro said.

"My name is Teresa Montalvo," the girl said. She curtsied gracefully.

"My name is Lauro Cavazos. I'm from the Laurel Ranch in Texas."

"I know who you are, Señor. Everyone is talking about the Tejano who trains the new horses. They say they are the best horses ever to come here," Teresa said.

"Well, thank you, but my father taught me, and I just added a few tricks of my own. Do you live in town?" Lauro asked.

"Yes, we have a casita down in the barrio," she said. "Perhaps the Señor would like for me to come back later and see if he needs anything?" She gave a smile that promised more to come.

"Well, yes, I'll see you later," Lauro said.

"I'll be back." Before Lauro could say anything else she was gone.

Lauro strolled down the street. The outside of the Las Palmas cantina was made of mud stucco. It had a mesquite log roof, thatched with palm and anything else that would keep out the rain. Inside, it had a dirt floor and some old tables and chairs. A bar took up most of the wall. Full length mirrors were turned sideways behind the bar with all kinds of liquor bottles.

There were three mariachis in one corner drinking and playing their guitars and singing love ballads about a woman who did a man wrong. It was nice and cool in the cantina. The dirt floor was kept moist and the big windows opened sideways.

The Coronel was seated with one of the girls who worked there perched saucily on his knee. He smiled when he saw Lauro come in the door. "Welcome, my friend. Welcome. Come sit down and listen to the music. Bartender, bring my friend a tequila," the Coronel said.

"No, thank you, jefe. I'll have a beer instead," Lauro said.

"Okay. Whatever you want." They ordered a tequila and a beer, which was kept cool in the well behind the cantina. The hours passed in talk about women, horses, work, and weather. "Well jefe, salud," Lauro said as he raised his beer in a toast to the Coronel's health. The Coronel returned the gesture with his glass raised.

"Tell me, Coronel, have the bandidos and the Indians been active this year?"

The Coronel replied, "Not as bad as you might think. Well anyhow, los Indios have not. There are two bands of bandidos that have given us all trouble. You must be careful going to Tejas. If they knew you carried all that gold, they would have your head." The Coronel raised his tequila and drank it down.

Finally, they ate *cabrito al carbon*. It was like veal, but with more flavor. The cabrito was salted and peppered, rubbed with garlic and chilis and then covered with a light coating of lard. Lauro enjoyed that more than anything he could think of, except beef. With *frijoles, arroz,* guacamole, and freshly made corn tortillas, it was a meal fit for a king. Lauro ate until he had to loosen his belt.

"Another round, my friend, on me," Lauro said. "Camarero, that was delicious. I've eaten cabrito only once that was as delicious as yours. That is the cabrito my mother cooks." The bartender, who was also the owner, smiled.

The Coronel was rather drunk, and with all that food, he was very sleepy. "Well, my friend, it's time to go to bed. I think I'll sleep over here with my Rosita to rub my back. See you in the morning. Go ahead and listen to the mariachis and sleep in my quarters. I'll wake you in the morning so you can get an early start," the Coronel said. He walked with his arm around Rosita as she guided him toward her room.

Lauro sat there for another hour listening to the music of the mariachis. They told of life and death, loves long gone, and great deeds of heroes of the people.

Finally, Lauro moved to pay his bill, but the proprietor waved his hand. "No, señor. It was a privilege to have served you, such a great horseman as you. It is an honor that I can tell my children for years to come."

Lauro thanked him and started to the door, weaving a bit. To refuse the man's generosity would have been an insult. He staggered out the door. There were very few lamp lights showing down the street --just those shining through the shaded windows. Lauro moved from one to the other, light to dark. When he was halfway down the street, he felt the whisper of death graze him on the neck and spin him around. He hit the ground, drawing his pistol, not knowing where the shot had come from. He rolled into the dark and lay still.

No one came out to see what had happened. Lauro lay there and tried to see if something moved. After a short while, he heard a horse galloping away. He rose slowly, feeling his neck. It was only a scratch, but it was bleeding. He moved to the shaded light and looked at the blood in his hand. "That was how close I came to dying," he thought. He kept out of the light all the way back to the fort.

He was challenged by the guard. "It's only me, soldier. Didn't you hear that shot?" Lauro asked.

"Si, señor, but that happens all the time. Some drunk vaquero will fire a shot, or someone shoots at the coyote in his chicken pen. We don't get excited about a shot. Señor! You're bleeding. I'll get the doctor."

"No, never mind, it's just a scratch. I'll take care of it," Lauro said. He made his way to the Coronel's hut. He thought he saw a shadow move across the window. He drew his pistol and moved like a cat toward the door. He opened it with a quick push and went inside. Pistol ready, he looked around the room. All he saw was one beautiful, scared girl by the bed. Teresa had her arms across her breast, with one hand at her mouth ready to scream.

"Teresa. What are you doing here?" Lauro said.

"I thought you wanted me to come back tonight, so I told the guard that I had to take your clothes to you because you were leaving early in the morning. You weren't here, so I waited." She saw his neck and the blood. "Oh, Lauro, you're bleeding." She rushed to him and softly felt along his neck.

"Someone evidently doesn't like me," Lauro said.

"Sit down on the bed, and I will make it stop bleeding," she said. He sat down, and she rushed to the wash basin with towels and the pitcher for water. She took the towel and wet it, bringing the pitcher with the water. Kneeling by the bed, she began to clean the scratch, touching the wound very lightly. "Does that hurt?" she asked with great concern.

"No. Not much," he said, looking into her eyes.

She cleaned the wound and then looked up at the ceiling. "There's one!" she said. She stood on a chair in the corner of the room, and pulled down a spider web. Gently, she pressed the web into the wound. "That will stop the bleeding and you'll be well in no time," she said.

"Thank you. You have been very kind. I'm glad you're here," Lauro said.

She looked into his eyes. "Oh Lauro, I would do anything for you." She took his head in her hands and kissed him. It was a long slow kiss, because she knew that this was his first time. She slowly began to take off his shirt. Her fingers were warm and gentle as she removed it. Her touch lingered on his muscled shoulders, then down his arms. They kissed again slowly at first, then with a passion that Lauro had never felt. He pulled her closer. She pulled back and removed her blouse. She wore nothing underneath and guided him down to her cinnamon tipped breast. He had never seen, or felt anything as soft and wonderful in his life. He started kissing each breast and breathing hard with passion. They pulled apart and took off the rest of her clothes. Slowly she guided him into making love.

When Lauro awoke, he reached over to find Teresa was gone. He rose and looked around the cottage. She was nowhere to be found. The things he remembered from last night made him blush and brought a smile to his lips. He touched his lips and thought of the curves of her body. He could hardly wait to take her in his arms again. He would ask her to go to Texas with him.

Lauro heard a knock on the door and went to open it. The sergeant was standing there with a man behind him holding a tub filled with water.

"Buenos dias, Lauro. *Como amancistes?*" the sergeant said with a smile on his lips, knowing what had happened the previous night.

"*Con salud,* Sergeant, where is the Coronel? Is he up yet?" Lauro asked.

"Why, of course. He is waiting to have breakfast with you. I brought water for your bath."

"Thank you, I'll hurry just as fast as I can," Lauro said.

When Lauro appeared at the mess tent, the Coronel was drinking coffee sweetened with goat's milk and sugar. "Buenos dias, Lauro. *Como amancistes?*" the Coronel said.

"Muy bien, gracias, usted?"

"Muy bien," the Coronel replied.

Lauro sipped his coffee. He knew not to say anything, as was the custom, until the Coronel was ready to start talking. At last, after his second cup of coffee, the Coronel spoke. "Well, chico, you out rode my men, you out drank my men, you sang the songs like a nightingale, and you stole my mistress. What do you have to say for yourself?"

Lauro brought the cup of coffee down from his lips, surprise on his face. "I didn't know, mi Coronel."

The Coronel laughed and looked down his stubby nose at Lauro. "Well, it was all right, being I didn't need her services last night. I, myself, was preoccupied. So I told her to spend the night with you." He slapped Lauro's leg. "Did you have a good time, my friend?"

Lauro looked in his coffee cup, took a sip, and composed himself. "Yes, jefe. Everyone had a good time." Lauro was broken hearted. He had given his heart to a whore and didn't even know it. She probably was laughing her head off. Lauro had a lot to learn about women.

"Well, what time are you going to leave, so I can give you your money?" the Coronel said.

"As soon as I finish my breakfast," Lauro said. He ate a good breakfast of *carne guisada*, fresh made flour tortillas and beans with lots of *chile petins*. When he finished, he went to the stables and saddled Lobo, who nuzzled his hand as he put the bridle in his mouth. Lauro looked at him and put his head against Lobo's neck. "I thought she loved me. She said so last night. What went wrong? I don't understand how she could say those things, make love to me and belong to someone else. I just don't understand." He patted Lobo on the neck, put the reins on him and mounted. He headed toward the Coronel's office.

3

SCARFACE

"Well, my friend," the Coronel said. He handed Lauro the gold coins in a belt.

Lauro accepted the belt, counted each coin and put the belt around his waist under his shirt. "Thanks, Coronel, for buying the remuda; I hope they will do whatever you ask of them."

"I'm sure they will. These are the last of the contracts. I'm afraid there will be no more."

Lauro was taken by surprise and looked at him with his mouth open. "What do you mean, there will be no other contracts?"

"No, my friend, I have orders, and we will no longer buy our horses from the Americano. I don't know why, but we will regret it, I can tell you that. Now, sign the bill of sale so that you can be on your way. Vaya con dios, my son. I hope we will meet again."

"I will miss you, Coronel," Lauro said. "I don't know what to say. Vaya con dios." He signed the bill of sale.

Lauro picked up the papers, took his copy, and handed the other to the Coronel. After shaking hands, Lauro headed toward the door and waved good-bye. He mounted Lobo and headed for the fort gate and down Main Street. There was hardly anyone on the street that early in the morning.

Looking down the road, Lauro didn't notice Teresa pull the curtain back in her window. She followed him with her eyes all the way down the street until he was out of sight. "Good-bye, my love. My love will always be with you. Our love could never be. Go with God. May he always protect you." A tear ran down her cheek.

Lauro rode across the hot desert. When the sun was almost straight above, he found an overhang of rocks and took the saddle off Lobo. He gave him water in his hat and oats to keep him close by. He leaned against a rock and looked out across the desert.

At noon there was nothing moving in the desert. If it did move, it was crazy. It was the hottest time to be out in the Llano Colorado. A green desert lizard crawled slowly across a rock in the shade where Lauro rested. He watched Lauro with one eye while the other watched where he was going. Lauro saw the lizard and marveled that it could live out there without water. It must know something nobody else knew.

Lauro never took his sight off the horizon, checking for any movement out in the desert. He was always watching, always alert for anything that might move. He was thinking about Teresa and why she didn't tell him she was the Coronel's whore. All of a sudden, he saw a wispy cloud of dust rise on the horizon, and he knew what it was.

Lauro saddled Lobo and moved back to the rocks, well hidden. In the outcrop of rocks, he pulled back until he could watch the lizard again. He had wiped out his tracks when he first got there, and the hot wind would wipe out the rest of his tracks along the trail.

After about an hour, Lauro decided they had gone the other way. The lizard scampered to a different part of the rocky desert floor, but Lauro didn't move. He put his hand over Lobo's nose to keep him from whinnying, drew his pistol, and waited. He heard the ringing of Mexican spurs with the flatter sound of Texan spurs. The jingle of the curbs of the bits and other sounds that told him it was a bunch of bandidos looking for someone.

He could smell horse sweat and unclean bodies. "He ought to be somewhere about here. I don't know how I could have missed him the other night," a voice said. It was a voice Lauro recognized.

"Well, you did, and it's a good thing, too. We wouldn't have been able to get to that money if you had been able to hit what you aimed at."

"Yeah, I guess I wasn't thinking, but it made me mad to think how that damn kid messed up my plans to kidnap that Kleberg girl," the leader said.

"You were always a lousy shot," another voice said. Everyone laughed but Scarface.

Lauro moved to a shelf of the outcrop of rock. He wanted to see who was following him. He crawled up one of the tall rocks and peered over the edge. He saw five riders. Two wore Texas hats and the rest had Mexican sombreros. They rode single file so that they wouldn't make too much dust. Lauro picked out Scarface immediately, a big man with a visible scar, redheaded, complete with a big Mexican hat to protect him from the sun. He was carrying a knife, rifle, a single action buffalo gun, and bandaleros with extra shells. There was also a Navy Colt revolver he must have taken from some poor soul. He was riding a mustang bred for long distance traveling. The type that would run all day before he gave out and then would allow you time to find another caballo.

Lauro watched them move on down the trail, hoping they wouldn't see any of his tracks as they kept on moving. Lauro waited quietly. There was a half-breed Apache with them, and Lauro knew that if there was one track on the trail, the half-breed would find it. They kept moving until they were out of sight. Lauro breathed a little easier. He looked around and then he felt the afternoon breeze begin to move. It was time for him to get out of there. When he looked back, all the bandidos had gone over the horizon except one, and Lauro knew that he had been found out. The half-breed was going around in circles looking at the ground and waving at the other men.

Lauro removed his hat and, filling it with water, gave Lobo a drink, and then drank some himself. He didn't know when they would have a chance to stop and drink again. Keeping the outcrop of rock between him and the bandidos, Lauro moved at a fast trot, with one eye on the bandidos and one on the trail. He knew that whoever had the freshest horse would survive that day. He tried to judge the distance between himself and the outlaws and to keep out of rifle range. When they started galloping, he started galloping. When they trotted, he did the same. He kept the distance constant for most of the afternoon. Lobo was doing fine, and Lauro kept to the trail.

Scarface looked ahead at his intended victim and called to his men to hold up a minute. They slowed to a walk. "That son-of-a-bitch is smart. He's staying just far enough to be out of rifle range. We have to get to him before dark, or we will lose him."

"I know a way," the half-breed said.

"How?" Scarface asked.

"There is an arroyo just ahead. It goes around the trail, and maybe I can get him in rifle range."

"Okay, we'll walk the horses to give you time to get around. Then when we hear the rifle, we'll come running, get that?" Scarface said.

"Si, Colorado, I will not miss."

"You better not, you hear?" They came to the arroyo and the half-breed fell back slowly and rode into the arroyo. Scarface and his men kept going.

Lauro kept his eye on the distant riders. "It's not too long until sunset, Lobo. We might just make it." He glanced back and noticed there was something different about the bunch that was following him. He couldn't put his finger on it. He glanced down the trail, and then looked at the men again. Why were they bunched up like that? Making all that dust?

Then Lauro knew what it was. There was one missing. Somewhere, the half-breed had left the group. Lauro kept an eye out for anything new that might move. Soon, he came to a place where the trail dipped down into the arroyo. He was out of sight of the bandidos. He pulled off the trail around the bank of the dry creek and waited. He thought he knew what they were planning.

Very soon, he knew he would hear the jingling of the half-breed's spurs and the noises riders always make. He waited with his hand next to his gun. The half-breed came around the bend in a gallop and came to a very sudden stop when he saw the boy just sitting there on his horse. As he reached for his pistol, the half-breed then felt something jerk him off his horse. He hit the ground with the wind knocked out of him. He had been shot and was about to die. He had never seen a pistol drawn with such speed.

As Lauro rode toward him, the half-breed looked at him. "Hey boy, you are fast with that pistol. Where did you learn that?"

"Vallejo Garcia showed me how to shoot," Lauro said.

"Ah, Vallejo, my old friend, I thought he was dead. He was the fastest pistolero in all Old Mexico. You can tell him he taught you too well," the half-breed said.

"I will, but what is your name?"

"Antonio Guerreo of Camargo. Are you going to finish the job?"

"I ought to, but I don't believe in killing a wounded man. Besides, it will slow them up. Good luck . . . Antonio Guerreo of Camargo."

Lauro took off, going as fast as Lobo could manage. He knew the bandidos would be coming when they heard the shot. Antonio looked at the boy from his position with one elbow beneath him, the other hand holding his gut where the bullet had caught him. Soon the riders came upon him. "Aye, Colorado, that kid is fast. I didn't even see his hand go for his gun," Antonio said.

"Too bad, Antonio," Scarface said. "But that's the breaks." Then he shot Antonio through the head. The others just looked at Scarface.

"What did you do that for?" one of them asked.

"What you want to do, have him slow us down and let that kid get away with all that money?" Scarface said. He put the spurs to his caballo and galloped after Lauro. The others looked at the body, then at each other, and rode after him, but they couldn't catch Lobo. Soon it got dark, and without their best tracker to guide them, they had to stop.

"Well, there goes a whole lot of money that should have been mine," Scarface said.

"You mean ours, don't you?" another outlaw said.

"Oh sure, I meant ours, but it's gone anyhow. Maybe we can pick him up in the morning. Let's make camp and try again," Scarface said. The men made a dry camp, thinking of all the gold that got away.

Lobo was breathing hard. The night had turned cold. Lauro was still moving, using the stars as a guide. After several hours, he knew that he had to stop and let Lobo rest. The mustang had served him well. He stopped near a seepage of water hidden in some rocks and took off the saddle and bridle so the horse could eat. He took him to the little spring and let him drink, sparsely at first because he didn't want him to founder. He would be allowed to drink a little bit at a time, then stop and rest, before drinking some more. When Lobo had drunk his fill, Lauro rubbed him down. He waited a little while before he fed him his oats.

He kept Lobo close while he ate the *carne seca* and camp bread. He made no fire. He knew that the bandidos didn't know of the spring. There were only animal tracks around the little seep in the rocks. A tiny pool about the size of a large hat had gathered at the base of the seep and overflowed into the rock once again.

Lauro rested and thought about the half-breed he had shot. He had been taught how to protect himself. He had never shot a man before, and he didn't like the feeling. He knew that he had to get back alive with the gold. Too many people were relying on him. The half-breed had chosen his life and knew the chances he would take. Lauro felt sad, but he knew he had done the right thing. Slowly, he dozed off to sleep.

Lauro woke feeling there was someone or something beside him. He moved slowly, removing his hat from his eyes. There was a rabbit moving to the pool of water. Lauro didn't move. The rabbit got to the water, looked around and then bent to drink. Just then, a covey of quail came out of the brush and surrounded the pool and also drank. Lauro didn't move because it would make the animals run and maybe alert the bandidos that he was there. Finally, they got their fill and wandered off.

It was just after dawn. Lauro retrieved Lobo and put the saddle on him while the horse drank. He gave him some oats, then crawled to the edge of the brush and looked for the bandidos. They were nowhere to be seen, so he put on his hat and went back to Lobo. He put on the bridle, put the reins on and mounted, carefully covering his tracks until he was away from the spring and then headed toward Matamoros.

He still had a lot of traveling to do before he reached home. Just about dusk, he could see the fires of Matamoros. He was half way there. He rode toward the bridge that would take him across to Texas. When he got closer, he looked again and saw him. El Scarface was waiting for him. He must have ridden all night straight to Matamoros, killing his horse but getting there before Lauro. Lauro spun Lobo around and raced back. Scarface let out a bellow and started after that ''damn kid.''

Lauro knew the border pretty well, so he raced for the spot where he crossed with the remuda. There was heavy brush along the river, with tall trees, mostly mesquite and Rio Grande ash. Lauro looked back and saw Scarface and one other man after him. The others must have given up and stayed behind. The path was narrow and covered by vines and brush. Lauro felt a bullet go by. He kept low and raced Lobo toward the Rio Grande, looking for a path away from the river. The trail curved just enough for Lauro to take off to the side. He brought Lobo to a stop and turned to face his enemy, waiting until they had gone by him.

He spurred Lobo forward and came up behind them. The brush was so thick that they had to run in single file. Lobo caught the last rider in a few strides. He never noticed till Lauro brought his pistol down on his head. His body made a thud sound when he hit the ground. Scarface turned around in his saddle and brought his gun to bear again on Lauro. But he lost control of the gun when he felt a great blow to his shoulder. He fell off his horse and almost was run over. Lauro had just winged him. Stopping Lobo, Lauro came back by Scarface, who looked up at the kid. ''Well, finish the job. I would.''

''No, I'll let you live but you remember this face, and if I ever see you again I'll kill you, you understand? I'LL KILL YOU, — YOU BASTARD,'' Lauro said.

Scarface looked at the retreating rider and thought, ''I'll get that kid if it's the last thing I do.'' He picked himself up and headed toward town with his shoulder bleeding. He had to get help.

4

LAURO'S GRANDMOTHER

Lauro went down the river, making sure he was out of sight of the authorities and Scarface. He wanted to get across without any further delays. Swimming across the Rio Grande was getting easier every time. He made it without any trouble and was back in Texas.

He felt happy and excited that he had taken care of the great responsibility his family had given him. Their well being was taken care of for the next year. He had accomplished a man's job. Lauro put on his clothes, putting the money belt around his waist, buttoning on his shirt, and then putting on the brush jacket for his ride into Brownsville.

He stopped at the railroad shipping office and was greeted by Mr. Carter. "By golly boy, you made it," Carter said as he slapped Lauro on the shoulder and shook his hand. "Boy, it's good to see you. Everyone was talking about the failed kidnapping and your part in saving the Kleberg girl. Mr. Kleberg was looking for you, but you'd taken off without a good-bye or anything. Nobody claimed the bodies, so they buried them in the Mexican part of the cemetery." Lauro flinched. Even in death, Mexicans were separated from the Anglos.

"Well, thank you, Mr. Carter. I'll go into town so I can clean up, go to Mother's Cafe for some grub, and then see my grandmother. I'll be heading home after that. See you later," he said.

Mr. Carter looked at him, waved a hand and started back into the office. He stopped and turned around. "Boy, just wait a minute."

Lauro stopped. "Yes, sir?"

"Lauro, you're a bright young man. You've got an eighth grade education, you have been offered a chance to better yourself. I know why you won't take anything from Robert Kleberg. It's because of the

San Juan de Carricitos Land Grant. Son, there's nothing you can do to get that land back, but I can give you some good advice. Go see the man. He owes you something, and he's grateful to you for saving his little girl. In this life, you only get so many opportunities. You must take advantage of them while you can. Don't be a fool like the rest of these saddle bums. Do something with your life. Take a chance. It won't hurt you." The old man turned and walked away, back into his office. Lauro watched his back. It was humped over with worry. The railroad had a pension when railroad folk retire, but most of the time, they just died on the job.

Lauro turned Lobo toward town. Back at Mother's Cafe, he went through the same greeting. Mama Garcia had a large home in back of the cafe and she always had room for anyone she liked. Lauro took a bath, shaved, and changed clothes. He remembered Teresa's hands on them, just like her hands on him. He shook his head, repacked his clothes and went to the cafe. He sat in his corner where he could watch the door. "Never sit with your back to the door," Vallejo had taught him, "You don't know who's hunting you."

"What will you have, my *lindo muchacho?*" Mama Garcia asked. She came over and put her big arms around him. "Whatever you want. Anyone who would face down a bunch of bandidos and save the Kleberg girl from certain death can have anything he wants."

Her normal voice carried clear across the cafe. Everyone who heard her raised their heads and looked at Lauro. He just looked at the board where the menu was on the wall, and turned four shades of red.

"Mama, please bring me the largest steak in the house, some beans and rice, and stop making such a spectacle out of yourself," he said.

Mama sat down. "Well, it's the truth. You did save that girl."

"That's the past. I just want to get something to eat, go see my grandmother, then get a good night's sleep," he told her.

Mama left to see that her husband did the job right. He was the cook and a damn good one. Mama couldn't do without him. In a few minutes, she returned with his food. "There, my boy, eat with gusto. You probably haven't had a good meal in days," she said. Lauro didn't tell her of the cabrito he had in Fort San Miguel; he just obeyed her orders and began to eat. He was a hungry man.

After the meal Lauro stepped outside of Mother's Cafe and looked around the street. He was rested and full. Mama must have fed him the biggest steak in Brownsville and it was delicious. He rolled a Bull Durham and lit it.

Lauro mounted Lobo and headed down to the residential part of town. He came to the plaza and started toward Jefferson Street. He passed the cathedral, making the sign of the cross as he approached. Lauro knew the Son of God was always present in everything and everywhere. He didn't go to church much, not since he was a little kid. He did his praying away from people and priests. Still, he loved the inside of the cathedral.

Lauro rode Lobo to the stables in back of his grandmother's house, unsaddled, wiped him down, and made sure he had plenty of water, hay and oats. Lobo had more than paid for his keep during the trip. Lauro patted his neck. "Thank you, old friend, for getting me back safely."

Shutting the stable gate, Lauro started toward the house. He paused to admire the large white structure set on piers to avoid the flooding common in the area. The yard, which was surrounded by a white picket fence, was filled with lush tropical plants with a path open to the wide steps up to the porch running all the way around the house. He loved the peaceful quiet of that yard.

As he approached, Lauro saw his grandmother where he knew she'd be, standing still, erect, and beautiful at the top of the stairs waiting for him. Never had he seen a more picturesque woman. Her black dress fell from a slim waist to brush the tops of her high-heeled shoes; a white lace collar matched the hair barely visible under the black mantilla she had worn for the last ten years to indicate she was in mourning. Time had been kind to her. Her blue eyes, aristocratic nose, and porcelain skin proclaimed her noble Spanish heritage; her posture declared her authority and demanded respect.

Lauro climbed the stairs, removing his hat and smiling at her. "Good evening, Grandmother. How are you? Well, I hope." She looked at him with her hand to her breast, breathing heavily, staring at the image of her husband who had been killed by bandidos in a trap. Lauro looked like just him. His every move was like Nickolas, her beloved.

Her smile lit up the night. "Lauro, my love, come kiss this old woman before I faint." She took him in her arms, kissing him on the lips, cheeks, and forehead. He was like no other grandchild that she had. He was the hope of the Cavazos Clan, the one who would keep the last of the San Juan de Carricitos Land Grant in the family. She stepped back to look at him. "My, you've grown since last I saw you. There is something about you. You've become a man. Your birthday is tomorrow, but you have grown beyond your years. Be careful. Don't grow too fast."

Lauro looked at her. "Oh, grandmother, you would have me stay a child forever."

"Yes," she said. "I would have you running around here, getting in my beautiful plants, climbing the avocado tree, eating the avocados and getting sick because you ate too many."

"I know, they're great, the finest I ever tasted," he said.

She was very proud of her avocado tree. Arm in arm, they walked toward the door. "Tell me, how was your trip to Mexico, was it worth the trip?" she said.

"Yes," Lauro said. "Definitely. I got top price for the horses." He pulled out the money belt after they were in the house.

"Oh my, how heavy it is," she said as she handled it. "You must have gotten gold like I told you." Grandmother did not believe in paper money, not since the war between the states. She had changed every bit of the family's money into gold and had survived the post-war carpet-baggers and their high taxes.

"Will you put this in the bank?" he said and winked at her. "Oh, I have taken part of it for mother so she can pay the hands and buy what she's going to need for the coming year. There will be enough left for something she can get for herself. You know how the family is about her. Anything she wants, if we can afford it, they will get it for her."

Grandmother smiled. She was crazy about Panchita. "Well, she deserves anything she gets, living out on a ranch forty miles from nowhere, putting up with your brother and sisters. What a life."

"Come now, Grandmother. You lived on the same ranch for twenty-five years before grandfather's death and raised your children on that good clean air."

"Oh yes," she agreed. "It was a magical time. When you're young, you don't know any better. When you've the love of a man, you can survive anything - almost."

Lauro knew what she was talking about, but didn't pursue the conversation. He loved the old house that her father had built for her as a place to bring up the children so they could go to school. Still she wouldn't stay very long and headed back to the ranch. A maiden aunt stayed with the children and taught them and any other child that wanted to learn to read and write.

"How is Tia Alicia? Is she still as sweet as ever?" he said. Alicia was his grand aunt, his grandmother's sister. Lauro had always loved the sweet old lady who had taught him how to read and write and speak

proper English as well as Spanish. He read everything that he could get
his hands on, all the classics, Shakespeare, and many more.

"Oh, she went to Mass like she has for the last—I don't know how
many years now. She'll be in later. Come, I'll fix you something to
eat." She started toward the kitchen.

"I'm sorry, Grandmother, but I have already eaten," he said.

"Oh, that Mama. She enjoys getting it over me, that she fed you
first. Well, what's a grandmother to do when all the women are in love
with her grandson?" She smiled proudly.

Lauro blushed. "Well, she cooked the meal, but it wasn't as good
as yours, Grandmother."

She laughed. "Yes, I bet you couldn't finish the meal because it
was so bad." She ate with Mama every Sunday after church. They had
always been good friends of the family.

Lauro loved the way the house was decorated, with large leather
chairs and sofas, in the Mexican style. Most of the decorations had
something to do with the history of the Cavazos clan. The horns of
some bull that gave his grandfather a good story to tell hung on the
wall near the portrait of Jose Narciso Cavazos, the first owner of the
Land Grant. He was on his trusty steed in full Spanish armor, looking
like an eagle about to devour something.

Then there were portraits of the successive aristocratic generations
including a portrait of his grandfather. All had a great air about them,
the look of an eagle. Lauro was sixth-generation Texan, yet was
considered something less than second class citizen by most Anglos.
That prejudice however did not dim his pride in being a Texan.

Tia Alicia came to the house just as Lauro was getting sentimental.
"Oh, mi hijo, it's so good to see you," his aunt said, as she enfolded
him in her arms.

"Tia, how are you? You look more beautiful than ever," he said
between all the hugs and kisses.

Tia Alicia smiled at him. "You flatterer of women, how you do
know the right things to say. It's all those books I told you to read.
You're still reading, aren't you?"

"Yes, of course, every chance I get. I'm now in the process of
reading 'The Last of the Mohicans' by James Fenimore Cooper. So far,
it's very exciting."

"Yes," his aunt said, "but not as exciting as what's going on
around here."

"How could you go through all that and not inform your poor aunt and grandmother who love you so much; how could you?'' his grandmother said.

Lauro looked at his grandmother and saw the hurt, worried look on her face. ''Because I knew that you would be worried until I got back from Mexico, and I didn't want that extra burden.''

''Lauro, what you did was the talk of Brownsville for days. You knew that Mama would race over here to us with the news. She was over here at break of day to tell us, and not even a hello from my grandson. How could you?''

''I'm sorry, Grandmother,'' Lauro said. ''I just didn't think when I left here with all those horses and the trip on my mind. I didn't want to worry you more. Besides, I'm here now, all safe and sound.''

His grandmother and aunt looked at him, then at each other. His grandmother took him in her arms, held him for a while and forgave him. She couldn't even pretend that she was angry at him. ''Well, come over here and tell us all about it.''

Lauro told them how everything fell into place and how he had saved the girl's life. They sat with their hands to their throats till it was over.

''My, how brave you were,'' his aunt said.

His grandmother sat there, smiling broadly. ''Well, it was the right thing to do, even if it meant helping the Klebergs,'' she told him. ''That poor little girl. I just hope this doesn't give her nightmares. I still have dreams about your grandfather and I wake up in a cold sweat.''

Lauro reached over and held her for a while. ''There, there, it's all right.'' He felt her shaking and crying, even after all these years. ''You never told me what happened the night grandfather was ambushed.''

His grandmother looked at him and brushed his face with her long smooth fingers. ''*Mi hijo,* how painful are those memories. But you are old enough and you have become a man. Now, you should hear the story of that terrible night.''

Lauro still held her hand in his. He waited. ''It was ten years ago. Your grandfather had come into the house at the ranch headquarters. They had been rounding up for days, and your grandfather had come in with the chuck wagon to get supplies to continue the drive. They came close to the ranch and had a good chance to get the supplies they needed as well as a chance to see that everything was all right at home.''

''Oh, your grandfather made such a grand looking vaquero in his sombrero and spurs, his brush jacket, and chivarras, coming into the house with the rain still falling off the brim of his hat making a puddle around his boots. He came in and grabbed me around the waist and kissed me. Ah, such a kiss. Full of love and passion. I returned his kiss as if I would never kiss him again. 'Oh my love, how I have missed you, I love you,' I remember saying to him.

"He gave me another kiss that took my breath away. He said he had to leave because the men were waiting for him. He just wanted to be sure the children were okay. He looked worried. They were all asleep in their rooms, except for Nickolas, Jr., the oldest, who was with grandfather on the roundup. He grabbed me and kissed me again. He smiled down at me. He was so tall, like you, and looked like you. Every time I see you, I see him, and I know he's not lost to me.'' She sighed and closed her eyes.

Aunt Alicia and Lauro waited patiently while she composed herself and continued with the story. "There was a knock on the door; a very loud knock like someone was in a hurry. Your grandfather looked toward the door, looked back at me, and opened the door. There stood a young Anglo cowboy. He didn't work for us. As you know, at that time, we still had a great part of the Land Grant in our possession, and we hired a lot of people to work it.''

"What do you want?'' your grandfather asked the cowboy. The young man stood there on the porch wet all over. He said he and his friends were looking for work. He said they were fresh out of the army and would work for food. Your grandfather looked him up and down and stepped on the porch and looked at the rest of the men. They were a sorry bunch he was looking at, but he needed hands. He needed to get those cattle to the San Antonio market or lose a great part of the ranch. There had been a three-year drought, and he had borrowed money from King on the hundred fifty thousand acres that was just north of the reseca. The Sauz Ranch was the last part of the Land Grant, except for a thousand acres where the ranch headquarters stood.

"Your grandfather agreed to hire the group and pay them in food and a salary once they got to San Antonio. I walked up after hearing the conversation. The young man took his hat off. He had bright, bright red hair. I asked his name to put it on the books. He was polite and well mannered, but there was something about him I didn't like. He said his name was Bill James, and he handed me a list with the other men's names on it. No home addresses, but that was not unusual in those days. Still, I didn't like or trust that man. I took the list, not touching him. He left and headed for his horse. I watched the bunch of men while they rode off.

"Your grandfather pushed me back gently inside the house. I felt a chill go through me, and I was scared for my beloved. I begged him not to hire the men, but he didn't have a choice. He needed all the men he could find. He smiled at me and promised to be back soon.

"He started to leave, smiling back at me, then turned and took me in his arms, looked into my eyes, and told me to kiss the children for him. 'Remember wherever I am I will always love you, so proud that you chose me to love. Take care of yourself,' he said. He kissed me like he knew something I didn't, turned with spurs jingling, pulled down his hat against the wind, and stepped out of my life."

Lauro looked at his grandmother. He saw the pain and sorrow in her eyes. "That's all right, grandmother. Let's forget it. We'll talk of something else."

"No," she said. "You need to know the truth of what happened."

Tia Alicia sat quietly, dabbing her eyes with a lace handkerchief, not saying anything. Grandmother continued. "They rode off into the night with slickers on and spurs jingling. I watched them until they were out of sight, and then walked back into the house. With that feeling of dread still hanging on, I went to say a prayer for my beloved.

"About three days later, your father came galloping in to the ranch headquarters, came to the porch shouting for us. We rushed to meet him with terror in our hearts. When cowmen come in a rush it is usually with bad news. Nick, Jr. came in searching for you and your mother. You were just a boy of about eight years at that time. He breathed a sigh of relief when he saw you and your mother were safe.

"I grabbed him, 'What is it, what's wrong?' I demanded. Your father stepped away from my grasp and took you and your mother into his arms. He had been told that you and Panchita had been hurt in the buggy, and he was needed at the ranch. Bill James had brought the word. He said that a man in a buggy he met at the Santa Gertrudis Creek had brought news of the accident. Grandfather told your father to go, that he would hold the cattle this side of the Santa Gertrudis Creek and wait for him.

"I will never forget the look on your father's face when he realized he and your grandfather had been fooled," she said looking at Lauro.

"Your father said, 'That bastard lied. It's a trap.'

"He said he'd go back and then told me to stay and protect the ranch. To find help if I could. He kissed your mother, and told me not to worry.

"He rushed toward the corral with Juan, the Caporal, and the remaining hands helping him change horses. He took off with three horses unsaddled trailing behind him. He had sixty miles to go and not a minute to waste. The horses that he took were the best. They would be dead before their run was through."

Lauro could see his father risking his life to get back to his own father, just as he would have done. Nothing meant more than family. When death called for a man, that was all he had left.

"Your father killed every horse that he rode that day except one. Don't ask me how he kept from killing that one. He barely made it back to where he had left the herd. They had made camp on the Santa Gertrudis Creek. Your father went into the camp with his gun drawn, but there wasn't a person or a thing moving. The herd was gone, all five thousand head of steers. The *remuda,* and the chuck wagon, too.

"Nick, Jr. moved through the bodies laying where they had been murdered, in their sleep, fourteen good men with families. He couldn't find your grandfather, so he went off to where the herd had been held. It was easy to find because cattle tore up the ground fast. As he rode up to the place, he was watching for tracks just as your grandfather had taught him. He noticed where one man had dragged himself to some brush near the creek. Nick, Jr. followed the sign. He found Manuel Canales laying against a mesquite tree, gut shot. Your father said he rushed to him and asked him what had happened. Nick, Jr. tried to raise him to a sitting position but Manuel told him to stop, that he was dying. Manuel raised his arm and pointed toward the creek, letting his arm fall.

"Nick, Jr. hurried to where Manuel had pointed. There lay five men, four dead in a circle spread out, one still alive. He went to him and turned him over. His father looked into his eyes, the mark of death on him. He actually said he would get up and go with Nick, Jr. to find the thieves.

"Your grandfather could barely whisper, but he told your father what happened. He had let the regular men turn in because they needed the rest. He kept Manuel and that son of a bitch Red and his gang with him. It was a mistake.

"He was worried about what your father would find back at the ranch, so he wasn't as alert as he should have been. They came in two bunches. They started shooting at the camp, then cut Manuel down. Your grandfather got four of them before Red shot him in the back, and your grandfather fell. While he was lying there, he pulled his knife and hid it under his leg.

"Red told him he had to get your father away because he knew they could not handle your father, your grandfather, and Manuel. Your grandfather asked him to bend down so he could talk to him. When he did, your grandfather cut Red, gave him a slash across the face from neck to forehead that he will have to look at for the rest of his life. Then Red shot him again.

"He told your father, 'I know I'm going to die, my son, and I'm sorry that I lost the herd. I'll miss your mother and me not growing old together, and I'll miss you, your brother, and sisters, growing up and having families of your own. You're the head of the family now. Take care of everyone. I love you, mi hijo.' He tried to rise but fell back and died.

"There was nothing Nick, Jr. could do. He just brushed the dirt from his face, holding his father in his arms, not wishing to let him go.

"Your father remembers every word your grandfather told him, and I remember every word your father told me. And now I've told you."

Lauro just sat there staring into space with a look of utter hatred on his face. "Grandmother," he whispered, "I ran into that scarfaced, red-headed son of a bitch in Brownsville and again in Mexico. He was the one who tried to kidnap the Kleberg girl and later tried to kill me in an ambush at night. I had my chance to kill him when he tried to take the gold from me, and I let him go."

"I wish you had. I wish you had!" his grandmother said. "That man has caused more tragedy to this family than you know. Your father bought a wagon from a farmer and loaded the bodies into it. He wasn't going to let them be buried in a strange land. I knew it was bad news when I saw the wagon. Your father looked as if he hadn't slept in days, but still he didn't stop until he was in front of the house. Then he just looked up at us as we stood on the porch, all of us, Panchita, holding tight to your hand. Juan went to the wagon. There was a tarp covering the bodies with their boots sticking out. I cannot tell you of the sorrow I felt. It was like my heart had been ripped from my chest. My world had been destroyed, my love was dead.

"I knew what my duties as a mother were. We are here for such a short time. At any time we could be called on to meet our God. The women must bear pain more than man, yet they know that life must go on. There are things that must be done for the living as well as for the dead.

"I came down the stairs and lifted the tarp on the last body. It was my beloved, yet it was not the man who loved with all his being, whose arms held me in love, the man who worked and slaved to make a home for me and our children. I dropped the tarp and looked at Nicolas, Jr., who had come up beside me. I took him in my arms and felt the tension go out of him. He had cried his grief out. Now he wanted revenge. The hate was so strong you could feel it in the air. He said grandfathers last words were of his family.

"We buried them in the old cemetery near the road in the east pasture where every Cavazos has been buried from the day we were given the Land Grant.

"There were many people at the burial. All of the families of the men killed, the Bishop from Brownsville, and the Kings. After the service, everyone left except for King himself. He came forward with hat in hand, an old man walking with one cane in each hand. He walked to the bottom of the steps and looked up at me. He said he was sorry for my loss, but he had a long way to return to the ranch and had to talk business. I didn't invite him in, so we just stood there.

"King looked at me for a long time, as if he was making up his mind about something. Finally, he said, 'Señora Cavazos, you know of the mortgage Nicolas took out on the Sauz Ranch, the last part of the San Juan de Carricitos Grant? Can you meet the note?'

"Your father stepped forward and with a furious look on his face that made King stumble backward a step or two, said, 'You know we can't. Our herd of steers is gone and the cows and calves go with the mortgage. I wonder how the cow thieves knew we were moving those steers. Tell me, Captain, do you know how they were informed?'

"Your father didn't have on his pistols or there would have been a gunfight right there. King's *pistoleros* stepped forward, hands on their weapons. King held his hand up and stopped them. 'I know you are in great pain, young man, so I will overlook that remark,' said King.

"I had told him that we would keep our part of the bargain. He could take that part which was mortgaged. We would keep the thousand acres which is our homestead. I looked into his eyes and said, 'If I find out that you were behind the killing of these fine men and my husband, I swear that I'll hunt you down myself and kill you. Is that clear? Now, get off the San Juan de Carricitos Land Grant.'

"King put on his hat and walked to his buggy. He was helped up into the buggy by his vaqueros. He tipped his hat and left, only to die a few months later. We never found out if he had sent that bunch of bandidos after the herd, and I wonder still."

Lauro looked at his grandmother, took her hand in his, and kissed the fingers. He looked into her tear-streaked face. "Thank you, Grandmother. I'm glad you told me the whole story. Now I know who was to blame. I swear to you that I will find that red-headed son of a bitch and kill him."

His grandmother looked back at him. "You did not know. We were just trying to protect you. Now you are a man and bear a man's burdens.

"Now help me to my bedroom, Maria can help me to bed, I am very tired." She rose. Lauro helped her to her room upstairs. Maria came and helped him to take her to the bed. She sat on the edge looking up. She took his face in her hands, looking into his eyes. "You are so much like your grandfather." She smiled, kissed him, let him go. He closed the door softly, a look of bewilderment on his face.

Did the Kings have anything to do with the killing of his grandfather and those good men? Lauro wondered about it, and had a hard time sleeping that night.

The sun was just coming up when Lauro awoke, washed, shaved, and combed his hair. He heard noises in the kitchen and walked to the kitchen door. "Good morning, Juanita. How are you this morning?"

Juanita turned toward him and curtsied. "Bueno dias, Lauro. Como está usted?

"Mu bien.. Hay café?" Lauro said.

"Si, como no." She handed him a hot cup of coffee.

Lauro went out on the porch, sipping his coffee and thinking about the previous night and what he must do. Juanita came to the porch and told him that breakfast was ready. He followed her into the breakfast alcove and there was Tia Alicia. "Bueno dias, *hijo. Como aman-cistes?"* she greeted him.

"Bueno dias, Tia. *Mu buen, gracias,"* he answered.

Grandmother came into the room and the morning salutations started again. Juanita served *huevos rancheros,* hot Mexican sauce, flour tortillas with fresh butter, and refried beans. Lauro had two plates.

Tia Alicia and grandmother kept the conversation moving along, trying to prolong his stay. Finally, Lauro was through. "Thank you, Juanita."

"Por nada, señor," she said. Juanita was the best cook in Brownsville and had cooked for his grandmother for twenty years. She loved to watch how much he enjoyed his breakfast.

Lauro looked at the matriarch of the family. "I must go, ladies.

Will you excuse me?''

Jose Montalvo, the handyman, had already fed and watered Lobo. Lauro saddled him, making sure everything was right. Lobo was rested and glad to see him. Lauro tied his saddle bags and bed roll on with the slicker on top, easy to get to in case of rain. He led Lobo out of the stables to the porch where grandmother and Tia Alicia were.

"Well, I must go. Thank you for telling everything, Grandmother. I will find that bushwhacker one of these days," he promised.

"I know you will. Just remember that he's a snake and will strike whenever he can, without warning," she said.

"I will remember, Grandmother, I promise."

Then he reached for a good-bye from Tia. They kissed each other and she handed him a book of poems. He looked at it and smiled. "This is great, Tia, thank you so much."

"Happy Birthday, *mi hijo,*" she said and kissed him again.

His grandmother waited for him to get through with his good-byes to his favorite aunt. Finally he turned and faced her. "Well, my sweet, I must leave you for a while. I have a mission that I must complete, and you will learn it when I have done so."

"Go with God, my beloved, but first I must give you your birthday present." She reached into her purse and brought out a beautiful, engraved watch.

Lauro looked at the watch with delight and surprise. "Grandmother, I didn't expect this. Thank you so much." He kissed her.

There were tears in her eyes. "Look inside the cover."

Lauro pushed the window button on top. The lid flipped open to show the face of the watch. Inside the lid was an engraving that said, "To my beloved Nicolas, *mi amor, mi corazon, mi vida,* my love, my heart, my life!" Lauro read the words so long ago spoken from her to his grandfather and looked at her with tears in his eyes. "Thank you, Grandmother. I shall cherish it forever."

"Whatever you have in mind, always remember you are a Cavazos," she said. "You have Spanish royal blood running through your veins. Let no man or woman make you bend to them. Stand straight and proud."

"Yes, Grandmother, I will never forget." He put the book in his saddle bag, hooked the watch chain to his pants, and dropped the watch in his pocket. He turned once again to the ladies of his life, kissed them again, mounted Lobo, and rode off.

Lauro couldn't get Scarface out of his mind. He rode to Mother's café, dismounted, and went inside. The minute he walked into the café, all heads turned toward him. Lauro walked up to the table were Mama was sitting. "Bueno dias, Mama," he said. "Bueno dias, *hijo*. I thought you were leaving this morning," Mama said.

"I am, but I have to talk to you."

"Sit down. I'll get you some coffee." She left, came back with a steaming cup, saying, "I know your grandmother would not let you get away without feeding you breakfast, that's why I didn't offer any." She put a cup before Lauro. "What do you want to talk about?"

"Mama, you know about my grandfather's death, losing the Sauz Ranch? You're the finest friend we have. Why didn't you tell me?"

Mama looked at him with hurt in her eyes. "Mi hijo, a long time ago, your mother, who is my best friend, asked me not to. She was afraid that you would feel that it was your place to seek revenge. She has had enough sadness in her life. We knew that in time you would learn about what happened."

"Yes, I learned it, but too late. I had the bastard on the ground, begging me to kill him, and I didn't know that he was the cause of my grandfather's death, a grandfather I loved, to learn from, to experience the happiness of knowing him. He took all of that and much more from me and my family. If I had known, I'd have shot him where it would have taken him a long time to die." Lauro looked out the window.

"Forgive me, hijo, it was not my place to tell you."

Lauro came out of his thought and looked at her. "I'm sorry, Mama. I know that it wasn't your place to tell me. My mother is always protecting me. But there is something I want you to promise me," Lauro said.

"Of course, *hijo*. Anything. What is it?"

Lauro held her hand in his. "Mama, you have a chance to hear things in this business. Promise me you'll get word to me the minute that bastard crosses back into Texas."

"Of course I will. I want to get him, too. He killed my sweetheart, Manuel Canales. I will never forget that," she said with sadness in her voice.

"Your sweetheart? I didn't know," he said.

"Yes, we were to be married when he got back from the drive. It took me a long time to forget. With time and kindness, my husband came into my heart, but there is still a part for Manuel Canales. I will let you know if I hear anything."

"Thank you, Mama. Just let Vallejo know. He'll know where I am.

But don't tell Mother, promise me.''

"Okay, I promise." Lauro kissed her and left the café. The women looked up again as he was leaving.

Lauro rode out of Brownsville, looking forward to leaving the town behind. He enjoyed visiting, but he felt happiest out in the brush. He thought of what he was going to have to do, then pushed Scarface out of his mind. Too many men had lost their lives because they weren't paying attention to where they were going. Lauro left the main road and headed toward the *resaca.*

5

LAURO MAKES A DECISION

Things were changing as farmers moved into the Rio Grande Valley. Looking around, Lauro realized that as man built toward what he saw as his own betterment, he destroyed the circle of life, a little bit at a time. All the birds, both songbirds and predators which abounded in South Texas, and all the animals that now were so abundant—would they still be here in fifty years?

Lauro rode all night. He didn't want to make a camp. There were too many people that knew he was carrying money. It was quite a temptation for those people who would do anything for a dollar, much less for five hundred dollars in gold.

Dawn was breaking as Lauro rode on to Cavazos land. He felt good to be home. He guided Lobo toward headquarters, noticing the condition of the pastures. It was a good year with plenty of rain. There was grass to last through the coming winter.

He rode into headquarters, seeing the barns and sheds and the corrals with the sick pens, where stock with a wound or with screw worms were kept. The screw worm was caused by a screw worm fly attracted to an open wound, where it laid its eggs. The eggs would hatch and the larva would dig into the wound, causing more damage to the poor victim. If not caught in time, the screw worm would cause death in the host animal. The parasite could clean out a rancher in no time. There were only three cows and a horse in the sick pen.

He kept riding until he heard the sound of a rifle being cocked. Drawing his pistol at that moment, Lauro spun Lobo around to face the danger that could await him. There stood Vallejo with a 30-30 rifle in his hands and splints on his left leg.

"Hey boy, you were just a second too late, but not bad," he said, grinning. It was a game they had played for years when Vallejo was teaching Lauro how to handle a pistol.

Lauro looked at his old friend and mentor. "Vallejo, you crazy loon, I could have shot you."

"Well, you didn't, did you?" Vallejo replied. Lauro came off his horse and embraced the older man.

"Hey, hey, you want to knock me down? Me with a broken leg and can't even defend myself," Vallejo laughed at the boy he had practically raised. Lauro stepped back and looked at him. He loved this man.

Although Vallejo was in his late thirties, he was a real saddle bum. He had traveled all over the west punching cows and he knew just about everyone, including many a bad hombre. He wouldn't say how he happened to know them. Lauro looked at the tall cowboy with the leather-like skin, brown as a chestnut with a happy smile on his face. "How are you boy? It's good to see you."

"I got top prices for the horses," Lauro said. "The Coronel, who by the way said to tell you hello, was very pleased, so he paid a bonus of ten dollars. All in gold."

Vallejo said, "Why it's a miracle you got here alive. I'm proud of you, boy. You did good. Let's go up to the house and see your folks. They're very anxious to see you."

They headed toward the house—a broken down cowboy and a young man in the flower of his youth. They reached the house to hear a squeal of delight and see a figure coming down the stairs in full flight.

Estella, the youngest of the girls, threw herself into Lauro's arms. "Oh, Lauro, I'm so glad to see you." She covered his face with kisses. Lauro laughed and held his squealing sister. He heard more squeals and more bodies came flying down the stairs. Patricia and Rachel came flying into his arms. Laughing, they welcomed him home.

"Hey, take it easy, will you? I'm back now," Lauro said.

"Oh Lauro, it's just that we are so glad to see you are safe," Estella said. She had black hair that shone in the sunlight and nestled on her shoulders, soft as the evening breeze. She had a small round face with a perky, upturned nose that wrinkled whenever she laughed.

Rachel was the follower of the group. She would go along with anything the others planned. Her curly black hair would spring and bounce with her every step or movement. She had the same classic beauty that all the Cavazos ladies had as their heritage.

Patricia added something special to the beauty of the Cavazos girls. Hers was a fiery temper, quick to flare and then to die with a mischievous smile that came out of the teasing. She had fair skin and blue eyes that could make every man's head turn.

The sisters were all excellent horsewomen and could fire a rifle as well as any man. Their father, Nicolas, made sure that they learned the basics of survival.

Lauro's mother came to the top of the stairs at the end of the porch. She looked happy to see her son home safe and sound. She offered a silent prayer of thanks to the Virgin Mary. Lauro ran up the stairs, put his arms around her and swung her off her feet.

"Put me down, put me down," she cried with joy. "I want to look at you." Lauro put her down and faced her, his eyes shining, a little tear starting to show. Panchita took his face in her hands, looking at his eyes. *"Mi hijo,* thank the Virgin Mary you are back safe and sound. I prayed the whole time that you were gone. Are you hungry? Do you want something to drink?"

"No Mother, I'm fine. Where are father and Steve? I thought they'd be here this time of day. It's almost supper time."

"They should be here before dark. They're looking for animals in the Novilla pasture that might be infected with screw worms," she said. She then turned to Vallejo at the bottom of the steps. "Please take his horse, feed and water him good. He carried my son safely to me. Let him get some rest."

"Si señora, I will take good care of Lobo. He looks like he needs a rest." Vallejo took the gelding into the barn, took off his saddle, rubbed him down and watered and fed him. "Well, old friend, you did your job," Vallejo said. "You brought Lauro safely home. I thank you," he smiled.

Lauro and his family went to the living room. Lauro took off his hat, hung it on a deer head by the door and brushed his curly black hair with his hand. He looked at the familiar surroundings and finally felt at home again.

He heard voices in the yard outside, Vallejo talking to Nicolas. "Lauro is back. He's in good shape, and he's in the house. I'll take the horses." Spurs jingled on the porch.

The screen door opened. Nicolas stood inside the door. "Hijo, thank God you are safe." The men rushed to meet each other. They embraced, the father kissing the young man on the cheek. "My son, how good to see you, how are you? Did you have any trouble? Did everything go as you planned?''

Lauro released his father and looked toward the second man in the door. ''Hey, Steve.'' They rushed to embrace. ''How are you? Boy, it's good to see you, too. How are things here? Did you take care of things while I was gone?''

Steve stepped back a little. ''Of course. We took care of everything. You act as if we can't manage without you,'' he said.

They laughed together, slapping each other on the back. ''Well, I knew you were short handed so I tried to get back as soon as I could.''

Nicolas looked at his son. ''We got along fine. If we needed any help, we used some of the *mojados*. Some of them are good with cattle and horses, and we get along fine.''

Lauro breathed a sigh of relief. ''That's great Papa, that's great.'' It meant he could go ahead with his plan.

Steve was the second of the children to be born in Lauro's generation of Cavazos. Two years younger than Lauro, he was not as tall and slighter of build with brown eyes and a friendly face. When they were children, Steve followed Lauro everywhere and grew to walk, laugh and mimic just about everything Lauro did. He knew he would always be second to Lauro, but he was not jealous of his older brother. They were very close.

Nicolas put his arm around Lauro and guided him into the living room. ''I want you to tell me everything that happened,'' his Mother said. ''Did you go by your grandmother's? How is she? How is your Aunt Alicia, did she send my letters?''

''There is a note from her in my saddle bag, in a book of poems she gave me for my birthday. As for you, Mother, she told me to kiss everyone hello, so I still owe you some kisses.'' Everyone laughed and rushed to be kissed all over again.

Panchita looked up from her kiss. ''Mi hijo, yesterday was your birthday, we will celebrate at dinner time. It will be such a celebration, my son. You are eighteen years old. It's hard to believe.'' A tear began in her eyes and Lauro kissed her again, holding her back a little.

''Mother, I will always be your baby boy as long as you want me to be.'' She beamed at him and rushed to the kitchen to see how the cooks were doing with the supper. The girls went to help their mother. The men stayed in the living room so they could talk without the ladies to interrupt them.

Nicolas picked up a beautiful crystal decanter and three glasses, and poured the wine made of home grown grapes. They drank it when they had special guests or had something to celebrate.

Lauro took off the money belt and handed it to his father. "There is some of the money for the horses—five hundred dollars in gold. The rest grandmother is keeping in the safe at home."

"But son, this money should belong to you. You trained those horses."

"No, father. We are in this together. It was your land, your corrals, your feed and water that was used. I know how important the gold is to you to pay the taxes those crooks charge us and to pay the hands. We need supplies for the coming winter, as well as clothes for all of us. I know that mother would appreciate something nice for herself, although she would never ask for it. Please, Father. No arguing with me, it is only right."

Steve was looking at the money. His father put down his glass and embraced Lauro. "Thank you, my son. You have saved us again. You have acted like a man. I'm proud of you."

Steve looked at Lauro. "How much did you get per horse? I bet the Coronal liked them. How much?"

"I got top price with a bonus of ten dollars each for completing the contract on time." Lauro decided to wait to tell his father there would be no more contracts from the Mexican Army.

"Wow, that's great. I wish I could have gone with you," Steve said between sips of his wine.

"No, Estevan," his father said. "I couldn't do without you. You were needed here. Let's have another drink."

"Happy Birthday," said Steve. They raised their glasses.

After supper and the cutting of the cake, the girls excused themselves, going into the kitchen to clean the dishes. Panchita asked for the letter that Alice sent her. She loved to receive letters from Brownsville. Lauro and the men went into the living room to have coffee and a little brandy.

Suddenly Panchita let out a small scream and rushed into the living room. The men looked up.

"What is it my love? Is it bad news?" her husband asked with a worried look on his face.

"Lauro, you naughty boy," she said with a smile on her face. "Here you were the hero of Brownsville and you didn't even tell us."

"What are you talking about?" Nicolas asked. "What hero? By God, I want to know what's going on."

Lauro looked at his mother, then his father. Last, he looked at his brother. "Well, it's a long story, but it's something I want to talk to you about."

Lauro told them about the Kleberg girl and his trip into Mexico. He told them about the kidnappers being bandits and how he had run and escaped from them in Llano Colorado, finally escaping into Texas. He was careful to leave out any part about Teresa and Scarface.

Vallejo had come in and listened to the whole tale. Everyone was totally mesmerized. A long silence followed the end of Lauro's story before his father spoke in a rasping voice. "My God, son, you really had a trip, didn't you? So, the Klebergs were impressed with you. Good. Let them know how a Cavazos sets in the face of danger. With courage. Go on my son."

Lauro looked at his mother who just sat there with her hand to her throat, hardly breathing, but with pride on her face. "Well, that's all there is to tell, except my plans now that I know everything is all right here at home," Lauro said.

"What plans? What are you talking about, hijo?" his father asked.

"I thought I would ask Mr. Kleberg for that job," Lauro said.

"Why?" his father demanded. "You belong here with the rest of us. This is your home. This is where you were born and someday a fifth of it will be yours."

"I know, Father, but I want to know what the rest of the world is like. I want to learn new things, and meet new people. I have only been south of here. I want to go north and see new lands."

His father looked at his mother. "Well, it's getting late and we have to get up early. We'll discuss it further in the morning." It was obvious he was not happy that his son would consider working for the Kings.

His mother came to Lauro, kissed him, and took her leave without saying a word. She went to the master bedroom downstairs. Lauro and Nicolas embraced, and his father left, following Panchita. The other children said goodnight and went to their bedrooms.

Lauro noticed Vallejo going out the door quietly to the swing on the front porch. That was what he did whenever he wanted to talk. Lauro followed him, closing the screen door slowly behind him. Vallejo was rolling a cigarette and looked up at Lauro. "Okay, *hijo.* What's the real reason you want to leave? Are you in trouble?"

"No, it's just something I have to do," Lauro said and sat down next to Vallejo. "Grandmother told me about the night Grandfather was killed." He felt his friend flinch. "I know all about it and about

Scarface too and how we lost the last piece of the San Juan de Carricitos Land Grant. I have to know if the Kings had anything to do with my grandfather's death, with the taking of our land, and the deaths of those fine men that were with my grandfather. I won't rest till I find out.'' Lauro said with a grim expression.

"Some things are best left alone," Vallejo said, "but knowing you as I do, I know you won't rest until you have your answer."

Lauro looked at Vallejo. "I also know about that red-headed son of a bitch with a scar my grandfather gave him. I want him most of all."

Vallejo sat up then and looked straight at Lauro. "Don't mess with that hombre. He's bad medicine and has the luck of the Irish to go along with it."

Lauro shook his head. "I ran into him, in Brownsville and again in Mexico, not knowing who he was. He tried to kill me when I spoiled his little kidnapping deal. He learned I was carrying a whole bunch of money and tried to kill me in Mexico. So you see, I have double reasons to find him. I have to kill him."

"I know you're angry with the Kings, but I don't think they had anything to do with the killings and the stealing of the herd. You don't expect to find Scarface there, do you?" Vallejo asked.

"I don't think so, not after the fiasco in Brownsville when he tried to kidnap the daughter. I don't think he's very welcome on the King Ranch. They have probably offered a reward for him. He knows better than to come into Texas without an army. If the Kings had anything to do with the killings and the theft, I will find out. If so, then the whole deal is off. It won't bring my grandfather back, but the land will have to be restored to the rightful heirs and my grandfather can rest in peace." Lauro said.

Vallejo put his hand on Lauro's knee. "Well, my boy. You have a lot to prove. It won't be easy. There's been a lot of water under the bridge, but if anyone can find out, you can, so go to it. Just be careful and watch your back. I wish I was going with you."

"I do, too. I'd feel a lot more comfortable if you were, but we need you here to help father keep this ranch running. It's the last of the great Land Grant, and I'll feel a lot better knowing you are here."

Lauro looked at Vallejo out of the side of his eyes while he rolled a cigarette. "I ran into an old friend of yours in Mexico, he told me to tell you hello."

"Who's that?" Vallejo said.

"His name was Antonio Guerro of Camargo. He was a little slow on the draw. I left him in a dry arroyo in Mexico, still alive. I imagine he was taken care of by his friends. He was part of the gang that tried to rob me," Lauro said.

"Old Antonio. I haven't seen him since we fought the Apaches in Camargo many years ago. He was the best damn tracker in Mexico," Vallejo said.

"I know," Lauro said. "He tracked me, didn't he?" Vallejo laughed.

The next morning, Lauro was up early with the men of the clan. He had a fine breakfast of *huevos rancheros* and some homemade flour tortillas, and drank many cups of hot coffee to wash it down.

He had packed his clothes in his bedroll with the slicker on top and walked out to the barn to find Lobo rested, ready to go. He saddled the horse, walked him to the house, and tied his rope around Lobo's neck with a nudo de caballo.

His father met him at the door. "I can't talk you out of this, can I?"

"No, Father. It's something I have to do for all of us. I must have answers, and the Klebergs are the only ones who know the truth," Lauro said.

His father put an arm around his son. "Very well. Go. Seek your answers. And if you find anything, find evidence, too. We'll have to prove it in court, if we can find an honest judge. It's rumored most are owned by the Kings, but maybe we can take it to federal court. We'll worry about that later. Your mother is waiting for you in the kitchen."

The girls were still asleep. He had said good-bye to them the previous night. He went into the kitchen. "Mother, it's time I got started."

His mother turned toward him with tears in her eyes. "So soon? I thought you would stay a few days at least before you left."

"I can't let Robert Kleberg forget that he owes me for saving his daughter's life. I must go now. Tell the girls good-bye for me and that I love them, would you, please? If I do it, they won't let me leave."

"I understand," his mother said. "Go with God, may the Virgin Mary protect you and keep you well." They embraced and kissed. Lauro was out of the kitchen before more tears flowed.

Vallejo and his father were waiting by Lobo. They had taken the rope off, putting it on the saddle horn. It was tied in a neat coil by a thin strip of leather strapping. Lauro looked at Vallejo, then at his father, the two men who had taught him everything, but mostly, to be truthful to one's self, respect others' rights no matter what color or creed, to be honest, and to love your family. That was the reason he was leaving on a personal mission to find some answers about the death of his grandfather and the deaths of the men who were with him when it happened.

Vallejo spoke first. "Well, my friend, you're all ready to go. Your bed roll and everything you'll need are ready. There's some grub in the sack, and I put plenty of shells for the pistol and the 30-30 rifle in your saddle bags. Your rifle is in the scabbard all oiled and ready."

"Thank you Vallejo, I will miss you." He embraced him in farewell. Vallejo looked away quickly so Lauro would not see the tears in his eyes.

"Go with God, my son. Remember—never forget who you are and treat all men as friends until they prove differently."

"I'll remember," Lauro said. He embraced his father. "Stay well, Father." He turned to Lobo and mounted. "Don't worry about me. Take care of the family, tell the men good-bye for me. I'll write to let you know how I am getting along. If I find out anything I'll let you know right away. *Adios, mi compadre, mi padre, adios.*" He turned Lobo to the north.

6

THE WILD HORSE DESERT

HOME OF THE KING RANCH

It was hot and sticky in the Wild Horse Desert of southern Texas. It was a majestic place with buffalo grass and a prairie that stretched for hundreds of miles. There were mottes of native oak, as well as mesquite, laurel, hawthorn, huisache, tesaheo, and other kinds of cacti. The grass was as high as a horse's belly. Rain would turn the prairie into a paradise with every kind and color of wildflower. The grass after a rain would make a cattlemen's mouth water. There were herds of deer, flocks of turkey, and other wild game in abundance.

These were among the reasons that led Rio Grande riverboat Captain King to invest in land in South Texas. In 1853 he acquired his first land grant, the Santa Gertrudis. By 1912 the King Ranch consisted of over one millions acres in four divisions spread across six counties: the original Santa Gertrudis, site of the Ranch headquarters, the Encino Division, the Laureles and the Norias Divisions.

Lauro followed the Camino de los Bueys for a while before deciding to ride along the coast and try to catch some fish for supper. He loved speckled trout freshly caught, straight from the sea to the pan. Beef was great, but every now and then it was good to have fish.

He was quite a way from the coast, but he knew he could get there before dark. There would be enough time to set out trot lines baited with mullet that feed in the shallows of the banks. He was sure that Vallejo had put two or three throw lines in his saddle bag.

The Laguna Madre is a shallow body of water that separates South Texas from the Gulf of Mexico. It was a long ride to the east and it was

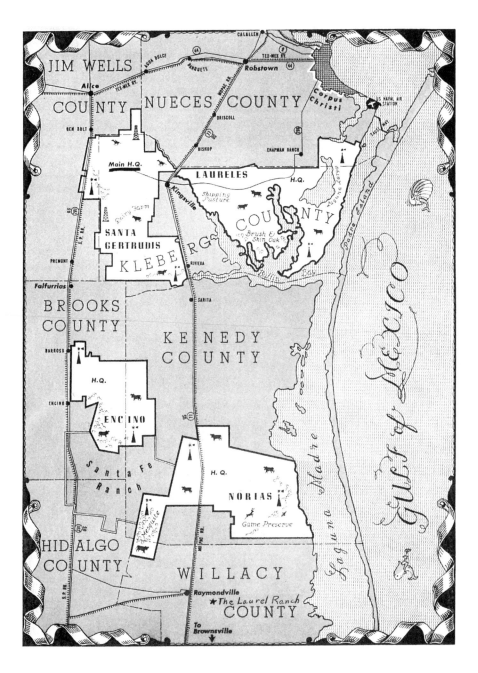

Outline of the King Ranch
* The Laurel - Cavazos family home

late before Lauro arrived. He still had to catch his supper and make camp. He found an oak motte to protect his camp from the wind, a place well hidden but giving him a good view all around. The salt water lapped on the shore, and the area was alive with birds. Lauro loved to listen to the gulls, and they gave warning whenever anyone approached.

Using a throw net, Lauro caught mullet and shrimp to bait his lines, saving the larger shrimp to boil later. Almost immediately he caught a speckled trout, followed by a redfish and two more trout. Eventually he caught a flounder, another redfish, and a tasty fish called black drum. He stopped with those, after all, he didn't want to catch all the fish in the sea.

Building a small fire which wouldn't be visible from very far, he cleaned the fish, packed them in seaweed and mud, and put them into the coals to cook. He set the shrimp to boil in fresh water and made coffee. He enjoyed a huge supper with plenty left over for breakfast.

Rolled in his blanket, Lauro stared at the fire, unable to sleep. Thoughts of the Kleburg girl kept him awake.

She is so spoiled, he thought. Rich girls like that never spoke to people like him. He wasn't a peon—he was a Cavazos, who settled the land long before the Klebergs ever heard of the Wild Horse Desert.

As he lay there staring into the fire, suddenly Lobo's head and ears became alert, and he looked up from grazing. The horse was listening for something out in the darkness. Lauro moved quickly out of the fire light with his Colt in his hand, grabbing the ammunition belt. He made a dash to the dark part of the camp. Laying on the ground, he watched the direction where Lobo was still trying to see what had made the noise.

Lauro cursed himself for having been so careless. Staring into the fire had made him totally blind in the darkness. Anyone or anything could attack him now and he would never know who, or what had done so. He was at the mercy of the unseen person or animal he was trying to identify. He waited. His eyes finally began to clear. In the darkness he could make out that it was a man who approached—but a man like no other Lauro had ever seen.

Out of the darkness came the oldest-looking man Lauro had ever met. He was taller than anyone else he knew, at least seven feet tall, with long gray hair flying in the breeze and a face so wrinkled his eyes were almost invisible. His skin, almost black from the sun, resembled parched leather. He was dressed in furs and had seashell charms and jewelry hanging all over him—from his belt and as necklaces, bracelets, and earrings. In his hand he carried a spear with jagged ends, sharp enough to penetrate any flesh, human or animal.

Standing in the firelight with his large bare feet planted in the sand, he looked like Lauro imagined a Karankawa Indian would have looked. He remembered his grandmother's stories of these fierce people and the harsh treatment they gave to captured enemies.

If I move, Lauro thought, he'll throw that spear, and I'll have to kill him. I don't want to do that. I'll have to see what else I can do.

He rose slowly, his Colt revolver in his hand, pointed at the ground but ready if it was needed. He spoke quietly in Spanish.

"Buenos noches, señor. Welcome to my camp. The night is cold, come warm yourself by my fire and have something to eat."

The old man brightened at the mention of food. Moving toward the fire, he crouched down and placed the spear beside him, then sat there, waiting. Lauro realized he would have to serve his unexpected guest. It was good he had left some fish for breakfast. The man looked like he hadn't eaten for several days.

After finishing the last of Lauro's fish, the Indian curled up by the fire and went to sleep immediately. Lauro looked at him, wondering what would happen next. Finally he dropped his extra blanket over the man and settled himself on the other side of the fire, intending not to sleep that night. However, time passed slowly and soon Lauro, too, drifted to sleep.

Lauro woke with a start the next morning. His extra blanket lay across his legs, his Colt in his lap. The fire blazed anew. There was not sign of the Indian. Before he could really feel relief at still being alive, Lauro realized that Lobo was gone.

"Son of a bitch. Now what will I do? I should have killed the bastard when I had the chance."

Lauro turned in a slow circle, hoping to find some trace of which direction his horse might have gone. There, over a dune to the west, he saw a pair of horse's ears appear. Lobo slowly came back into camp from the low spot he had gone to for a drink of fresh water. Lauro went to meet him and removed his hobbles before tying him close to camp. He wasn't taking any more chances on losing his horse.

Just then, Lauro heard a noise behind him and spun around with the Colt up, ready to fire. There stood the old Indian with a mess of fish on a leather string, which he held out to Lauro. The younger man was surprised to see he was still there, but he took the fish, cleaned them and put them to bake in seaweed and mud. Then he handed the old man a cup of coffee which the Indian accepted gratefully.

Only after he finished the first cup did the man speak. "I am called La Ganza, Chief of the Karankawa. What are you called?"

"I am called Lauro, son of Nicolas Cavazos. Where do you come from? What are you doing here? You could have killed me while I slept. Why did you spare my life?"

"You were kind to me, and anyhow, the Padre said it is wrong to kill unless in self defense."

"Padre?" Lauro asked. "Where did you know a Padre? I thought your people believed in only your Spirits."

"Listen, and I will tell you my story. This is how I came to be the last Karankawa."

"The last of his tribe," Lauro thought. "There haven't been sightings of Karankawa Indians for many years. Is he the last of his tribe?" He thought of the book he had read—*The Last of the Mohicans.*

The Karankawa continued his story. "We were a people who roamed all over the land the Mexicans call Nuevo Santander. We were very happy people. We laughed and fished for the tender meat of the great water, hunted the deer and hogs of this land. All we wanted to do was to live in peace and be left alone. We moved far away to the place where the sun rises on the Isla de Sol. We were happy there. Other tribes didn't go with us, and they soon were killed by the iron sticks. We did nothing to make them angry at us, and we thought we were well hidden, and they would never find us."

"But one day they came. We were just rising to go and fish for food. Their sticks spit fire, and killed my tribe, all but a few of us. The men who were strong and would make good slaves they let live.

"I was little more than a child then, but I tried to escape many times. Always they caught me. They whipped me, drove me on with very little food and hardly any water. We were driven into the land of the Apache. There I worked on a big hacienda for a man called Cortez. He was a great warrior. I worked the land, digging the earth, planting the food everyone ate. It was hard work for a child who had never done it before. Soon I got used to the planting, but I never gave in to the whip and they began to leave me alone.

"One day, a man in black robes came out to the field. By now, we spoke with their talk and he asked our names.

" 'I am La Ganza, the Chief of my tribe,' I told him. 'I will fight anyone or anything.'

" 'You are a fine looking warrior, my son, but you fight no one

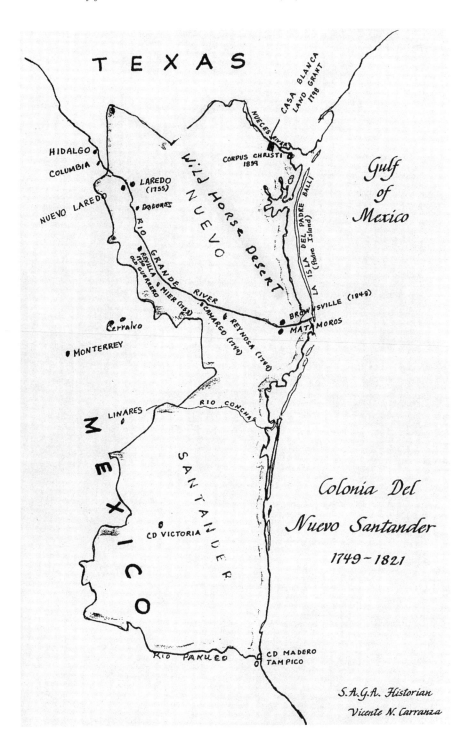

TEXAS

CASA BLANCA LAND GRANT 1798

NUECES RIVER

HIDALGO
COLUMBIA

Wild Horse Desert

CORPUS CHRISTI
1839

LAREDO
(1755)

NUEVO LAREDO

Dolores

NUEVO

RIO

LA IS LA DEL PADRE BALLI
(Padre Island)

Gulf
of
Mexico

REVILLA
OLD GUERRERO

GRANDE

MIER (1752)

CAMARGO (1749)

RIVER

REYNOSA (1749)

BROWNSVILLE (1849)

MATAMOROS

Cerralvo

MONTERREY

LINARES

RIO CONCHAS

MEXICO

SANTANDER

CD VICTORIA

Colonia Del

Nuevo Santander

1749–1821

RIO PANUED

CD MADERO
TAMPICO

S.A.G.A. Historian
Vicente N. Carranza

here. You must cast your Spirits away and join the Holy Church of God.' He told the guard to take me to the church, that he would be responsible for me. So, I was free of the fields, but I was still a slave of this Cortez.

"The Padre was kind to me," the Karankawa said. He stirred the coals of the fire with a stick. "He tried to teach me about his God. I listened to the Black Robe's talk and decided he was the same Spirit that we talk to when the Sun rises from its home and goes to sleep when the dark comes. He must be the same Spirit who put the fires in the sky to light our way in the dark. I tried to explain it to the Padre, but he would get mad. One day he took me before a lot of Black Robes and asked me if I accepted his God. I told him, yes, because I believed he was the same Spirit that guides the Karankawa.

"Soon after that, the other slave men began dying. They got small sores all over their bodies, and they were as hot as the fire that cooks our food. The Padre tried to heal them, but he kept saying, 'It is the will of God,' when they died. But I knew what it was—the white man's sickness. If they were but taken out of that land they would live. I caught the sickness also, but fought it because I was determined to escape and come back to the land of my birth. I got well and the Padre couldn't believe my good fortune. 'God's will,' he said. I lived there for many moons and one day the Padre died, of old age, they said. So, they brought another Priest and he lived a long time, but I lived longer than all of them.

"One day, I decided it was my time to die. So I packed food and just walked away. No one tried to stop me. I just kept walking. After many days and nights, I came to the river they call the Rio Grande. I made a boat of reed and floated to the mouth of the Great Waters. I crossed over and kissed the land of my people. I walked until I saw your fire in the dark. I noticed that you had food. I was too tired to hunt so I came to your fire."

Lauro was amazed. The old man had to be over a hundred years old and was still strong as a bull. A new respect came into Lauro's eyes. He was looking at the last Karankawa.

Lauro spoke in Spanish to the old man. "Grandfather, you are a great warrior to have lived longer than your enemies. I respect you. May I live longer than my enemies. We must eat now."

They finished the meal, and Lauro started to break camp. He saddled Lobo, tied his bedroll on the back of the saddle, and poured sand on the fire to make sure it was out.

The old man stood there all this time watching him. He hated to leave the old man, but he knew that to help him get to his place of the last sunrise was to offend him. He must reach it by himself. Wrapping the last of the fish in a piece of soft leather he kept for just such a purpose, he handed it to the old man. "Take this as a sign of the great respect and friendship I have for you. May your journey be a good one."

The Karankawa took the package. Putting the fish down, he took off one of the sea shell necklaces, one with all the colors of the rainbow, and handed it to Lauro. "Take this small gift in return for your friendship and the respect that I in turn hold for you, my son. Let no man take it from you. I give it to you so it can bring you good fortune and long life. I will not need its Spirit where I am going."

Lauro looked at the necklace. He knew to refuse it would be an insult to the Chief. "I thank you, Grandfather. I will protect it from my enemies as you have done these many years." Lauro had nothing of like value, but he noticed the old man kept looking at the paper tag of the Bull Durham tobacco in his pocket. Smiling, Lauro handed it to him.

"Take this, Grandfather, to enjoy on your journey." Tobacco was used in spiritual ceremonies by the Indians. It was greatly prized.

There was a smile on the wrinkled face. "Thank you, my son. May the Spirits of the necklace protect you. May your troubled spirit find the truth."

Lauro was taken aback by the words. How could the old man know about his mission to find out about the killing of his grandfather and the loss of their land? "I thank you, Grandfather. Go in peace. Go with God." Turning to Lobo, he mounted and started his ride along the shoreline of the Laguna Madre.

Lauro looked at the necklace the old Indian had given him. It was the most beautiful necklace he had ever seen. The chain which came from Mexico was made of gold so delicate he could easily break it. It was more like something a woman would wear. The shells were a perfect compliment to the chain. His mother would love it.

Lauro reached into his saddle bags, finding what he was looking for, a soft small leather bag he kept to protect something of value. He dropped the necklace in it and put it back into the saddle bag.

7

ACROSS THE WILD HORSE DESERT

Lauro rode the coastline of the Laguna Madre thinking of the old Indian and how the sands of time changed everything. The Indians were the first people of this land. They clothed themselves in furs and animal skins. Their tools were of simple materials, suited to very basic needs. They had staked a part of the land for themselves, probably taken away from another tribe, who in turn probably went to another place and took the land from that tribe.

They lived in peace and tranquility until the Spanish came. The Spanish took the land away from the tribes, and put their ways and beliefs into the land. Then the Anglos came, and the vicious circle continued.

Through all of this, some things lived on. The love of family, a desire to be free, the choice of belief, and the love of the land.

Lauro's thoughts were interrupted by something crashing through the brush. A bunch of cattle came crashing through near to where Lobo and Lauro were standing. The well trained horse stood there, waiting for a command from his rider to go after them. Lauro kept a firm rein on Lobo.

The cattle were large cross-bred citizens of the brush. They were all different colors with long horns. They looked filled out more and were heavier than the native cattle. Some were white with red, and some with a hump on their back above the shoulders. There were also gray cattle with humps more prominent than the others. All sorts of colors. Lauro had seen the colors before but not so uniformly on so many cattle. They all had one thing in common—the brand on their sides. Branded there for the life of the cattle, never to be removed under the penalty of death if anyone tried to remove or alter the brand of the King Ranch—"The Running W." That brand was on everything the King Ranch owned. It was registered with the State of Texas so that all men would be aware of King Ranch property.

Lauro was impressed with the type of cattle. He knew that Robert Kleberg, Sr. was experimenting with new types of cattle, cross-breeding them with the native Longhorns. Whoever was picking the bulls was doing an excellent job.

After the cattle moved out of sight, Lauro left the coast and rode on toward Norias Ranch. The land began to change slowly—a little oak scrub here and there, and more mesquite appearing. The soil turned to sandy loam. There were more hackberry, olmas, cactus, and grass. It was almost the best cattle country he had ever seen. The Cavazos place in San Perlita was better. It was black land and grew grass as high as the belly of a horse. Nevertheless, this was still good land.

As he rode inland, the brush got thicker until he had to follow a game trail to move at all. When he smelled smoke he went toward it and found a camp for a hundred men, all working to clear the brush, cutting it and piling it to be burned.

Lauro hated to see the brush cut down, but in some areas it took over the grass and didn't leave much feed for the cattle. He consoled himself with the thought that it would come back.

Lauro loved the smell of a camp like this—the smoke everywhere, the smell of coffee, beans and rice, *pan de campo* and *carne guisado*. They were the smells he grew up with.

The Caporal saw him ride into the camp and went over to see who the stranger was and what he wanted. Lauro pulled Lobo up to a watering trough to let him drink and rest. He dismounted and loosened the cinch, taking the bridle off his head, but leaving the reins on his neck so that Lobo could drink better.

"*Como está,* señor?" the Caporal asked. "Welcome to *el campo.* How can I help you?" He saw that this was no saddle bum. This was a real vaquero.

"Bueno dias, Caporal," Lauro replied. "I'm riding to Norias to speak with the Patrón about a job in the *corrida*. Do you know if he is there?"

"No, señor, I don't know if he is there or not, but you can talk to Mr. Caesar Kleberg, the Caporal of the Division, and he can tell you. Why not let your *caballo* rest and eat with us? It's almost noon and we have plenty."

It was a custom that no man coming into your camp went away hungry, be he friend, stranger, or peaceful enemy. You could fight after you ate, if that was your mission.

After the meal, Lauro looked up at the head cook as he drank his coffee and rolled a cigarette. "That was good, gracias."

The cook looked at him. "*Por nada*, señor. Would you like the *conejo*?" he asked as he pointed to the Brer Rabbit molasses.

Lauro was pleased to have dessert, and he didn't want to hurt the cook's feelings. "Si, señor. That would go good with a perfect meal." The cook gave him a big smile. It wasn't often he got such a compliment. He went to get the dessert. There was nothing better than the cowboy's dessert. The cook put the can of Brer Rabbit molasses and fresh hot *pan de campo* in front of Lauro. Two helpings later, Lauro pushed his plate back, sighed, pushed his hat back on his head, took a swig of coffee and rolled another cigarette. "That was good *comida*. Thank you," he said, looking at the Caporal.

"*Por nada*, señor," he said. "The *Patrón*? I am sure he is working cattle in Santa Gertrudis with all three *corridas*. They get together when they have a roundup so they can help each other. The *corrida* at Encino had an outbreak of screw worms and couldn't join them. The screw worm has been bad this year. We have to keep a sharp lookout for them all the time."

"Yes, I know, we have had more trouble with the screw worm, seems more than usual," Lauro said.

"Where are you from, señor? You look like you have traveled far," the Caporal asked.

"San Perlita, on the *Camino de los Bueys*, a ranch they call Laurel," Lauro answered.

"Oh yes. You must be Lauro Cavazos," the Caporal said with excitement in his voice. He stuck out his hand to shake hands with Lauro.

Lauro took his hand, with a surprised look on his face. "Yes, but how do you know my name? No one knew I was coming," Lauro said.

"Well, the story got around. You know how vaqueros don't have anything to talk about around the camp fire. So they tell the news that they heard. They also like to liven up the truth, so that they can tell the best tale at the campfire. Well, the boys were talking several weeks ago about you saving the *Patrón's* daughter single handed. That was a real battle, and how you came out victorious. Was it bad?" The Caporal said. Lauro took a sip of coffee. He didn't want to spoil some vaquero's tale, so he just nodded. "Well, by golly, I can hardly wait to tell the *mojados* who you are. They were wondering anyhow," the Caporal said.

Lauro got up, and shook hands with the cooks, thanking them again. Then he moved toward Lobo, who was grazing nearby. The Caporal followed him, shaking his head and smiling.

"Well," Lauro said. "Don't believe everything you hear." He mounted Lobo, reached down and shook hands with the Caporal one last time. He rode off without saying anything more.

Lauro rode on toward Norias headquarters, noticing how the brush was taking over in some places. The *mojados* at camp would have to work for the rest of their lives, and they would never get rid of the brush. All along the way as he rode, he noticed the cattle. They were just as good as the ones he saw along the coast.

He reached a good place to camp just before sunset. There was a lake and big oak trees with branches hanging low under the moss. It was a beautiful place. He built his small fire, cooked some quail, and watched the wild game and waterfowl on the lake as he thought about the Karankawa Chief, wondering if he got home and met his God.

Early the next morning Lauro broke camp. He figured it would take him about four hours to reach Norias headquarters. Since his grandfather's gold watch showed it was only six o'clock, he took time to bathe in the lake. The water was cold, but once he was used to it, invigorating. He washed his clothes and spread them, and himself, in the sun to dry. It didn't take long in the dry heat of South Texas.

Thoroughly relaxed after his bath, Lauro was in no hurry so he decided to ride through what was once the San Juan de Carricitos Land Grant, the one-time holding of his family. The Cavazos family believed that Captain King had obtained much of his land, including San Juan de Carricitos, through undue use of gold and political influence.

They understood why he would want it. When the rains came at the right time, lasting through the late spring, it was a cattleman's paradise. Without the rains, however, the summer heat burned up the grass, leaving nothing for he cattle to eat.

As he rode through Wild Horse Desert back to the shore and then along the Laguna Madre, Lauro enjoyed the rich variety of animal and bird life around him. Land use on the King Ranch gave some protection to nature. In effect, it was a wildlife sanctuary.

Lauro compared this area to the damage in the Rio Grande Valley caused by land speculation and farming. Already the *resacas* were drying up and soon the natural cycle of life on the land would be destroyed completely. The Laguna Madre, at least, had to be protected. If the Cavazoses still owned the San Juan de Carricitos Land Grant, Lauro would have ensured its survival.

Lauro made the Ranch Headquarters about one o'clock the next afternoon. There was barbed wire running along for about five miles, and it made him take a more westerly course. When he got to the corner which turned back north, he followed the fence until he could see the Norias Headquarters. He followed along a long winding road and soon came to the Headquarters.

The headquarters for the Division included houses for the regular workers and their families as well as a Company Store. Workers were paid a monthly food and supplies ration as well as a salary. It was a fairly generous allowance, and if they ran short, they could charge additional against the next month's salary at the Company Store. As a result, they made good money, especially compared to the people of Raymondville, the nearest town. In fact, the King Ranch and its workers kept Raymondville alive.

Also at the headquarters were a large set of pens for working cattle and the pen for sick animals. In the pastures were the purebred Shorthorn and Brahma bulls to do their job, improving the herd.

In the barn they kept the stud horses for breeding, with pens running out of the stalls for exercise. Lauro found the Main House, where the Division foreman lived, with the Division office in the same building as the store, close to the railroad tracks which ran through the headquarters. He left Lobo at the hitching post and went into the office where Caesar Kleberg slept in a chair with his hat pulled over his eyes.

"Excuse me, sir, " Lauro said.

Caesar Kleberg jumped about two feet. "What! What happened?" When he saw Lauro, he yelled, "Dadgumit boy, don't you know better than to sneak up on a body when they're taking their siestá?"

Lauro looked at the foreman who was rubbing his brown eyes. He had a paunch, was sunburned a dark brown like all western men, with a strong face and heavy shoulders. Lauro liked him right away.

"Sir, my name is Lauro Cavazos, from the Laurel Ranch in San Perlita. I'm looking for Mr. Kleberg. Is he here at Norias?"

"No, he's not. Last I heard he was in Santa Gertrudis working cattle. You said Lauro Cavazos?"

"Yes Sir," Lauro said.

"Why boy, I knew your grandfather and know your father and

mother. Fine people. Is your mother still as pretty as ever?''

Lauro smiled. He knew the old foreman meant it as a compliment. ''Yes sir, she sure is, and they send their regards.''

Caesar Kleberg smiled, with every wrinkle showing in his sun-browned face. He was a nephew of Robert Kleberg, Sr. ''By golly boy, I've heard some good things about you. Why, I haven't seen you since you were a baby. You sure have grown tall, like your grandfather.'' A faraway look came to his eyes as if he was remembering something.

''So, were you aware of the circumstances of his death? If you are, I would appreciate you telling me. I was just eight and my grandmother and my parents don't like to talk about it, so I just have to go by what people tell me.''

Caesar Kleberg looked at him. ''Boy, it's better that you don't know. I only know that he was a hell of a man and was killed by that son of a bitch, Red James. That's the lowest skunk I ever had the misfortune to hear about. I sure would like to get my hands on him.''

Lauro decided that he was telling the truth. ''This Red James, is he the same man they call Scarface?''

''Yep, the very same. Your grandfather sure fixed that son of a bitch with the ladies. He can't look in the mirror without remembering he murdered your grandfather and those brave vaqueros.''

''Why, he can't even get a whore to look at him, so he has to pay double to get a piece of ass.'' He laughed with a great roar, slapping the top of his leg. Lauro laughed with him.

''Say, how come you want to see the Patrón?'' Caesar said.

''Well, about a month ago, I did a favor for Mr. Kleberg, and he said to come see him if I ever wanted a job,'' Lauro said.

''Well boy, I heard what you did. He came by here on the way back to Santa Gertrudis. That was a hell of a thing you did. He likes you. I'd hire you myself, but he said if you showed up to send you to him. So, you'll find him at Santa Gertrudis working the Canleo pasture.

''Why don't you take your horse over to the stables. Let him rest a day or two. He looks like he could use it, and I'll show you around,'' Kleberg said. Lauro was hoping that he would say something like that so he could talk to the old man and maybe find out more.

Lauro took Lobo to the barn and found a stall for him. He took the saddle off, rubbed him down well, and fed him some oats and a bunch of hay. It was cool and pleasant with all the horse smells and the smell of the leather saddles and tack that hung all around the walls. Lobo would be very comfortable there.

Lauro moved down the middle of the barn, looking at the thoroughbreds housed there. He had never seen such beautiful animals, long of limb and strong. He could see the possibilities in crossing the native stock with the thoroughbred made for speed, strength, and endurance.

Caesar Kleberg came into the barn just as Lauro was looking at the last stallion. "Well, what do you think? Will they be able to breed a new type of stock? Things sure have changed since my time," Kleberg said.

Lauro looked at him, smiling. "These are magnificent animals. I can see what Mr. Kleberg is trying to do."

Caesar Kleberg looked at the stud Lauro was looking at. "Well, boy, you're the only one who can see it. He hasn't gotten much yet but a bunch of legs and heads. I'd be afraid to ride one of the progeny to the camp; he's liable to break a leg getting there."

Lauro laughed. "Well, he isn't there yet. He's still experimenting. Maybe if he crossed the progeny again with different stallions, he might get somewhere."

Lauro and Mr. Caesar, as Caesar Kleberg was called, walked toward the Main House and cow camp, which were quite a distance from the working pens. "My uncle is a smart man," Mr. Caesar said. "I know he studied in a big university up north and got to be a lawyer. He's supposed to know about the law, not breeding horses."

"Still, he's on the right trail I think," Lauro said. "I find it very interesting."

"It's dinner time. Let's go to the Main House and get some beans," Mr. Caesar said.

Lauro shook hands with the cooks, making sure he didn't leave anyone out. It was very impolite to ignore someone, especially among the cooks.

They ate at a separate table from the headquarters crew, who were the only ones at the ranch. Everyone else was out in the field and the *corrida* were working cattle. The meal was delicious. Cooking over mesquite gave it a special flavor.

After the meal, everyone waited for the breeze to start and the meal to settle. The only thing to do was to take a nap. Mr. Caesar was the first one snoring.

After the siestá, Mr. Caesar had his buggy brought around to the Main House door. "Come on, son, I'll show you around." They spent four hours riding around looking at the cattle, fences, and other things that Mr. Caesar could see needed repair.

Lauro spent the next day washing his saddle and saddle blankets and repairing his gear.

The next morning, at the big house where he had slept, he had breakfast in the kitchen before saddling Lobo to leave. He stopped at the office on his way out. "Well, Mr. Caesar, thank you for the hospitality. I was sure glad to meet you at last. I've heard my folks talk about you all my life."

"Anytime, son," Caesar said. "I sure hope Uncle Bob sends you down here after he hires you. We could always use a good man, and you sure remind me of your Grandpa."

"Thank you, sir, again, for everything. I hope he does send me down here with you."

They shook hands again and Lauro walked out on the porch. Mr. Caesar followed him. "Lauro," the old foreman said. "When you get to the Santa Gertrudis, look up Güero Mendietta. He might know something about that night your Grandpa was killed. Be sure and tell the *Patrón* everything is okay here."

"I will, sir. Thank you again," Lauro said. He waved good-bye, and headed north. He had about sixty miles to go across the Wild Horse Desert.

Lauro made good time. Lobo was in a frisky mood with all the rest he had gotten at Norias. They moved at a fast pace. About noon, they stopped, Lauro shot a rabbit for his noon meal and built a small fire under a tall oak. Salt bacon wrapped around the rabbit made a tasty meal.

Lauro waited for the breeze to pick up so as not to tire Lobo too much. He laid back and took a nap. He awakened with Lobo nudging him lightly, ready to go. Lauro tightened the cinch and mounted. They traveled till dark, making camp next to a lake of fresh water. Lauro made sure that Lobo's hobbles were tight. It was a long way to anywhere.

The next day, Lauro got to Sarita, a camp named after the Kenedy girl. When he saw it, he thought about Reina and wondered where she was. She was probably in one of those fancy schools up north.

Besides the bunk house for the cowboys and the upstairs office, there was another house for the Mexican family that took care of the camp. Eppe was the caretaker, sometimes cook, and his wife did the washing for the cowboys when they were there working. There were two unmarried girls in their early twenties.

Lauro rode up to the wood shingle house where he saw Eppe working in the front yard. ''Buenos tardes, señor,'' he said to the caretaker.

''Bueno tardes. How can I help you?'' the caretaker asked.

''I am Lauro Cavazos from San Perlita, and I'm on the way to Santa Gertrudis to talk with the Patrón about a job. I wondered if I could water my horse?'' Lauro said.

''Of course. Help yourself. The trough is over by the road leading to the house. Would you like some coffee?'' Eppe said.

''Why yes, that would be good.'' Lauro hadn't had any coffee since he broke camp early that morning. He would welcome the break. He took Lobo to the wood water tank. It was leaking all over the place, but it served its purpose. It was fed by a hand pump. Lauro washed his face and neck, ran a wet hand over his hair, and raised his head. There were the two girls with the coffee smiling at him. One had the cup and black coffee pot and the other held a can of milk and sugar.

Lauro didn't want to hurt their feelings. He smiled and took the cup. The girl holding the coffee pot spoke. ''My father will be here in a little bit. My name is LaLa, this is my sister, Maria.''

They both curtsied and Lauro nodded his head in recognition. ''I'm Lauro. Thank you for the coffee.''

Both girls were pretty and well endowed. They were wearing low cut blouses. With jet black hair and lively brown eyes, they were two girls bound for some cowboy's sack.

Their father came up then, having given them enough time to get acquainted. ''So, you're on your way to Santa Gertrudis to talk to the Patrón about a job. Why don't you stay here till fall roundup and help me? You can ask him then,'' Eppe said.

''Well, thank you, but I was told to report to him. It looks like you have your hands full, I mean with the work and everything,'' Lauro said. He took a drink of his coffee so they wouldn't see his face.

''Lots of work, from sun up till sun down, never a time for rest, always something to be done,'' Eppe said. ''Wouldn't you like to stay for the night?'' He looked back and saw his wife standing in the door, big and fat with her hair standing in the breeze. She was a picture of horror.

''No, thank you, I have to go on. The Patrón is expecting me,'' Lauro said.

He poured the rest of the coffee from his cup on the ground, handed the cup to Lala, who took it as if it were gold. She looked into Lauro's eyes. He turned quickly, put the bridle back on Lobo, mounted and looked at Eppe and his daughters. "Thanks again, ladies." He tipped his hat, and with one last look at the wife standing in the door, he shuddered. "That's what the daughters will look like in ten years," he thought. "What a shame." He waved at them one more time and headed north. He was still a good twenty miles from Santa Gertrudis Ranch.

Vallejo had told him which way to go, and Lauro was anxious to see where his grandfather was ambushed. He crossed Los Olmos Creek in the late afternoon and headed across the pasture to make better time.

Along about four in the afternoon he started hearing cattle, and the noise of a round-up. It was a sound that a cowboy never forgot. The mother cows bawled for their calves, the calves bawled for their mothers, and the cowboys yelled as they drove the cattle toward the round-up grounds. He had found the Canelo pasture, the largest pasture of the Santa Gertrudis Division of the ranch. He rode on the top of a sand hill. There below him was the herd.

The cows were looking for their calves, and the calves looking for their mothers. A cow will always go back to the last place where she left her calf.

The cowboys moved the herd slowly but surely toward the area where they would work the cattle. Lauro noticed the *remuda* moving at a distance. There must have been five hundred horses in that group —he had never seen such a large *remuda* before. The Remudeo and two helpers kept the *remuda* a good distance downwind from the camp house and the cooks who were fixing the evening meal. They didn't dare get too close to the cooks and make dust in a cow camp.

Lauro started down the hill toward the herd. If he wanted to find the Patrón, he would be with the cattle. The first man to see the stranger riding to the herd let out a high-pitched yell. It was a warning there was a stranger out there.

8

THE KINEÑOS

A rider broke from the rear of the herd at a gallop, headed toward Lauro. His rifle lay across the saddle aimed just a little off center of Lauro's belt, his finger on the trigger.

"Buenos tardes, señor. How may I help you?"

Lauro saw a large man with the deep tan of a gringo who had spent his life in the sun, his hat pulled low to shade his eyes. His broad shoulders and big, steady hands gave evidence of years of hard work. Silver hair topped a strong face with kind eyes. Without even knowing him, Lauro felt this was a man he could trust.

"Buenos tardes, jefe," Lauro replied respectfully. "I'm looking for Mr. Kleberg. He told me to look him up if I was in this part of the country."

Four riders, all mounted on excellent caballos, all young, came to stand around the white haired man, their rifles at ready. Lauro didn't take his eyes of the older vaquero.

"What is your name? Where did you come from? How did you know where we were?" the leader demanded.

"Caesar Kleberg told me where to look for you. I could hear the herd a mile away," Lauro said. "I could see the dust rising a great distance in the air, and I know all the signs of a corrida. Besides, any blind man could find where you were," Lauro said, looking at the rest of the men for the first time.

One of the young hotheads put the spurs to his horse, jumping forward and bumping Lobo with his mount. "Let me teach this boy some manners," he said with a sinister smile. He brought his rifle to bear on Lauro.

"No!" the white haired man shouted. "Leave him alone. He knows Mr. Caesar from Norias. I'll take care of him. Get back to the herd. Get going." He signaled with his hand to get back to the herd. Then he looked Lauro over from head to foot. "By the looks of your outfit, you're not from around here. Where do you come from and what is your name, boy?"

"My name is Lauro Cavazos from San Perlita, the Laurel Ranch. I come to find the owner of this ranch," Lauro said.

"Well, he's not here, but he should be tomorrow. Come to camp and spend the night. You're welcome if you are who you say, and the Patrón knows who you are. My name is Güero Sisto Mendietta. I'm the Caporal of the corrida, and while you're here you will take orders from me and no one else, is that clear?"

The Caporal spoke in a clear voice so there would be no mistake about who was boss here.

Lauro knew the name. "Do you mind if I ride with you and give you a hand with the herd?" Lauro asked.

"No, just looking at you tells me you know how to handle yourself around cattle, so come on." He put the spurs to his caballo and Lauro rode after him. Lauro noticed the Caporal never took his eyes off him.

Lobo was small compared to the Caporal's horse. That must have been the result of the breeding at Norias. The horse was at least one hand taller than Lobo, with more muscle.

They moved behind the herd. Lauro estimated that there must be eight hundred head, a good number to work. He wondered if these were all the cattle in the pasture. After all, it covered a large area and conditions were good.

As with most drives, the older men brought the tail of the herd forward. They had more patience working with the young calves that were hard to move. The calves darted in all directions except forward, looking for their mothers. They wanted to stay the last place they had seen her until she came back for them.

The rest of the herd moved at a pretty good pace. The point man, who was usually the segundo of the drive, kept the lead steers moving at just the right speed to keep the herd together. He knew the pastures like the back of his hand—where to work the herd, the close water holes, the best way to take the herd without having to slow down. The lead steers—the bueys—were trained to follow his call and the rest of the herd would follow the leaders.

The younger cowboys rode around the herd about fifty to a hundred paces from each other. They practiced roping imaginary cows at the edge of the herd; the swinging ropes helped keep the cattle bunched up. However, a cowboy never swung his rope inside the herd, or in the remuda, as this scared the animals and caused them to run.

Lauro loved the excitement. It was a feeling of being a man—the dust, the bawling cattle, the colorful picturesque movement before his eyes. He had worked cattle before at Laurel Ranch, but never in such great numbers. It was what he was born to do.

"*Cuidado*," he heard someone shout. He saw a calf make a dash for the next county. Lobo automatically followed the calf and in two strides turned it back to the herd. Lauro heard several yells go up as soon as the calf was back in the herd. "Nice going. Did you see that caballo? What a start. I wonder if he trained it?"

Lauro heard all the comments at once; and he was pleased with Lobo and his performance. He looked at the Caporal, smiling.

"That was a nice piece of work, chico. Where did your horse learn to do that?"

"I taught it to him. I broke him and trained him. I've had this horse ever since he was a colt and I was a young boy. He was born to one of our brood mares," Lauro said with pride in his voice.

"Well, for a Spanish blood, that's a very good caballo. You did well, but can you rope from him and run the brush? Is he an all-around horse?" the Caporal asked.

"Yes," Lauro said. "I can do all those things. He's a great caballo. Lobo and I have traveled many miles together, and he has never let me down."

The Caporal was impressed with this youngster. "He will do okay to ride the Rio with," he said. The Caporal drew out a sack of Bull Durham and started rolling a cigarette, keeping an eye on a cow that was straying from the herd. When she took off the Caporal took out after her. He turned the cow in three strides without spilling a leaf of tobacco.

Lauro grinned. "That also was a piece of work. You let her escape so that you could show off your mare. What is her name?"

"La Perla," the Caporal said, smiling. "You see, we have good horses, too. We ride all our potrancas and train them so we know what kind of cow sense our breeding stock has. That way, we can select the best riding stock and breed them to our best stallions. The stallions are also trained to cut cattle and rope so we can see what kind of temperament they have."

Lauro was impressed. "I'd like to ride one of your stallions. I bet that's a thrill, to feel so much power in one animal."

"Well, you handle your caballo pretty good. I'll talk to the Patrón about you; we will see," the Caporal replied.

Lauro was pleased. He picked up the pace driving the cattle toward camp. The herd got to the trap, which was about five hundred acres of clear fenced pasture, next to the working pens. The cattle would be easy to round up the next morning.

As they neared the trap, the Caporal moved ahead to stand on one side of the open gate, the segundo on the other. The vaqueros would drive the herd slowly through the gate into the trap so the Caporal could get a good count of the herd.

Once inside the trap, the herd was held for about a half-hour to allow the mother cows and calves to find each other again. Occasionally a calf would try to break away before entering the new pasture. Then the cowboys would have to rope him and drag him through the gate.

Gradually the herd settled down again and the vaqueros could slip quietly out of the trap. The cattle were left to graze as if nothing had happened.

9

THE CANELO PASTURE WORKING

Lauro was tired and thirsty and ready for camp. He was pleasantly surprised to come over a sand hill and find a stuccoed camp house with smoke rising from the chimney. The odor of food cooking made his mouth water; he knew how good the food was at camp.

The men unsaddled and rubbed down their horses, then turned them into the trap to graze and drink from the earthen tank. Next they stored their own equipment, warbag and bedroll. Lauro joined the men who went to the kitchen for a cup of coffee and a piece of pan de campo to tide them over until supper was ready. There he found the smallest cook he had ever seen.

"And you, son of a mule, what are you looking at? Haven't you ever seen a man that women fall all over themselves to sleep with? Huh?"

Lauro sputtered. "I'm sorry, señor, but you took me by surprise. I almost ran over you. Please excuse me. My name is Lauro Cavazos from San Perlita." He stuck his hand out in a friendly manner.

The cook looked at the hand, then looked up at the tall, slim young cowboy, and smiled. "Buenos tardes, chico, Juventino Villareal at your service. You didn't have to tell me that you weren't from around here. I knew it the minute you showed some manners. These so-called vaqueros around here would never have thought to meet someone they didn't know." All the men laughed and the talk picked up. A few of the men started introducing themselves to Lauro.

Most of them had earned nicknames. The cook was named "La Chista" after the tiny wren that flew from bush to bush in South Texas. Then Shorty came up with his pal Toro to shake hands. La Mula and

Colorado were walking by and stopped to introduce themselves. Each of these names had a story behind it, and Lauro knew that he would eventually hear them all.

Lauro met everyone and then sat at the table with the Caporal while the rest of the men gathered around to listen. Cowboys liked to gossip, though they never would admit it. And they wanted to get to know the new man.

"I understand that you had quite a time in Brownsville with the Patrón," the Caporal said. "I knew who you were when you rode up. The Patrón had told me to keep an eye out for you. I want you to know how thankful we all are to you for saving Reina."

Lauro was surprised that the word had already spread and his face showed it.

"I didn't mean to embarrass you, but it was a brave thing you did," Güero said. All the men were nodding and smiling. La Chista put another cup of coffee in front of Lauro. He had taken a liking to the tall slim cowboy.

"Thank you." He smiled at the cook. "It wasn't much. Any of you would have done the same thing," he said, looking at the men, one by one. They looked like a bunch of good hard-working men. He felt like he was home.

They finished the evening meal and turned in early. They were going to be very busy in the morning.

The morning started with strong coffee. In a cattle camp, the swamper, or cook's assistant, was awake by three o'clock to build up the fire and start the coffee. By that time the two cooks were up and starting breakfast. The cowboys, and even the Caporal, knew not to interfere with the cooks in their cocina. The cowboys who rose especially early drank their coffee quietly so as not to disturb the other men.

While a few men ate early breakfast, most of the cowboys collected their gear and got a caballo from the remuda. Then while most of the men ate, the few would hold the herd.

The vaqueros collected colts from the remuda that morning. This time would be used to teach the horses more of what they needed to know about working cattle.

"Lauro," the Caporal yelled from across the pen. It was hard to hear.

"Rope that sorrel with the small star over there in the corner of the pen." Lauro's rope was already flying in a loop over the sorrel's neck.

"Nice throw," Shorty hollered. "Couldn't have done better myself."

The men led the colts back to the camp, making a big swing away from the kitchen, so the dust wouldn't make a mess for the cooks.

Lauro put the snaffle bit on the colt he'd be riding when he got around to where his saddle was hanging behind the building. Once the snaffle bit was on, Lauro took the rope off the colt so he wouldn't get tangled up in it and get dragged to his death. Then he grabbed the reins in his left hand so he could turn with the colt if the colt bolted. After his filly was saddled, he put the rope back on by tying a knot, nudo de caballo, around the neck of the filly. Then if she sat back on the rope she would not choke herself.

He heard a wagon or stagecoach coming down the road—the same stage he had seen at the Laurel Ranch. There were no outriders now.

"Here comes the Patrón," someone said. "Get the coffee ready. Mamie, go and bring the Patrón's horse."

The Patrón went to the table and started putting on his spurs. La Chista put a cup of coffee in front of him. "Buenos dias, Don Roberto."

"Buenos dias," the Patrón replied. "Is breakfast about ready?"

"In a few minutes," the cook said, while cleaning the table with a wet cloth. This was a formality they went through every time, a sort of sign to show respect for the Patrón.

Güero came up, putting on his chaps and giving the morning greeting. They sat down to have another cup of coffee. No one drank more coffee than a cowboy at camp.

"Como te que?" the Patrón said.

"Bien, Patrón. We picked up 848 head, making a total count for the herd of 2,009 head for the month in the pasture," Güero said. The last count from the fall round-up had been 2,050 head.

A true count of cattle in a pasture was impossible because of the brush, the death rate, and the calf crop. That was why cattle rustling in a small number was never detected on a giant of a ranch like the King Ranch.

"Well, that's not bad," the Patrón said. "Did you send men down the arroyo all the way to the large Palo Blanco?"

"Si, Señor," Güero said "We covered it real good."

Lauro came around the corner of the kitchen with a cup of coffee and saw the Patrón. Kleberg looked up about the same time. "Well, chico, when did you get here?" he asked with a smile.

"Just yesterday afternoon. I picked up the herd about half way to the trap," Lauro said.

Reina put her head out of the stage. "Lauro," she said, rushing out to stand by her father.

Lauro was surprised to see her. He took off his hat and smiled at her. "Hello, Miss Reina. It's good to see you looking so well," he said. He had never seen a girl dressed in jeans before, with a man's shirt and hat. She looked different from when he had seen her last. It had been a couple of months. She had started filling out the shirt. Her golden hair was in a pony tail, hanging out the back of the western Stetson hat. Her boots were hand tooled—Rios's boots, he could tell. They were exquisite on her tiny feet.

The Patrón interrupted his thoughts. "Well, you got here just at the right time. This is the next to the last round-up of the spring. We take the weaners to headquarters after we get through working this herd, and we need every man that we can get to help us. Welcome to the kineño. I hope Güero has taken care of you."

"Yes sir, they made me feel right at home," Lauro said. "The horseflesh is the best I've ever seen, and the food is delicious."

La Chista beamed and rocked on his heels.

"How did you think to breed the thoroughbreds to the native stock?" Lauro said.

"It's a long story. We'll talk about it sometime. Right now, we have to get the cattle rounded up before it gets too hot," the Patrón smiled.

The vaqueros did everything for the Patrón. His and Reina's saddles and other equipment were unloaded from the top of the stage and their horses saddled. Robert Kleberg, Sr. and his family expected this sort of treatment. He was the Patrón, the one with the final decision on the very lives of these men and their families.

Robert Kleberg, however, was a cattleman. He was also Captain King's lawyer and had married the Captain's daughter. He learned the business by doing a cowboy's job. The Dama King now ruled the King Ranch with an iron fist, with the help of her devoted son-in-law. Hers was a wise choice since Robert Kleberg had a vision lacking in many men in that world.

Now his expanded duties prevented him from doing many of the tasks he loved, such as breaking his own horses. He had to depend on others, and he saw in Lauro someone he could depend on. He would watch the boy and hope that this lad could gain the men's respect.

The sun was just sending the first rays of sunlight into the far horizon, making a brilliant color of red light in the sky. It was the time of day Lauro loved best, quiet, with hardly any breeze. He turned toward the filly he had been given.

Everyone was watching Lauro prepare to mount. He curled his rope and tied it with a thin leather strap on the right side of the saddle horn. He put the rope reins over the filly's neck, turned her to the left and mounted as always from the left side. Just as his foot felt the stirrup, he felt her bunch her muscles. He knew he was in for a ride. He wasn't expecting her to buck, so he had not bothered to keep her head up. She ducked her head and sunfished. Lauro stayed with her and dug his spurs into her, watching her head pulling on the reins and trying to stay in the saddle.

The men were yelling and laughing. Reina screamed. "Stay with him, cowboy."

He rode that filly in the prettiest ride anyone had ever seen. The filly did her best to throw him off, but he was like a tick on a dog's ear and she just couldn't do it. Soon, she tired and Lauro rode her out into the pasture. The men quit laughing and started after him, some galloping, some walking their horses, all as if nothing had happened.

"Oh Father, did you see that ride? He was beautiful. He was in command the whole time. He was wonderful," Reina said with a flushed face, eyes big and flashing and breathing a little too fast.

Kleberg looked at his beautiful daughter riding next to him. He reached across and put a hand on her knee. "Yes, it was. It looks like I can still pick them."

"You pick them?" his daughter said. "I'm the one who told you to hire him the first day we saw him on the way to Brownsville. I haven't been wrong in my choice yet," Reina smiled.

Kleberg could understand his daughter's excitement. The boy could handle himself in any situation. He hoped his daughter wasn't feeling puppy love for him. She was too young to know what men were like.

The Caporal stopped a little way inside the trap. The men joined him to receive their orders. The Patrón took orders like the rest of the men.

Martin Mendietta, Jr. was the Segundo, and a natural cowboy. He had been taught by his father. Martin could ride, rope, pop the brush, train good horses, and was flashy enough to get the rest of the men to listen to him. One day he would take over as Caporal. For now, he also took orders.

"Martin, you take half the men and spread out from the fence to me," the Caporal said. "I'll take the middle. Julian, go drive the bueys to the round-up grounds and hold them there. Take Augustin, Chito, Manuel, and Toro to stop the herd from going past the lead steers. Okay, let's go, and Martin, be sure and hit those spots of brush by the watering place."

The men rode off. Reina rode along beside Lauro, and the other men spread out in a scrimmage line, making just enough noise to make the cattle move away. Things were going smoothly.

Reina didn't move too far from Lauro, keeping her eyes on both her father and the young cowboy. "What made you accept a job to work with the kineño? You all have a good ranch in Willacy County. You didn't need the job."

Lauro looked at her. He was glad she came with him; he couldn't take his eyes off her. "Oh, but I did. I needed to get along with my life and see what I could learn from the rest of the world. I'm glad I did. Your father is way ahead of everyone in his breeding programs. I find his ideas on genetics just like my own."

She looked at him with a new light. "Where did you learn about genetics?"

"From my grandfather, who was educated in Mexico City. He had many books on animal husbandry and on genetics. And on work being done in England on their livestock," Lauro said.

"He must be a very smart man to look that far ahead," she said. She noticed he was looking down at his saddle horn. She saw the hurt on his face. "Oh, did I say something wrong?" she asked softly.

Lauro looked up and into her eyes. "He's dead. He was murdered, ambushed by a bunch of cowardly bastards." He had a vengeful look on his face. She looked at him, not knowing what to say, except she was sorry.

Lauro could see the herd gathering on the lead steers, with a few vaqueros galloping to gather a calf here and there. Everything was going smoothly. Finally, the herd was gathered and the men took position so that the Caporal could count the cattle again.

Shorty moved close to Lauro, who was guarding the herd. Reina had moved to where her father was, and he was talking quietly to the Caporal. Lauro's eyes followed her, and he didn't see Shorty move next to him until he was right on him.

"Hey, Amigo, that was a good ride this morning, eh? The boys were putting you to the test. That filly always bucks in the morning.

Güero was going to put her out and sell her to the horse buyers, but he just hasn't done it yet."

"Thanks, Shorty. I figured the test would come sometime, but not before breakfast." He laughed. Shorty laughed with him and passed his Bull Durham to him. Shorty was bending over his saddle horn looking at the herd.

"She is quite beautiful, isn't she? Everyone in the corrida is in love with her. One can't help wanting her. She is forbidden fruit."

Lauro's face flushed, and he grinned. "Oh, she's just a child. I was just talking to her."

"Ah, yes," Shorty said. "But what a child. She's grown up, and you are in trouble. She finds you very handsome. I think she has a crush on you, but walk lightly my friend. That could be dangerous for one so young."

Lauro just sat there and looked at the herd milling around. "Thanks for the warning, Shorty. I didn't come here to get in trouble with the Patrón. I just want to learn and find the place where my grandfather was ambushed and killed. I'm not interested in anything else."

"Your grandfather?" Shorty asked. "Is that Nicolas Cavazos, who was ambushed by bandits several years back over by the Santa Gertrudis Creek?"

"Yes," Lauro said. "I have a mission to learn and then move on and find the killer. I know who he is, and I'll find him."

"Well, good luck," Shorty said. "I hope you do. I'll help anyway I can."

"Thanks," Lauro said. "I might take you up on that."

The signal was given to move to camp. Most of the men took a break, while those who had eaten breakfast first took over watching the herd.

The Patrón was a smart man. He had to be to run the ranch. He knew the men and would listen to what they had to contribute. He went to a table where the cooks put out coffee for him.

"Chista, tell me what do you think of that new hand?" he asked, taking the coffee to his lips.

Chista stopped on the way into the kitchen, wiping his hands on the apron he was wearing. "Well, Patrón, I just met him and I already like him. I feel like I could trust him in the middle of a fight with my life in the balance. I like him. He's a real leader. I think the boys would follow him into hell if he asked. But he wouldn't ask."

The men and Reina came from the back of the camp where they

had been unsaddling their caballos. All were laughing and talking, with Reina right in the middle of them. The Patrón smiled when he saw her. With their spurs jingling and chaps still on, they started to put down their ropes and bridles. After breakfast, they would pick new colts to train. The older hands would pick gentler more experienced horses in case one needed help.

The Patrón noticed how the men let Lauro go ahead of them when they stopped to wash up. That was a sign of respect. He planned to train this horse-trainer to be his right hand. He needed help to run the place.

La Chista started putting bowls of beans, rice, carne guisado, and camp bread on the table. Güero sat across from the Patrón so they could talk. Reina sat next to her father, and Lauro just took a place in line with the boys.

The Patrón saw him standing in the line to get his breakfast. "Lauro, come over here and sit down with us. I want to talk to you."

"Yes sir," Lauro said. The men nodded. He was being picked for special duties, so he sat with the Patrón. Reina smiled when Lauro sat across from her. He pushed back his hat and his black curly hair fell down his forehead.

Kleberg served himself and passed the bowl of carne guisado to Güero. Güero passed it to Reina and she to Lauro. She nodded, looking at him. She loved all these cowboys and looked at the older men as "fathers" for they had taught her everything.

Kleberg looked at Güero. "The Mesquite pasture looks good. The cattle will be fat and sassy when we go into that one. It will take longer to round up because of the brush. I wish there was something we could do about that. Maybe some day we will."

Taking a bit of pan de campo he looked at Lauro. "Have you ever cut cattle before? You seem to have done everything else."

· "Yes, sir. Down in the valley at the Laurel Ranch we work all our cattle from horseback. That's the best way to have a look at your herd."

"That's right. You all own the last part of the San Juan de Carricitos Land Grant," Kleberg said.

Lauro looked him straight in the eye. "Yes, sir. We're going to keep it, too. It's not going to get away from us like the rest of the Land Grant."

"I know, my father-in-law, Captain King, tried to buy it from your grandmother many times," Kleberg said. "Even offered many times over what it's worth. She's a hard woman to deal with. By the way, how is she?'' He was watching the young cowboy's eyes closely.

"She is fine, sir. She's from the old school, tough as nails but every inch a lady,'' Lauro said.

"It is my understanding that she was an elegant, beautiful woman. I wondered why the Captain always wanted to deal with her personally instead of sending me. I think that he was taken by her beauty,'' Kleberg said.

Lauro didn't say anything. He just looked at Reina and smiled.

When they were finished with breakfast, the Patrón got up from the table as his stage driver and companion, Adan, handed him his chaps and spurs. He started putting his spurs on. "Lauro, take the Mariposa and ride her. She needs some work, and I haven't had time to work with her.''

"Yes, sir,'' Lauro said. He looked at Güero wondering which one was the Mariposa.

Güero yelled at Julian, the remuda helper. "Cut the Mariposa out for Lauro and see to it that he has the right kind of bosal.''

Julian nodded and went to get the right mount. Lauro had a long way to go to learn all the horses in the remuda. There were five hundred of them, and a good Caporal was expected to know them all.

Julian brought the Mariposa to where Lauro was standing by his saddle. "Here is the filly you were told to ride. Remember her well, for she's yours as long as the Patrón doesn't ask for her. Train her well. The Patrón will judge your horsemanship by the way you train one of his cutting horses.''

Lauro thanked him and put his rope on her neck, taking off Julian's rope and handing it to him. She was a beautiful filly, well muscled with a broad head and eyes that shone with just a little bit of apprehension and excitement.

"Well, my beauty, it seems that we are going to see a lot of each other.'' He reached out and rubbed her nose with his hand. He let her smell his hand and brought her close so that she could get his scent. He brushed her back and took his time, talking to her and brushing her down. They took a liking to each other right away.

The men were moving off toward the herd with the Patrón leading the way. Reina stayed behind and waited for Lauro. He looked so good in the saddle, tall and straight, his long legs hanging naturally, his shoulders so broad and straight. She felt the heat rising to her cheeks as he rode by her, pulling his hat down over his eyes. Reina moved close to him. "Well, what do you think of her?" she asked.

"Boy, is she a beauty. I've never seen such great horseflesh in my life, and she seems to have some cow sense. I'll find out in a while when I start working cattle," Lauro said.

"Don't worry, she has cow sense all right. Daddy doesn't ride anything that doesn't. Manuel Quintanilla broke her and got her ready for the bosal when Daddy took over. He thinks she'll make an excellent cutting horse. It's quite a compliment he chose you to teach her. You'd better know what you are doing."

Reina took off at a trot with his eyes following her back and tight buttocks and her golden hair bouncing up and down with every step of her caballo. That too, was a beautiful sight.

Lauro made a few figure eights to get the feel of how much Mariposa knew, trotting slowly, and feeling her with his knees. She responded beautifully. Manuel had done his job. Lauro took his time working her, and letting her get a feel for him.

By the time Lauro had given Mariposa her warm-up, the Patrón and Güero had already cut out the lead steers and put them upwind where the cattle that were cut would smell other cattle and run toward them. Once they saw and smelled their own kind, they would stay put.

With that done, they returned to the herd. The vaqueros were surrounding the herd a good fifty yards away, the cattle milling around while the mother cows found their calves. The Patrón and the Caporal were in the middle of the herd looking for cows and bulls that weren't suitable to keep—old cows, a dry cow too old to breed, and bulls that were too old for breeding. Kleberg was also looking for the pair of cow and calf that would fit into his breeding program. That went on all morning until the Patrón had culled all the unwanted cattle out of the herd.

The boys would work the culls with the colts, but never to the point they lost the colts' interest in what they were doing. That was the way to train good horses. They would each work one colt for a while, then take turns getting a fresh mount from the remuda.

There is nothing closer to a vaquero's heart than a cutting horse that performs well. That's why the vaqueros took so much effort to train the young horses. A mature animal, well-trained, could almost work without guidance from the cowboy. Rider and cutting horse together were western poetry in motion.

After the Patrón had culled all of the rejects, he turned to Güero. "Get Lauro in here to start cutting out the weaners. We'll see what he knows."

"Yes, Patrón. It shall be done," Güero said. He turned toward where Lauro was guarding the bueys and signaled for him to come into the herd. Lauro saw Güero waving toward him, and he knew it was his turn. He moved toward the center of the milling cattle.

Reina was watching all that was going on, and she smiled at Lauro. "Go get'em, cowboy. Show them what you can do."

Lauro and Güero cut weaners for a good hour, then went to change horses. Martin and the Patrón did the cutting while they were away. When they returned, Lauro and Güero continued the work. By the time they got through it was nearly noon, too late to start the branding.

While a few cowboys held the herd, the rest moved the culls and weaners upwind to the holding pens. If they smelled the herd and broke for it, it might became an unstoppable stampede, and a day's work would be wasted.

Reina rode up to Lauro. She had changed horses a dozen times, and was riding a pretty buckskin filly. "Nice job out there, Lauro. You really impressed Dad and the rest of the men. You handle your horses beautifully. It was great just watching."

"Thank you. I had my job done for me already. The Kineños really know how to handle their horses," he smiled.

A weaner broke out of the smaller herd and headed for the main bunch of cattle. Lauro turned with the solid red bull calf. The boys yelled their approval, and the calf ran in next to the lead steers. Lauro noticed the quality of the calf. It was big for its age; the head was very masculine, and the body was deep and wide. It was the best conformation on a bull calf he had ever seen.

It was noon and time for La Chista's excellent food. Lauro had noticed a calf about six months old being towed into the camp when they had gone out to the herd that morning. He knew they'd have very fresh beef to eat for the next few days.

The vaqueros unsaddled their horses and turned them loose in the horse trap. "Hey Chista, is the food ready? We have a lot of work to do," Lolo Trevino said.

"It's ready, you bunch of unclean peons. Go clean up or you won't get to eat my food. Shorty, be careful the water doesn't make your face fall off. You seldom wash it and your face doesn't know what water is." Chista laughed.

Shorty laughed with him. "Look, you cook, and just serve the slop, and let the men go back to work."

Shorty waited his turn at the water pump with the rest of the cowboys. Dust caked on their faces, hands, and necks. Lauro handed Reina his wet bandanna. She took it and started cleaning her face.

"Thank you, kind sir. That really feels good, especially in this hot weather."

Lauro smiled and looked to the kitchen. "Boy, does something smell good. I hope he has enough for me."

"Don't worry. Güero knows to keep fresh meat for the camp." Reina said as she handed back his bandanna. Their hands touched, their fingers lingering.

He washed his face, then drew back and looked at the bandanna. Her perfume was all over the cloth. He wiped his face again, taking the fragrance in. It was a wonderful smell.

They ate in silence, not because they didn't have anything to say, but because the food was too good to talk. There is nothing like freshly roasted beef along with beans, rice, pan de campo and plenty of chili pentins. Of course, there was plenty of strong hot coffee . After the meal, some of the men poured Brer Rabbit molasses over their pan de campo for dessert.

After the noon meal was over, Lauro slipped into the kitchen, sipping on his coffee. "That was really good Chista, thank you."

Chista looked up, surprised. Compliments were few and far between in a cow camp. "Well, gracias, Lauro. It's my job and I enjoy doing it for this bunch of vaqueros. They're a pretty good lot. We ride for the brand here. Everyone does his or her job." He smiled, looking at Reina.

Lauro looked at the girl sitting across the table from her father. "Yeah, she can really handle a horse, can't she?" Lauro moved toward the back of the camp house. Finishing his coffee, he put the cup in the big pan to wash.

Güero came around the corner of the camp house and saw Lauro. "Saddle Payaso. He is the best roping horse in the remuda. Julian will show you which one he is."

"Okay. Thank you. I can't wait to have my own string of horses," Lauro said.

"You will. It just takes time to know which ones will be suited for what job. Till then, you'll use my string. I don't have the time to ride them all, and they have to be worked, or they get fat and sassy," Güero said.

10

FIRST LOVE

When Lauro had saddled up, all the men had left. Only he and Reina were still in camp, besides the cooks who were in the kitchen. Reina came around to where Lauro was saddling up. She reached out and gently grabbed Payaso's tail and started pulling out the matted hairs.

"Güero gets too busy to take good care of his horses. He needs to get them in shape," she said.

Lauro was through putting his rig on the horse and he smiled, watching her pulling the hairs. "What girl would do that?" he thought. "Even if she is the Patrón's daughter."

"Here, let me do that. We have to get back to the herd," Lauro said. He reached up to grab the tail from her, and his hands closed over hers. She turned right into his arms, putting her arms around his neck. They kissed, a very small kiss at first, then she drew him closer. Finally, Lauro drew back and let out his breath in a rush. "You shouldn't have done that. You could get me fired. I just got here," he said.

"I've been waiting to do that ever since Brownsville. It was worth the wait," she said, smiling.

Lauro drew back. "No, we mustn't. We better go," he said. He put the reins on Payaso, mounted and moved toward the gate that led to the herd.

He wondered what was happening to him. He was short of breath, and all he could think of was her and the touch of her lips. He felt light-headed and a little dizzy.

Reina caught up with him, riding beside him. She smiled. "I'm not sorry it happened. I think I'm in love with you. I can't help it, and it feels wonderful. So there. Meet me by the first motte of live oak, the closest to the camp tonight after everyone is asleep. Please," she begged. She pulled her hat over her eyes and spurred her horse lightly into a trot.

Lauro looked at her riding off and could not believe his ears. It was the first time he had been in love, and the blood was pounding in his head.

The men had the fire going when Lauro got there. Men were working all over the branding area. One man throwing tie ropes here and there around the area, while another prepared the vaccinations for the different kinds of cattle diseases. Other cowboys prepared the smelly mixture of sulfur and oil to put on castrated calves or on any open wound that the cattle might have. That would protect any animal from the screw worm. The smell alone was enough to keep the flies away.

The King Ranch was one of the first to practice preventive medicine in the livestock business. They were way ahead of everyone, even hiring their own veterinarian, J. K. Northway, from the new Kansas City Veterinary College. He was young but very knowledgable about animal health.

All the different brands of the King Ranch were being put into the fire. The famous "Running W" was branded on the left side so everyone could see it was King Ranch property. The pasture brand was put on on the rear of the left leg. The Canelo Pasture didn't take a rear brand—it took an ear notch. That was part of the record and breeding program. It made it easier to tell what pasture and what bulls they were from, so that the best heifers in the breeding program wouldn't be bred to their kin. Lauro found the selection and record keeping for the breeding very impressive.

Beto Mendietta, the camp swamper, supervised all the preparation for branding, but each man knew what his job would be. Some of the older hands were holding the herd while the younger men did the branding and the heavier work on the ground.

The weather was perfect for working cattle—hot and dry. There wasn't a cloud in the sky. It helped keep the screw worm from infecting the brands, the castration, or any open wound.

Lauro helped to hold the herd with the older men. No one went into the herd without the Caporal or the Patrón's signal. They would rope first, and when their horses got tired, they would signal a cowboy to take over so as not to interrupt the work. Lauro waited patiently for his turn in the herd. It was quite an honor to start roping in the herd, and the Patrón wanted to see how good he was.

Kleberg was the only one who picked the bulls for breeding. Naturally, he was the one who picked which bull calves would be allowed to grow into a herd bull. He had an instinct for the way his cattle would develop. As a bull calf was dragged to the branding fire, the Patrón would call out "Toro" and it would be given a chance to grow up as a bull. If he was silent, the calf was castrated.

Beto Mendietta, a good roper himself, signaled that the irons were hot, and were ready for the first calf. The fun began. There was nothing a vaquero liked better than physical contact with the cattle, the pitting of one's strength against a wild beast. The Patrón edged close to an unsuspecting cow and unbranded calf that had just mothered up. He threw a quick loop over the calf's head and started dragging it toward the fire.

The waiting men were already swinging their ropes toward the calf as he was dragged by in front of them. Just as the calf came by, Shorty threw his rope at its back feet, catching both feet in the loop and pulling it tight to bring the calf to a standstill. Another man grabbed the calf's tail and brought it down on the right side. A third one jumped on the calf and put his leg in between its hind legs. He took the rope off the head and tied the calf so they could brand, castrate, vaccinate, and give it the pasture ear notch. Then they released it to go back to the herd. The calf was away from the herd only a short time.

After about thirty minutes, the Patrón signaled to Lauro as he waited at the edge of the herd. "Lauro, get in here and rope some of these calves. I can watch better from over there by the fire and pick my bull calves. Just go slow in the herd and drag the calves out in a slow walk." The Patrón had dirt on his face that made a black mask around his bandanna. The dust rose from the herd milling around in the sandy soil in a spiral cloud that reached high into the air.

Güero pulled a calf toward the branding fire, giving Lauro a smile. "These are good calves. They're heavier than the last herd we worked. Go get them. We have a lot of branding to do," he said.

Lauro roped calf after calf, dragging them toward the fire. After a while, Güero left for the remuda to change roping horses. Martin Mendietta came in and took his place. They didn't want to tire the horses too much; they did much of the heavy work.

Lauro thought it probably looked like chaos to anyone outside a ranching outfit. But for the King Ranch, it was a well-oiled machine, branding three hundred head of calves on this one round-up. Everyone knew his job and did it smoothly—the ropers on the ground, the castraters, the vaccinator, the ear notcher, and the boy that put the sulfur and burnt oil on the castrated calves. It was a good time for all—part of the west that only a select few would experience and remember.

One of the calves eluded the loop and ran around in the herd, making a dash for the outside. Lauro was right behind him, roping him neatly. The men yelled, laughed, and shared in a job well done.

"Quick on the calf," Reina said. "Don't run your horse too much. Save your arm for more throws." She watched Lauro with big blue eyes, taking in all the action. She joined the yelling and laughter when someone missed with his rope or got kicked loosening a calf.

She wasn't ready to join the roping in the herd; it was too dangerous for a young girl. However, she did help in the branding, putting the sulfur and burnt oil on castrated calves, turning loose the calves, and being careful of a kick. With dust on her face, sweat running down her face and neck and down through her shirt, she was a picture of beauty. Lauro kept looking at her when he dragged a calf to the fire. He loved to just watch her. He had never seen a girl work cattle.

When they were through branding the calves, Güero signaled Lauro to tighten his horse's cinch and follow him. Slowly, they rode through the herd, looking for grown cows with horns twisted and growing into their heads. They were easy to spot because the screw worm had already invaded, and there was blood down the outside of the wound. If it wasn't taken care of, the cow or bull would be killed by either the horn growing into the skull or the screw worms getting to the brain.

It took teamwork to bring a full-grown cow or bull down safely. One man on his horse would rope the animal and pull it toward the branding area. There, another would rope the back feet and everyone helped to bring it down. Then one man would saw off the deformed horn and treat the wound before the cow was released, head first. That day they were lucky and there were no bulls to be treated.

It was all done, another pasture finished. The men held the herd until the cows and calves mothered up and their bawling stopped. They slowly moved them away. One of the men opened the gates of the trap so the cattle would leave by themselves, taking a few days to graze and move with their calves. Some of the men would return a few days later and clear the trap out to be sure that no calf was left behind.

Beto loaded the open branding wagon with all the brands, medicine, oils, sulfur, ropes, and tools. Everything had its own place, making it easy to find. If a cowboy didn't put a tool back in its proper place, Beto wouldn't let him use the equipment again.

The sun was setting in the west when they got back to camp, unsaddled their horses, and released them in the remuda trap. The horses were as tired as the men and walked slowly toward the tank to drink and roll in the sand.

The men walked slowly back toward the camp, tired, every muscle sore, but with a sense of having done their job well. They were closer to going back to the Headquarters and their homes and families. They had been away for three months, and they had one more pasture to finish before they could go home.

The men waited until Maria Lusia, Reina's duena, signaled that her charge had finished her swim in the tank, dressed, and was getting her hair combed. The cowboys could use the tank now. Lauro got some of his clean clothes and dove into the tank, dirty clothes and all. The rest of the men joined him. The wet clothes were hung on bushes to dry, then they dove back into the tank. The water was cool and it felt good to wash the dust off. All clean and hair combed, they put on their clothes and hats and made their way back to camp. They could hardly wait to sink their teeth into Chista's cooking.

Even the Patrón was tired. He had cleaned up before the others and was drinking coffee, waiting for everyone else to get back.

"Come and get it, you bunch of no good vaqueros," Chista called. "My assistant could finish that herd quicker than you all."

Reina stepped out of the stagecoach, and everyone stared. Her hair lay soft and lovely on her shoulders. She wore a light summer skirt, blue as the color of her eyes, and a white peasant blouse pushed down to expose her shoulders. Maria Lusia, in her role as duena or chaperone, had tried to dress her charge more modestly, but Reina had gotten her way again.

Lauro stared at her and pulled his hat off. He waited for her to sit down. She sat next to her father and turned on her best smile.

"Well, father, how many calves did we brand? Were you pleased with the calf crop?"

The Patrón looked at her with pride, but did not like the low cut blouse and looked at duena Maria Lusia with disapproval before giving in to his daughter. "Well, darling, it's been a great summer, plenty of rain, and the cattle produced twice the calf crop we usually get. It's been a good year so far, and now we have just one more pasture to round up."

"Oh, can I help?" she asked.

"Now, Reina, honey, you know your mother would have a fit. Besides, you have to get ready to go to college in New York. It's your first year, and you have a lot to do. Your mother wouldn't speak to me if I didn't take you back right away. We leave tomorrow."

"Yes, father," she said. She was looking at Lauro, who had a look of disbelief on his face.

He had found her, only to lose her to college. He should have known she couldn't stay in his life. He didn't even notice Chista looking at him with a sad look on his knowing face. Maria Lusia showed her disapproval of the way Reina looked at that new vaquero with the handsome face. She knew that meant trouble if the Patrón saw her.

After the meal, the men broke up to drink coffee, play cards, and listen to Chito play the guitar. He was very good and played at the dances at the Headquarters. The Patrón and Güero sat and talked about the round-up and what had to be done with the weaners and the cut-out cattle.

"Martin, Sr. will be at the Mesquite windmill in the morning with his corrida to take the cattle to Santa Gertrudis," the Patrón said. "You can turn over the cull herd there. When do you think you'll be ready for me?"

Güero looked like he was counting the days in his head, but he knew exactly how much time it took. He looked at the Patrón. "Maybe two weeks, depending if we don't get a storm, or the wheels on the chuckwagon don't fall off. We'll be ready for you to look at the herd on the second of August."

"Okay, I'll be there early the morning of the second so we can begin cutting the cattle that morning, branding on the same day. That will be the round-up for this summer." The Patrón drank a cup of coffee and smoked a Bull Durham.

"Well, I think I'll turn in. It's getting late and I need to get back to the Santa Gertrudis early. Buenos noches, muchachos," the big man said as he rose from the table and started toward the sleeping quarters.

"Reina," the Patrón said. "It's time to hit the sack." The Patrón would sleep in the bunkhouse with the men, and the women would sleep in the stage.

"Okay, Papa," said the girl smiling. "I'll be along pretty soon. I want to enjoy my last night with the corrida before I have to go to school.''

"All right, but don't stay up too late. We have to get an early start." Her father bent over and kissed the top of her head.

"Goodnight, Lauro," he said. "You did well today. I'll see you in the morning."

"Yes, sir," Lauro said, half rising from his bench. "Sir, I'd like to talk to you before you leave in the morning, if I may?"

"Okay. Check with me before we leave. See you in the morning." He headed toward the bunkhouse.

Lauro watched him until he had gone inside the walls of the camp. "Your father seems like a nice man," Lauro said to Reina while rolling a Bull Durham.

"Yes, he's the best father any girl would ever want," she answered. She was noticing his lips as he licked the cigarette and could not wait to kiss them again.

"I'll head for the oak motte after Maria Lusia has fallen asleep. She always falls right to sleep as soon as she sees that I'm in bed. Please be there, my love."

Lauro looked around to see if anyone heard her. He pulled his hat over his eyes. "All the horses of the Wild Horse Desert couldn't keep me away."

Her breath caught as she put a small hand to her breast. "I'll hurry," she said. She rose from the table and headed for the stage where Maria Lusia was waiting for her. The full July moon slowly rose, brightening the night. The old timers would call it a "Comanche Moon." The perfect moon for lovers.

Lauro disappeared from camp like a thief in the night. He put his boots on away from the camp, where no one was watching. Then he waited in a state of anxiety, afraid she might not come. A coyote sang his lonesome mating call, while Lauro paced under the big oak tree. Suddenly, he saw a flash of white coming toward him. He let out a big sigh. She had come. Reina ran into his arms. Never had he felt the softness of a girl like this one. Her lips reached for his, and he answered her kiss with tenderness. The feeling was so wonderful, he must be in love. Slowly, he started feeling the curves of her body. His passion matched hers with every kiss and the tide of young love soon overcame them. Slowly, they lowered to the warm soil of the Wild Horse Desert.

A cicada started rubbing it's wings together making the humming sound known only to their kind. Soon other cicadas began their humming in the night. Then, the coyote howled to the other coyotes, and they all began the "lonesome song."

The lovers had shut out the world except for the spot underneath the oak tree where they lay and listened to the night sounds. She lay in his arms and noticed his tanned skin in the moonlight. Both were exhausted from the spent night of love. She sighed in her contentment and looked in his eyes. "Oh, my love, I had no idea that it could be so wonderful. I feel full of your love. Make love to me again." She smiled and reached for him.

"Whoa," he said. "Give me a little time to rest. You've worn me out." He kissed her on the nose, pushing back her hair from her eyes.

Her eyes filled with tears and she sighed. "My love, what will we do if we are pulled apart? I can't bear to be away from you, not even for a minute." She stroked his arm.

"I know," he said. "I can't ask your father for your hand in marriage so soon. It wouldn't go so well. Besides, I'm just a cowhand. But that wouldn't matter if I took you to our ranch in San Perlita."

She smiled. "Oh Lauro, that would be wonderful. I would go any place with you."

He kissed her again and looked at her beauty as she lay in his arms. He couldn't get enough of her. They made love again. It was a magical night, never to be forgotten.

At last, spent, he looked at her. "We must wait. I must make my mark and earn your father's respect before I ask for your hand."

"That shouldn't take very long. He likes you already and has plans for you," she said.

"Yes, but he has plans for you, too," Lauro said not letting her go.

He reached down and kissed one of her luscious breasts. She put her hand on the back of his head, delighting in his touch. At last he kissed her on the mouth, a long sweet kiss.

"Oh, my love, I keep thinking about what your father said about you going to that college in New York. I know you have to go, but I don't know if I can live through it. I'll be here for you, and I'll write to you every day. I love you so much," Lauro said.

She looked into his eyes. "I won't go. I'll tell him I'm in love with you and we're going to be married. He can't make me go," she said, grabbing him in a strong embrace.

Lauro looked into her eyes. "You can't. You must go. Give me time to work into this organization; then I can go to him and ask for your hand."

"I knew I loved you in Brownsville. Somehow, I knew I would see you again. I couldn't get you out of my mind. When we returned to Kingsville, I kept looking for you along the Camino de los Bueys. But you weren't there. I was so disappointed. Oh, Lauro, I love you so. Let's run away to your family's ranch. I don't care what happens. I can't lose you."

"No, mi amor. I can't do that. I owe your father at least a year's work. I took this job and I must fulfill my part of the bargain." He wanted to tell her why he really came to the King Ranch, but he held back. He promised himself he would tell her in time.

The sun would soon be awaking the morning when Lauro rose and started putting on his clothes. She also rose and reached for her underclothes. "We must hurry before the cooks awake," she said.

When they were dressed, he took her in his arms. "I love you. I will love you till the day I die, mi amor, mi vida, mi corazon."

She kissed him. "I'll see you at the working of the cattle at the Mesquite Pasture. I can hardly wait." She turned and ran back to the camp.

The last he saw of her was running through the wildflowers in the soft rosy light of dawn, a picture of loveliness his heart would remember forever. He moved around to the back of the camp. He slipped into the kitchen and was surprised to find La Chista there with a cup of coffee in his hand. "Buenos dias, Lauro," he whispered. "Would you like some coffee?"

Lauro looked at him, not knowing if he would wake the Patrón and tell him or not. He took the hot coffee in his hand. "Buenos dias, Chista. How are you this fine morning?"

"Muy buen," he said. He turned toward the fire and poured himself some coffee, not saying a word. Lauro let out a silent sigh and drank his coffee. The morning had begun.

After the men had saddled up and eaten breakfast, Güero talked to the Patrón. He turned and walked to where his horse was being held for him. All were mounted and ready to go.

Güero mounted and adjusted his pants to the saddle, looked around and spoke to Martin. "Take half the men and start rounding up the cattle against the west fence. Be sure and look for baby calves born last night. They usually drop like popcorn after a working. Be alert.

"Lauro, the Patrón has time to see you. Catch up with us as soon as you can."

The cowboys went to their assigned duties. Lauro watched them ride away, turned, and looked toward the stage. Reina wasn't to be seen. He dismounted and walked toward the front porch. He tied his horse before he moved toward the camp, there to find the Patrón sitting at his usual place at the table, looking off into the distance, drinking coffee.

Lauro took a deep breath and let it out. He wanted to please the man, not because he was her father, but because he wanted his respect as a cattleman and the owner of a vast ranch. Lauro knew he had much to learn—all the pastures' names, the windmills, and the daily operation of Headquarters. There was so much to learn. He moved toward the table.

"Patrón, you sent for me?" Lauro said.

"Yes, Lauro. You said you wanted to talk to me. I have time while the ladies dress. They are the slowest things I've ever seen. How can I help you?"

La Chista put a cup of coffee in front of Lauro, looking up at him under his hat and winking. Lauro smiled and took the coffee to have time to gather his thoughts. "Well, Mr. Kleberg, I wanted to talk to you about what kind of plans you might have for me. I'd like to work my way into management if you have the need."

"Well, young man, you get right to the heart of the matter, don't you?" The Patrón pushed his hat back and took a sip of his steaming coffee. "The way I see it, you have lots to learn. Running this ranch is a job that I can't do by myself. I have different foremen at every Division of the ranch. They're all good men and know how things are done around here. However, I always need more good help."

11

HOW IT ALL BEGAN

"This ranch is getting too big for one man to run everything," Kleberg said. "There is so much I want to do and so little time. You've been running Laurel Ranch, and from what I've heard, you do a good job. But this operation is on a completely different scale. We have a million acres here, much of it from old Spanish land grants, including your family's. That's something you'll have to learn to live with."

Lauro was taken aback by Kleberg's words. He coughed in his coffee and flinched when Kleberg mentioned the San Jan de Carricitos Land Grant, but he managed to keep his mouth shut.

Kleberg flipped his cigarette off the porch. He thought of the plans he had for the future, the development of new breeds of cattle, and making the huge ranch operation work. Henrietta King inherited everything when the Captain died, including Robert Kleberg to manage the ranch and keep it together. It was a great responsibility.

"I'll tell you, Lauro, I like the way you handled yourself in Brownsville and the way you train your horses. Also your skill in working cattle. The men seem to like you; you'll find some jealousy but not much. Most of them are hardworking men whose families have been here since the beginning, when King brought a whole village from the state of Tamaulipas, Mexico, here to work the ranch."

Lauro rolled a cigarette, looking at Kleberg from beneath the brim of his hat and thinking about how the Captain acquired all his land. He knew he'd never have a better chance to ask for the story.

"Say, Mr. Kleberg, when and how did Captain King start this ranch? It must have been a hell of a job," he asked.

Kleberg took a sip of his coffee, pausing for a moment,

remembering. He had heard the story years before from Captain King, and from Augustin Quintanilla.

THE STORY

It began in 1853. King had a partner, Captain G. K. "Legs" Lewis, a former Texas Ranger who had been appointed captain of a company of Texas Mounted Volunteers to patrol the area for bandits, crooks, Indians, and murderers. He moved the group into a cow camp known as the Rincon de Santa Gertrudis. Captain King persuaded the owners to sell him the land, over 15,000 acres, at two cents an acre. In addition King and Lewis claimed nine blocks of unpossessed land along Santa Gertrudis Creek that was not part of the Rincon, but had been designated to use as payment for services to soldiers of the Republic of Texas.

In April of 1855, someone finally stood up to Lewis. J. T. Yarrington shot and killed him in Corpus Christi for seducing Yarrington's wife. Lewis left no will and no heirs, so King claimed his share of the property.

King and Lewis had begun stocking the ranch before Lewis was killed. King bought cattle in Mexico and had them delivered to Santa Gertrudis to be turned loose to roam. He had no choice about that; his men were *pistoleros* and knew nothing about handling cattle.

There was a great drought in Mexico in 1853 and 1854. Most rancheros in the state of Tamaulipas were trying to get rid of their stock. Augustin Quintanilla, the head man of a small village between Camargo and Mier, heard about a Tejano who was buying cattle.

Quintanilla found King in a cantina having a beer with other rancheros. Quintanilla and two of his *primos* approached the table and asked if he was buying *ganado*. King asked if they were good cattle and Quintanilla replied, "We have the cattle, but because of the *sequia*, they're not in the best shape. If you have pasture and water, they will look much better in time."

King was impressed by his honesty and agreed to inspect the cattle.

The village was much like others King had seen in Mexico. The huts were thatched with palm leaves and had mesquite and dried-mud walls. Children ran around laughing and playing; dogs barked, and chickens flew out of the way of the horsemen coming down the dusty road.

The animals had to be driven miles every day to water. King watched the vaqueros round up the cattle for his inspection. They were the sorriest herd he had seen, but the men were magnificent to watch. King had never seen a bunch of men work cattle the way these men did. They knew every move to make. They collected the herd in no time, carefully, and without losing a single head in the round-up.

These vaqueros enjoyed their work. It was as if they were one with the cattle they were working. He needed men with this knowledge; his success depended on finding this type of cowboy, the *"vaquero de verdad."*

King rode around the herd, not looking at the cattle, but sizing up the men. His years at sea had taught him how to pick good men. The trick would be to get them to move their families to Texas. King realized that Augustin Quintanilla was the key to his plan. He looked straight at the younger man and said, "I'll buy the whole herd for whatever price you name, if you will deliver them to my ranch in Texas."

Quintanilla protested, "But, Señor, the whole herd? Most of the cattle won't make it to Camargo, much less to Texas. You will be cheating yourself. Besides, we couldn't leave our women and children behind for that long a time."

"I'll buy every cow, horse, sheep, goat—even the chickens—everything you have if you'll move the whole village to Texas and work for me, and help me build my ranch."

Quintanilla looked at this crazy gringo. King looked back at him and saw that Quintanilla was thinking about what he proposed.

"I'll throw in more for you to think about. Your people will have a home at my ranch for as long as they want. Your families will be taken care of as long as they wish to live on the ranch, even if you die. I swear it on the Holy Mother of God." King wasn't a Catholic, but he knew they would believe him if he used the name of the Holy Mother.

"Señor, that is quite an offer. I will have to talk to my people. Let us go into the village."

Most of the men in the village gathered in the jacal. The village leaders sat on hand-woven blankets; the rest of the men stood in the back. Augustin Quintanilla's wife served a tea made of "hierba buena" as they could not afford coffee.

Augustin Quintanilla introduced the Captain to the villagers. "My people, I want you to meet El Señor King. He is a ranchero from Tejas, and he has a proposition for us. I want him to tell you about it so there are no mistakes.''

"My friends,'' King said, "I have a ranch in Tejas about one hundred fifty miles from here on the Santa Gertrudis arroyo. I wish to buy all of your livestock—cattle, caballos, burros, everything—if you will move the village to the Rancho Kineño.''

There was a murmur of surprise in the jacal. King signaled for silence and continued. "Mi amigos, I know this is a lot to ask of you, that you leave the homes that have been in your families for a hundred years, but let me explain.

"I have a dream. I want to build the biggest ranch in Texas, a ranch that will live for hundreds of years, but I need your help. I need your knowledge of animals. It will take all of us to build this great rancho.

"In return for your hard work, I promise that you and your sons will always have jobs with the Rancho Kineño. I will pay you one dollar a day in gold, and a ration of meat, flour, salt, pepper, lard, beans, rice, sugar, and coffee, and will provide a place for your families to live.

"I know you will want to talk about this. I will wait for your answer outside.'' King rose and left the jacal. As he stepped into the hot, dusty afternoon sun, he could only hope and pray that the village would accept his offer.

Augustin addressed the meeting first. "My people, you have heard the promise from the gringo. What do you have to say? You, Juan Mendietta, what do you think?''

"What have we here? Nothing. We work and work, and we have nothing to feed our women and children. I say let us go,'' Mendietta replied.

Flores Vela spoke up. "He offers us all these things. But can we trust what he says?'' Again a murmur through the crowd in the jacal.

"If he is a man of his word it would be a chance for our children to be raised in America. I hear that if children are born in Texas, they become Americanos. Is this true?'' Manuel Garcia asked.

"That is an important question,'' Quintanilla agreed. "What does the council have to say?''

Thomas Alvarez looked at the rest of the council for approval before he rose to address everyone. "My people, I do not want to leave my village, where I was born, where my father was born and his father before him. It is hard to trust this man, to go to work for him in a strange place that may not even exist. But what do we have here?

"We have no money. We barely have food for our families, only frijoles and tortillas. The corn won't bloom in this drought, and soon we will have to begin killing the sheep and the cattle. What will we do when they are gone?

"This man offers us something of value, a new beginning for us and our children. We will have dinero in our pockets, real gold that we can feel and spend. I speak for the council. If he can agree to a few more points, let's go."

Augustin stepped outside to find King. "Señor, will you come in? We wish to ask you a few more questions, please."

"Of course. Ask me anything you wish." King came into the jacal and sat down, looking at the council and at the rest of the crowd.

"We will sell you our *ganado*—all the cattle, sheep, horses, and burros, except the goats. But we get to keep the horses we ride to the rancho, so that we can leave if it is not the way you say.

"We wish to have homes like we have here, and a village council. If there is something that displeases you, or if one of our people does wrong, you will let the village council handle the problem. If one of us should die, our family will be taken care of and allowed to stay on the rancho. And when you die, as we all must, your children and your children's children must see that your word is carried out."

King thought for a minute before he answered. "I agree to all your conditions, and I swear by all that is Holy that my promise will be carried out generation to generation for as long as my rancho lives."

"Very well," Augustin said. "Señor King, you have bought yourself a village. From here on you will be called Patrón."

King smiled, greatly relieved. His dream was on the way with these men behind him. They shook hands, and everyone wanted to shake King's hand or to touch him.

"Now, Augustin, how long will it take you to be ready to move?" King asked.

"We will be ready by tomorrow morning. The cattle and sheep are already rounded up."

"Good. How many people are we talking about?" King wanted to know.

"Not counting the old ones who won't leave their village but would rather die here, there are close to two hundred men, women, and children."

"Okay. I'll take fifteen men with me to Camargo to buy wagons, supplies, and tools, including guns to protect ourselves from Indians and bandits. You send five of your best carretas with the biggest jarras you have and fill them with water to drink. The livestock will have to suffer from water hole to water hole. I know they can make it because cattle have been delivered before to the ranch.

"Who among you knows where to cross the Rio Grande? We need a good place, shallow with a good bottom to hold the wagons and all the livestock."

"Señor, I know such a place," said a young vaquero.

"What is your name?" King asked.

"Juan Mendietta at your service, Patrón. I fish the river a lot, and I have crossed to the other side many times. It is a good, sandy bottom. There are many tracks to show the ganado have crossed there, too," the young man replied.

"Good," King said. "We will cross where you say, Juan. Just be in front when we get there."

"I will be back in the morning with the men and supplies. Each familia will get a ration of food for the trip. We'll kill a beef every other day. We aren't gong to starve our people."

Augustin Quintanillo smiled and nodded when King said "our people." Already he was taking responsibility for them.

The next morning the wagons were loaded and in line. The cattle, horses, and sheep would be kept down wind, and the people would travel to the side where the dust wasn't blowing.

The children ran around the wagons, laughing and playing. The adults were sad to be leaving the only home they had ever known. Some wept as they said good-bye to the old people who had decided to stay. Already the village looked abandoned. Even the dogs were quiet as everyone waited for the Patrón to give the signal to move.

King looked at his people. He was responsible for them, and they now trusted him to take them safely to their new home. He thought he knew how Moses must have felt when he led the Israelites out of Egypt. These people and the King Ranch shared a common destiny.

Everyone was ready. They would travel on horseback or donkeys, in the wagons, and on foot, But he vowed they would make it to the King Ranch if he had to push every wagon across the Wild Horse Desert himself. With a look at Augustin who nodded his agreement, King gave the signal to start.

Slowly, like a giant snake which had just awakened from a long sleep, the wagon train began to move. The vaqueros started the herd on the trail—the cattle, the sheep, the remuda, and the *manada*. Everyone let out a *grito,* and the drive was on the way.

They crossed the Rio Grande where young Juan Mendietta had suggested. The bottom was solid and could have stood up to a dozen such crossings. The boy beamed as he took his place at the front of the line and led his people across the river.

King didn't think that they were in any danger from bandits or Indians; they usually raided only unarmed wagon trains. But his people were ready for any trouble that might arise. Augustin placed outriders far out where they could barely be seen, but close enough so that if they gave a grito the people could circle the wagons.

The vaqueros had trouble with the ganado when they started moving in the grasslands. In some places the grass had not been grazed. The horses and cattle were very hungry, and they would stop to graze every few yards. The cowboys constantly urged them forward, and they made very poor time.

King recognized the problem and didn't say anything about the delays. Instead he looked around at the land they were crossing. Even in the drought there was a lot of grass; it was the best land for cattle he had ever seen. They were on the San Juan de Carricitos Land Grant.

They made camp early. King knew that the cattle and the rest of the livestock would move better the next day if they were allowed to graze overnight. He signaled to circle the wagons.

Soon there were fires going at each wagon, and the women began the evening meals. King and Augustin rode around the camp seeing to it that everyone was set up for the night. The outriders tied fresh horses to the tailgates of their wagons so they would be ready in case something happened in the night.

"Patrón, my family and I would be honored if you shared our food and our camp," Augustin said. King thanked him and unsaddled his horse, tying him to the back of the wagon along with Augustin's caballo.

King and Augustin sat on rugs laid out by Señora Quintanilla. She handed them cups of coffee and smiled. "This time we have real coffee to offer you, Patrón."

King smiled back and thanked her. "There will be coffee from here on out. I promise you this." She beamed a smile in reply, looking much younger. They had killed a steer before they started out that morning. With that and a ration of staples, for one of the few times in their lives, they would have a full stomach.

The meal was delicious—fresh flour tortillas, pinto beans, rice, and carne guisada. King ate till he could eat no more. When he was through, he handed his plate to Augustin's wife. "Gracious, señora. Muy bien servido."

He looked across the fire at Augustin. "How many men will stand guard on the first shift tonight?"

"Myself and eight more. Then we will be relieved and ten more will stand guard till daybreak. Early in the morning is when an attack will happen if it is going to," Augustin replied.

King woke to a beautiful morning. The sun was just sending its rays into the eastern horizon, and it was still dark in the camp. Men washed and shaved by the light of kerosene lanterns, and everyone had finished breakfast and broken camp by full light when the Patrón gave the signal to move out.

As they rode along, King studied the sea of grass. Even in the drought there was still grass for grazing. The problem was water. The cattle would lose any weight they gained from the abundant food on the long journey to water. If he could find a way to get water to the livestock, King realized he could control the San Juan de Carricitos Land Grant.

Suddenly his thoughts were interrupted by a *grito* from the point man; there was trouble ahead. He spurred his horse lightly into a trot until he could see about twenty men approaching at a gallop. They made a grand picture with their *sombreros* and the *conchos* sparkling on their Mexican saddles. At first King thought they were bandits but quickly realized they were too well-dressed. With *bandoleros* strapped to their chests, *chivarras,* big rowel spurs, and Springfield rifles held in one hand, they made a fearsome bunch of *vaqueros*.

King rode forward with his arm raised, palm flattened out in the sign of peace.

"Buenos dias, señor," one of the vaqueros greeted him. "Are you the Patrón?"

"Yes," King replied. "How can I be of service?" He looked out of the corner of his eye to see that the rest of the outriders for the wagons had come in to protect their Patrón. He felt a sense of pride that his men would fight for him if necessary.

"I am Manuel Cantu, the Caporal for Don Jose Narciso Cavazos, and you are on his land, señor."

King had heard the name and was impressed. "Yes, but we are just crossing it to get to my rancho about a hundred miles from here, to the north on the Santa Gertrudis arroyo."

"Si, I have heard of you. You must be Captain King. We welcome you to the San Juan de Carricitos Rancho. You have a loyal bunch of vaqueros. They have come to fight for you,'' Canto said. He looked them over and chuckled to himself.

"Yes,'' the Captain replied. "They don't look like much right now, but let me assure you, they will fight to the last man to protect this herd and their families.''

Manuel Cantu was impressed. He had looked in the eyes of some of King's men. "Very well. You may pass with your herd of cattle and sheep, and with your *Kineños*. May God go with you.''

King liked that—*Kineños*—his men, his people.

"Thank you, Manuel. Extend my thanks to Señor Cavazos. We don't want any trouble; we just want to cross his land. After all, it is an awful lot of land for one man to claim.''

"Yes, it is. The King of Spain gave it to him for all time,'' Cantu said.

"Of course, but who did the King of Spain take it away from before he gave it to your Patrón?'' King asked, smiling.

Cantu shrugged. "Who knows, my friend? But this land will be in the Cavazos family for many, many years to come. Now you must go. It is a long way to your rancho. Adios. Perhaps we will meet again.''

———————

Kleberg took another sip of his coffee and remembered what the Captain had told him. "They are the finest cowboys in the world, and loyal to the brand. Without them, there would be no King Ranch. Remember that—without the people we are nothing. That is why you have to earn their respect. Can you do that?''

"I'll try, Patrón,'' Lauro said. "I won't be weak just to earn their respect or to make them like me. I will judge each man by his actions and make a decision.''

"That's all anyone can ask of you. They will be able to tell; they are a very fair people. If they respect you, they will follow you to hell.'' Kleberg took a sip of his coffee and looked at Lauro. "Work with the corrida and watch me and do as I do. You will learn, and in time I will be able to tell if you are the man I'm looking for. Okay?''

"Yes sir. I'll try my best. You don't have anything to worry about,'' Lauro said.

"Good, I expect great things from you.'' Kleberg thought a while. "Oh, and Lauro, what's mine is mine, and that means my daughter, too. I guess you know that from Brownsville. I'll kill any man who tries to hurt my family. Is that understood?''

Lauro paled but managed to smile. ''Yes, sir. I don't blame you. You have a beautiful daughter.''

''Well, you better get back to the corrida and I have to get back to Headquarters and see how everything's going there. I'll see you at the Mesquite round-up.

''Go with God.''

''Thank you. You also, go with God.''

Lauro turned to leave when Reina stepped out of the stage with a sad smile on her face.

''Oh, Lauro, before you go, will you help Adan put the valise on top of the stage, please?'' She looked into his eyes. Lauro walked to the stage and took her luggage from her hand, taking all of her hand and lingering there. Then he smiled and turned away with a heavy heart, longing to take her in his arms.

12

BRUSH POPPING THE MESQUITE PASTURE

Adan had moved to the other side of the stage to get on the roof, and for just a few minutes, they were out of sight of the others. Reina moved quickly, melting into Lauro's arms and kissing him. "I love you. I'll write you every day if I can't be at the Mesquite round-up."

Adan moved to the back of the stage. They parted quickly, looking upward where Adan would appear. Lauro breathed a sigh of relief. Again, the lovers had taken a chance and won. He wanted to go to Kleberg tell him that he loved his daughter and wanted to marry her. He handed the valise up to Adan, then took his hat off and stuck out his hand to Reina. "Well, Miss, it was great seeing you again. I hope we get to see you at the round-up at the Mesquite pasture."

She took his hand and held it, thinking that no one was watching. The curtain of the stage drop opened and duena Lusia stepped back with her hand to her throat. She frowned, and a worried look came to her face.

"What shall I tell the Patrón," she thought. But first I will talk to my "Nina," maybe no harm has been done. She sat back on the seat and thought better of saying anything to the Patrón. After all she might lose her job, and hers was one of the better jobs on the ranch.

Lauro moved away from the stage, hurrying to the colt he was riding. Gathering the reins into his left hand, he mounted and looked over toward the stage as Adan was taking his whip out and moving out of the cow camp. Reina looked at him from the window in back, waving. He waved back, feeling his heart sink.

He caught up with the herd just as they were getting settled down and mothered-up. Güero had sent riders to open and tie the gates. He didn't want them to close anytime soon, separating a calf from its mother. The mother cow would come back if she didn't find her calf in the herd. Later, someone could return to close the gates and make a round in the trap to be sure all the cattle were out.

Now the fun would began, moving the weaners, the old and barren cows, and the old bulls into the small trap. The bueys were moved out through the gate of the small trap into the big trap. Güero sent Lauro and half of the men to round up the herd out of the little holding trap. The rest of the men were holding the lead steers, waiting for the coming of the weaners and the cull-out cattle.

Lauro rode the fence around the small trap, but his mind wasn't on the job. It was on Reina and the night in the oak motte. He glanced at the place where they had made love the night before, then he sighed and started singing a love song, "Tu solo tu." His voice was loud and clear as a bell. The men in the trap all looked up and let out a yell. They really liked the singing. They loved anyone who could sing the corrida songs, and Lauro was singing a favorite. It was beautiful when sung from the heart. Although the men thought he was just singing for his pleasure, he really was in love and singing it to the world.

Finally, they had all the cattle at the gate of the large trap. One of the men moved carefully around the herd. He opened the gate slowly, careful not to let the cattle rush into the trap where they would just keep on running.

Slowly, he let the older cattle through the gate so they wouldn't run, but would stop where the bueys were, on the other side of the gate. There they created another herd where the weaners would stop and look for their mothers.

Every man was ready for the arrival of the calves. That was a critical time. If they held the calves, they would have no trouble handling the herd. However, if they let one escape, the rest would follow, and they would be delayed by having to round them up again.

Slowly, the cattle poured out of the small trap until the last one had passed the gate. After the cattle were let out to settle down the men called to the bueys. They began to move ever so slowly. The older cattle followed, then the calves. The vaqueros moved with them quietly, ready for anything that might happen.

They moved the herd up and down the large trap fence, getting them accustomed to moving as one herd. When the Caporal felt that they had settled down, he opened the east gate slowly, and waved at the men to cut out the bueys. They were held in the Canelo pasture about twenty yards from the gate. When the cattle were allowed to leave the trap, the grown animals went to the bueys and stopped, while the men on the outside of the trap would stop the charge of the calves. They turned the herd north, toward the Santa Gertrudis Headquarters. Soon the cattle would settle down to the pace of the bueys, bawling, raising dust, and fertilizing the road home.

The day started getting hot, so Güero told one of the cowboys to ride up front and tell Martin to slow down the pace. Martin was the point man for the herd, possibly the most important job was his responsibility as Segundo to set the pace. The Caporal watched the whole picture, hollering at the young vaqueros to stay alert as one of the weaners might take off. By staying alert, they could stop it from running off before it started.

Lauro couldn't get over how beautiful the country was. He wished Reina could be with him to enjoy the flowers and all the different kinds of birds, the deer running and jumping with their white flag of a tail waving good-bye. Javelinas ran away from the herd in packs. Hawks flew above, picking up insects kicked up by the cattle in passing. The sandhill cranes flew away from them. It was more exciting and better than a day at the market. He was in love, and the world was beautiful.

It was ten miles to the headquarters and five to where Güero would turn the herd over to Martin Mendietta, Sr. He was waiting for them at the Mesquite windmill. Then it would be his responsibility to take the herd to the Plomo feedlots, where they would be separated, with the calves left in the feed lot to gain weight before being driven to the railhead and shipped.

The corrida was approaching the Mesquite windmill, when they began to hear soft whistling, clear and shrill. Martin's corrida was there, and Güero thought how good it would be to see his cousin again. Slowly, they turned the herd over to the smaller corrida. The cattle had become accustomed to moving down the road, and wouldn't be any trouble to a small bunch of vaqueros. They had been driven five miles, and after drinking water at the Mesquite windmill, they would be too tired to run.

All the men waved at cousins, brothers, uncles and fathers, as they were all kin in some way. Güero rode toward Martin, Sr., when the cattle rushed to the water tanks to quench their thirst.

"Buenos tardes, Martin. It's good to see you," he said, extending his hand.

"Buenos tardes, primo. Welcome to the Mesquite pasture," Martin,

Sr. said.

He shook Güero's hand, then waved to his son. "How did it go, primo," looking into Güero's brown eyes. "Did you have any trouble with the ganado?"

"Oh, just a little, coming out of the Canelo pasture. You know how they act leaving their home pasture."

"Yes, I know. I remember the time in the Santa Cruz pasture when we lost a whole day's work when the weaners got away. We had to round up again to get them back."

Güero laughed. "Yes, I remember, it was a stupid job by you and me. Oh well, we were young and didn't know any better. It was your idea to let the calf go so you could chase it. The trouble was, the calf was faster than your colt."

"Hijo, the Caporal was mad at us. We felt the whip on our behinds that day."

"Where is the Chista? I see the smoke of the camp, but I can't see him." That was a standard joke because the Chista was so small that the underbrush hid him.

"Oh, you look closely and you can see him working underneath the cactus cooking his famous pan de campo." They all laughed.

Some of the men stayed behind and held the herd while the cattle drank, grazed, or lay down to rest. The others made their way toward the smoke where the Chista had set up camp by a large Mesquite tree. There wasn't a camp house close to the Mesquite pasture, so they camped near the Mesquite windmill. It had taken Güero's corrida about six hours to drive the cattle that far.

There was no better time, Lauro thought, than when the vaqueros rode toward a camp set out in the brush country. The smell of the burning fire, the quiet banging of the pots and pans, the smell of the food cooking on the mesquite coals, the jingling of the bits and bridles, the spurs jingle—it was music to Lauro's heart.

Each man unsaddled his mount and laid the saddle upside down, putting saddle blankets and the bit on top. They took their ropes to catch the horses they would ride that afternoon. Then laughing, each hugged the other cowboys that had arrived. They hadn't seen them for about a month, and that was too long for primos to go without seeing one another.

La Chista looked up from the fire and smiled underneath his old hat. His eyes darted back and forth to each new arrival, waiting for an opening to make a joke. "Hello, you son of a lopped ear mule. Where have you been? It took you long enough to get here," he teased, smiling from ear to ear.

"Buenos tardes, you shrimp from the Laguna Madre," Martin, Sr. said.

"Have you finished burning the frijoles?"

"Burn the beans! Why you broken-down *vaca de monte*, they should have retired you long ago."

"Well, who would be around to listen to your chirping, you little *parjaro de monte*?" They embraced.

"How are you, *hermano*? You look well," Martin, Sr. said.

"You, my friend, how are things at Santa Gertrudis?"

"Well, everything is okay, but we lost old Jose Esquivel two weeks ago last Friday. He just closed his eyes and died right there, taking care of the goats at Santa Cruz. We didn't have time to let you know that he passed away. We had to bury him right away. He was five days dead when we found him," Martin, Sr. said, looking at the men.

"He was a good man, and a great herder of goats," Martin, Sr. said. All the men nodded.

Beto Mendietta had put the chuck wagon where the tarp was rolled out in the shade. That was where the Caporal and the bosses sat and drank coffee, talked, and ate. The rest of the men sat on hand-made stools of wood and tanned leather that folded up when they weren't in use.

Quickly, La Chista started putting the serving bowls on the table for Martin, Sr. and Güero. He knew the first group had to get back and give the other men a chance to eat. The Caporals could linger at the table.

"Lauro, come over here and meet Martin Mendietta, Sr., the Caporal of the Headquarters corrida," Güero said. "This is Lauro Cavazos from San Perlita. He just started working for the kineño a few days ago."

"How are you, señor?" Lauro said. They shook hands across the table.

"Mucho gusto, I'm glad to know you," Martin, Sr. said.

"Are you any kin to Nicolas Cavazos, the first owner of the San Juan Carricitos Land Grant?"

"Yes sir, he is my grandfather, but not the first owner of the Land Grant. My great, great, great, great grandfather, Jose Narciso Cavazos, received the Land Grant from the King of Spain."

"Well, if they were like your grandfather, they were good men,"

Martin, Sr. said.

"Thank you, my father will be glad to hear that he was a very well liked man by everyone, except for the man that killed him, Scarface Colorado."

"Yes, I heard of him," the older man said. He shook his head. "It was a bad thing he did. I'll tell you one thing, he better not show his face around here. The Patrón has put a price on his head."

Lauro was taken aback by that bit of news. "You said the Patrón put a price on his head?"

"Yes, after the kidnapping attempt in Brownsville. I heard that you had something to do with the rescue of Reina, which we all appreciate," Martin said.

"It was nothing," Lauro said. "I just wish that at the time it happened I had known who he was. I would have followed him into hell to get him."

Martin Sr. liked the young man; all the Kineños liked valor and bravery in their children. He was a man true to their code. Martin Sr. looked at his son, who was sitting across from him. "Well, I guess if we don't get started, we won't get there. We have a long way to go."

Güero smiled. "Well, I'll take the herd to the Santa Gertrudis, and you round up the Mesquite pasture, okay?"

Martin Sr. laughed, slapping his leg. "Oh no you don't. I know who's got the easier job to do." He threw his last bit of coffee away.

"Thanks, compadre," he said to Chista. He waved to the men to get going, hugged his son, and turned to shake Lauro's hand. He pulled his hat on and went to work.

Everyone watched as the herd moved slowly to the northeast, wishing they were going with them to see their families and to sleep in their own bed.

"Well, it's as he said, if we don't leave we won't get there," Güero called out. He moved to where his horse was tied. Lauro gathered his rope and stood by his horse, enjoying the sounds of the corrida. With their hats pulled down, so the wind or brush would not knock them off, their brush jackets, chaps, spurs, the scarves around their necks and leather gloves, they looked like an army fixing to do battle.

They mounted and headed toward the jumping off point a little way from camp. Güero was in front; the others followed behind in a double file, talking, laughing, and enjoying the afternoon. They were thinking about family and what they were going to do on pay day, which was the end of the month, just two weeks away. Lauro was thinking of

Reina and her warm arms and breathless kisses, and the touch of her skin. He could hardly wait for the round-up to be over.

They came to an old wagon road just wide enough to get by the brush on either side. It was thick with every kind of wild obstacle that a man on horseback had to pass through.

Güero stationed each man within yelling distance of the next. "Keep alert. Don't let the cattle get by you. Stay in sight of the next man when you can." Julian and Chito had taken the bueys on ahead toward the far road on the other side of the pasture, to wait for the gathering of the herd. Güero stopped for the drop of the next man. "Lauro, you go through here, and keep the men on your left and right in sight, and don't get lost."

Lauro waited, looking at the brush before him. There was something quiet and serene about it. Nothing moved except the branches of the mesquite when the wind picked up.

He crossed his leg over the saddle horn, rolled a Bull Durham and looked into the brush. It was thick like a jungle, except this jungle had thorns, from cactus, mesquite, and wild rose vines. It was like being in a cathedral of green. It made Lauro feel small and frightened, knowing that God's power was infinite and beautiful, that He was truly working to provide for all of his creatures.

Lauro loved brush work, it was the next best thing to the actual working of the cattle. He looked to his left; there was Shorty sitting, smoking, and waiting for the big push. He looked to his right; Güero was waving. And then he heard the mournful yell to move forward.

The *grito* to move sent goose bumps down Lauro's spine. He put out the butt of his Bull Durham on his leather chaps, pulled down his hat, waved at Shorty, and moved into the brush down a game trail he had spied while he was smoking and waiting for the yell from Güero.

The trail was just wide enough for a man on horseback to maneuver in and out of the prickly pear that was in the way. He ducked out of the way of the hanging mesquite limbs, always looking ahead, smelling the wild smells, knowing that no cattle had passed there in a few days and noticing the tracks that were left by deer, quail, snakes and javelina.

Lauro saw the cattle moving toward him in single file. He hollered, making the cattle stop, look at him, then move the other way, away from a cowboy yelling his fool head off.

"Ya, no you don't. Go the other way. Ya, move. Hey Shorty, they're coming your way. Ya, look out. Ya, there's another bunch, ya." They finally turned and moved in the right direction. Lauro breathed a sigh of relief.

Lauro kept moving, it was very exciting to never know when cattle would move in your direction and try to get by. The cattle knew what was going on. The Kineños were here, and it was round-up time in the Mesquite pasture. After three or four times turning the cattle back, Lauro began to wonder if this portion of the round-up was ever going to end. He was sweating under his hat, brush jacket, and his seat in the saddle. It was thrilling, but hard and hot work. This was the life of the cowboy in brush country.

Soon he could hear the other men yelling. "Look out, Chito, they are coming toward you." Then he heard Chito hollering. "Ya, ya, no you don't, get back there, move. Lookout, Shorty, they're coming toward you." It was Shorty's time, then Lauro's, then Güero's, and so on down the line. The deer had already raced out, the turkeys had flown away, and the javelina had scattered in all directions. But the cattle smelled and saw the lead steers had gathered on them, too late, knowing they were caught.

Some of the cows and calves made it through the brush to get away from the vaqueros, but they were seen and let go for the bigger portion of the herd. There were some stragglers that waited until they were almost in the herd before bolting away.

The men let out soothing noises to calm the cattle down. The cows and bulls milled around the lead steers, the calves tried to find their mothers, and everything seemed in complete chaos. But, gradually, the herd settled down. The men took the time to roll a smoke, talk and be sure no one was missing. Güero started counting riders. All okay. Then he thanked God for getting all the men safely through the first push.

"Well, Lauro, how did you like your first push through the brush?"

"Not bad, at least I didn't get lost," Lauro thought back. "Well, a couple of times I almost did, but Shorty kept an eye on me." The men laughed.

"You'll learn the pasture in time," Shorty said, laughing with the rest of the men, a kind of nervous relief in his voice.

They had just come through a dangerous part of cowboying, like busting broncs. It gave them a sudden rush of adrenaline, knowing they had done a good job.

The cowboys surrounded the cattle, not giving them a chance to escape. Güero let them smoke their Bugle or Bull Durham and relax for a little while. He looked at the herd, noticing the crippled cows, the wormy ones, and the number of calves in the push. Also the ones that had not mothered-up, and the cows with horns that had grown down and into their heads. These would have to have their horns removed and doctored. Some had screw worms already showing in the wound. All this he noted while the other men rested, laughed, and talked back and forth.

Lauro took this in, noticing the difference in the man who was in charge and the rest of the men. Güero was always thinking of what answers to give the Patrón, the condition of the herd, the calf crop, the injuries, and the work they were going to be doing.

After a while Güero signaled Martin, Jr., to move the herd toward the trap at the Mesquite windmill.

Water had been discovered on the ranch several years ago, and with the fencing of the ranch which was still going on, there were windmills scattered all over the ranch. All of them were named so that they could be used to start a pasture.

The calves had mothered-up pretty well and Güero and the rest of the vaqueros were not too concerned that the herd would take off. Güero never moved a herd until they mothered-up and settled down.

Lauro moved to the rear of the herd with Güero, and the older men who were pushing the calves that tried to hide in the brush. Every once in a while a cow came rushing back to see if her new born calf was still with the herd. Güero smiled and nodded his head when he saw Lauro move to the rear where they were. "Lauro, this is where the actual work is and where you learn about the cattle and their stupid ways," the Caporal said with a smile on his face.

They reached the trap at the Mesquite windmill in the late afternoon, counted the cattle in the trap, and rode over to the camp, a short way upwind of the dust. They unsaddled, led their caballos over to the gate leading into the trap, and turned them loose with the rest of the remuda. Beto Mendietta, the corrida swamper, had put some light troughs on the ground, and the men fed the remuda oats and green alfalfa. Each man looked to his own string of horses and made a good inspection of each mount to see if it had any injuries. At last they moved toward the camp, tired but content with the round-up. They had about four hundred head, not bad for a day's work.

They washed up in the ground tank at the windmill. The turtles and snakes took off for higher ground, away from this bunch of laughing wild cowboys jumping into the cool water. It felt good to get rid of the dust and grime.

They could smell La Chista's cooking, and they were anxious to taste the food and see if it was as good as the last meal. It was. After the meal, the men rolled cigarettes, and sat down to a game of cards, or dominoes, or checkers, before going to bed early. They knew tomorrow would begin early.

Lauro and Güero drank coffee and talked in low voices of the day's work and when they would be ready for the Patrón. Güero said, "Tomorrow we will hit the south end of the monte, all the way to the fence. It is the hardest part of the round-up. The farthest to drive the cattle. After that we will round up the western part of the pasture, then the eastern part of the Mesquite. Then, finally, it should take about seven days to clean up the wild ones. If nothing goes wrong, we will be ready for the Patrón on Friday."

Lauro perked up at the news. Maybe, just maybe, he might get to see Reina before she left for that New York college. He drank some coffee so that Güero would not notice, but Chista, who was always the last to go to bed looked at Lauro and smiled.

Lauro thought to himself, "He knows, that little bird knows. I hope he can keep it quiet."

Lauro smiled back at him and finished his coffee. "Well, time to hit the *cama*. I'll see you in the morning. What time do you get up, Chista?"

"Oh, I start about 3:30, why?"

"Will you wake me when you get up please?" Lauro asked.

"Sure," Chista replied, "I'll wake you when coffee is ready. Buenos noches."

"Buenos noches, Güero," and Lauro headed for his bedroll. He put out his ground sheet, then brushed his teeth with baking soda, washed his mouth out, and laid down on his bedroll. He looked up at the stars so bright out there underneath the mesquite and wondered if Reina was looking at the same stars. If only they could take a message to her. He found the North Star, the symbol of which he had given her that night of love. "Oh, star so bright, take my love to her, please tell her I'm always thinking of her," as he closed his eyes and went to sleep.

He dreamed the Patrón was holding Reina by the arms, not letting her go to him. He was running toward her with his arms reaching out, never able to reach her. Someone was holding him back. "Wake up, Lauro, you asked me to wake you," Chista said as he shook him.

"Oh, Chista, I was having a nightmare. Thanks, I'm awake now." He lay back down and looked at the stars again, but they had disappeared. He put his clothes on and shook out his boots to get rid of anything that might have looked for a warm place to make its nest.

Chista had a big fire going. The coffee was made and he handed Lauro a cup before he began making his pan de campo. Lauro sipped his coffee as he sat on one of the camp stools, looking into the fire.

"Buenos dias," he said to Chista.

"Buenos dias," Chista answered while adding a little water to the flour, "How do you feel this morning?"

"Okay, but boy, I sure slept hard," Lauro said.

"Yeah, you were tired last night. I could tell." Chista kept mixing, taking his time, to let Lauro wake up.

Lauro looked into the campfire, and his thoughts were of Reina. He was in pure, sweet, young love. Never before had he made love like that wonderful night in the *monte* at the Canelo camp. He was overjoyed knowing that she loved him, but in lover's pain, that she would soon be gone.

Chista made big dough balls in the big mixing pan, drew a cup of coffee, and walked over to Lauro. "You know that she can never be yours," he said, in a low whisper to Lauro. Lauro looked up into the eyes of the one man that had seen them running from the oak motte.

"So you know," Lauro said. "I don't know what to do, Chista, I'm lost in the love I have for her. I'm glad it's out now; we don't have to hide. We can just come out and say that we are in love and plan to marry."

"Didn't you hear what I said?" Chista replied. "I said, she can never be yours. Don't look at me like I'm crazy. Do you think the Patrón will let her marry a cowhand and a Spaniard at that? Even if you are of mixed blood the Patrón would not go for it. And in this, the girl would have nothing to say about it. You see, the power of the ranch is so strong that even if you ran away together they would find you, and in time she would forget you."

Lauro looked at La Chista. "Look Chista, I know that right now I'm just a cowhand, but in time I will be someone. You wait and see. I will, I know I will."

"I hope so, Lauro. I like you; you're someone to ride the Rio with, but you better keep it under your hat till you see how the wind blows. Don't worry, I won't say anything to anyone, I give you my word. Just watch yourself. Okay?" Then he looked at Lauro and smiled as he walked off. The rest of the camp began waking.

After they ate their breakfast and saddled up, they moved out with the Caporal leading the way. As the sun was just peaking its daybreak colors over the horizon, the men were rested and ready to go. They talked in whispers, since at that time of the morning, their voices would carry a long way. Güero dropped his men in their places, raised his hand, and started the round-up of the brush to the Mesquite pasture.

Julian had moved the lead steers into the right position, and four other men besides himself were in position to turn the rushing cattle toward the lead steers.

Lauro moved forward knowing that Manuel Mendietta was on his right and Shorty Muniz was to the left. He could hear the crashing of the deer and other wildlife rushing to escape the gathering that was taking place. Lauro saw a bunch of cattle running across the trail he was on. "Manuel, lookout, they're coming toward you, watch it. Turn, you wild ones."

He could hear Manuel shouting and making all kinds of noise, slapping his chaps, waving his hat, making a funny sound with his mouth.

Lauro knew that there were too many cattle for one man, so he tore through the brush, cracking the limbs, hearing the noise that cattle hooves make pounding the ground. He felt his horse bunch up to jump over the cactus, and he braced himself, tightening his knees, relaxing and going with the movement of his horse, never taking his eyes off the cattle. It was like thirty different things going on at once. Popping the brush was exciting and fast.

They had turned the rush of cattle and saved the push. Lauro smiled at Manuel and moved back to his position, always keeping his eyes moving, watching for movement of anything in the brush.

So went the morning, always going in the general direction that they wanted the cattle to go, weaving in and out of the cactus and *graneno*, mesquite, and other obstacles. Never taking their eyes off the cattle once they spotted them. In other words, "*Pela el ojo.*" Lauro could hear the clanging of the lead oxen's bell, welcoming the new arrivals out of the brush.

It was well past noon when the men came out of the brush, after the wild game and cattle, in that order. Chista had moved the camp just a little way from the place where they were holding the cattle. It was always a welcome sight.

While the noon meal was being eaten the men took turns holding the cattle. Everyone got to take a short siesta before saddling up to hit it hard in the afternoon when the wind started up again.

They spent a whole week rounding-up, and another week roping the ladinos and dragging them toward the lead oxen. It was always hard work, but this was the life the vaqueros lived. This was what they were born to do; this was the life in the kineño. They were the real backbone of the King Ranch, men as skilled as any professional in the world.

Güero put the pencil down after counting the last of the herd into the pasture trap and smiled at everyone. They were bunched up like quail around the Caporal. "Well, men that about makes it; with the dead ones we saw and counted, we are just ten short. We will pick them up next time. The Patrón will be here tomorrow to work the herd. So, clean your saddles and equipment, rest up and get ready for some hard work."

Lauro was happy that they had done so well in rounding up the herd. They had just missed ten head to make the count or tally come out right.

La Chista had moved the camp at least twenty times during the round-up. Finally, he ended up back at the Mesquite windmill under the same mesquite tree where they had started.

The men were glad for the break and took the afternoon to check their horses, repair bridles and lariats, and make sure everything was in top shape for the work they were going to do. This was the end of the summer round-up and they were anxious to get to Santa Gertrudis Headquarters and their families.

They slept after taking care of their chores, ate, and then went back to sleep, or played cards or dominoes, and talked. They were getting ready for tomorrow when the Patrón would get there. They rested.

It was still dark the next morning when they heard the stage coming. Even in the dark they drove the horses at a pretty good speed. The driver, Adan, knew the road well. The stage stopped down wind from the camp.

"Whoa, you bunch of bones, this is where we stop," Adan said with a sense of pride that the team had made a safe trip with no trouble at all. He smiled at the men who were already saddling up and ready to round up the trap.

The Patrón stepped out of the stage, "Buenos dias, good morning, how is everyone?"

"Buenos dias, Patrón," the men said in unison.

Lauro had just finished saddling his colt since he was going to ride in the round-up of the trap. He looked up from rolling his lariat and smiled as Reina stepped out of the stage looking for him. Never had he been so glad to see anyone. "Buenos dias, Reina," Lauro said, with a

A sea of red Santa Gertrudis heifers in the pen

hunger to reach for her and hold her.

"Good morning, Lauro," Reina said, with a different sound in her voice, as if she was saying to him—"Hello, my love, how I missed you."

"Patrón, Reina, hay café," Chista said and put the coffee on the table. "Breakfast will be ready in just a few minutes," he said.

Güero moved toward the Patrón, "We were just going to move out to round up the trap, do you want to saddle up?"

"No, I think I'll stay here and enjoy my coffee. Reina does want to go help the men," answered the Patrón.

"Oh yes, please, Güero . . . if Julian would saddle my Rosita I would appreciate it," Reina said. Adan started taking their saddles from the stage.

Some of the men had already started to move out because they had a longer way to go around the trap. Lauro spoke to the Patrón and waited for Reina to saddle up. How glad he was to see her. She was putting on her chaps, having put on her spurs in the stage. Lauro couldn't help but notice how the chaps hugged her buttocks. They seemed more pronounced with each button that she fastened. Lauro wanted to hug her. She looked so beautiful, she was the best looking "cowboy" he had ever seen.

"Well, let's go . . . *Vaminos*," she said, looking at Güero, who with the rest of the men, was waiting for her. When they paired off, Reina naturally paired with Lauro. He did not look at her until they were away from the others. They headed for a mesquite motte in the middle of the trap.

They both entered the motte chasing the cattle out of the brush. Quickly, Reina came to Lauro, in the middle, where they were well hidden from the men. Lauro took her in his arms; her mere touch went all the way to his loins where his manhood started to fill his khaki pants. He kissed her for a long time, not wanting to turn her loose. Their horses finally pulled them apart.

"Oh, my darling," she whispered, "How I want you," she said, at last pulling away by necessity of the horses' action.

Lauro cleared his throat and said, "I'll meet you tonight, on the opposite side of the water tank after everyone goes to sleep, my love."

She answered "I'll be there, darling," and they rode out of the motte like nothing had happened.

Everything went well working the cattle. All knew their jobs and did them. Only two wrecks happened, for while riding colts, accidents were bound to occur. While rounding up the trap Chito's colt started bucking when the men were yelling and waving their hats. Chito had been watching Shorty chasing a yearling, so he was not ready for the action, and was bucked off. The men quickly caught the bucking colt while yelling and teasing Chito. He got back in his saddle, none the worse for the unseating.

The other mishap happened while Lauro and Güero were cutting out weaners. They had just cut a bull calf out of the herd; the men picked up the calf to take to the lead steers when all of a sudden it turned back to the main herd. Yoyo Silgerio was pushing his colt too close to the calf, and Lauro yelled to Yoyo to warn him, but too late. The calf cut back, cutting the colt's front legs out from under him. It happened so fast no one had a chance to do anything.

The colt went down, and Yoyo went head over heels in a jumble of hat, chaps, jacket, and man in a perfect somersault. Right over the head of the colt, to land on his feet.

Everyone laughed a nervous laugh, thankful that Yoyo had landed without injury to himself. The bull calf got up and was roped and dragged to the bueys. That was the only way to win an argument with an animal after a wreck like that. It was settled with a rope.

"Get along little dogie, it's your misfortune and none of my own," Lauro sang. Quickly the calf was roped and Yoyo, embarrassed but none the worse, mounted his colt and moved back to the main herd.

The branding went well and the men were glad to return to camp, tired but happy they were going home.

Silently the lovers met that night, in a night of love and promises all young lovers make, never to be broken, but alas, they often are.

The next morning the stage pulled out before the men had finished the preparations to break camp. Lauro waved to Reina as she hung out the stage window with tears falling down her face. With a smile she waved and to herself said, "I love you, mi amor, mi vida, mi corazon."

The main herd was let out of the trap, the remuda gathered, and the changing of the horses to ride part of the way to the Headquarters. It was a good day's ride to Santa Gertrudis Headquarters.

They rounded up the cattle that were cut out of the main herd the day before, and held at the gate leading out of the small trap. The corrida was ready to go home.

Beto and the Chista went ahead to where the corrida would break for lunch. Then they would pick up and move to the Plomo Feedlots, where they would wait for the men to join them.

It was a slow, hot, boring, job moving the cattle down the stage road. The cattle were sore from all the jousting they received from the day before, and this made them even slower until they loosened up.

Lauro helped Güero at the back of the herd, the dust always present and the noise always loud. But he did not mind, he was a happy man and it showed.

"Why are you so happy?" asked Güero between moving a calf to go forward. "You act like you don't have a worry in the world and you have a secret you are not telling anyone."

Lauro laughed and replied, "I'm just happy that I'm here with you and these men. It is a real pleasure to be part of the kineño. I'm happier than I have ever been."

"Why is that?" the Caporal asked as he threw a closed loop at a calf that was lagging behind.

"Well, I didn't know what I was getting myself into when I left the Laurel Ranch. Everything has turned out better than I thought it would. I knew it was a big outfit, but I didn't know that I would like it so much. The food is great and the vaqueros are the best in Texas, and the Patrón is, or seems to be, a good man."

He glanced at Güero and thought to himself, "Shall I tell him about being in love with Reina? He seems to like me . . . I don't want to spoil that, maybe I had better wait, maybe later, maybe later."

"Well, just wait till we get to the Headquarters; it's a beautiful place and the Kineños hospitality is given to anyone who comes by, or has become a kineño. You will be welcomed with open arms."

"I am looking forward to the kineño hospitality, they say the ranch has never turned anyone away if they were hungry or needed a place to sleep."

"If you come in peace, anyone from a Priest to an outlaw is welcome," Güero said. "But be fair warned, for anyone that doesn't come in peace, the justice of the gun will be fairly dealt out."

Lauro thought to himself, "I wonder if the outlaw that killed my grandfather ate and slept at the ranch after he did his dirty work. I need to find out these things."

"Güero . . . can I ask you something?" Lauro said.

"Sure, shoot," Güero said as he stopped a cow from leaving the herd.

"Well, do you think Scarface Colorado might have anything to do with King and the killing of my grandfather? I mean, did the Captain know anything or have anything to do with the killing or taking of our herd?''

Güero had this far away look on his face, his hat shading his eyes so that Lauro could not read them.

Vallejo, his old mentor, had told Lauro to always ''Watch a man's eyes'' if you wanted to learn what the man knew. He could see nothing in Güero's.

''You must learn that we are just vaqueros. We take care of the horses, the cattle. We do not know the mind of the Patrón or the mind of the thief. But I'll tell you one thing. Once you have laid your life on the line for these vaqueros, they will ride from here to hell for you. You have proven yourself to this outfit. We accept you as one of our own. If we hear of anything that can help you, we will let you know and ride with you to the end of this injustice. The men know of your quest. Do not worry, we are with you.''

This was a very long talk for Güero. Lauro's head came up, and he looked at this man who was more man than almost any he knew. A new respect for the Kineños became part of him. He had some allies; it was a good feeling, he was not alone. Now, maybe, he could find out something. Maybe, he'd better not mention Reina yet. He hated not to be able to tell this man about his love, but he knew the timing was not right. ''Later,'' he said to himself. He was afraid to lose this man's respect and he needed a friend. I'll tell him when the time is right . . . I promise.

13

THE SANTA GERTRUDIS DIVISION HEADQUARTERS

After an hour or so the cattle settled down to a steady pace, the men still alert for a wild calf. The vaqueros would have fun picking out the one to run away, then bet on who would have to rope it and drag it back to the herd. All in all, they made good time, finally seeing Chista's fire.

They unsaddled and picked the horses they would ride to the headquarters, had some fun with Chista, ate, and started the drive again. Along the way, Lauro continued his learning process. Güero pointed out the different landmarks, windmills, the joining of pastures, and how many head of cattle were in each one. It seemed every pasture and windmill had a story.

Last year one windmill crew had just finished the job when they saw a deer. Scared by the activity going on around the well, it ran across the well site and jumped into the mud pit and was stuck. The men roped the deer and pulled him to safety, but immediately killed and butchered it for their camp. So the windmill was named *Venado*. Other spots were named after someone who was just born or died, trees, horses. Lauro had to learn them all.

Finally, a little before the sunset, they saw the headquarters, and they came to the first set of pens about a mile from the main buildings. Lauro had never seen such a series of pens.

Güero looked at him and smiled. "You have never seen feed lots before?"

"No," Lauro said. "What are they doing here?"

"This is where we will work the cattle tomorrow to separate the weaners from the barren cows, the old cows and the bulls that are no good anymore. We put the good calves in the feed lots to grow and then decide which ones we keep for breeding and which ones we send to market. All the calves from the second half of the year are here, and we have a lot of work to do.''

"How many do you have?'' Lauro asked.

"Well, Martin, Sr. and his crew have been working the cattle they brought here from each round-up. They work each herd, and I haven't heard the full count. I'll find out when we work this herd with his corrida, but right now, the men want to get to their families.''

A line of wagons, horses, mules, donkeys, and people of all sorts, shapes, and ages were coming to see the corrida. They all waved, and the men waved back when they recognized their loved ones. This was a bad time for the cattle to be put through a gate and into the pens. Güero knew this and kept shouting at the men to watch what they were doing and not lose control of the herd. The bueys were pushed out of the herd and led into the large holding pen.

Slowly, the cattle started following the lead steers into the pens. The vaqueros didn't push them until the last stragglers started cutting back. Then the men rushed toward the last of the cattle, pushing them into the pen. Güero breathed a sigh of relief. They had completed the summer round-up.

Lauro sat watching the men rush their horses toward the shouting, laughing, crying people. Never had he seen such an outpouring of love. He felt happy for the vaqueros, yet sad that there was no one to greet him. He missed Reina and his smile slowly disappeared.

Güero shouted at him, waving him over to join him. Lauro spurred his horse toward the Caporal, who was in a wagon talking to a striking middle age woman. "Lauro, I want you to meet my esposa.''

The smiling Caporal pointed toward a thin, comely woman with black hair and big brown eyes. Her eyes never left the big Caporal with his arm around her. She gave a slight dip of her knees to Lauro, recognizing that this young man was important to her husband.

"Serina, this is Lauro Cavazos; he is now a Kiñeno, but he was born in San Perlita.''

"Buenas tardes, señora. It is a great pleasure to meet you. It seems like I already know you. Güero has spoken many times of your beauty, and truer words were never spoken.'' Serina gave a big smile, and her eyes shone as big as the moon.

"Welcome, señor, to the Rancho Kiñeno. Any friend of my man is always welcome," she said.

Güero looked at his beloved, laughing, then turned toward Lauro, "You know how to please a woman, amigo." You will stay with us till you can find a place. Come on, I want to take a bath and get this dust off me." He slapped Serina on the rear and she gave a slight cry.

The rest of the men were moving toward the ranch headquarters where some of the colony was located. Lauro could see a large structure. "Güero, what is that in the distance?" he asked.

"That is the Casa Grande where the Patrón and his family live. We have to go there, you will see." He mounted and in one big swipe of skirts and laughter, picked up Serina and placed her in front of him. She put her arms around his neck and rode there, happy as a lark. The people let out a big howl of approval and everyone started toward home. Laughing, kissing, and hugging, they traveled down the road toward Santa Gertrudis Creek. A bridge spanned the deep creek for wagons, stages, and anyone that needed to cross the wooden bridge to travel to the southern part of the King Ranch.

Lauro looked at the bridge with deep concern on his face. "Güero," he said.

"Yes, Lauro, this is Santa Gertrudis Creek. About a mile east of here was a crossing for cattle where your grandfather met his fate. It's called the *Paso de los Muertos.*"

"I want to see it," Lauro said. He started toward the east end of the creek.

Güero caught hold of the reins. "No, amigo, let it go for now. We must go see the Patrón and report to him what we have accomplished, and we must give him the tally of the cattle. We must also give him a report of the drive. Do not worry, we will go to the Paso de los Muertos as soon as we have done our job as Caporal of the Kiñeno. Understand?" Güero looked at Lauro earnestly.

Lauro looked at his friend and understood. "Alright, if you say so. I just have to see the spot."

"I know, my young friend, but this is a time for celebration, a time for song, laughter, eating, and making love. There is plenty of time for the serious business."

"Okay," Lauro nodded. "I will leave it for now."

"Good. Now we go home." The procession moved across the bridge, laughing, yelling and singing. Lauro's mood lightened a bit and he started singing with the rest of the group. They were going home.

As they passed the Big House, Güero let Serina down in a wagon.

"I'll be home as soon as I can. Get ready for us, my little dove. We have company coming. Cook us something to eat." He reached from the saddle and kissed her, and with a wave of his hat started toward the Big House, calling for Lauro and Martin Jr. to follow him.

Lauro had never seen such a mansion. It was beautiful, a three story gray structure made of lumber, glass, and brick with a touch of old Victorian architecture. There were five verandas, two in the front of the house, and a veranda on the second floor connecting the two wings and two on the other side. There were windows on all sides that reached to the floors, with magnificent doors at each end of the mansion and at each end of the connecting verandas. Four chimneys stuck out of the tall roof. There were large attics, with windows on all sides for guards to watch for Indians or bandits, but mostly for King to look out at his vast empire. The grounds were immaculate with green plants that made the Casa Grande look like the plantations in the old South. With cheap labor, they kept the grounds beautiful. There were large mesquites dotting the landscape, palms, tall and stately, and banana trees along the sides and front of the mansion. It reminded Lauro of his grandmother's yard, with green everywhere. It was a gorgeous place, so serene.

The only things that seemed out of place were the cannons on the lawn and on the inside windows of the lookouts, pointing toward the four points of the compass.

"The cannons came from Captain King's ship," Güero said. "He used them during the Civil War when he sailed for the Confederacy from Galveston to Brownsville. When he started the ranch he built the Casa Grande for Mrs. King and moved the cannons here, for protection. That is why the Santa Gertrudis was not a wise place to attack; it was well fortified. The enemies of the ranch knew not to attack main headquarters."

Lauro felt small when he rode through the massive gates. "So this is where Reina lives," he thought. "How can I provide for her after seeing this?" But young love could rationalize anything. They would make out alright. She loved him and nothing of material wealth would matter. He would make her happy without all this.

They rode down a long driveway to the rear of the mansion and tied their horses to the rack. Without taking off their chaps or spurs they walked to the connecting veranda in the middle of the Casa Grande. Juan, a primo of Martin, Jr's, greeted the dirty vaqueros on the porch, shook hands all around, then went to get the Patrón. In a few moments Juan returned with drinks for all. "The Patrón will be here soon. Sit and enjoy the cool evening.''

Lauro was a bit embarrassed. He looked at the sofa and chairs. They were upholstered in leather and very clean. Güero moved to sit and enjoy his drink of whisky and water. He motioned to Lauro. "Come, sit down, Lauro.'' Martin had already done so.

"They are used to hard working people coming here to report to the Patrón. It's alright. Sit.'' Lauro sat in a big comfortable chair. It had been a long time since he sat in his grandmother's chair, and he felt like hers were as good as this one he now sat in.

Lauro was starting to relax when he heard light footsteps in the next room. He looked from his drink to see Reina enter the veranda. He rose with the rest of the men. "Hello, Güero, Martin, Lauro, how are you all?'' She was beaming and very happy to see them all, but especially Lauro. She kept her blue eyes on him and stuck her hand out to shake hands with everyone. Her hand lingered in Lauro's hand. She looked a little more mature. It seemed she was starting to grow into a young woman, sure of herself, with some confidence he hadn't noticed there before. She was a woman who had loved and been loved. "How was your drive?'' she asked Güero, but not taking her eyes off Lauro.

Lauro felt out of place in the great mansion. Yet, looking at her made everything seem alright.

Güero answered her question without skipping a sip of his drink. "Fine, we had no trouble at all.'' The Patrón walked onto the veranda.

"Buenos tardes. *Como te fue?*'' He shook hands with all.

"Muy bien, Patrón. There were a thousand three hundred forty head put into the pens at the Plomo. Do you have the count of the cattle that Martin brought in?''

The Patrón motioned for everyone to be seated. Lauro sat in the big chair. Reina sat next to him in a smaller chair, and he hoped no one noticed her moving her chair closer to him.

"Two thousand ninety head is the count he gave me. Added to your count, that's three thousand four hundred and thirty head. Not bad for a spring round-up in the Mesquite and the Canelo pastures. We should have a total count of twenty thousand weaners for the spring round-up. Not bad, but I still feel that we've been hit by bandidos in those far pastures. But no matter. We'll catch them. What time do you want me at the Plomo?''

"Well, we could be ready for you about eight o'clock in the morning,'' the Caporal said.

"Good, have the junk cattle cut out. We'll go through them first and the weaners last.''

"Yes sir. I'll have it ready for you. Is there anything else?" Güero put his empty glass on the coffee table and stood.

"No, I'll see you manana. Lauro, will you wait a minute, I want to talk to you. Goodnight, men.''

They all put their empty drinks on the table and Güero and Martin, Jr., moved for the door. "I'll wait for you, chico," Güero said. He put on his hat and patted Reina on the shoulder, while moving to the screen door.

Lauro's face had turned red. He wondered if the Patrón knew about him and Reina. "Yes sir," Lauro said to Robert Kleberg, Sr.

"Lauro, I'm having a reception for the end of the spring working here at the Casa Grande on Saturday, and I want you to be here. The men will have a barbecue with their families at the schoolhouse, and we'll join them later. We'll have Mariachis, good food, dancing. Reina will be in charge, along with my wife, and I want you to help them with the arrangements.''

"Yes sir," Lauro breathed a quiet sigh and smiled at Reina. He put on his hat and walked out.

Güero and Martin, Jr., were waiting. Martin held Lauro's horse. There was a big grin on Lauro's face.

"Lauro, what are you so happy about? You look like you just ate the biggest piece of Chista's *pan dulce.*''

"The Patrón just invited me to a party here at the Big House. I have to help with the arrangements Saturday morning. I love any kind of fiesta," Lauro said as he mounted his horse. He could see Reina looking out the window and waving at them. It seemed she was always waving out of a window at him. He smiled and waved back, and they moved down the drive that went into the grounds.

A flock of peacocks ran across the lawn, making their high-pitched cry, warning anyone that strangers were in their domain. They were the watch-dogs of the Casa Grande.

Lauro noticed the big building at the end of the drive. "What's that building over there?''

"That's the *tienda* where we get all our supplies for the camps, our rations for our families once a month, or if we run out during the month we charge it against next month's ration. The different camps, like the corrida, the windmill crew, Martin, Sr.'s headquarters corrida and the fence camp get all the supplies we need. Also we get saddles, ropes, chaps, spurs, and all the things to keep the corrida going and to keep the ranch running.

That building over there is the Patrón's stables, where they keep the carriages and their vaquero equipment and the studs they buy to upgrade the stock of the Kiñeno. Up there, just a little way up the road, is a one-room schoolhouse made of lumber brought from the Port of Corpus Christi. That is where I learned to count and read. So I could keep good counts for the Patrón,'' Martin, Jr. said.

Güero looked a little embarrassed. He had learned the hard way without the help of a teacher. He could count, but could barely read, yet kept the most accurate records of all the livestock on the ranch.

''Who's the teacher?'' Lauro asked.

''A very pretty lady by the name of Miss Dale. She came from up north, but she's really good.'' Martin said.

''Yes, she would have to be to teach you something,'' Güero chuckled, poking fun at his young Segundo.

''Is that where you have your dances and all festivities?'' Lauro asked.

''Yes,'' Güero answered. They passed some other buildings and the Caporal pointed to them, explaining what they were. ''That one is the carpenter shop. They make gates of all sizes, gates for the pens at the Plomo, the Caldero pens, and gates for all the pastures. In fact, that's all one crew does is make gates. They are the best carpenters in these parts. Next to it is the forge. They make everything to hang a gate.

''In fact . . .''

''I know,'' Lauro interrupted. ''They are the best blacksmiths in Texas. Okay, okay, so everything is the best.'' They all laughed.

''Buenos noches,'' Martin said to both men.

''Don't go into town. You won't make it back in time for work,'' Güero said.

''Don't worry, I'm tired. I just want a bath and some home cooked *tortillas de harina* and then to bed. See you in the morning.'' He waved and disappeared into the night.

''Martin's not married, even though he could have anyone he wanted on the ranch. He likes town girls, cantinas, and music. Ah!, to be young again like you two,'' Güero said sighing. He chuckled to himself, and Lauro laughed with him.

''Will there be any of the family at the schoolhouse barbecue? I mean like the Patrón and his family?'' He hoped Güero wouldn't get the meaning of his question.

''Yes, the family will be there, after they get through with all the festivities up at the Big House. They all come for the dancing and eating. There will be lots of people from town, Mexicans as well as Gringos. There will be a number of people from Alice, Corpus Christi, and the surrounding towns.''

"How can anyone feed that many people?'' Lauro asked.

"It's easy when you have all the people helping and you're as rich as the Patrón. You'll see. It'll be a fiesta like you have never seen.'' Lauro saw some lights up ahead and Güero pointed out that this was the colony where some of the workers and their families lived. "We are almost home. There is the house and stables.''

Lauro saw the outline of the house and some fencing and the roof of the stables. They unsaddled, fed, and watered the horses, then gave them a rubdown before turning them out in the lot. Lauro could barely see, but Güero knew where everything was, so he just followed the Caporal around. He found his warbag and bedroll on the porch.

"Who brought these things?'' he asked Güero.

"The boys and Beto dropped them off. Come in. *Mi casa, su casa.*''

Lauro entered the comfortable wooden home.

The furniture was plain, with a lot of leather on the chairs and beds. The soft cotton mattresses had big leather covers to keep cool in the summer, and were taken off during the winter. It smelled nice—the leather and fresh *tortillas, carne guisada,* the beans, rice with green peppers, tomatoes, garlic, all from the garden at the side of the house. Serina tended to the garden during Güero's long absence. She and the other women would gossip while they helped each other tend their individual gardens. They took some of the produce to the market place in town to earn extra money.

"Welcome, señor,'' Serina said with a smile. "Welcome to our home, pase con paz.''

"Muchos gracias, señora. I thank you and your husband for having me,'' Lauro said, looking at the gracious lady in front of him.

"Put your bedroll over there on the bed by the window so you can see the stars and think of past romances.'' Güero pointed as he took off his chaps and spurs, hanging them in their place on a deer horn on the wall. A working cowboy kept his equipment close by, in case it was needed in a hurry.

Serina took a big pot off the stove and, going into the next room, which was their room, poured the water into a big wooden tub. She tested it to see that it wasn't too hot and satisfied that it was just right, signaled for Lauro to be first to take his bath. He started taking off his clothes before she closed the door.

Never did anything feel so good. The water was just right, the lye soap strong and clean smelling. He took his time. Lauro could hear Güero and Serina playing and giggling in the other room.. He felt good after the bath, and the food smelled even better.

"Hey Güero, come on in here and help me throw this water out so you can take your bath." The Caporal came into the room, picked the tub up by himself, carried it to the window and threw the water out. "My beloved, is the water ready?"

Lauro stood there with his mouth open. That tub was heavy, and Güero handled it like it was nothing.

After their meal, Lauro leaned back in his chair from the big wooden table. "Hijo, that was really good! Thank you, Serina, I'm so full I can hardly walk."

Güero was very pleased the meal went so well. A Kiñeno took pride in his woman, that she was able to cook, sew, and manage his house and garden.

"Come, we will go out on the porch to smoke and talk." He moved toward the door that lead to the front of the house. The night was cool and there was a breeze blowing. They sat in the big chairs that a primo of Güero's had made in the carpenter shop.

Lauro started rolling his Bull Durham. "That was a great meal. Does she cook like that all the time?"

"Yes, she likes to watch me eat. That's why I'm so big. When I'm here, all she does is cook and make me happy. She's a beautiful woman, I'm very lucky. That is what you need, amigo, a lady who will take care of you the way my woman takes care of me."

Lauro's mind went immediately to Reina. He lit his cigarette. "Well, maybe I have."

"Oh?" Güero perked up at the young vaquero's acknowledgment. "I've known since the Canelo pasture, you young people think that you are the only ones who fall in love, but remember we have been there before you."

Lauro was startled. He had no idea that Güero knew. "I wanted to tell you, but you were always talking to the Patrón. Again on the drive home I tried but there was no chance. Besides, I knew that you wouldn't approve."

Güero blew a stream of smoke in the air. "It's not for me to approve or disapprove. It's not my affair. But if I were you, I'd think long and hard, my young friend. She is used to having everything she wants. Can you give her that?'' He flipped his cigarette out into the night. "It is getting late. We better turn in. Buenos noches, chico.'' He rose and turned toward the door.

Lauro sat there thinking about his love for Reina. He didn't know what to do. He knew she could have anything she wanted, and he couldn't give her that. Still, she could change. "What will I tell her if I find out that King was behind my grandfather's death?'' he thought. "I just have so much to think over. This is such a fabulous place. Would she leave? How long could I keep her happy before she would want to come home?'' He rose, flipped his cigarette into the yard. "I love her so much. We just have to work it out,'' he thought.

Lauro felt someone shaking him. He didn't know where he was at first and rolled over to see Güero grinning at him all ready to begin the day.

"Buenos dias,'' Güero said. "It's time to rise and shine, sleepy head. Breakfast will be ready soon.''

He washed his face in the basin outside by the porch, brushed his teeth, combed his hair and put on his hat. The clothes Serina had washed the previous night felt good. He smiled. It was just like home, the women did all the little things that men had no time to do. They were just done so that the man could go about his business. He wondered if Reina had ever washed clothes. Probably not.

He walked toward the shed where Güero was feeding the horses. "There's a bucket hanging on the post over there,'' Güero said. "Feed the milk cow and she will be still while you milk her. I'll feed the rest of the animals.''

After breakfast, they started toward the horses, Serina walking with them, she and Güero holding each other. They mounted their horses. "Go with God,'' Serina said, kissing the Caporal and putting her hand on Lauro's leg, to include him in the blessing. Lauro thought of his mother and the women left behind to worry and wonder if their men would be safe.

When they got to the feedlots at the Plomo pens, the rest of the men and Martin's little corrida were already there, smoking and talking in low voices. The day was cloudy and it looked like it might rain. "Buenos dias,'' Güero greeted them.

"Buenos dias,'' they answered in unison. The men put out their smokes and waited for orders.

"Martin, you take some of the men and start rounding up the rest

of the cattle in the trap. Martin chico, you take the rest of the men and
start up the opposite side and meet your Dad in the corner of the trap
and bring the cattle to the pens. Lauro, Julian, Augustine, and I will get
the gates ready and move the cattle from yesterday in the pens forward
to the chutes they will go through first.''

Güero explained to Lauro what they were going to do. "We will
open the gates to the big pens, let about half of the cattle into the back
pens and the rest into the front pens. Then we'll push the cattle into
different pens till we get them crowded into the long alley that leads to
the small crowding pens and cutting chute. This will be where the
Patrón will stand and judge the cattle. He will pick good heifers, good
bull calves, good steers to stay in the feed lot, and the old or barren
cows and old bulls that will be shipped. You will get sick and tired of
opening and closing gates."

They worked from sun up till sun down. Güero was right, Lauro
had never seen so many gates and pens. All day they moved cattle out
of one pen and into another, depending which way they were trying to
move the cattle. The dust was thick and breathing was difficult. It was
hot and dirty work.

Lauro watched the Patrón judge the breeding stock, the good heifers
and bull calves he would keep, the others to feed for a while then drive
to the railhead.

At last they finished. The cattle were put into their pens where they
would stay for ninety days. Then they would be put through the cutting
chute and culled again.

"Okay, Güero, thank you," said the Patrón. "I'm late for a dinner
party, I'll see you tomorrow. Lauro, come up to the house tomorrow
and the Patróna will talk to you about the party for the people outside
the ranch. She'll explain everything."

"Yes, sir," Lauro said. He looked at Güero, who was rolling a
cigarette and not looking at him.

14

THE FIESTA

The next morning, all cleaned up with hat in hand, Lauro stepped into the connecting veranda. He was greeted by the Patrón's wife, Alice. She smiled at Lauro and held out her hand. "Welcome, Lauro. I'm glad to meet you. Reina has talked about nothing but you, and I wanted to personally thank you for what you did for my daughter in Brownsville. I will be eternally grateful to you."

Lauro turned red as he took her hand in a firm hand shake. "It was nothing, ma'am, I'm glad that I could help." He could see where Reina got her beauty. This gracious lady was a real beauty, and her mannerisms reminded him of his grandmother. She asked if he had had coffee and breakfast.

"Yes, ma'am. Serina served a big breakfast for Güero and me. Thank you."

"Yes, I forgot that you're staying with Güero and his wife. It's too bad that they have no children. She would be such a good mother. Well, shall we get started?

"First I want you to go to town. I have a list of things I'll need. Be sure and give this note to the owner of the store, Mr. Zimmerman. He'll fill the order. Beto will drive the wagon and Reina will go with you. She has to pick up a new dress she ordered from New York. We received word it had arrived."

"Yes, ma'am," he said as he turned redder.

He heard Reina calling out for her. "Mother!"

"In here, honey." Reina came bouncing into the room. She never looked lovelier. She wore a yellow skirt and blouse that matched her hair, which was tied back on her head with a yellow ribbon. Lauro melted on the spot.

"Good morning, Lauro. How are you this delightful day?" She took his hand in a shake that sent chills down his spine.

"Good morning, Reina. You're looking well," he said. He released her hand and stepped back a little so as not to be tempted to take her in his arms.

"Thank you, did mother give you the list?" she said.

"Yes, I have it here." He held up a piece of formal stationery covered with writing. The Patróna noticed that they made a beautiful couple. Reina, so much the young beauty and Lauro, the tall slim cowboy.

Alice Kleberg thought to herself that Lauro was very good looking. He will drive the girls crazy at the party, including her daughter. "I'd better tell Maria Lusia to keep an eye on them," she said to herself.

Lauro rode Lobo while Reina, Beto Mendietta and the ever watchful Maria Lusia rode on the seat of the wagon. It was a wonderful morning. Lauro felt alive, anticipating future possibilities. He couldn't take his eyes off Reina as they made their way down the road to Kingsville, three miles from the Ranch Headquarters.

"Is the town very big?" Lauro asked. He rode close to the wagon to speak to Reina.

"Yes, it's gotten pretty big, but not as big as Brownsville," Reina replied. "You'll like the people in the town, they're all so friendly. We even have a drug store where we can get a soda if you'd like.

"The ranch owns several businesses in town like the bank, lumber company, and saddle shop. We now have a railroad, and there's a dry goods store where we will pick up the dress I ordered."

Reina smiled at Lauro, who knew full well that she would wear it just for him. He felt more happiness than he had ever known. Reina continued to smile and talk to Lauro from the wagon. "Kingsville was started by Grandmother Henrietta King, who gave the land to the Kleberg Town and Improvement Company. But, of course, my father is head of the Land Company."

That was the first time Lauro had heard the name of Henrietta King. He knew that Captain King had been married. After all, he was in love with his granddaughter, yet no one had ever mentioned Mrs. King. Lauro looked at Reina with puzzlement on his face. "Your grandmother, you never mention her. Where does she live?"

"Grandmother King lives at the Big House with us, or really we live with her. I'm sorry, we haven't talked about her, have we?"

Lauro shook his head, "No, I thought she must have died or something because no one ever mentions her."

"Well, she is the real owner of this ranch. My father is the manager, but she gives all the orders. She's a very strong woman. I never knew a man or woman who knows more about ranching and breeding livestock than my grandmother.

"I go upstairs and see her every day. If I don't, she sends for me. But I do love to talk to her. She is such a dear. She is the one who enabled the railroad to come to the Wild Horse Desert. With my father's help, of course. They decided to build a town, and staked off the lots for the town with one stipulation—that the selling of alcoholic beverages was prohibited on Main Street. But everyone still drinks the stuff. I can't stand the smell. Do you drink?"

Lauro thought of Mexico and smiled. "Well yes, but only on special occasions."

Reina looked at him and laughed. "I thought so. Well, just don't do it in front of Grandmother King." Maria Lusia looked at them and bit her lower lip.

The town of Kingsville had about one thousand inhabitants, including the railroad people. It was a prosperous little town with many businesses that served both the townspeople and the ranch. In the eastern part of town there was the barrios. Many of the Latinos worked for the railroad, as did those from a small Negro section on the south part of town. The only businesses that had any real money were the King Ranch and the railroad. Everyone else owed the bank, which belonged to the King Ranch.

They made their way down a wide Main Street to the red brick Ragland's Department Store. John B. Ragland greeted them at the door. "Welcome, Miss Reina. It's good to see you. Come right in, we've been expecting you."

John Ragland was a born salesman. He was a short, dumpy man with a bald head, round face, and ears that stuck out. The two other employees made a big commotion getting the box with the dress down from the shelf where it had been put for safe keeping.

Reina smiled and introduced Lauro. "John, this is Lauro Cavazos. He is helping me with the supplies for the party tomorrow night."

Ragland looked at the tall, good looking cowboy standing there looking at the ceiling of his store. "Glad to know you, young man. Welcome to Kingsville." He stuck out his hand.

Lauro took his hand. "Hello, Mr. Ragland, how are you?" Lauro said, still looking at the ceiling of the little store.

"Fine. Do you find our ceiling to your liking? You keep looking at it."

"Yes. I've never seen anything like it. Beautiful. What is it?"

"I bought it in New Orleans. It's copper tin."

"It's beautiful. I like the floral design," Lauro said.

"We're very proud of it, there's not another like it within a hundred miles."

Lauro thought of his grandmother's ceiling which was just copper, but he wasn't going to correct the friendly man.

Reina looked at him. "Why don't you and Beto go do the rest of your chores while I try on my dress?"

"Yes, ma'am," Lauro said. He put on his hat, shook hands with Ragland and walked out of the store.

"Nice young man. Who is he?" Ragland said.

"He works for the ranch," Reina said, as she went through some lace on the counter. "He's a very good cowboy, and his family owns a ranch in San Perlita."

Lauro and Beto drove the wagon down the street to the Kingsville Meat Market. They could get the spices they needed there. The Ranch Store would take care of the rest of the things needed for the big Fiesta. He gave the list to Mr. Zimmerman, and finishing their chores, they went to fetch Reina.

Lauro and Beto waited patiently for her to come out. She appeared about two hours later. "I hope I didn't keep you waiting very long, but you'll be pleased with the results." She smiled at them.

Lauro grinned back at her. "No, ma'am, we didn't mind at all, did we Beto?" Beto just sat there, bored to death with all the woman business. Maria Lusia bit her lip.

In the next hour, Reina introduced Lauro to just about everyone in town, saying it was important for him to meet everyone. With Reina's packages and the few items from the grocery store they finally loaded the wagon, picked up some things at the saddle shop, and started back to the ranch. Lobo, who had been tied at the hitching rail next to the wagon, seemed glad to be back on the trail as he snorted and pranced about for the benefit of the bystanders on Main Street. When they arrived back at the ranch, Beto and Lauro brought the packages into the house.

"Oh, Mother, the dress is even more beautiful than I remembered, and Mr. Ragland waited on me himself, since Mrs. Ragland had gone to

Galveston to pick up some merchandise for the store. Just wait until you see the dress.''

The next morning the preparations for the party started in earnest. Never had Lauro seen so many people doing so many different things while preparing for a party. The day before the Patrón had picked ten steers for the barbecue, well fed and fat. The Headquarters crew had butchered the steers away from all the working and dust at the Plomo pens. Nothing was left behind, as the head, guts, blood, hooves, horns, and hide were all put in the wagon. The hide was kept away from the good meat, and the tripa, heart, liver, kidneys, and sweetbreads were all cleaned thoroughly for the Mexican stew. The head was to be made into *barbacoa.* The only things burned were the hooves and horns. The hide would be stretched and cleaned and later made into rawhide for the saddles, ropes, whips, and other things needed for the operation of the ranch.

The men of the Headquarters crew had dug long pits at the school yard to build mesquite fires where the barbecue and dance were to be held. Guests would be seated at long tables and benches where they could sit, eat, drink or just visit and listen to the strolling Mariachis. The Rancheros Band was in the school house providing music for dancing. The Kingsville Power Company that furnished the lights and power to the Headquarters hung electric lights in the trees, making the whole place look like a fairyland.

La Chista, and every cook of the ranch crews, did the cooking. They had plenty of help from the hands, who wanted to get a taste before the guests arrived. Great pots of beans, rice, *pan de campo,* tamales, *barbacoa,* barbecue meat, *carne guisado,* sangrita, potato salad, and sweets of every kind were being cooked and made ready. It was to be a grand feast.

Lauro went to the Big House to help decorate. He was hanging crepe paper out on one of the verandas with the help of the servants. He had never been so tired of a job, hanging the crepe paper, in all his life. He had been at it ever since returning from Kingsville. He hadn't seen Reina since they returned. Miss Alice, as the Patrón's wife was often called, had put him in charge of hanging the paper. He had to admit the house and yard looked like the carnival back in Brownsville. Just as he drove the last nail into the porch wall, he felt the ladder shake. Grabbing the sides, Lauro looked down uneasily, to see Reina standing there with a big smile on her face.

''Hey, Mister. If you're not doing anything, can you help me with something, please?''

"Yes ma'am, I'll be happy to,'' Lauro said. He hurried down the ladder. "How can I help?''

"I have to move some chairs outside on the lawn, and I wonder if you can help me?'' Reina asked.

"Yes ma'am. Just lead the way.''

She turned and led the way into the large living room where they were alone. She spun around, taking him by surprise and went into his arms, kissing him until she finally stepped back. "Oh, Lauro, I wanted to do that, I've wanted to ever since you got back from the round-up.''

"I thought you'd forgotten me,'' he said, pulling her back to him and holding her tightly.

"How can you say such a thing? You know I love you and was just dying to see you,'' she said with a sweet smile.

He touched her face. "I miss you so,'' he said. He kissed her again. They heard voices coming from down the hall, and they got busy moving the chairs.

"When can I see you?'' he asked, watching the hall and talking in a whisper.

"Tonight, after the party. Come to the orange grove behind the house. There's a pump house for the water system there, and I'll meet you at one o'clock. Now hurry and go so that no one can find something else for you to do. I'll see you tonight. Be here at six so you can tell the men what to do.''

"Okay, I have to help park the buggies and see to the automobiles. I don't know how to drive some of them, but I guess they all work the same.'' Reina started laughing. They laughed so hard it brought tears to their eyes. Lauro was still laughing when he left. "I'll see you tonight,'' he said. He went out to mount his horse and leave. It wasn't the joke they enjoyed so much, it was just being together.

The party started shortly thereafter, with people coming from as far as San Antonio, Corpus Christi, Alice, Premont, and from all over south Texas. They came early and stayed late. They kept the party going until the wives pulled them away from the bar which was set up outside. Some of the guests stayed at the Big House, but most stayed at the Kings Inn in Kingsville.

The first carriage that arrived were people from Kingsville. They had started the party early at the hotel and were on their way to a grand time. Lauro heard a motor car coming up the drive. He told one of the boys to take the horse carriage to the back and he would wait for the automobile. It came up the drive, backfiring and scaring the horses before it stopped in front of Lauro at the foot of the steps to the front door of the Big House. The driver wore white coveralls to protect his fine suit. "Here, boy, take this "Liz" and be careful with it. It's the finest piece of machinery in Texas."

Something about the man's manner upset and insulted Lauro. "My name is Lauro Cavazos, mister. I don't answer to boy."

The short, plump man looked at the young cowboy and smiled. "Well, what have we here? Oh yes, you're the boy that was in town with Reina yesterday. I've heard about you. But I didn't know the hired help would accompany a member of the family to do her chores."

"Maybe you don't know the Klebergs well," Lauro said.

"Let me tell you something, I am J. B. Bell and I am the legal advisor to the Kings in all their business matters. I don't like your tone of voice, young man." Bell was turning purple, he had never been talked to in this way by anyone, especially a ranch hand.

"Manuel," shouted Lauro, "take this car to the back." He thought to himself, "I wouldn't touch it with a ten foot pole."

"Si, señor, I will take care of it," Manuel said. Four of the men pushed the Model T Ford to the back of the house.

Bell glared at Lauro and took the arm of his wife and headed to the front door mumbling to himself. "Wait till I talk to R. J. about him. I think we better get rid of him; he looks like a dangerous young man."

Manuel de la Garza had observed the scene, and when he came back from pushing the automobile he told Lauro, "That bastardo is the lawyer for the ranch. He treats all the Mexicans like we were dirt under his feet," Manuel said. "The Klebergs aren't that way. They are good people. But Bell, he answers to no one but the señora King, so he is insulting and has no manners. He's a very powerful person. It seems he has very good friends in the State Legislature, the Governor's office, and law enforcement. It's said he has the favor of the United States Congress and even the President. Si, señor, he is a very powerful man. They also say that he was the one who acquired most of the Land Grants that made up the King Ranch."

"How is it you know so much about him, Manuel?" Lauro said.

"My name is de la Garza, my family owned this land the ranch headquarters is on." He spat a glob of spit behind Bell's path. "He made it impossible for the families of the original Spanish Land Grants to keep the land, after Texas stopped recognizing Spanish Land Grants. It is said that he had very good friends on the Borland-Miller

Commission that investigated the ownership of the grants.

"Of course, many records were lost in one of Captain King's steamboat accidents. That made it easy for Bell. We had to sell everything or get nothing for our years of work to settle this part of Texas. All the Mexicans hate him. What we have always wondered is what were the records doing on that steamboat?

"Borland and Miller were personal friends of Bell's. They worked together to take the Spanish Land Grants from the rightful owners and to claim the grants invalid. It is rumored Bell held favor with local courts, judges, and lawyers, all educated in Anglo-Saxon law, so we didn't have a chance." Manuel shook his head sadly. "Naturally, when the land became available King bought it at a very cheap price. If there had been any way to keep the land, we would have done so."

Lauro knew he was right. Maybe it had been Bell who had plotted the takeover of the Spanish Land Grants. He would have been able to buy the officials and make a hefty commission by seeing to it that King got first chance of refusal.

Lauro finished the job of parking automobiles and carriages, but he thought a lot about what Manuel de la Garza had said. "It was not King's fault after all. The deal was there, so he took it. Who wouldn't?"

Lauro made his way through the orange orchard, thinking how glad he was there was a full moon. He could see fairly well, and the pump house was visible from there in the moonlight. He sat and rolled a Bull Durham, struck the flame of his match and smoked his first cigarette of the night. So far it had been a very busy night for him. As he waited for Reina he began thinking of the party and the people he had met, in fact, all the things that had happened this night.

He wasn't in very good spirits after the altercation with J. B. Bell when Reina came to him and took his hand in hers. "What's the matter? You look like you just lost your best friend."

"It's nothing," Lauro answered, still angry at J. B. Bell.

"Well, alright. Let's go join the party in the Big House," Reina said.

"No thanks, I would just as soon go to the school grounds. I told Güero I'd see him there," Lauro said.

It was a shock to Reina to be rejected by Lauro. He had never talked to her that way. "Lauro, what's the matter? Is it something I've done?" she asked.

Lauro felt like a dog because of the way he had talked to her. "No, nothing, sweetheart. I'm sorry. I didn't mean to jump at you. I just heard something that made me lose my temper, and I can't tell you what it is. Please try to understand. It's not your fault," he said.

"Okay, I won't ask you what it is, so let's forget it. Go ahead and meet Güero and the rest of the vaqueros. I'll be up there as soon as possible. Save all the dances for me and be careful of the girls. They're going to be all over you tonight. Remember that you're mine and I'll scratch their eyes out." She turned and ran back up the steps to the Casa Grande.

Lauro heard the music before he got there. It was loud and they were playing a ranchero that shook the timbers of the old schoolhouse. There was a slight breeze that blew the smoke away from the dancers and the delightful smell of roasting meat over an open pit was enough to make a person's mouth water. There was the familiar sound of shuffling feet on the hardwood floor, in perfect beat with the music. It made him homesick for San Perlita. He moved toward the open windows that reached to the floor; inside the Kineños were having a fiesta. Güero was right in the middle of all those dancers with Serina, who was smiling from ear to ear. Martin Sr. was dancing with a young lady who was holding on to him for dear life every time he twirled her around. They were all having a great time.

Lauro had never seen so many pretty girls at one dance, and with all their mothers watching them. Güero saw him and waved for him to come out and dance. Lauro laughed and motioned that he would just watch.

All the people from the ranch were there as well as many faces he didn't recognize. The dance ended, and Güero came over and pulled him in the window. "Hey amigo, come in and dance, the music is great and we are all having fun. I want to introduce you to some of my primos. They work for the railroad, lumber yard, bank, and other businesses in Kingsville. They didn't want to live the life of the vaquero. Oh well, that's their fault. Gustavo!" He yelled over the band who had started on another tune. "I want you to meet Lauro Cavazos. He's with us now." They shook hands. Gustavo's grip was strong.

"Hello, Gustavo, how are you?" Lauro asked.

Lauro moved his navy Colt over to one side. The Patrón had asked him to come armed, sort of an insurance against anything that might happen. They didn't know all the people from town, so he just wanted some protection for his people.

The girls had heard about the new vaquero who had come from San Perlita. They looked him over and liked what they saw. He cut a pretty good figure with his Stetson hat, khaki pants, and shirt with collar buttoned. His boots shone in the light and his navy Colt was high on his right hip. He was a handsome man.

Some of the men were drinking behind the outhouse. It was alright as long as they kept it out there and not in plain sight. It was considered an unwritten law that no one got drunk with all the kids and wives around, so Lauro kept an eye on the men.

Martin Jr. came by with a real beauty who had skin the color of cinnamon and black hair that shone in the light. "Hey, primo, how are you?" Martin Jr. said. He punched Lauro lightly on the arm.

Lauro could tell that he had more than a drink or two, but he was just having fun. "Hello, Martin. It looks like you have your hands full. Think you can handle it?"

"Si, señor, he can handle it," the woman said. "Would you like to try it?" She smiled at Lauro.

They all laughed, Martin, Jr. the loudest. "How about that, amigo, can I pick them?"

"You sure can, Martin, but just be careful you don't lose her to someone else," Lauro replied. Martin took off in a fast shuffle in perfect time with the music.

He heard shouting and laughter outside. The Patrón's party was arriving. He came in saying hello and shaking hands with everyone. Miss Alice came right after him hugging and kissing the children. Their arrival livened up the party and everyone started dancing. Reina came in right behind her mother and father and the rest of the family, saying hello to everyone. She was looking for Lauro when J. B. Bell grabbed her and started dancing, leaving his wife standing there by herself. Lauro felt sorry for her. He didn't like Bell dancing with Reina, so he went out on the dance floor and cut in.

"May I dance with you?" he said to Reina.

"No, you can't" Bell said. "I got her first." He started to dance off with Reina when she pulled away and left him just standing there alone as she melted into Lauro's arms.

They glided across the floor as if they were one. Lauro held Reina lightly, but she pulled him tighter.

"Not so close, everyone is watching," Lauro whispered.

"I don't care, I just want to be held by you. I want to yell to the world that I love you," Reina said.

"We can't, Reina, you have to give me time to prove to the Patrón that I am worthy of you."

"Oh, I can hardly wait for later tonight! I hope you can find the pump house; don't be late."

"I'll be on time, I already checked earlier where I will meet you."

"Just be there." She smiled.

They danced every dance until finally the cooks told everyone to come and eat. There were yells and laughter, the happy noise of people lining up to eat the best food north of the Rio Grande. After everyone had eaten, a few of the guests sat around the tables, drinking and talking about cattle prices, horses, the last time it rained, the Mexican bandits, how the border was getting wilder, and the unrest in Europe.

"If we're not careful, those damn Mexicans will try to take Texas back and there won't be anyone to help us," Charles Flato said. He owned the hardware store and other businesses in Kingsville.

"Yes, we're way down here with no one to hear us if we yelled. What do you think, Bob? What will we do if they come across and raid us?"

"It seems there's more unrest than ever before," Kleberg said. "A little here, a little there. I don't think there will be any real organized invasion from Mexico, but just in case, I'll write the Governor for more Texas Rangers to patrol down here. In fact, I'll ask him to send some more troops to Fort Brown and maybe that will discourage the Mexicans."

All the men nodded. When Robert Kleberg, Sr. spoke, everyone listened. "Good idea, Bob. We'll show those greasers who is boss in this country," Bell said, holding a glass of whiskey in his hand and weaving back a step from the table.

Kleberg looked at him and spoke in a commanding voice. "Bell, I think you should keep your mouth shut. Remember, this ranch wouldn't be here if it were not for these people. I think you've had enough."

Bell stepped back as if he had been slapped in the face. He was smart enough to know where his livelihood came from. Slowly he put down his drink. "Sorry, Bob. I guess it's time to go home." He had turned red in the face, then bit his tongue and turned without so much as a goodnight, grabbed his wife, and left.

"Bob, you kind of jumped all over him didn't you?" John Maltsberger said.

"Oh, he'll get over it. Sometimes he gets to me. He shouldn't talk like that. These people are decent, hard working and loyal to a fault. I'd bet my life, and my family's on it," Kleberg said. He flipped a Bull Durham cigarette out in the school yard.

The dance continued after everyone had eaten. The party was just getting good when there was a disturbance in the west wing of the school. Lauro left a couple of young girls he was talking to and the band stopped. On the way, he met several of the men from the corrida. "You men better come with me. I think there may be trouble."

They followed him into the crowd that had gathered, trying to see what was happening. In the center of the crowd, a man with a knife faced Martin, Jr. They were circling each other trying to find an opening. Martin was unarmed, and it looked like the other man knew how to handle a knife.

"What's going on here?" Lauro shouted.

Martin looked toward the shout and the man with the knife attacked. Lauro reached out, grabbed the extended arm, and at the same time drew his navy Colt, butt first. He came down hard on the man's head with the butt of his Colt. There was a crack that sounded like a rifle shot and the attacker fell to the floor, out cold.

Everyone stared at the crumpled man on the floor and at Lauro who stood over him ready to hit him again. It had happened so fast that no one had seen Lauro draw his Colt and hit the man. Lauro holstered his pistol and looked up to see the Patrón, who was standing there and had seen the whole fight. He looked at Martin, Jr. "Are you alright?"

"Si, señor. It was pretty close there for a while, but Lauro saved my life. I didn't have a chance without my knife. I didn't think I'd need it here." He turned to Lauro. "Mucho gracias, primo. I owe you one."

Lauro knew he had a friend for life. "What will we do with this one Patrón?" Lauro asked.

"Take him and tie him to that mesquite tree over by the outhouse. We'll let him sober up before letting him go. Javiel, we don't want him ever on this ranch again, is that understood?"

"Si, señor, we will keep him there till in the morning." Javiel, Güero and several of the men picked him up and tied him to the tree by the outhouse. Lauro watched them and wondered if that tree, with low large branches had ever been used for something else, like a hanging. He had heard stories in years past of the King Ranch dealing with outlaws in their own way.

Javiel came over to Lauro, "Every time there is trouble, there you are. You're a good man to have around. Why don't you join my outriders?"

"No thanks, Javiel. I'll stay with the corrida," Lauro said.

Javiel nodded and shook Lauro's hand. "Good job, Lauro. I must get back to the Big House.''

Everyone crowded around Lauro. Reina couldn't even get to him to see if he was alright. Kleberg put his arm around Lauro's shoulders, smiling with pride. ''Son, you did a great job, not only saving one of my best vaquero's life, but the barbecue. You have a great talent to think fast in times of trouble. I'll remember this night and so will the rest of the Kineños. You are a brave lad.''

''Thank you, sir. It was nothing. I was just lucky, I guess.''

Lauro threw the cigarette butt out into the orange orchard away from the pump house. He didn't remember grabbing the arm with the knife, but he remembered hitting the man on the head. It all happened so fast. ''I hope I didn't hit him too hard,'' he thought, ''but he had it coming.'' He saw someone moving through the orchard, it was Reina. She came into his arms. Her lips were as sweet as honey, and he couldn't get enough of her kisses.

''Oh, Lauro, you were so brave. You just amaze everyone, Papa included. I don't know what he would have done if Martin had been killed. Probably that drunken guy would be hanging right now.''

''But what about the law? Don't they have something to say about it?'' Lauro said, kissing her on the neck.

''The Ranch is a law within itself. Besides, no one could hold back the corrida if something had happened to Martin.''

''I'm glad I could help.'' He kissed her lips. ''You were late. Where were you?''

''I couldn't get away from Grandmother King. I told you I have to go by and see her every night before I go to bed. Now, put me to bed,'' she whispered. Slowly, he lowered her to the ground, there in the sweet scent of the orange trees.

They made love and lay in each others arms, looking at the stars between the branches. ''I'm so tired I could go to sleep right here. It's so peaceful. From now on, this place will be ours, like the Canelo pasture,'' he said kissing her cheek.

''I know,'' she said in a sleepy voice. ''I could stay here forever, I love . . .'' They heard a yell and the fire bell began to ring.

''Come on we have to get out of here.'' She started putting on her clothes.

Lauro had his pants buttoned before she was through talking. They didn't say a word while they finished dressing. He kissed her, and they ran toward the Big House.

When they broke out of the orchard they were horrified. The Casa

Grande was on fire. "Oh, my God," Reina cried. "Oh, my God. Not the Big House. What are we going to do?" She started running toward the blazing house. Lauro heard her scream. "Grandmother!" She looked toward the top floor.

Lauro grabbed her just as Javiel came running toward them. "Javiel, keep her here, no matter if you have to sit on her, don't let her get near the blaze. I'll be back." He ran for the burning mansion.

"Lauro," she yelled, struggling in Javiel's arms. "Let me go. I must get to my grandmother." She finally quit struggling and stood there. She knew that she could do nothing but pray.

Lauro rushed into the breezeway and headed toward the stairs. The smoke was blowing away from the main part of the mansion, and it looked like the fire had started in the kitchen and spread up the north wall. He raced up the stairs onto the second floor. There was some smoke coming into the hall of the second story. He met the most of the guests coming out of their rooms. "Get out, the whole place is fixing to go! Hurry! Get out!"

He was starting up the third flight of stairs when he saw Mrs. Henrietta King coming down the stairs. She was dressed in black from the tip of her shoes. A tall frail woman with a walking cane coming down the stairs, not hurrying and showing the calm and composure that proved her the matriarch of the King family. A few gray hairs were hanging from beneath the mantilla, and as she brushed them away she looked up and saw Lauro.

"Good, young man, help me down these stairs." He grabbed her arm and helped her down the stairs of the burning mansion. Smoke was beginning to fill the stairs just as they reached the second story. They turned and headed down the last flight of stairs. Lauro looked at the old lady. She was crying, yet there was no panic on her face. Smoke was beginning to fill the hall and the stairs.

They were at the bottom of the stairs when Kleberg came running into the room. "Thank God, Mother Henrietta. You're safe, I'll take over here. Lauro, get the men to start getting what papers we can save out of the office. Hurry."

But the old lady interrupted. "No! Let them burn. There is nothing we can do. It's not worth a life. Let's hurry out of here." They hurried out of the hall and into the breezeway. The fresh air rushed into their lungs, and it felt like a cold splash of water on the face. Lauro saw Mrs. King take a big breath of air and started to cough. They rushed out of the breezeway into the yard. They were safe.

Reina rushed to her grandmother, embracing her, laughing and crying all at the same time. "Oh, Grandmother, we were so worried. Thank God you're safe." As she looked at Lauro, "Thank God we're all safe." Lauro saw tears racing down her face and smiled knowing that she was safe, too.

"Hurry, get the men on the bucket brigade. There's not enough pressure coming from the few hoses we have," Javiel said. He and everyone knew it was of no use. There was no equipment to fight a fire like this. They only had a few hoses and with electric lines fallen, there was no electricity to run the pump. They watched in shock and disbelief as the flames consumed the wooden mansion. Still, all of the family and guests were out safely, so they were thankful.

Lauro watched the old woman. He noticed she was holding a black bag that she would not put down. The flames had spread to the roof. It was like a giant torch. Like a signal for ships at sea. Lauro thought of the Captain King and wondered if he was standing watch to guide his ship to safety.

Mrs. King looked up and threw a final kiss to the old mansion and turned to go rest in the commissary. Reina took her arm to help guide her over the immaculate yard and into the building. She was almost eighty years old and had seen many tragedies in her lifetime. There was no use watching the mansion burn—too many memories, too much pain, tears, laughter, love, all going up in smoke.

There was nothing left standing but two tall black scorched chimneys. The next morning was as gray as the mood of everyone at the King Ranch. It looked like it wanted to rain. Lauro wished it would. Lauro and the rest of the men were drinking coffee at the camp which had been set up in the yard to feed the men who had fought a gallant fight but lost. Tired and sleepless men sat around waiting for orders from the Patrón. Finally, he came out of the commissary, walking slowly toward the camp. Chista served him a cup of coffee as he sat on one of the benches and rolled a smoke. Everyone had blackened faces and smelled of smoke. They were very tired and sad about this happening to the family.

Güero sat next to the Patrón. "Patrón, the men wanted me to tell you how sorry we feel that this has happened to you and your family."

The Patrón looked at these men who were almost like family to him. He was proud of them and the way they fought the fire, even though they knew that they could not win. "Thank you, Güero. Thank all the men. I will pass your sympathy on to the Patróna and the rest of the family." He sipped his coffee and looked at the remains of the mansion. Then he threw the coffee away, stood up, turned, and looked around. "Where is Schultz? I want to talk to him."

Everyone looked around and looked at each other. "We don't know," Güero said. "You know, I didn't even see him last night. It's funny, he is the chief gardener and he was nowhere around."

"Where is he?" No one knew. There was a murmur that rose out of the men. "Do you think he started the fire, Patrón?"

"Well, yesterday Miss Alice chewed him out about not doing his job. She told Schultz that she was giving him two weeks notice."

Güero looked at the men. They knew what to do—search till they found Schultz. Lauro started to go with the men, but Kleberg stopped him. "Wait a minute, Lauro, I want to talk to you."

"Yes sir," said Lauro, "What can I do for you?"

Chista brought some more coffee for both of them.

"I just want to thank you for helping Mrs. King last night. If you hadn't, no telling what would have happened."

"Oh, it was nothing, she was practically down the stairs. She's a remarkable woman, like my grandmother. They're made of something that no modern woman has—steel."

The Patrón laughed. "You're absolutely correct. They are a hardy breed. I wish my sons were that way."

"They will be, they're just too young yet, you'll see," Lauro said.

"Yes, maybe," the Patrón said thoughtfully. "By the way, Mrs. King wants to talk with you. She's in the big bedroom on your left when you go up the stairs in the commissary."

"Me, what for? I didn't do anything that anyone wouldn't have done," Lauro said.

"Yes, but you were there, and you answered the call. You always seem to be at the right place at the right time. It's extraordinary. You are a lucky young man. I've watched you and your work is very good. You learn fast and the men like you and follow your orders willingly. When you get back, I need to talk to you of other things. I'll be out here going through this rubble to see if I find anything that might have escaped the fire. It looks like we lost everything of value —our clothes, jewelry, paintings, important papers—everything. God, what a mess. The fire is still hot, and I won't to be able to look until it cools down. By that time, it will be complete daylight and we can do a thorough search. You better go see Mrs. King. She's expecting you."

15

PASO DE LOS MUERTOS

Lauro got up and threw the remains of his coffee on the grass of the lawn, turned toward Chista, and looked into his eyes. "Thank you, Chista." He pulled his hat down over his eyes and headed for the commissary to see Mrs. King.

He knocked on the door and was told to come in. She was sitting by the window in a big rocking chair looking at the burned out building. Taking off his hat, he greeted her, "You sent for me?"

She turned and looked at him, staring just a moment before answering. "Yes, Lauro, come in, sit down. I wish to know you a little better." Lauro sat on a chair across from her. There was a table with a coffee pot and cups for serving between them. The room was bare except for a bed, wash stand, table, four chairs, and a dresser.

"Do you take sugar?" she asked as she poured his coffee.

"No, ma'am, just black, thank you."

"That's good. Too much sugar is bad for the blood, and we all drink too much coffee. But coffee is one of life's few pleasures." She handed him his cup.

"First, I want to thank you for your help in getting me out of that fire last night." Lauro started to protest, but she held up her hand to stop him from talking. "You were there when I needed you. I won't say another word about it. The fire is too painful to talk about. Too many memories."

Lauro was amazed at how much the woman was like his grandmother—strong willed and unbending. Even in the face of disaster, she held her head up like a queen talking to one of her subjects.

"How is your grandmother? She has never forgiven the Captain and me for the death of your grandfather and the loss of the Land Grant." Lauro's face turned red, he almost dropped his cup. He rose from his chair. There it was, the very reason for his being there. It was the moment of truth. Before he could say anything, she put her hand on his hand. "Sit down young man. I'm not through. I know how you feel. If that had happened to me I'd feel exactly like you. Let me finish, then you can talk." Lauro sat back down and regained his composure.

"That's better. Now listen. When Texas declared all Spanish Land Grants disallowed after the Texas Revolution until they were investigated for their validation, the Captain saw a chance to build something and he took it. He didn't make the laws of Texas. Yes, he used his wealth and influence in shaping the outcome. He saw something that no one else could see in this vast, dry wilderness.

"It was just business. You're too close to it to see it. J. B. Bell came to him with the information that the San Juan de Carricitos Land Grant would be up for sale soon, and asked if he would be interested in buying in that part of Texas."

She sipped a little coffee and continued. "He had acquired the Santa Gertrudis from the de la Garzas. I know it went for practically nothing."

Lauro sat at the end of his chair and just held his coffee cup, not drinking. He was spellbound by her words. "But again, you must remember that there was nothing here. With money, sweat, and tears, we built something and we are still building. We have a town, a railroad, businesses of all kind, and more people are coming into the town all the time. Some day we will develop a type of cattle that will grow fat in this hot dry desert.

"The Captain had great plans for this Wild Horse Desert, but God had other plans for the Captain. So I carried on, and God willing, I will finish what the Captain started."

Lauro felt that she was not talking to him, but to someone else in this room. Yet, it was just the two of them. He felt a chill run down his spine as he realized she was talking to the Captain.

"Please be patient, Lauro. I'm an old woman and it's not easy for me to speak of painful things. But I want so much to see my granddaughter Reina have all the things that she deserves, including happiness, love and children of her own." Mrs. King took a sip of water from her glass. "We acquired the Santa Gertrudis Grant through J. B. Bell."

Lauro was captivated by her voice. She was telling him everything he wanted to know.

"Everything we have done has been through him, lawfully and above board. He would come to us and say this or that piece of land is available, and we bought it. J. B. had many friends. We didn't question his methods, but they were not ours. We know that he had great influence with the Borland-Miller Commission, which was appointed to investigate the validity of the Land Grants. We had no part in their findings and conclusions. Yes, J. B. made a lot of money off the Captain in commissions.

"The death of your grandfather was a terrible thing, but we had nothing to do with it. The Captain was outraged that it happened. Your grandfather was a friend and fellow cattleman. It was people like your family and the rest of the Spanish nobility that built this great land. We are all care-takers of this land, and we must protect and nourish it so that it will grow for generations to come. I'm sure we made mistakes along the way, but let me say that it was not intentional. So try to see it our way. Don't hate us for taking opportunities.

"Would you like some more coffee?" It was a signal that she was through explaining and that she was ready to listen.

Lauro's coffee had gone cold in the cup. He put the cup down on the table. "No, ma'am, thank you. I know that it was business, but can't you see how we feel? Man's greed is never your fault, it's always someone else's. It was rumored your money was the factor that made the Commission rule the Land Grants weren't valid. The sinking of the records in the steamboat accident—what were they doing on the steamboat anyhow? Was that part of the whole deal? Did the Captain know about it? Was Bell part of the conspiracy to take advantage of the Land Grant owners?

"After all, my family fought for this land along with the Sequins, the Carvajols, the DeLeons and the rest of you. They were all assured by General Sam Houston that if they fought, they would be protecting their rights to the land. What happened to his promise? Again, the Anglo took advantage of our difference in languages and customs.

"We can do nothing about the way things turned out but, by God, I can do something about my grandfather's death. I will have my revenge on his killers. His blood cries out for retribution, and I will see to it. I changed my mind about the Captain when I heard he had offered a reward for the capture of the killers. The Kineños have been nothing but kind to me. This is a great place to work and live. Mr. Kleberg has been nothing but honest and truthful, and he has some plans for me in the future, I believe. I want to do my best, so that I can do the job for you, but I need to be someone in this organization, someone who the people will look up to. I know I can't recover what we have lost, but I can see to it that it is not abused and is protected. Like you say, for generations to come. Now, if you will excuse me, I have to see what the Patrón has for me to do." Lauro rose and headed toward the door.

"Lauro, well said."

He stopped and turned. She continued. "I know you will go far. Just remember who you are, and let me explain something to you about my granddaughter who is very precious to me. She is headstrong, just like the Captain. She thinks she knows what she wants, but she is bound to break a lot of hearts between now and that date her destiny is reached, whenever that will be. Be careful that you are not one of those broken hearts."

Lauro looked at her, understanding she was giving him a message. Without a word, he went out the door, taking the stairs two at a time, thinking about what the old lady had said. It had started raining as he raced to the camp and sat at the table under the tarp, not looking at the Patrón or Chista. Kleberg said nothing for a while, then spoke. "Lauro, tell Güero that I want him to take you to the *Paso de los Muertos*."

Lauro looked at him, thinking, "So, you were in on it, too."

"Why," Lauro said. "Why now?"

"Because I want you to get over this, to live a life for yourself, not for your grandfather. I understand how you feel. You will get revenge if God wills it. It does no one any good to carry this on your shoulders, and I'm sure your grandmother would agree with me. I know you feel that your quest for the truth of your grandfather's death will not be complete without your visiting the actual place of his death. Now is the time to put it to rest. So tell Güero, and go with God." The Patrón began to roll another cigarette, staring out at the falling rain.

"Yes sir, I'll go and see if I can find Güero." With that he pulled his hat over his eyes and went to the corral by the stables to get his horse.

As he rode to find Güero he was thinking about what Reina's grandmother had said to him. The old lady knew. "Don't ask how she knows, but she knows," he thought. "But that bit about breaking hearts, surely she wasn't talking about us. Reina loves me too much. It can't be." Güero was sitting on his front porch watching it rain.

"Did you find Schultz, the man you were looking for?" he said to

Güero.

Güero looked at him and nodded, but did not mention it again. Lauro wondered what happened to Schultz.

"The Patrón wants you to take me to the *Paso de los Muertos*. He said he will take every available man to clean up that mess the fire made. All other work except the feed crew is to stop. With this rain, the fire will cool down quickly. I'm ready when you are." He sat down in the other chair and rolled a smoke. The rain continued. Neither of them spoke.

Güero stared out in the yard. Finally, he tossed his cigarette out into the rain. "Okay, let me get my poncho and we'll go. I don't think this rain is going to let up." He rose and went into his casa. He came out shortly putting on his poncho and stepping into the rain.

Serina came to the screen door. "*Vaya con Dios.*"

Lauro looked at her. "Thank you, Serina. We'll be home before dark."

They rode through Headquarters, looking at the burned out mansion as they rode by. "What a shame," Güero said. "All the years they lived in the casa with all of the historic things they had collected, gone up in smoke."

They went over the bridge at Santa Gertrudis Creek, then cut to the east. Güero took a path that went along the creek bank. It was tough going. The bank had been washed out from sudden flooding from the creek. Güero stayed high on the bank, in case of a sudden flash flood. He shouted over the rain. "This creek runs all the way to Baffin Bay and empties into the Laguna Madre and that empties into the Gulf of Mexico." Lauro's mind was elsewhere. He just nodded and followed the big Caporal.

Lauro thought to himself, "We are going to the place where it all started. It could have been different but we are dealt the hand we must play. If grandfather had not stopped on this side of the creek, if they hadn't hired that redheaded son-of-a-bitch, if King had given him more time, if he had not sent Father home to see if we were all right. So many ifs, but '*Que sera, sera*' what will be will be. Surely God and the Virgin Mary will let me see this through," he thought. "We lost my grandfather, we lost the land, and all because someone knew grandfather was going to take a herd across Santa Gertrudis Creek."

About a mile from the bridge, Güero held up his hand. "This is the crossing. This is the *Paso de los Muertos*."

Lauro stopped, then moved a little away from Güero, studying the

water-filled crossing where all the dreams of the Cavazos died. No
cattle could safely pass that part of the creek. The waters had flooded
there and caved in the sides, digging deeper and deeper until it had
become a giant hole. He looked around to see if he could tell where the
camp had been, but the weeds and mesquite had taken over the area. It
was still raining, making Lauro pull his hat down lower over his eyes
and the collar of his poncho up to keep the water from running down
the back of his neck.

Güero moved over by a big mesquite tree. "This is where they
found your grandfather and the four bastardos who died before he did.
He must have been a hell of a man, *muy macho.*"

"He was," Lauro agreed.

Tears ran down his cheeks mixed with the rain. It was strange to be
at the place where men had laughed, eaten, worked and died.

Lauro stepped down off his horse and he moved to the place where
his father had found his grandfather. Lauro knelt in the mud, said a
silent prayer. He rose and moved toward his horse, put his arm around
its neck, laid his cheek against the warm body and cried. Güero moved
away to let the grief come out of the boy.

The rain began to let up. Güero was watching the creek rise and the
debris of limbs and tree trunks floating down the path when he heard
Lauro mount his caballo. He turned and smiled. "Hey, chico, it looks
like a good rain; you know how to tell you've had a good rain?"

Lauro looked at him. He didn't want to spoil Güero's joke. "No,
how?"

"When you see the cow piles floating down the cow trail; that's a
good rain." Güero slapped his leg and laughed his head off. Lauro
laughed and felt better.

After a while, they headed back to the ranch. When they got to the
bridge, Lauro looked at the big Caporal. "Thank you, Güero. It was
something that had to be done; I had to go there."

"Hey, chico, I'd have thought less of you as a man if you hadn't
gone. We all have our crosses to bear. You will find the bastardos who
killed your people. God acts in strange ways. This Scarface will get
what he deserves, wait and see."

He changed the subject and moved down the road, making small
talk and singing a song or two. It had been a long two days, and when
they got back to the ranch and Güero's house, they turned in early.
Lauro fell right to sleep; not even dreaming. Later, something woke
him. He was so drowsy he couldn't think of what it was, then he heard

it again. Looking out the window, he saw a shape.

Someone was scratching on the screen. "Lauro, Lauro. Wake up. It's me, Reina. Wake up." Immediately, he was awake and he put his finger to his lip, signaling her to be quiet.

It was still raining, and he motioned toward the shed and started putting his pants and boots on. When he was dressed, he quietly slipped out of the house. He went to the shed by the corral where she was waiting for him. "Darling, what's wrong? What are you doing here?" He took her in his arms.

"Oh, Lauro, they're going to take me to Corpus Christi tomorrow to stay with relatives. I have to get a complete new outfit for school, then I'm going directly to a girl's school in New York. That's a million miles from you. What are we going to do?" She held on to him as if it was the last time she would ever hold him.

Lauro's heart sank. New York might as well have been the moon. "I don't know, why so soon?" He thought of the fire and all the clothes and things that women need. He saw she had to have those things. It was heart breaking to think that she was leaving tomorrow. She started crying.

"Shhh! Don't cry, my love. There's nothing that we can do." He kissed the tears from her eyes. "We knew that you were going to leave for school, the fire just made it sooner. Anyhow, we had these months together, and I have to make a place in this organization. We knew we would have to be apart for some years. Our love will keep us going. Please don't cry. Everything will be alright, you'll see." He held her tight.

Slowly, she stopped crying, and Lauro handed her his bandanna. She blew her nose and smiled at him. "I knew I'd have to go, but it's so hard to leave." He kissed her again. Their passion rose and they couldn't get enough of each other. They made love like it would be the last time. Afterward, they lay in each others arms in the warm hay, whispering and listening to the rain.

"Don't you mess with any of these girls on the ranch or in town. If you do, I'll shoot them, I promise."

He laughed. "Don't even think that. I love you. There's no one else for me."

"I'll write you every day, and you can write to me at school. That way, I can tell you how much I love you as many times as I want."

"Yes, sweetheart, I'll write as soon as I get your address. I can't very well ask your mother or father for your address, now can I?"

"Oh, no, that would spoil everything. I'll write to you as soon as I can." He kissed her again and again. She left just before sunrise. The last he saw of her was as she galloped off into the early morning darkness, waving his bandanna, tears falling down her face.

The Author cutting a weaner bull calf from the herd.

16

THE PLANNING OF THE RAID

MATAMOROS, MEXICO - JULY 1, 1915

The fly buzzed around the man's face and landed on his lips as he snored. He didn't even bother to brush it away. He was used to the nasty little things. It was siesta time in Lupe's Cantina, in the barrio that lawmen wouldn't enter without an army of men. The floor was dirt, well packed by a thousand feet packing it down. Lupe Chaves kept the floor wet so it would pack well and make the place a little cooler. Lupe finally brushed the fly away before it entered his mouth. It was hot in Matamoros, especially in July. Everyone was asleep except a table of five men who were talking in low voices.

Three of the men were Mexican with big sombreros and dirty tight breeches and very loose shirts. Not a breeze was blowing. The smell was so strong the flies wouldn't land. The men had scraggly beards and mustaches. Another man, an Anglo, wore the same kind of clothes. His sombrero hung down the back of his neck on a strap of thin leather. His red hair was wet with sweat and hung down in his tanned face. No one mentioned the scar. The last man wore a dark wool suit, white shirt, tie, high top shoes and a Homburg hat. He was as pale as a ghost. He had a very short neck, square jaw, and blonde hair. A smile never crossed his lips. His name was Eric von Lutter. He was an agent for the German High Command. He hated the place—he hated Mexico, the Mexican people, the customs, the food, the flies, and the heat—but he loved the Mexican women.

Von Lutter had been sent there three months earlier to carry out a mission. He was to cause as much havoc to the American government as he possibly could. He thought this would not be easy with these idiots that sat across the table from him.

He looked around the cantina, but there wasn't much to see—an old wooden bar that ran along the wall without even a rail to rest one's feet, some matador paintings hung on the walls, and Mariachis asleep in the corner of the bar. He could never get used to these people sleeping in the middle of the afternoon. He sighed, took another drink of the foul smelling tequila. How he hated being here.

Still, the peons were useful. They would raid the border, causing trouble and drawing American attention away from Germany.

The German spoke to Scarface. "How soon can you start? It is imperative that you begin right away!"

Scarface Colorado looked at him and drank his tequila straight. "What's your hurry, kraut? We have a lot to do, and we can't start until I talk to my contact in Kingsville. I have to know what's going on at the King Ranch before we cross the border. I'll send a message to my contact to meet me in Brownsville. As soon as I talk to him, we'll move. You krauts have really gotten things stirred up. Why are you doing this? We haven't raided into Texas in a long while."

"I'll explain it to you if you will listen. Germany is going to conquer Europe. It belonged to the German people for thousands of years. We just want to regain what is rightfully ours. Just like Mexico—Texas belongs to the Mexicans. It was lost because of the stupidity of your General Santa Anna who betrayed all loyal Mexicans and sold out to Sam Houston at San Jacinto. That is why we are supporting the Mexicans on raids in Texas."

The German sat back in his chair, straight as an arrow. He took another drink of that stinking tequila, but this time with lime and salt.

Scarface took another drink, looking at the German through narrow eyes. "Listen, bastardo, I know what your game is. Don't come in here trying to pull the wool over my eyes. You came to Matamoros six weeks ago, flashing money, buying drinks, meals, and women, trying to get cozy with this bunch of sons-of-bitches. No one comes in here to be pals. They finally pointed the finger at me. They told you I am the meanest, ugliest bastardo in Mexico, that I would just as soon stick a knife in you as look at you. So, you offer me money, women, lots of tequila, rifles and ammunition, horses, supplies for a long trip, all for giving back Texas to the Mexican people. Bullshit! You're doing it for yourselves. You could care less for these peons; they're not worth that stinking roach on your shoe."

The German jumped up and started pounding his foot on the dirt floor with a look of disgust on his face.

"Sit down," Scarface said. "You're going to listen to me now. From here on out, I'm giving the orders. I'll tell you what we need, when we need it, and how much. You just come up with the money you promised me and I'll do the rest. Is that clear?"

Von Lutter had never been talked to by anyone that way. He started to jump up again to protest, and a big hand from Scarface sat him down again. "Sit down, kraut. I'm not through yet. Give Texas back to the Mexicans—don't make me laugh. You're doing it for the Kaiser and that bunch of sausage eating sons-a-bitches. You want to keep America busy here at home, not meddling with what you're doing over there. If you can keep America out of the war, you just might conquer Europe. We're nothing but a diversion for you. If we get killed, so what? You could care less. So, don't say it's for the Mexican people." Scarface spit a big wad of tobacco on the German's shiny shoes.

Von Lutter sat there. He knew that if he moved he might be a dead man. "Now, now, my friend. There's no reason to get angry. We're friends. We are alike, you and I. We both want to reach our goals. I want to obey my superiors and carry out my mission. You want revenge against the King Ranch for offering a reward for you. You also want to find a boy who beat you at your own game, not to mention all the gold you'll find on the King Ranch, the fine horses I hear they have—all the loot which will be yours. You don't have to share it with this bunch of cutthroats. It can all be yours. Think about it. You'll be a very rich man."

Scarface sat back in his chair, thinking to himself. "Yes, why not use this bastardo. He is right, there will be much riches from this raid. I want to find the boy who ruined all my plans. I want to shoot him in the gut and watch him die, just like the old man from hell who gave me this scar." He reached up and touched the scar that ran down his face. "Now, every time I look in a mirror I see that old man and remember how he laughed at me, even when I shot him full of holes. If I would have had more ammunition, I would have shot him again. But, all in all, he was a better man than any of these bastardo's that called themselves men. Especially, that gringo foreign son of a bitch." Scarface had lived in Mexico so long that he thought of all foreigners as gringos.

Scarface turned his attention to the German. "I want those new rifles. You know, the ones you were talking about. What do you call them?"

The German looked up and smiled at Scarface. He would like to have killed the murderous scum right there. "The 7 mm. Mausers have arrived. When you have completed recruiting your followers, then you will get all the rifles and ammunition you need. There is a special military cartridge for the Mausers."

"Good," Scarface said. I'll need a hundred rifles, and supplies for each man to carry, also two horses for each man. We can pick up the horses in a raid on the Kiñeno. I won't have any trouble getting men. These poor bastards don't have a pot to piss in; they'll do anything to get a horse and a new rifle." With that Scarface got up from the table, downed his glass of tequila and left, leaving the German sitting there alone thinking to himself.

"What have we done," he thought. "I hate to think what will happen to those people in Texas when this bunch of cutthroats are turned loose. Still we must conquer the world for the betterment of the German race. We will deal with these peons later." He looked around the cantina, ". . . although we might not want this part of the world." He drank another shot of tequila.

Scarface turned to his men before he mounted and said, "Go back to the hideout and wait for me. I'll send word when I'm ready for you to meet me and where." Then he mounted, spit a big wad of tobacco on the ground and rode toward the border.

Scarface crossed the border into Brownsville with a bunch of wagons carrying cotton from Mexico to the Port. His big sombrero covered his red hair, and he pulled his serape up around his face. As soon as he could safely leave the wagons he headed for Miller's Hotel where his contact would be staying. He came every month and stayed a week to take care of King Ranch business.

He hadn't seen Bell since the night he sent for him about the old man Cavazos taking those cattle to market. Now that was a profitable venture, but it had been a long time ago —too long, and he was broke. He needed a big deal to put gold in his pocket.

He rode down an alley behind the hotel, tied his horse, and walked to the front, ducking his head and hiding his bright hair under the big sombrero. He squatted next to another peon on the porch of the Miller Hotel. There were beggars there, ready to run errands or do any kind of small jobs, but right now they were taking a siesta; it was too hot to move. He took a short nap waiting for Bell to come out.

Bell was talking to two other men as they left the hotel saloon, laughing and waving his arms. His cane and a big Havana cigar were stuck between his stubby fingers. He wore an expensive white suit and a white Panama hat, his fat belly sticking out over his belt. The perfect image of the rich political lawyer.

His arrogant manner said it all. He was J. B. Bell, the wheeler and dealer friend of the King Ranch. Money and power were behind him. Scarface almost drew his knife and slit him from groin to chest, but he held back. He needed this man for now. He would get rid of him later. He stood up, right in the way of Bell, bumping into him and staggering back a little so that the surprised lawyer could see who staggered into him. "Watch out, you clumsy fool, get out of the way."

Bell was about to strike the beggar with his cane when he saw the scar. He stepped back. "Oh, it's you." He looked around to see if anyone else had recognized Scarface, but no one had noticed anything.

"Get rid of them now," Scarface whispered, nodding toward Bell's companions.

"If you all will go ahead, I'll join you in a little while," Bell said to his companions. "I need to send this man with a message to the train master." The men waited. "No, go on ahead, I want to be sure he gets the message straight. I'll join you directly." He waited till they were out of hearing range. "What the hell are you doing here? Do you want to let everything out of the bag, you fool?"

"Listen, son of a bitch, I need to know when the payroll will be at the Norias headquarters," Scarface said.

Bell looked at Scarface with a surprised expression. "What are you up to? Why do you need that kind of information?"

"You don't need to know. Just find out when the payroll gets to Norias. I'll be at our old meeting place tonight about an hour after dark. Be there." Scarface stepped back, turned, and left the same way he came.

"That fool. He'll ruin everything. He's going to rob the payroll. But what can I do?" Bell thought for a while and made his way toward the cantina where he was going to meet his friends. He got to the door and stopped. "Maybe he'll get killed and I won't have to worry about him anymore. Yes, why not get him the information, let him go, and then notify the Rangers that he's coming. Anonymously, of course."

He turned and walked toward his office. "I'll just send a wire asking when the payroll stage is coming in, that I want to send a package back with the stage." He took out another cigar and lit it, took a couple of puffs, smiled, and went up to his office.

Scarface didn't trust Bell. He had done his dirty work for him when they rustled cattle from that old man at the pass. He knew something was funny when Bell said he didn't want any of the money from the stolen cattle. Later, he found out that the old man's family had to forfeit a note to Captain King when they couldn't come up with the money they were going to get for the cattle. It was pretty slick of Bell.

The Captain had no idea they were going to rustle those beef. He wouldn't have stood for it. He got the cattle, King got the land, and Bell got the gracious thanks from the Captain for thinking of letting old man Cavazos have the mortgage on the land.

Scarface backed deeper into the shadows, away from the shack where they had met in prior years. Most of the walls had been ripped out and used for firewood. Mesquite, bamboo, and ragweed had taken over the yard. He heard a horse approaching. Bell whistled, giving the signal they had used before. Scarface drew his pistol and answered with his signal. He stepped out of the shadows.

"What's the matter, Red? You don't trust me?" the lawyer asked.

Scarface holstered his pistol. "About as much as I trust a rattlesnake. Get down. I don't like to look up at you." The lawyer stepped out of the saddle. He was quite agile for such a fat little man.

"Did you find out when the payroll gets to Norias?" Scarface said.

"Yes, but first I want to know what you're planning. I don't want to get into a mess like last time. You weren't suppose to kill anyone."

"Listen, Bell, when you do the type of work I do, there's no promise about anything. You think that old man would have let me just walk in there and take his herd? Hell no. He fought me tooth and nail. I hope I never meet his kind again." He spit a chew of tobacco to one side, raising dust. "I underestimated that old man, but it worked out to both our advantage."

"Yes, I know you messed up," Bell said. "Now, tell me what you're planning. I don't want a bunch of killing like last time."

Scarface would have killed the lawyer right there, but he needed him. He let the remark go by. "Listen, I know that you're a big man in this state, thanks to me. If I hadn't stolen that herd, that bunch of rancheros would have paid off the note, and you wouldn't have looked so good to King. Well, let me tell you something, you might be a big man to some people, but I know you for what you really are. You're worse than me. You hire men to do your dirty work while you sit back and reap the harvest. That sir, to me is a coward."

Bell turned red in the face, but held his temper. "Now, now, Red. We mustn't fight amongst ourselves—there's too much to gain and we can't let your plans go astray. The payroll will be at the Norias headquarters about the sixth or seventh of next month, and there will be only the usual vaqueros with the stage. You shouldn't have any problem. That's what you wanted to hear, isn't it?''

"Yeah, you're right. You're good at what you do, but so am I. Let's just leave it at that,'' said Scarface.

Bell mounted his horse. "Good luck, Red. I hope you get what you want, but don't ask me to do anything else for you. We're even. I don't want to hear from you again. Are we understood?''

Scarface smiled and spit again. "You'll keep in touch. You'll find in politics you need men like me. I'll hear from you again, don't worry about that.''

Bell looked at the outlaw for the last time. "No, Red, I don't think so. I'll be in Austin in August. I wish I could say it's been nice knowing you, but I can't. You'll get exactly what you deserve. You're a dying breed. This is a modern world. There will be great changes made in this country and there will be no room for your type of bandidos. There will only be room for the politicians, the lawyers, and judges. We are the ones who will rule this country.''

Scarface got a bad feeling with those words. They made him suspect that something might go wrong. "That's what you think, gringo, I'll be around when you are under the ground.''

Bell turned his horse and rode away. He let out his breath when he was out of rifle range. That crazy outlaw would kill him if he knew what he was planning. It would be best to wait until a few days before the raid to tell the Rangers about Scarface's plan. It was perfect. He would be rid of the son of a bitch forever. The last link to the rustling would be gone and no one could ever discover his part in the killings.

Scarface approached the Rio Grande at a crossing frequently used by outlaws. Luckily, since he had no wish to be seen, there was no moon that night.

Once across the border back into Mexico he headed for Lupe's Cantina. He still had to round up the men he wanted, his old gang. They were older now, and some had died or been killed, but they were still the meanest bandits in Mexico. He'd last seen them chasing that kid three years ago.

His hatred for the kid still burned his insides. It was like some power protected the boy from harm. That reminded him of the curse the old man put on him after he shot him the last time. He couldn't forget the ferocious look in the old man's eyes, like an eagle when it was wounded and cornered. He shuddered, trying to block the thought.

It was almost midnight by the time he reached the cantina. He tied his horse behind a shed by the corral; he didn't want people to know he was back in town. Slipping in the back door, he spotted the German running his hand up a whore's skirt. Scarface didn't mind him doing that to a whore —that was the way they made their living—but that was his whore.

"Let's go to my room, Aleman," she said. "Then we'll have a lot of fun."

"Let's go my little pigeon," he said. "I will treat you well and pay you with gold." All of a sudden, his chair was jerked from under him. He fell hard, right on his back, taking the bottle of tequila and the glasses with him. He came up in a hurry with his Luger in his hand, ready to shoot, when he felt a blow on his wrist. The Luger went flying across the room, and he felt a cold piece of iron next to his temple.

"Don't move or I'll blow your German ass away, do you understand? Just nod your head up and down if you do." The German agent nodded very slowly. "Alright, my friend. Let's have a drink and forget this unpleasantness. Excuse me a minute." Scarface stepped toward the whore. He grabbed her hair and slapped her. The slaps and her scream echoed through the cantina.

"There, bitch. You know better than that. Don't let me catch you doing it again." He jerked her up close to him by the hair and a large knife appeared like magic in his hand. In one swift cut he managed to slice off a large part of her beautiful black hair.

The girl screamed and put her arm around him. "No baby, please don't cut my hair again, please." Tears were coming down her face.

He shoved her away into a corner. "Stay there till I tell you to get up." She sat in the corner feeling of her hair. The cantina was silent.

"Okay, Aleman. Let's have a drink," Scarface said with a smile on his face. He sat down after righting a chair. Von Lutter had retrieved his gun and put it in the holster inside his coat. He had watched Scarface deal with the woman. It almost made him sick.

Von Lutter was one of several German agents up and down the border sent by the German High Command to cause havoc from Brownsville to El Paso, New Mexico, Arizona, California, and into Colorado. They were to organize the Mexican people to start a war with the United States to take back the lands "stolen" from Mexico and keep the Americanos so busy that they couldn't interfere with the German plans for Europe.

The lowlife of the border, the very poor, those with nothing to lose, would take the riches from others, be they Anglos or Mexicans, who had settled north of the Rio Grande. The German agents offered these bandits a dream of taking back what had never been theirs. They were nothing but thieves hiding behind the mask of patriotism.

As soon as the table was set upright, von Lutter sat down and signaled for new glasses and another bottle of tequila. The bartender added it to his bill and hoped no one would kill the German before he had paid it.

His embarrassment by Scarface fueled von Lutter's hatred for the outlaw. However, he swallowed his pride and spoke with a smile. "I apologize, my friend, I did not mean to covet your girlfriend. Please forgive me."

The bandit looked at him and finally raised his glass. "Okay, just don't do it again. They're nothing but whores, but that one, she is my whore. Understand?"

"*Javohl, mein Herr.* It will not happen again, I promise. Now, to business. The rifles won't be here tomorrow as I promised. I just received word that the shipment will not be here until a day later."

"That's okay. It will give me time to organize these no good bastardos. I'll leave first thing in the morning. Now, I have some business that is personal and very private." He went to the corner and grabbed the woman's hand. When she was standing, he pushed her toward the stairs. "Come on, bitch, let's go to your room. Lupe, send a bottle up to Tonia's room. If anybody asks for me, I'm not here." All eyes were on him as he walked up the stairs dragging the whore. She was still crying.

The next day about noon, Scarface started out on his journey to the mountains west of Matamoros. It would take him two days to cross the desert, and along the way, he remembered chasing the boy who got away with all that money. It was the same boy who had messed up his plans to kidnap the girl in Brownsville. He would find him when they took over the King Ranch. He would have enough money to offer a reward for him, and everyone would look for the boy.

He didn't go into San Miguel. The soldiers were there, and he didn't want a bunch of questions, so he skirted the little town. He could have used a drink of tequila, but it was better not to be seen.

A little before sundown, Scarface rode down a dry gulch in the foothills of the mountainous desert. He was getting low on water and his horse needed to drink. Scarface always took care of his horses. He knew that without a horse in that land he would die. He wanted to find the watering place as soon as possible. Where there was water, he would find the rest of his old gang. He kept an eye open for Apaches even though he was on their friendly side. Still, if they woke up on the wrong side of the blanket, there might be trouble. It was best to avoid any contact with them.

He finally got to the spring where the camp had settled. It had grown since last he was there. He whistled once, loud, interrupted by two short blasts. He was answered by three whistles, the signal to approach slowly. Scarface was home. He stopped at the spring to drink with his horse next to him. He felt a shadow approach him slowly. "Well, I'll be damned, if it isn't Scarface!" a voice said. In the next minute, he was hollering that it was all right, it was just "*Cicatriz.*" They began shouting and laughing, firing their weapons in the air.

"Hey, Scar! How you doing?" The comancheros shouted at him from above where they had been hiding. "You old bastard. Where you been? I thought someone had finally shot you." They all laughed.

Scarface turned and saw Juan Vasquez with a big grin on his face. Juan was a young comanchero whose mother was Apache and his father Mexican. Scarface knew that Juan was afraid of no man, except maybe him. "Hell, cabron, how have you been?" Scarface said.

"Okay, how about you? Where you been? How come you haven't been here in a long time?" the young comanchero said, frowning.

"Hey, Juanto, don't look so worried. I have been working. When I left I told you that I wouldn't be back until I had something that would make us all rich, didn't I?"

"What you got? Tell me," Juan said. "You can tell me, I won't tell anyone till you say I can, okay?"

"No, Juanito. I don't want to say anything till I talk with your papa." He put his arm around Vasquez's shoulders, leading his horse by the reins. They walked up the trail to the comancheros' camp. It led to a high plateau and was the only entrance to the camp. The view looked out over many miles of the landscape. They had to be able to see who was coming from a long way off. There was a back way out of the camp, but it wasn't used unless there was an emergency. "You've grown, Juan. You're taller than when last I saw you," Scarface said.

"Yes, I'm doing all right, but I get tired of the same boring things here. I need something to prove to Papa that I'm a man."

Scarface laughed. "You'll get that chance, joven. I have big plans for all of us."

They finally made the climb. Scarface was breathing heavily by the time they reached the top. He stopped to get his breath and looked around. The comancheros could make hell look like home. There were adobe jaccals all the way around their area of the main camp. There was a meeting place in the middle. A spring was close by, a place for livestock to drink and a place to get drinking water and to wash clothes. The corrals were also close by, in case they had to catch their horses and saddle up in a hurry. It was one of the permanent camps, and the comancheros felt safe there.

Pancho Vasquez, the leader of the *comancheros*, greeted him. "Scar, long time no see," Pancho was a shrewd trader. He was a big man with a big belly and always tied a rope around his waist to support his pants. He tied another rope over his shoulders like suspenders without any slack to keep the pants up. His ears stuck out from his head, and his nose was too big. In fact, the Indians called him, Nariz Grande.

"Hello, Pancho. How have you been? It's been a long time," Scarface said.

"Yes, it has," Pancho said. "We were beginning to think you were dead, but you are welcome here as ever. Come, let's have a drink of Mescal for old times, eh?"

They sat at a table that Pancho had taken in a raid. It had chairs to match. In fact, all the furniture, dishes, bowls, glasses, and utensils were stolen. "Sit, my friend. Let's drink and talk of old times, times when we could raid anywhere we wanted and no one would bother us. There was no law and no Texas Rangers to chase us. Those were the good old days. Woman! Bring us a bottle of Mescal."

Spotted Horse, Vasquez's wife, was an Apache chief's daughter. They were married by the chief under the Law of the Tribe. She had been a quite comely young girl when they married, but like most of the women after much child bearing and living the life of the comanchero, she had lost her beauty.

Spotted Horse brought a bottle of Mescal and two glasses. Juanito looked at his mother, pleading for a glass. She looked at Pancho and he nodded. Juanito smiled and rubbed his hands together. Vasquez poured drinks all the way around, raised his drink in salud and drank it down. Scarface drank his and then another, finished it, and sighed. "It's been a long journey and a dry one."

"Hey amigo, take it easy. There is more where that came from," said Pancho, chuckling. He poured another round and sat back. "Where in the hell have you been? You look awful."

"I've been in Matamoros," Scarface said. "I ran into an Aleman who offered me the biggest deal I've ever run across."

"What's Aleman, Papa?" Juanito said.

"It's a German, a gringo from the other side of the world," Pancho said. "Can you trust him?" Pancho put up his hand to silence Juanito's next question. Juanito sat back and asked nothing.

"He came into Lupe's Cantina about six month ago," Scarface said. "I watched him and he started buying drinks and asking questions. He finally came right out with it. He was looking for men who wanted to become rich and didn't care how. Of course, I started to listen more carefully then. He said his country was going to conquer the world. First Europa, then Los Estado Unidos. He said Mexico would be their allies, and they would give all the land they lost to Texas back to the Mexicans."

"Can you trust him?" Pancho said again.

"No, but once we take what we want, we'll kill all the Alemans and take over," Scarface said.

"What about horses, and rifles, ammunition and supplies? Who's going to buy these things?" Pancho asked.

"He is," Scarface said. "New rifles that fire as fast as you can load them, all the loot we can steal, horses, gold, silver, cattle, anything we want, but here's the good part. We will raid the Rancho Kiñeno as many times as we want, till they lose everything and go broke, and the Aleman will pay for it. All we have to do is what we do best—kill and rob."

Pancho took another drink, thinking. "You mean they will furnish the horses, guns, and ammunition, everything, and all we have to do is raid?"

"Yes, that's right. We'll be rich," Scarface said. He took another drink.

"How many men will you need?" Pancho said. "I have to keep part of the men here to guard the camp. Also, they'll want to know what their cut will be. You can't leave out the men who have to stay here. They must get a share, too. Also, my cut will be half of your cut. Because I know you, Scar. You'll get half of everything that the men haul away."

"Okay," Scarface said. "This is my deal. I'm getting the rifles and everything. I'm doing the planning, the hard work of finding out when the payroll will come, and where we are going to raid." He didn't want to name the place. If they knew, they wouldn't need him. He smiled.

"So, therefore, I get the biggest cut. I get three to one, you get two to one and the men the rest."

Pancho finished his tequila and poured another. "I like it," he said. "Okay, I'll talk to the men tonight. I'll call a meeting."

That night at the meeting, Scarface did most of the talking, explaining what the deal would be. The outlaws listened with great interest. Anytime a raid was planned, everyone was invited to come and listen to what the planners had in mind. If they didn't like the plan or the division of the spoils, they simply got up from the circle, which was around a big bonfire, and left. Only the old women and old men left this meeting early.

"Think of it, amigos. All we can carry off. We'll get wagons at the places we raid and fill them with gold, silver and all the things the rich Texans have gotten off the sweat of the poor Mexicans. If the Mexicans now in Texas don't join us, we'll kill them and all their families. If they join us we'll soon have an army to raid even more. Everything will be furnished, except a cook to make our meals. We'll have to do without our women. As soon as we have our army, we'll have many camp followers and our women can join us. The men that stay here to protect our women and children will share equally with the raiders. If you don't come out alive from the raids, your family will get your share and more."

Scarface told how everyone would share in the loot. The old weren't forgotten, because when they were young, they shared with their old ones. It was the law of the comancheros. Scarface knew that and played it to the hilt. Everyone nodded. No one left the camp fire. Scarface showed his teeth in an evil smile. His scar, the red hair and the camp fire all combined to make him look like a devil.

"Now, who among you does not want to go?" No hands were raised. "Good. We'll now draw beans out of a sombrero to see who stays and who goes. Juanito, pass the sombrero around," Pancho said.

"All right men, those who got the black bean go, and those who got the white bean stay." Juanito had palmed a black bean when they were counting out the beans before the meeting. He held up his black bean shouted. "I'm going, I'm going, my first raid. Papa, what do you say?"

Pancho looked at his only son. His woman wouldn't like it, and he would never hear the last of it, but the boy was old enough to go. And he had shouted that he had a black bean in front of all the men. He had to let him go or lose face in front of the men. "Okay, you go. Start getting your equipment ready.''

It took a week to get all the equipment and horses ready. They checked everything from bridles to saddles, and the hoofs of the caballos. Each one would carry a saddle blanket for the horse and to sleep on. They carried a serape to wrap around them for protection against the rain or cold and for protection from insects, sun, and wind. It served to cover them at night when they slept. They also carried an empty tequila bottle wrapped in leather to keep their drinking water cool. The leather cover kept it from breaking and reflecting sunlight and giving away their position.

They would eat nothing but beef jerky and dry roasted corn. If they wanted to eat better, they would steal it from the people they raided. They had a small sack of corn for their horses, just to tide them over till they had plenty on hand. They knew how to live off the land without giving their position away. Many a rancher or farmer never knew what hit them until it was too late. The comancheros were the deadliest enemy a settler could possibly have.

The next morning there was a mist when Scarface stepped out of the adobe *jaccal* where he slept. Already, the sun was breaking the horizon. He wore the navy Colt he had taken when he killed a pistolero in Reynosa, Mexico. He looked around the camp, and there were people all over the place. Some just squatted by their horses, others gathered the last of their equipment. It was a busy morning. Juanito was one of the *comancheros* who was ready. He was talking to his mother in a low voice when he saw Scarface, and left her just standing there. He had already saddled Scarface's horse; he untied it from the corral and began leading it over to him. Scarface's extra horse followed very close behind.

"Mucho gracias, chico," Scarface said. He began tying his gear to the back of the saddle. He was dressed as many of the other men were, in a sombrero, light shirt, tight riding breeches. He wore two bandoleros across his chest, a cuchillo in a scabbard, tied around his shoulders, a lariat on his saddle, the Colt on his side, and a rifle in the saddle boot. He was ready for anything that might come his way.

Finally, everyone was ready. The good-byes to their families were over, and their wives were crying softly. There was an eerie silence. They knew that some of them wouldn't return. They looked around for the last time, then Scarface let out a *grito* and waved the men forward. The other men let out their gritos and rode into the morning mist.

Two days later, eighty-two of the meanest, leanest fighting men, rode into Matamoros late in the afternoon. The people ran into their homes and watched them pass. Children were pulled off the streets and shutters were closed. Doors were bolted and stores closed early. Only the cantina stayed open. They knew business would be good.

Scarface knew that if he didn't get control of the men right now, they would become a mob. He told Pancho that he had picked a place for a camp a little way out of town close to where they would cross the Rio Grande.

The clatter of six hundred and fifty-six horse hooves made a lot of noise on the cobble streets of the old town. With dust flying everywhere and their big sombreros, the bandoleers across their chest, their cuchillos, the pistollas, and the rifles, they made a fearsome bunch of riders.

The captain of the soldiers at the entrance to Matamoros was nowhere to be found, so, the few soldiers stationed there just watched the comancheros go by. A sergeant wiped the sweat off his brow. Never had he seen so many wanted men together at once. He could make a big haul if they could arrest them, but he didn't step forward.

Their captain was peeking through the crack of the shutters above the El Patio Cantina. He wasn't about to come out. The Aleman had paid him well to disappear for a few days. With Conchita in his bed, plenty of tequila and food, who needs to come out and see what the noise is all about?

The comancheros rode through town, not waving or talking to anyone because the streets were bare of people. Scarface led the group to the camp site three miles from town. He didn't want to be too close to town. He had to see that German to settle the bargain.

"Okay, muchachos, pick your place to make your camp," Scarface said when they reached their camp site. He dismounted and started putting his things under a big cottonwood tree. He was watching the men out of the corner of his eye, especially the one they called "El Manco." Scarface knew his real name was Julian Cantu. He was a *mestizo*—a half breed. His father had been a Negro who had been accepted into the band of comancheros. His mother had been full blood Comanche. The mixing of the two bloods had produced a man with a very bad temper. His father had been wanted in the State of Texas for murder and rape, and for cattle rustling, which was a major offense in any western state. He decided to come to Mexico for a while and had found a home. His father had been killed when they raided a hacienda in Mexico, so he was raised by his mother who took on another man.

He had taken the name of Cantu because his original father never claimed any name. When he was just fourteen, he killed his step-father after he caught him beating his mother. He had been killing ever since. Scar never did like him so he decided to make an example out of him.

Julian didn't take his saddle off his horse and was still mounted, waiting to see who was going into town. The bandits' leader didn't want that gang of cutthroats going into town all at once. If they got to drinking, there would be no control over them. Scar did not want to draw undue attention to themselves.

"I told you to make camp," Scarface said to El Manco.

"Why aren't we going to town? It's been a long trip. Besides I hear there are some good looking *putas* in town."

"I said make camp." Scarface reached up and jerked El Manco off his horse. The young outlaw hit the ground hard. Spurs, bandoleers, sombrero all hit the dirt and went flying into the brush.

Scarface was on him at once and kicked him with the toe of his sharp pointed boots. El Manco kept rolling. When he was clear of his horse, he came up with his pistola in his hand. Scarface had already drawn his weapon, and he shot Julian Cantu right through the heart.

"Alright, is there anyone else that wants to go to town?" No one answered. "You don't get to go to town unless I say so, is that understood?" Scarface looked around to see if anyone was going to challenge his orders. No one said a word. Scar had the comancheros under his control.

"You, Andres, Pablo, two more of you men, bury him. I'm going into town to talk to the Aleman and see if the rifles got here. Then we'll go to town by drawing lots, twenty-five at a time." The men all agreed that was a good idea. Scar smiled.

Scar and Pancho got fresh mounts and they rode into Matamoros.

As Scarface and Pancho walked into Lupe's Cantina, Lupe waved and poured Scar a tequila at the bar. "Buenas tardes, jefe. Welcome back. It's been too long," said the owner of the bar. Scarface looked around the bar. Only one or two of his gang were there. The German was nowhere in sight. He went to the bar, shook hands with Lupe, picked up his glass and tossed it down. He nodded toward the bottle and Lupe gladly put it in front of him. Scar took the bottle and glass to the table where his friends were. Shaking hands all around, he poured a drink and handed the bottle to Pancho, who took a big swallow.

"This is Pancho Vasquez. He is my partner in this and he's also the jefe of the comancheros." They shook hands and passed the bottle around. "Where is the German?" They raised their heads toward the upstairs.

"Well, go upstairs and tell him I'm here, and I want him down here in five minutes. Make it pronto." One of the men got up to go upstairs. He stopped when he saw von Lutter coming down.

"No need my friend, I would recognize that voice anywhere," the German said. "Welcome back, I didn't think you were ever going to return. These times are so unsure, don't you agree?"

"Yes, but I know what I'm doing. You're not messing with just anyone. Don't forget that," Scarface said. "Did the rifles get here?"

"Yes," von Lutter said. "All that you wanted has been bought. It was shipped in by boat. We are ready. Did you get the men you went after?"

"I went after them didn't I?" Scar said. He looked over at Pancho, who was having another drink. "This is Pancho Vasquez, the leader of the comancheros. We need to see the rifles, and the money for the men so they can come into town and have a drink or two."

"Alright. Lupe has the money. When they spend the amount I gave him, we'll get some more. How long before you'll be ready to cross into Texas?"

"I don't know. Those new rifles—the men will have to learn to shoot them. We'll have to practice three or four days. Also, the horses have to rest, maybe a week."

"Fine, that's what I thought. How are you going to control them? I don't want any problems while you're here."

"Don't worry about that. I have everything under control," Scarface said. "They'll start coming in when I send for them. Now, I want to see the rifles. Where do you have them?" Scar rose from the table.

"In the back of the store room. That's why I picked this place. It has a lot of storage."

Von Lutter led them down the hall to a back door, which was boarded up with a big padlock. The German took a key from a string around his neck, unlocked the door and pushed it open.

Scarface's eyes widened. He took in a breath sharp with surprise. There were cases of potatoes, stacked to the ceiling, and stacks of smoked German sausages. "What is this? You promised me rifles, instead I get potatoes and sausage. What are you trying to do to me?"

Von Lutter started laughing, and it became louder and louder. "You dumkopf. Do you think I could have gotten them here in their original crates? There are your rifles and ammunition, dumkopf. There is everything I promised you.'' He went to the crates first, took a crowbar from the wall and pried the wooden lid off the crate that read sausage. Scarface smiled. Part of his mouth remained still because the muscle of his lips and cheek had been severed. It gave him a sinister, crooked smile.

"Hey, look at this,'' Scarface said. He reached into the crate and pulled out a rifle in its oily wrapping. He held it up above his head. "With this, I pay back what I got many years ago.'' He reached with the other hand and touched the scar that ran down his face. They went back into the cantina laughing, slapping each other on the back, their spurs jingling on the dirt floor.

"Lupe, bring plenty of tequila, rum, whatever you have. We are celebrating tonight. Manuel, I want you to go out to the old camp site, by the crossing to Texas—you know by the big mesquite. Tell the men to come into Lupe's Cantina, the first twenty-five that got the black beans. Then hurry back, we have a lot of planning to do. Lupe, tell the girls to get ready. They're going to be so sore that they won't be able to sit down. Tell Tonia I want to see her.''

The German's lips parted into a thin smile. He had shared her pleasures ever since Scar had gone. Von Lutter was in an excellent mood. He had the rifles, the ammunition, the horses and most important, the worst bunch of cutthroats in Mexico. Tonia came down the stairs. He smiled and drank his tequila. He was beginning to like the stuff.

17

KING RANCH

SANTA GERTRUDIS DIVISION

"Casa Grande"

It was a hot, sweltering afternoon that July 1, 1915. Mrs. Henrietta M. King walked down the wide veranda of her new mansion. It had taken three years to complete. Money had been no object. She looked at the red tile imported from Mexico. Most of the architecture was Mexican, with Moorish, Spanish Mission, and South Texas mixture all scrambled together to create a beautiful gleaming white stucco concrete mansion. Its red tile roof and tower stood over everything.

She smiled, pleased with the way it had turned out. The Captain would have been proud of the way Kleberg had handled everything.

———————

She remembered the day after the dreadful fire that had destroyed their old home. She had sent for Kleberg that day after she had talked to Lauro. At that time she was in the two story commissary, looking out the window at the burnt mansion when he arrived. All the memoirs had gone up in smoke.

Kleberg watched her and his heart went out to her. His family had slept in the commissary. It was a mess. The whole family had left that morning for Corpus Christi to stay with relatives and buy new clothes and see Reina off to school.

"You sent for me, Mother King?" her son-in-law said as he stood in the door of the bedroom.

SANTA GERTRUDIS — *"Big House"*

Santa Gertrudis Home that burned

"Yes, Robert, come in. Do you want some coffee?" she asked.

"Yes, thank you, I'm beat. We're trying to clean this mess up. Everything is gone; there is nothing worth saving. It's a terrible loss. I'm sorry."

"It wasn't your fault. It was that damn Shultz. Did they find him?"

"Yes, Mother King. He was hiding in town, trying to get out by train. Javiel brought him back and took him to the *Paso de los Muertos*. He'll never burn another home."

"Good. Hanging would be too good for that swine. We won't ever mention his name again. Is that understood?" Kleberg took a sip of his coffee, then nodded his head.

Mother King walked toward a wrought iron bench, and looked at the beautiful plants on the patio. It had been designed as a cool place to rest and remember. She sat on the bench, leaning on her cane and looked at the birds that collected in the cool, shaded area of the patio. She smiled and remembered.

"I sent for you to tell you about the conversation I had with Lauro. We must do everything in our power to keep him in our employment. He's smart, and you've said he knows cattle and horses. He is a leader, and he has courage. The men will follow him anywhere but most of all, they respect him. We need him for the future of the ranch. There will be changes we cannot even fathom or try to understand, but this younger generation will and must carry on when we are gone.

"I am so glad that Alice picked you for a husband. You plan for the future instead of living for the present. We built a town, now we have a lumber company, bank, real estate office, a farming community and most of all a railroad. Many other businesses opened this past year. I know the railroad cost me a lot of land, but you will see, it will be worth it. There's no telling where this country is going, but I tell you this, the King Ranch must change with the times or go down in history as just another pioneer. We must lead not follow. That is why you will need men like that boy. He needs time to mature. Give him that time, but you must keep him at all costs. Is that understood?"

"Yes, Mother King. I've already thought about that and I have plans for the boy, but one thing bothers me. I think he and Reina are becoming too friendly. I don't blame her. He's good looking and very dashing on a horse. I don't know what to do about it."

"Well, I do," the old woman said. "We must keep them apart. Time will take care of everything. Let me handle them; I'll see to it that Reina marries the right kind of man for her station in life.

"Now for other business." She looked out the window at the destruction of her dreams. "I want you to go to the best architect in the State of Texas. I want to build the finest home that people in these parts have ever seen. It must be fireproof so that we won't have to go through this heartbreak again. I want it to be a monument to the Captain and what he and others did for this country. Build a small home we can live in over by the orange orchard till the new Casa Grande is built. Spend whatever it takes. Build it so that it will last through the years, so people will realize the King Ranch is here to stay."

Those were the instructions Henrietta King gave to her son-in-law on the day after the fire.

Now all was completed. It was a greater mansion than anything that had been built before in the State of Texas. It was built where the original ranch house had been, with a fireplace in each of its twenty-five rooms and a bathroom for each bedroom. There were long halls, high ceilings, a large dining room, and a small dining room for just the family, and dens for private talks. The massive furniture was hand crafted by skilled carpenters. Marble stairways gleamed, mesquite wood planks in the salon came right from the ranch. A patio stood in the middle, filled with every kind of plant indigenous to that part of the country.

Verandas were placed where they would catch the prevailing wind in the hot, South Texas climate. The house featured stained glass windows, murals of ranch life, stuffed heads of wild game, and rugs on the floor made by hand in Mexico. Most of the architectural ideas came from a hacienda Kleberg had visited in Mexico, but it had a grandeur that matched the Wild Horse Desert perfectly. The white stucco could be seen for miles, and the tower that loomed over everything was still the mainstay of defense against the Mexican bandits and Indian raiders. Nothing like it had ever been seen in this country. It was a grandiose monument to Captain and Henrietta King and the blood, sweat and tears of the Kineños.

Mother King shifted her position on the bench and put more weight on the cane. She loved the little sparrows who darted here and there. They looked like they were so busy having fun, trying to survive the hot summer breeze.

She shifted her weight again to take the stiffness from her left leg.

It's hell to grow old, she thought. Why couldn't we all stay young? Then she thought of her granddaughter and Lauro. Her plan had to work.

Reina had stopped writing to Lauro almost three months ago. She had just left for a tour with her school to England. She would be gone for three months, and that should finish the romance. Mrs. King knew about the romance and how long it had gone on. Her spy had reported to her the minute that Reina and her father had come back from the Canelo pasture so long ago. Donna Maria Lusia had told her everything that had happened, everything except that they had met under the oak motte that night.

She saw how Reina had come back an entirely different person from the girl she had been. She really did love that young vaquero, but she had a position in life to uphold. Some things were more important than what a person wanted.

Mrs. King remembered how her father's ministries traversed all over the country, to finally settle in Brownsville, Texas. She had met a young Sunday School teacher and fallen in love; they had planned to marry and live a quiet settled life.

Then she met Richard King on the streets of Brownsville. He was a ship's Captain, a man of considerable wealth, and her father made her change her mind. She never quit loving the young teacher and wondered about him all these years, how her life would have been different. Sometimes you had to give up something dear to receive greater rewards, but still she wondered.

A cardinal dropped down from a branch and started searching for the food Mrs. King always brought with her when she came to the bench to remember. She reached into the sack and threw out some bread crumbs and sunflower seeds. The memories of the day after the fire returned.

After talking to Kleberg she sent for Jose Silguero, the manager of the commissary for many years, a thin man of middle age, with sharp features and a small mustache which made him look younger than his age. He came into the room as she watched the debris being cleaned from the burned out mansion.

"You sent for me, señora?" he asked.

"Yes Jose. Come in. Sit down. I want to talk to you about something of the utmost importance." She offered him a cup of coffee.

He knew it was important when she offered him a cup. She had never offered him coffee. "Thank you. Mucho gracias," he said with a surprised look on his face. He reached out and took the coffee.

"Jose, you have been with us a long time. We trust you. We educated you so that you could run the commissary, to keep the books. They're always correct. You also receive the outgoing and incoming mail."

"Si, señora," he said, looking at his cup and basking in her praise, not realizing what was coming.

"You have done an excellent job for me, but there is another job I must prevail on you to do."

Jose raised his eyes to look at the one person he would do anything for. "Si, señora. You do not even have to ask, just tell me and it is done."

"Thank you, Jose, but let me finish. You handle the incoming mail as well as the outgoing, don't you?" He nodded his head slightly. "Does anyone else handle the mail?"

"Yes, when I am sick or I have to go somewhere, my wife Juanita delivers your mail to the Casa Grande," With the mention of the Casa Grande he lowered his head in embarrassment. "I'm sorry, señora. *Perdona mi.* I didn't mean to cause you heartache."

"It's quite alright, Jose. I know that it was a shock to everyone. Now let's continue. Juanita and you are the only ones who handle the mail?"

"Si, señora, we are the only ones."

"Good, I want you to bring the mail to me. Is that understood?"

Jose looked at his Patróna. "But señora!"

She held up her hand to stop him. "I know, but I will return it to you when I look at it, that's all."

Jose's face lost its frown and a smile appeared, "Oh, well that's alright then, as long as the mail is returned to me so I can deliver it to the right person."

"Thank you, Jose. We will not mention this to anyone. You can tell Juanita what to do, but Jose, tell her if it gets out . . ." She looked at him with an expression on her face that he had never seen before. "I'll move you and her off this ranch so fast you won't even have time to pack your bags. Is that understood?"

"Yes, Patróna. I will tell her, do not worry. I'll take care of it."

"Good." She put her hand on his. "I knew I could count on you. Have some more coffee."

She fed the last of the bread crumbs and seeds to the birds, sighed and tapped lightly with her cane on the red tiles.

————————

The Jensen camp was 10 miles west of Santa Gertrudis Headquarters. The corrida had a bunkhouse to themselves and a kitchen for the cooks. The meals cooked in that kitchen were legendary with the cowboys up and down the trail, said to be the best grub south of the Nueces River.

The bunkhouse was made of stucco and had a two-sided fireplace that served the kitchen on one side and the bunkhouse on the other side. On occasion, when it was cold, the cowboys would drag a washtub inside to burn mesquite. This caused quite a bit of smoke, but the cowboys would still gather around to talk and swap lies and tell stories of their experiences on the trail. It was a favorite pastime.

That day, there was no need for a fire on the bunkhouse side. It was about ninety-five degrees outside. A porch ran the length of the house and there was an outhouse away from the bunkhouse. The porch was the best place to sleep, despite the rattlesnakes. The breeze would blow real fine in the evening when everything was quiet. Behind the bunkhouse was a rail made of pipe and stucco so the men could put their saddles on it and not tie the horses. They would just throw the ropes over it and make the horses think they were tied to the rail. It was a kind of bluff so they could saddle up quickly. You never tied your horse. It was too dangerous since he might balk and sit back and then go forward ''up the cowboy's front pocket.''

The kitchen had two large Dutch doors. One led to the large porch, and the other outside to the mesquite wood pile. It, also, had one large Dutch window and the large two-sided fireplace.

The bunkhouse had one large Dutch door and four small Dutch windows in the front and four more in the back wall. The windows were all made with a border about two feet high all around to keep the snakes out. It had a stucco floor that was smooth enough to dance on, and sometimes they did dance on it. It was built as strong as a fort and could stand a lot of gunfire from bandits.

There were the usual corrals for working cattle and one used as a holding pen. The first pen and the four pens on either side of the cutting chute were the actual pens used to work the cattle. All the cattle were first put in the big pen with water troughs, then brought forward in a rotation into a crowding chute, where they were separated into different

pens by four cutting gates, handled by two cowboys on top of the chute.
This gave the Patrón a total of five different ways to cut cattle. The
fifth way was straight ahead with the good bulls, and the mother cows
of the main herd.

This was an art to most cattlemen. The separation kept the herd
from bunching up and smothering the calves. The calves didn't have
much of a chance, but managed to survive in spite of what the older
cattle did or the treatment they received from the cowboys.

The cooks were a special kind of breed. There were usually two
with a helper who washed the dishes and brought firewood and kept the
kitchen cleaned the best way they could. Flies were everywhere —in
the food, camp bread, the coffee, and everywhere else. They got used to
it. They had to. After the wind picked up, the flies were gone. That was
the best time to enjoy coffee, after the siesta, when everyone gathered
their thoughts and talked in low voices so as not to disturb the men who
were still sleeping.

This was time for talk with the Caporal. The Caporal was the boss
of the cowboys, the man who knew the most about running a bunch of
wild cowboys, working the cattle and horses, and just running the
everyday operation of the corrida. He was a special sort of man. He was
tough, yet he had a sense of humor that came with being a cowboy all
of his life. He had to know when to round up the cattle and where they
would be heading.

The morning always started early. The swamper was the first to
rise. There were no clocks except in the swamper's mind, and it would
go off at exactly three o'clock in the morning. He would build the first
fire and put the water on to boil for the coffee.

The cooks were the next to rise, knowing that they were in for a
rough day, just like every day. They were proud of their trade and
didn't put up with anyone coming into their kitchen and telling them
how to cook. That included the Caporal. The *cocina* was their domain,
and if anyone messed with them, they took their life in their own hands.

La Chista and Modin, the second cook, were the first to make the
coffee and start breakfast. Making good coffee was an art. It was a time
consuming operation. The tone of the rest of the day was set by how
well the coffee turned out. Its success was an omen for the day.

The head cook was always the first to taste the coffee. Slowly, the
head cook would take the lid off the coffee pot and dip in for a cup.
Modin would watch him closely to see his expression. A grimace would
mean that it was a failure. If he started to roll a cigarette, it had passed

the test, and Modin would also reach for his Bull Durham.

Julian Buentello, the Remudeo, was a small, wiry man with dark skin. He was the next to rise. He would go to the pump, get the cool water and wash the sleep from his eyes, while looking toward the corral for his horse, Mosca. Then he would pick up a coffee can full of oats with one hand and some alfalfa hay with the other. Mosca, would snigger a little as the best Remudeo on the ranch spoke to her. After feeding Mosca, he would then take care of himself.

Julian knew every horse in the remuda, and when he rounded up the horses at four o'clock in the morning, he could tell if one was missing. He would holler, crack his long snake whip and yell. "Alright, you no good, ungrateful bag of bones. Get out of the monte or I'll come in after you." Sure enough, two or three slackers would come out of the brush galloping and bucking, full speed toward the corrals. All the remuda were there, so Julian had done his job.

Güero was the next one to get up, stretching out for his hat to put on and reaching for his boots. Most cowboys couldn't afford boots, so the ranch would issue them heavy rough out shoes. Most of the men preferred the shoes to work in and saved the boots for when they went to town on payday once a month. The boss, the Caporal, and the Anglos, could afford the boots and wore them for work as well as on the trips to town.

Güero would roll his bedroll up and put it next to the wall, step out on the porch and look for signs of the weather before going to the long table where everyone ate their meals. He always sat at the end of the table, against the wall and next to the door that led into the kitchen.

The kitchen was just one big room with a long mantel over a big fireplace with cooking areas on both sides. Cooking was done over the coals taken from the fireplace and put on either side to make the *pan de campo,* red beans, and *carne guisada.*

La Chista brought Güero his coffee in the usual tin cup.

"Bueno dias, Güero. Como amansistes?" Chista said.

"Bueno dias, Chista. Como amansistes?" the Caporal replied. "Looks like another hot day. Tell Beto to wake the men."

Beto loved to wake the men because it was his only chance to get back at some of the teasing they dealt him during the day, all day, every day.

Then la Chista would tell the second cook to start the preparations for making the *pan de campo.*

The men rolled up their sleeping bags and placed them up against the wall. They put on their clothes, hats and shoes and staggered out to the porch. Everyone said "Bueno dias" to the other for the morning greeting. It was a ritual each day. Not only was it good manners, but a sign that they were each glad to see the others and be part of the corrida. All told there were thirty-two men, most of them kin to the others in some manner. It was one of the reasons they were the best cowboys in the country. The fathers and uncles would teach the young ones. They learned the work of the cowboy first hand.

Few things are associated more with the working of cattle on a ranch than the smells. There was the smell of cattle, the sweet smell of horse flesh, the sweat of both men and horses, the dust, the burning of mesquite, and the smell of wild flowers. There were the smells from the kitchen, but mostly from the mesquite burning and the smell from the camp, with meat being roasted on an open fire and all the other food. It made a cowboy's mouth water just thinking about it.

After the cowboys' first cup of coffee, they would look around and spy Chista. Then the fun would begin. It was usually Shorty who started it. Shorty was a tall, rangy cowboy who loved to poke fun at la Chista. He was called Shorty because when he was young he was short, but as people sometimes do, he shot up and grew a foot taller than anyone else.

"Bueno dias, *pajaro*," Shorty said.

"Bueno dias, Shorty. The name is Chista, you bow-leg son of a jackass," la Chista replied.

"Well, you know, bird or buzzard or whatever kind of animal you are, how about some grub?"

"After you saddle up. You know the rules. Now finish your coffee and get after it. Güero is waiting to talk to you," la Chista said.

After they finished their coffee, the men picked up their ropes and started toward the corrals. All wore different hats, with their brush jackets and their chaps swinging on their legs. Some rolled a Bull Durham, and some swung ropes. Others talked. All were anxious to start the day's work.

Being a cowboy meant knowing how to work, how to prepare to work, and how to do the actual work. After they had their second or third cup of coffee, they would put on what they called their working uniform. Each cowboy was equipped with the tools of his trade —spurs, chaps, a saddle, saddle blanket, two head stalls, two regular bits, a thin rope to make reins, and a rope.

Then there was that very important part of the equipment—the brush jacket. It was made of heavy canvas material, hot during the summer but cool when it was rained on or just dunked into a water trough. In the winter, it blocked the cold north wind and offered protection when riding through tall, heavy brush. All the men wore it. The brush jacket separated the cowboys from the other men in town, and it was a way of identifying a Kineño cowboy.

That was their basic equipment to start, but as a boy grew into a man, he accumulated more of the working tools he needed. He would find gloves and slickers for the heavy rains and the fog and cold that could blow in within a few minutes on the Gulf Coast. Each cowboy carried a warbag. He learned to braid a rope and horsehair bosal, which is approximately ten feet long and three-eighths inch in size for training a horse to rein. Leather strapping was used for the different jobs because of its strength. The ranch furnished the saddle soap which preserved the leather and gave it a clean smell.

They had the best trained horses in the west. There were sorrels, mostly because of the sand burn. There were blacks, duns, bays, buckskins, and chestnuts. A beautiful herd of horses, built for stamina and speed. They were bred to be able to stand the jerking of a bull when roped, and be able to pull the bull where the cowboy wanted to take him. Thoroughbred stallions on native stock produced excellent quarterhorses.

Years ago, the ranch had only the Spanish stock that ran wild. These were trapped, then broke, and trained. They had the heart of a mustang, but not the strength or stamina. That's where the thoroughbred came in. The result of selective breeding was the quarterhorse. A finer herd of horses could not be found in the west. Each cowboy had about ten or twelve horses in his string. Güero had about fifteen in his string because he would cut cattle and rope calves for branding and castrating.

The Caporal had excellent horses. He was a good horse trainer, but most of all, he had a way of knowing when to choose a certain mount to train for whatever job he was going to perform. The picking of horses came with experience. Usually, he would let the young cowboys break the colt for the saddle and rider. Then he would take the colt and train him or her to his need. Güero needed good horses at all times, and he took pride in their training.

Lauro sat under a big, old mesquite tree inside the first pen where they caught the colts they were breaking. They had been at the Jensen corrals for over two months, breaking two year old colts to handle, and respond to a snaffle bit, saddle blanket, and saddle. Then they would try mounting and riding in the pens until they could rein, stop, go, turn, backup, and go forward on command. It took patience and repetition to train these colts.

It was July 1, 1915. Three years since Lauro had started working at the King Ranch. During that time he had learned the name of all the pastures, windmills, horses, and the way the Patrón wanted the ranch run. There had been good days during the spring roundup. Hot days during the summer, when they rode the colts in the early mornings and again in the cool of the late afternoons. The cattle roundups were in the spring and winter; Christmas and Fiesta time were in between seasons. There were so many different things to learn and ways to learn them. So much work each day.

It was the third year Lauro had done this job. Three years since he had said good-bye to Reina. His thoughts were always of her. He sat under the mesquite tree, smoking, handling a rope, and just killing time. It was siesta time, but he wasn't sleepy. His heart was broken and only time would mend it. He wished the breeze would start blowing again so they could begin work on the colts. When he was busy, he did not think of her, so he stayed busy all the time. Whenever there was a chore to do, he would do it. If there was a cow or calf or bull reported to have worms, he and one other man would rope and doctor it. He braided reins and bosals out of horses' hair, made hackmores out of rawhide, cinches out of horses' hair, quirts out of rawhide, and whips to drive cattle.

Güero came in the gate and closed it. "Hijo, it sure is a hot one today, but of course, it is always hot in July, especially on the first of July, eh Lauro." He sat next to the quiet, lanky cowboy who acted like the Caporal was not there. They sat in the shade, smoking, not saying anything, until Güero jumped up and put his arms out in a boxer's stance. "OK, put your dukes up, as the gringos say, come on put them up."

Lauro looked at him. "What's wrong with you, you going crazy? It's too hot to fight. Besides I wouldn't hit an old man."

"Old man! Just get up and fight, at least I'll know you are alive."

Lauro looked at him from under his hat, which was pulled down over his eyes. "OK, I'm sorry, I just can't get her out of my mind. Why did she act the way she did? Telling me she loved me, that I was the only one for her. Why?"

"Who knows the mind of a woman. They can change as fast as the weather in Texas. One day it's sunny the next it's raining. Haven't you learned that?" Güero looked at the boy that had become a man in these short years. He was proud of Lauro and loved him. He felt as if he were his own son. Lauro still lived with Güero and Serina. Every time he was ready to move out, they would find some reason to delay the move. He finally gave up.

Güero had taken him under his wing and taught him everything about how to run a corrida, the names of pastures, the windmills, the way the cattle would gather when rounding up, the names of horses in the remuda, the mares and foals, the stallions and their breeding lines. Lauro learned how to tell a cow is nursing a calf if the calf is not with her, when a cow is pregnant or barren, and which bulls wouldn't mate. There was so much to learn and often Güero would say, "You never stop learning. Keep an open mind. Be ready for anything, because when you least expect it, something will happen, you can bet on that."

Lauro had come to love Güero and Serina. They were like his second mother and father. As for the rest of the corrida and the Kineños, they were like family, every one of them. Often when someone had a problem, even though Lauro was younger than most, they still came to him and asked his advice. He had become a real Kineño and he loved the life he led. Still, he was miserable as any love sick cowboy could be.

At first, Lauro waited to hear from Reina. But her letters never came. He asked Jose Silquero if he had a letter. Jose would say yes, and his heart would jump into his throat, but it was mail from his mother or grandmother and nothing from Reina. That kept on for about two years. Slowly, he began to get the message. She did not love him. That's why she never wrote.

But she had written, letter after letter. Every day she would write to him asking why he was not answering her letters. She would say how much she loved him and missed him, and to please write to her and let her know he was alright.

Güero hated what had happened to Lauro, but he tried to tell him when he first found out about him and Reina that if the Patrón found out about the two lovers, he would have run Lauro off the ranch. But it had not happened, only because the Patrón had realized how valuable a man they had in Lauro.

Lauro could run the ranch while they were taking care of other business. The ranch had branched out into many things, and it was too much for the Patrón alone. Güero knew that Lauro was that man when he first saw him riding up to the herd that day so long ago. If he could only get him over this love for Reina—he sighed, and threw his smoke away. "Well, we can't change what has happened. We must go on. Forget her, and find a new woman. That is the way of life, and there is nothing we can do about it. In time, you will forget, I promise you, and you'll find another woman who will love you for what you are, and raise you strong children who will make you proud. You will see.

"Now, it's time to check the colts, doctor all the cuts and bruises and turn them out to pasture till next year. Okay? Also, we must break camp and head back to the headquarters, spend a few days with our families before we start the handling of the colts from the manadas. Go and tell the Chista to break camp."

Lauro was glad they were going back to headquarters. There might be word from Reina.

The next morning, Lauro rushed to the commissary to see if there was any mail for him. "Hey Jose, buenos dias, good morning. How are you? Buenos dias, Juanita. Is there any mail for me?"

"Si, Lauro, buenos dias, I'll get it for you," said Jose. Juanita looked at Jose sadly. "Here you go, Lauro, that's everything for the last month."

"Thanks, Jose, how about a sack of candy for the kids?" He always picked up a bag of candy from Jose for the kids around the barrio. "Thanks," he said not looking up. He grabbed the candy and walked out of the store, going through his mail. Again, there was no letter from Reina. His heart was crushed, but he really wasn't expecting one. There was a letter from his mother and one from his grandmother. He read the one from his mother first.

Dearest Hijo:

I hope this letter finds you well. I pray every day that God will keep you safe and well from all the evil in this world. Everyone is fine and we think of you each day. Thanks to God, our health is good. Vallejo sends his regards and wants you to come home and tell him about the Kineño. Is it as wild as they say? The cattle look fine and it looks like the summer will be hot, but we will make it through all right. Your father is working too hard, but you know him, he won't slow down.

We have been noticing some riders along the Camino de los Bueys. They seem to be looking for something. They never stop or ask directions. Papa and your brother are keeping a close watch on them.

Papa says that they look like they're from Mexico, but if they are, why don't they come and ask for work? I don't like them snooping around the place, but we can't stop them from coming down the road.

Well my love, I must go do my chores. Your sisters and brother send their love. We miss you. Take care of yourself and write when you can.''

All my love,
Your loving Mother

Then he read his grandmother's letter.

My Dearest Grandson:

I hope this letter finds you in good spirits and good health. Thanks to God, your aunt and I are fine. She sends her love, and mine is always with you.

There is something that I feel I must write to you about, something I feel in these old bones of mine that I must pass on to you. There have been some raids by Mexican bandits all up and down the border, all the way to El Paso. Some men and women have been killed, places burned, cattle and horses stolen. I cannot remember when it was this bad. It is rumored that it is planned by someone else and then carried out by the bandits. They say that they have good rifles and plenty of ammunition. I don't like what I hear. It's like the old days when we had to keep weapons by our sides all the time. I believe someone is stirring the bandidos into raiding the farms and ranches. I hope that trouble does not start up again. I've written your father to be on the lookout for any strangers and to keep their rifles close by. Also, not to alarm your mother. They have not raided around Brownsville, but he must be warned. I get most of my information from Mama at the cafe. She keeps me well informed. She sends her love. I must go now.

Please write when you can. I'll write to you if I feel you are needed at home. So far, there has been no reason to feel they are in danger, but we must be ready.

Take care of yourself. May God watch over you and protect you.

Your loving Grandmother

Lauro looked up from reading the letters with a worried look on his face. So, it's started again. But why?

Robert Kleberg, Sr. found Mrs. King at her favorite bench feeding the birds on the patio. "There you are, I knew I would find you in the coolest part of the Casa Grande." He sat next to her, taking off his hat, wiping the sweat off his brow, enjoying the cool breeze and the peace and quiet of the patio.

"You did a magnificent job on this place R. J. I don't know what I would have done without you."

Kleberg turned and looked at her. "It did turn out alright, didn't it?"

"Not bad at all."

He paused a minute to enjoy the companionship of this strong lady. "I got word from Caesar down at Norias that things aren't right. He's afraid that we're losing cattle little by little at the Sauz Ranch, the pasture closest to the Mexican border. They've taken cattle before, but not like this. Caesar writes we're losing about fifty head every other week. He needs help, and he doesn't like what is happening there."

"What does he mean, happening down there?" she asked, turning toward her son-in-law.

"Well, he said they're seeing more signs every day of someone scouting the ranch pretty well. He needs help, someone to watch and scout around, let him know who the rustlers are, and where their camp is. Someone who knows the country. He doesn't trust his men to tell him. So I was thinking, maybe we could send Lauro."

She was startled a little when he mentioned Lauro's name. "Why him? We need him here. He's done a fine job. We need him," she said again. She had a premonition that if she let Lauro go, she would never see him again.

"I know he's needed here but Caesar needs someone he can trust, he asked for him, and this thing will die down in a few months. Besides, he wants to see his family in San Perlita. It will do him good. He's not been the same person in quite awhile. I think he's homesick."

Henrietta King looked up from her black high-top shoes, and knew the answer to his homesickness. "Yes, maybe, it's a good idea to send him down there. He can learn how Caesar runs that division and visit with his folks. He already knows that part of the country, and he might be able to find out why the rustling has started again.

"Also, send a message to the Texas Rangers that I want to talk to whoever they send down there. I want Tom Tate to know what's going on. Besides Tom and Lauro are good friends. Together they might do some good."

"Alright. The corrida got back last night. I'll send word to Lauro that I want to talk to him." Kleberg hated to leave this cool spot, but he knew he had work to do.

Just as Kleberg got up from the bench to go, Lauro came walking down the long veranda toward them. "Good afternoon, Mrs. King. Patrón, excuse me, but I needed to talk to both of you," said Lauro.

"Good afternoon, Lauro," Mrs. King said.

Kleberg smiled, still a little cautious of why Lauro appeared just as he was going to send for him. Kleberg wondered what Lauro wanted.

My, what a good looking man Lauro has turned out to be, Mrs. King said to herself. He had gained a little weight; put on more muscle.

"If you will please forgive me for interrupting you, I'd like to ask for a leave of absence to go visit my family in San Perlita. I received a letter from my folks and they need me." He stood there with his hat in hand, waiting to hear what they would say. It made no difference what the answer, he was going. His people needed him.

"Well, Lauro, this is a coincidence. We were just talking about sending you down there for a while," Mrs. King said. "Caesar needs some help at Norias and he has asked for you. It's evident that you made an impression on him. This will work out quite nicely."

"Mr. Caesar asked for me? What for?" Lauro said.

"We have been losing more cattle than usual. He needs someone who knows the country to scout for him and try to head it off before it gets any worse. I'll request some more Rangers to help you. Tom Tate is there with Frank Martin, and with you riding together with them, there should be no trouble finding out who is causing this rustling."

Frank Martin was from Alice, Texas, and had worked at Santa Gertrudis for awhile, then transferred to Norias. He and Lauro had become good friends when he worked at headquarters.

"It seems that there is a lot of unrest along the border. My grandmother has written that things are getting worse. She's afraid that it will be like the old days. My folks' letter said they have seen strangers on the Camino de los Bueys, checking things out. I don't like it," Lauro said.

Mrs. King gave the instructions. "Well, I think that you should go as soon as possible. Say your good-byes and see that your equipment is ready. Take one of those brand new Winchester 30-30 rifles out of the commissary. Tell Jose I said it was okay. You can go by train or you can go on a caballo. If you go by train, you'll save days, but if you go by horseback you might be able to cut their trail and find out where they're coming from. But either way, I want you to stop at Norias Headquarters, help Caesar look around before you go down and see your folks.''

"Yes, ma'am. I already thought about that, and I know that it will take me three days on a caballo, and it's slower, but if I can spot the rustlers and do something about them, I won't have to worry about my folks.''

"Good thinking. Go ahead and stay as long as you feel it's necessary, but Lauro, remember to come back to us,'' Mrs. King said.

"Yes ma'am, thank you.'' Lauro turned to go. He stopped and turned around. "Excuse me, would you mind giving me Reina's address so I can drop her a line and tell her what we're doing, and that I'll be back?''

Mrs. King and Kleberg were taken back for a minute, then Mrs. King recovered. "Oh, I had a letter from her today. I haven't even had a chance to tell Robert. She has become engaged to a very wealthy man from the east and she wants us to announce the engagement next month. Right now, she is in England with her senior class touring the country. I doubt she would get your letter. I'll write to her about what we have planned. Go along now. You have much to do.''

Lauro and Kleberg were shocked. Lauro took a step back as if she had slapped him. He turned around, put on his hat, and walked down the red tile veranda without saying a word. When Lauro was out of hearing range, Kleberg looked at his mother-in-law and whispered. "Is it true, is she really engaged?''

"Yes, I'll explain later. I hated to hurt him, but I felt that it was best he knew. After all, it's going to be three years. You knew this was bound to happen, as beautiful as she is and as vulnerable, she's ready for anything. I just hope that she's not making a mistake, but we will see.'' She watched Lauro walk away. She felt a pain in her heart.

Lauro walked to the stables. He untied his mount, put his head against the warm neck and cried. He had never felt more alone. After a while, he mounted and rode to town. He went to Richard Street where the cantinas were. He walked into a bar, looked around, and took a table at the far corner of the room. The Richard Street Bar was a favorite bar of the Kineños, and Güero had taken him there before on payday. It was a typical cantina. Though Mrs. King had prohibited the selling of spirits or alcohol on Main Street in Kingsville, they tolerated Richard Street bars. There were six or eight of the bars open. Both Anglos and Tejanos were allowed to drink there. Mrs. King was smart enough to look the other way. She knew the men had to blow off steam somewhere.

Lauro sat in the corner of the Richard Street Bar drinking tequila and thinking of how he lost the only woman he would ever love. "Bring me another drink," he yelled at the bartender, trying to roll another cigarette. He had been in the cantina ever since he rode into town. He was drunk, listening to the one mariachi they had.

The bartender recognized Lauro when he came in. He was Güero's friend, and he knew that the boy was hell bent to get drunk. He had sent for Güero to come get his young friend out of there before he got into trouble. Petria, the only barmaid, sat almost in his lap, trying to get him to go to the back room, but Lauro was too drunk to go anywhere. She played with his leg, and higher, but he was not interested. He knew that he had never been so miserable in his life.

Güero came in the cantina and spotted Lauro talking to Petria about how rotten life was and how much he loved Reina, and yet, hated her, and yet loved her.

"Forget her," Petria said. "Let's go to my room and I'll make you forget this gringa. You belong with me. I love you," she said.

Güero stepped in front of them as they started to go to Petria's room. "Yes my little *paloma*, till the next man comes with money to spend, then you will love him, eh?"

Everyone knew the Caporal of the corrida. His word was law, so when Güero spoke everyone listened. "Come, hijo. It's time to go home. Supper is on the table and Mama will be very angry if I don't bring you home."

He bent over and threw Lauro over his shoulder and whacked him on the behind. Güero started toward the door, turned and looked around the cantina. There were just a few men, none from the Kineño. He looked back at the bartender. "Thank you, Elias, I will remember this. I owe you. This never happened, okay?"

"Okay, primo. Don't worry, it will be taken care of." Elias took his cigar out of his mouth and waved good-bye to the big Caporal.

Petria moved to the bar, a sad look on her face. "Give me a drink, I almost had him, *que chulo*. How cute he is. How handsome. I've been trying to get him in bed ever since he came here with the rest of the corrida. I need a drink."

Güero put Lauro in the back of the wagon, and covered him with a tarp. He looked at Lauro and put his hat on his head. "Sleep, my son. It is hard, but you will forget. You'll live through this, I promise."

When Lauro woke the next morning, he tried to move his head, but just the slightest movement sent a pain to his temples. He looked around the room and had a terrible thirst. He managed to get out of bed and head toward the pitcher of water by the wash basin. He drank till he could drink no more, then he went outside and threw up. "Never again," he said.

Güero stood on the porch, watching him. "How you feel, sick, huh? Well, come in and drink some coffee, you will feel better."

After breakfast, Lauro told Güero and Serina what had happened. The talk with Mrs. King and the Patrón. The news from the valley and what he had to do, and Reina's engagement. Serina put her arm around Lauro, not saying a word.

Lauro went about the business of packing. Güero saddled Lobo and packed what he would need for the trip. Güero was very sad that Lauro was going to leave, but he had his orders, and his family needed him. He had to go. He turned when he heard the door open on the porch. Serina was crying softly. Lauro put his arms around her, kissed her cheek, held her for a moment, then headed to the shed.

While Lauro tied his saddle bags and slicker to the back of the saddle, Güero told Lobo to carry Lauro safely to his destination. He checked his headstall and handed Lauro the reins. "Well, hijo, looks like you are ready. You got everything you need?"

"Yes, Serina made sure. I'm going to miss her. You take care of her and yourself, too." He strapped his Navy Colt on and tied the pigeon string to his leg.

"Sure, you know me, I always take care of me," said the Caporal.

Yeah! After everyone else, Lauro thought. "Well, I guess this is good-bye. Mucho gracias, primo. I'll put to use everything you've taught me, I shall never forget you." They embraced.

Güero cleared his throat to keep from crying. "Go with God, my son, remember, Pela el ojo, watch your back."

Lauro mounted, looked around, waved to Serina, took one last look at Güero and rode away. He adjusted the rifle so it would not rub Lobo raw, sat straight in the saddle and did not look left or right till he was away from the main headquarters. It felt good to be on the trail again as he crossed Santa Gertrudis Creek at the bridge. He kept going down the road moving to the south, passing the Plomo pens, waving at the feed crew, feeding the thousands of head of cattle.

18

NORIAS DIVISION—KING RANCH
We Reap What We Sow

Lauro had been at Norias for about four weeks. He had moved along the coast, trying to find tracks that would lead him in the direction of the cattle rustlers.

He found plenty of cattle tracks, but no horse tracks. He should have come across some signs that the outlaws were working this area. But there were none.

He had looked at one camp that looked familiar, remembering it was the camp where he had seen the Karankawa Indian Chief. He raised his finger to where the sea shell necklace had been around his neck. He had told the Chief that he would never take it off, but he had given it to Reina that night they were together in the Canelo pasture as a token of their love. Now, Reina and the necklace were gone. He thought she probably had thrown it away by now. He decided to make camp here.

It was nice being back along the coast, under the same trees with a small fire, well hidden so it could not be seen by anyone that was not welcome at his camp.

He looked into the flame of the fire, losing his night vision, but he couldn't take his eyes off the blue flame that appeared every once in a while. It was the blue of Reina's eyes. He shook his head, sat back from the fire. I better pay attention to what I'm doing, Lauro thought. He must not stare into the fire and lose his night vision. He let the fire die by itself, but his last thought was of blue eyes and blonde hair and a smile he could never forget.

The next morning Lauro awakened to a heavy fog. He built a fire from the wood he had gathered and covered with his saddle blanket. The fire felt good. The morning was cool with a light breeze blowing from the coast. He boiled some coffee and cooked some *pan de campo* and bacon. It was a quick breakfast, and he was ready to start his search.

The fog began to lift. He decided to move down the coast to the Sauz Ranch, another part of the King Ranch. It had been the southern most part of the San Juan de Carricitos Land Grant. It almost bordered Mexico, except for the Rio Grande.

Lauro figured it would be a good four day's ride even if he was not looking for a sign. He also wanted to see if his folks were alright at the Laurel Ranch. Their ranch bordered the Sauz Ranch division of the King Ranch. Their ranch was the last of the original Spanish Land Grant.

It took him three days to reach the property of the Laurel Ranch. As he rode he saw signs going toward the border. It looked like they were hitting more of the Sauz Ranch than anywhere else.

Lauro looked up and saw a rider in the distance heading toward him. He didn't recognize him, so he pulled into the oak motte and waited. He didn't think that the rider had seen him, but the stranger was coming right for him. Lauro looked down to see if his rifle was where he could reach it, then looked up, and the rider was gone. Lauro knew that he had made a mistake. "Never take your eyes off of someone you don't know. *Pela el ojo.*"

He heard someone behind him and turned to a familiar voice that said, "Don't move, amigo. Not if you value your life. Now I want some answers. First, where did you get that horse, and it better be the truth or you die."

Lauro said, "You old fool, would you shoot a boy you used to wipe the snot from his nose?" He turned in the saddle and saw a startled Vallejo holding a 30-30 rifle right at his middle.

"Lauro," Vallejo shouted. The next thing, the two men were embracing. They laughed and pounded each other on the back, and hugged each other again and again. It was so good to see each other.

Finally, Vallejo drew back and held him by the shoulders. "Let me look at you. Why you've grown into a man. You're thicker through the shoulders. Look at those arms. I didn't even recognize you, boy. It's good to see you." They embraced again.

They started a small fire to make some coffee, and rolled a smoke.

Lauro looked at his old friend and mentor. His heart was full of love for this man who taught him how to survive in the Wild Horse Desert. He was like a second father to Lauro. The spark was still in his eyes, those eyes that never quit searching for something out of place, something that was not right with the natural scheme of things around him.

Vallejo had come to their ranch just before Lauro was born. Lauro's father told him that Vallejo had arrived, wounded and about to die. But Lauro's mother would not let him. He had two wounds that would have killed any other man, but with her help, he recovered and never left the ranch.

No one ever asked how he got the wounds, but Lauro had a good idea. He remembered the half breed from Mexico that was part of Scarface's gang.

"Your folks are fine. You can see we're a little dry. We need a good rain or a hurricane, but I've seen worse. The cattle are in good shape. Maybe this month of August, we will get a rain to help.

"Now, what are you doing way over here? What happened at the Kineño? Did you find what you were looking for? Tell me the whole story." Vallejo started rolling a smoke and sat on his haunches waiting for Lauro to begin telling everything that had happened to him.

Lauro told his story. He poured his heart out to his old friend. He left nothing out, his love for Reina, and the heart break, the fire at the big house, the knife fight at the party, the trip to the *Paso de los Muertos,* the conclusion that the Kings had nothing to do with the killing of his grandfather. He told of all the friends he had made and the mission he was on now.

"What can I tell you. There is nothing that hurts more than a love gone wrong. It is in our songs, our stories, it is a part of our life. We must live with it, forget it, and go on," the old friend said. "You will live, you will see.

"Now, as for your cattle rustlers. I have seen strange things happening in this country. Wire cut, missing cattle, signs at the windmills. It looks like they're scouting for something. There's too much movement. They're not burning or looting like they did. I wonder what is going on. It's not like the bandidos I knew. They would not pass these things. Something is going on.

"They're not taking large herds of cattle. Just enough to be able to move fast. Like they were taking just enough to feed a large number of people. They seem to be waiting for someone or something," Vallejo said as he stirred the fire with a stick.

"None of us can figure out what they are waiting for. Your father and mother are worried too. They have made the ranch into a fortress. Someone is on guard all the time, while I scout to see what I can find. I'm cutting the same sign that you are. I'm wondering, maybe they're thinking of hitting Norias Headquarters. What do you think, Lauro?"

"Yes. That is exactly what I have been thinking. There are too many signs around here at the Sauz Ranch Headquarters not to mean something. They seem to be watching Norias as if they are waiting for the right time to make their move," Lauro said.

"Your father said that there was a great war going on in Europe and there is a civil war in Mexico between the Carranza Constitutionalist and the Federals of Huerta. They do not have time to watch the border and keep the bandidos from raiding the United States. Now, it is our turn. It does not look good, my friend," Vallejo said.

"I wish I could see my family," Lauro said. "But I think I had better warn the Caporal at Norias. You go to the ranch and tell father that I will come as soon as possible. I don't think the Laurel Ranch is in danger. It sounds like you're prepared anyway. They won't strike against anyone who is ready and waiting for them. That's not the way of the bandido. It would be too dangerous. They like it when they can surprise you."

"Okay, I will go home, but you must come as soon as possible. Your mother will be waiting for you and so will the rest of the family," Vallejo said.

They kicked a little sand on the fire, embraced each other again and mounted their horses to go in different directions, Vallejo to the family that Lauro loved, and Lauro to warn a bunch of people that he barely knew.

———

Lauro had ridden Lobo pretty hard to get back to Norias. To his disappointment, the Caporal had gone to Kingsville. There was just one of the hands there and it was his friend, Frank Martin.

Frank met Lauro at the corral. "Well, I'll be damned. How you doing, Larry? It's been a long time. I heard you were coming," Martin said.

Frank was a tall thin man with brown eyes and a ready smile for everyone. He was a man to ride the Rio with.

"Hello, Frank. How are you? Long time no see." The two friends shook hands.

"Where is Mr. Caesar and Mr. Goodwyn?" Lauro asked.

Caesar Kleberg was a nephew of R. J. Kleberg, Sr. and he had been put on the Norias Division as the manager of the division. Mr. Eppse Goodwyn was the cow boss and actually ran the division.

"I need to see them right away," Lauro said.

"They're in Kingsville. Gone to get the payroll and supplies for the store," Frank said.

"That's it!" yelled Lauro. "The payroll! When is it due here? How long does it take for them to get here? What's the date of the month? Do you have a telephone here?" Lauro asked. He had become so excited.

"Whoa, partner. Slow down. One question at a time. Now, to answer them. It is the sixth of August. The payroll doesn't get here till about the seventh or so, depending on if they are delayed in Kingsville. Yes, we have a telephone. In fact, we just got one. It's on the porch at Mr. Caesar's house. Now, what's going on?"

"I'll tell you later. Just show me how the telephone works," Lauro said as he pulled Frank toward the two story building that was ranch headquarters.

The railroad had split Norias Headquarters in two parts. Caesar Kleberg's office was on one side of the tracks and built on the bare flat sandy ground, totally exposed. The barns and corrals were on the other side.

"Just pick up the receiver and talk into the mouth piece sticking out there," Frank said. "Then crank the telephone until somebody answers. It will be Raymondville. Just ask for Kingsville and when you get the Kingsville office, ask for the King Ranch."

Lauro picked up the receiver and cranked the telephone, after a short time the operator came on. "Yes, stop cranking. You're hurting my ears," the operator said. "That's better. Now, how can I help you?"

"Give me the King Ranch office in Kingsville," Lauro said. He heard a buzzing sound and then someone said, "Hello, King Ranch office."

The King Ranch had built the Kleberg National Bank downtown on the corner of Sixth and Kleberg streets in 1911. It was a two story building with the ranch office upstairs and the bank downstairs.

"Hello, is Mr. Kleberg there?"

"No, I'm sorry. He's working cattle at the ranch. Can someone else help you?" the lady asked.

"Well, how about Mr. Caesar, is he there?" Lauro asked.

"Yes, but he's in a meeting and I can't disturb him," she said.

Lauro heard voices in the background. "Well, damn it. Who's there?" Just then he heard someone say, "Who's that, Nellie Jeff, I'll take the call. Hello, this is J. B. Bell. How can I help you?"

"Mr. Bell, this is Lauro Cavazos. I'm down at Norias. We are going to be in big trouble down here. I have to talk to Mr. Caesar right away. Can you get him?"

"No, I can't. He's in an important meeting and he asked not to be disturbed. Why don't you tell me what you're talking about and I'll pass the word to Caesar?" Bell asked.

"I was sent down here to find out who was rustling the cattle and there are signs all over the place. They're taking just what they need to eat. They're scouting the place to raid the Norias Headquarters for the payroll. We're going to need help. Don't send the payroll," Lauro said.

Bell's face turned red and he thought to himself, "The bastard has found out. I'll have to find out what he knows."

"Take it easy, young man. Just slow down. The payroll will leave this morning, but we can still stop it. That is, if you are sure of what you're talking about. Those men at Norias will be mad if we don't pay them on time. Did you see the bandits or you just guessing?" Bell said.

"I didn't see them, but I cut the sign everywhere. I just feel it in my bones. It makes sense that is what they're shooting at. We need help. All the men are working cattle in the farthest part of the ranch. They can't get here in time," Lauro said.

"Okay, Lauro. I'll relay your message to Caesar. We will get you help in a little while," Bell said.

"Thank you. I'll keep scouting and let you know if I find anything more," Lauro said and then replaced the receiver.

J. B. Bell looked at Nellie Jeff, the Kleberg secretary. "It's nothing to worry about. I'll handle everything."

He started to walk away. It would not be my fault if I forgot to tell Caesar about the boy calling. I have so many things to do. I just can't remember everything, Bell thought to himself.

All of a sudden Caesar Kleberg came down the hall. "What was that call? I heard my name mentioned," he said.

Bell looked at Nellie Jeff and interrupted her before she could speak. "Oh, Caesar, I was just about to go get you. That was the boy, Lauro Cavazos. He says that bandits are going to hit Norias Headquarters for the payroll and he needs help. I asked him if he had seen them and was sure. He said, 'No,' so it's probably just his imagination, if you ask me.''

Caesar Kleberg picked up the telephone and asked the operator to get the Texas Ranger Station in Brownsville.

"Captain Ransom, this is Caesar Kleberg." Henry Ransom was still in command of the Texas Rangers. "It looks like we're going to have trouble at Norias. One of my men has seen a lot of signs at Norias, and we need help," Caesar said.

"Yes sir, Mr. Caesar. I'll get some of my men and head down there. We'll get started first thing in the morning," the Ranger Captain said.

"Good. You can use our horses and eat there at Norias. I'll call Fort Brown and see if they can send some troops to help you. We have some men there at Norias, but the rest of them are too far away. I'll ask the railroad people to send a special train from Brownsville to carry all of you to Norias. There are two good men there that can help you. Also, Tom Tate should be around there. He is foreman of the Sauz Ranch and a hell of a good man, but that is about all the men you can depend on from us, right now. I will get things started here. It will take all day tomorrow. We will be there as soon as possible. Let me know if you need anything else," Caesar Kleberg said.

"I don't think that we will need any help, just stay there until I call you. I think we can handle a few Mexicans by ourselves," the Ranger Captain said and hung up the phone.

"Why that stupid son of a bitch. Who does he think he is, Sam Houston? He's going to need all the help he can get and then some," Caesar said.

Bell stood there and listened to the replies from Kleberg, thinking to himself, "That stupid bastard Scarface will get us all hung. I hope I never see that son of a bitch again. I don't think anyone can tie us together, but I better get out of here."

"Caesar, I wish I could help, but I have to be in Austin for an important meeting tomorrow. I'm leaving on tonight's train," Bell said.

Caesar Kleberg looked at the fat pompous little man with disgust. "Yes, go ahead. I'm sure we can do without you," Kleberg said.

In the next breath, he picked up the telephone and called Fort Brown in Brownsville and explained what was happening. They responded with a squad of men, eight of them from the 12th Calvary Station in Harlingen, Texas.

Caesar Kleberg called Lauro who was waiting for a call from

anyone to see if they were going to send help.

"Lauro, it's good to talk to you," Kleberg said. "Here's what is going to happen. I called the Rangers and they're coming to help. Also, the Army is sending troops to Norias. Tom should be around there somewhere. I will organize a train from here with volunteers to go and help. Tell Tom to get the remuda for the Rangers and the troops ready. I will be there as soon as possible."

"Yes sir. I'll tell Tom when I see him. But Frank is here and we can get the horses. You better bring all the help you can get. I'm afraid we're going to catch hell."

"I know you can handle anything that may come up, Lauro. You're a good man. Just hold the ranch till we get there," Caesar Kleberg said and hung up.

Bell came back to the ranch office that night to pick up some papers. He had told Caesar he was going to be in Austin tomorrow. He wanted to distance himself from the raid, just in case Scarface was caught and tried to put the blame on him. He had plenty of money in his briefcase if he had to leave suddenly. He started up the stairs. He always lost his breath when climbing them, and this time he took them too fast. He was half way up the stairs when he grabbed his left arm. The pain was unbearable, and he slumped to the steps, knowing he was having a heart attack.

He had had them before. The first was two years ago and the doctors told him to lose weight and stop drinking so much. He had not listened to their advice. He had to get his nitro pills the doctor had given him. He reached in his coat pocket where he kept them, but he dropped the bottle and watched it roll down the stairs.

He tried to get up, but didn't have the strength. He looked up and saw a light underneath the door. He had forgotten about the janitor. He always cleaned the office at night. "Help, help, I'm on the stairs, help." He had never bothered to learn the name of the old man who had cleaned the office for years.

"Help! Help! I'm on the stairs." The pain was worse. The door opened and the janitor stood silhouetted against the light in the office. The old man, bent and wrinkled, looked down at Bell.

"Help me, you old fool! Get my pills. They're down at the bottom of the stairs. Hurry!"

"Mr. Bell," the old man said, "you are having trouble. Are you sick? Do you need help? There is no one here but me."

"Yes, you must help me. Get my pills and then go for help at the

Sheriff's office. Hurry.''

The old man didn't move, he just smiled. ''Excuse me, do you know my name? No? Well, Mr. Bell, it is Jose de la Garza, one of the former owners of the Spanish Land Grant you cheated from us. You and your gringo friends in Austin. You and your crooked politicians who took the land that had been in our family for generations. You didn't even know who we were or even bothered to find out my name.

''Well, Mr. Bell, you are going to remember my name when you burn in hell. What good will all your money and power do for you now? All the pain and misery you have caused the de la Garza family and other grant owners, the Cavazos, Mindiolas, Falcon, the Balli family of South Padre Island, and many others. I'll be able to meet my God with a clean conscience. You, what can you tell him? That you were greedy and stole from the people who were the rightful owners. So, Mr. J. B. Bell, rest your soul in hell.'' He closed the door to the office, locked it, and walked past J. B. Bell lying on the stairs.

Bell had listened to the old man, reached out for help and got none. He would have given all he owned for his help, but he ''reaped what he had sown.'' He died there still reaching for his pills.

———————

It was August 6, 1915, in Matamoros, Mexico. Von Lutter sat alone at his usual table in the corner of Lupe's Cantina brooding about what Scarface had said to him three days ago when he left to raid the Texas ranches.

His superiors had sent a message to begin their raids as planned, to create as much confusion as possible along the Texas, Mexico border. He had demanded that Scarface begin.

Scarface told him he would start when he wanted to, that he was the chief of the bunch of cutthroats, and he would move when he was ready and not before.

The German agent did not know about the payroll. Scar told him to just sit there and buy the drinks and girls and he would let him know when he was ready. Von Lutter had protested by telling him he would cut him and his riffraff off the money if he didn't go now.

The next thing he knew he had a ''*cuchillo*'' at his throat. ''Listen, you pig, I'll tell you when to cut us off, you don't say or do anything until I tell you to, understand?'' Scar said. He pressed the knife harder to his throat, a small trickle of blood started down von Lutter's throat. He felt the blood start and he knew how close he was to dying.

"Alright, alright, we do not move till you are ready," von Lutter said as he tried to move away from the knife that was being held tightly to his throat.

Everyone was watching when Scar relaxed the knife and sat back. "That's better," he said.

"Lupe, bring us another drink and bring one for this fat German pig. He's buying again," said Scar. The cantina roared with laughter.

That was three days ago, a delay of over a week between when von Lutter had received his orders and Scar had finally decided to go. Von Lutter was still mad and humiliated. No one spoke to him that way. When this was over he would kill that scum and laugh when he did it.

A whore sat down beside him and reached under the table to feel his penis through his trousers. "Buy a girl a drink," she said.

Von Lutter looked at her with disgust. He was tired of all these Mexicans and their ways. He had been kicked around enough, and he was tired of it. He backhanded the whore and knocked her away from the table.

"Get away from me, you filth, I'm sick of you all. Leave me alone. I wish I had never come here," and he turned his back to the stunned whore.

It was a mistake.

She came off the dirt floor like a wildcat, knife in hand. She slit his throat from ear to ear and he never even felt it. He did see his blood gushing out on the table and all around him. He knew he was a dead man. "Oh, my God," he said, barely getting it out. Then he died.

Scarface looked at the bunch of horses they had stolen from the headquarters at the Sauz Ranch. He was mad because they had found nothing else. He would have to send them back with two men, but it was still better than nothing.

They had picked up more supplies at the Sauz—flour, salt, pepper, sugar, and coffee. That was all he would let the men carry because he knew it would be a horse race back to the border after the raid. They would pick up more horses so they could put the stolen goods in a wagon and travel fast. That was the way of the comancheros, hit quick, travel light, and run like hell.

Scarface didn't set fire to the headquarters at the Sauz Ranch. He didn't want to draw attention from the smoke. It would have been seen for miles.

They were camped at Coyote Lake, no fires, and horses hobbled close by. They ate *carne seca* and flour tortillas and drank water. Scarface lay on his saddle blanket, head on his saddle, looking at the stars and thinking about the next day. By his calculations, there would be around ten to twenty thousand in gold at Norias Headquarters. The King Ranch always paid their bills in gold, and there would be the silver and gold plates and silverware they used to serve their guests. He would be a rich man again. He hadn't hit a big jackpot since he stole that herd from the old man long ago. He reached and touched his face, and softly cursed that devil from hell. Maybe I'll kill that fat Aleman when I get back, he thought. He has a lot of cash to spend. It will be a pleasure. I'll kill him when I'm through with him. Give the land back to the Mexican people. What a joke. They'll keep it for themselves. Who do they think they are kidding?'' He didn't know that von Lutter had already gone to his reward.

The young boy had watched while they rounded up his mother and the rest of the people at the Sauz Ranch Headquarters. His father and the rest of the men were with the Sauz corrida to the west of the ranch, working cattle. It was too far for him to warn them of what happened, but it wasn't too far to the Norias Headquarters.

His name was Jose Lopez, and he liked to ride his mule while hunting armadillo. He was just pulling a big fat armadillo out of a hole when he heard the shouting when the bandits struck. He let the animal go and rushed to his mule. The animal shied away from him, but he was an excellent rider and he jumped on the back of the mule. ''Let's go, Conejo. Something is happening at the rancho.''

He stopped in the brush where he could watch what was happening. He watched as they pulled his mother out of the casa and put her with the rest of the people in the store, and took what they could carry. They didn't harm anyone, but Jose didn't like the way they treated his mother. He watched as they rode off, then rushed to the store and broke the lock to free his mother and the rest of the people.

His grandfather embraced him. ''Good boy, Jose. I knew you would come. Now you must go to Norias and warn Mr. Caesar that the bandits are heading that way. I'll send someone else to warn your father and

the corrida. Now go. Be wise like the fox and fast like the falcon."
They had taken all the horses, so all he had was Conejo. "Come on
Conejo. We have to make tracks. Let's go."

He followed the trail left by the Mexican bandidos. He had never
seen so many tracks left by horsemen, unless it was by the whole
remuda. He watched the bandits make camp at Coyote Lake. He
noticed that the one who gave orders to the bandidos had red hair and a
scar on his face. He looked more like a gringo than a Mexican, but Jose
couldn't tell from his hiding place in the mesquite. He waited till they
were asleep and crawled back to Conejo. He quickly took the bandana
off of Conejo's nose that kept him from braying and held the mule's
nose while he walked. He took the long way around the bandit's camp
before letting go and mounting. "Okay Conejo. Let's go. We have to
get there before the bandits. *Vamanos.* Let's go." The brave boy
headed for Norias as fast as Conejo could carry him.

NORIAS DIVISION—KING RANCH
AUGUST 6, 1915

Lauro and Frank Martin stayed close to the telephone, waiting to
hear from Caesar Kleberg. They looked toward the section house and
noticed that there was some kind of commotion going on. The railroad
foreman and his wife lived in the section house, which held their living
quarters, a kitchen, and eating quarters. That was where most of the
section gang lived and ate.

The section house was about as strong as a building could be, as
sturdy as most buildings the railroad built. Lauro crossed the railroad
tracks and headed to the section house. He had left Frank at the
telephone in case Mr. Caesar called. He noticed every one of the
railroad people were very excited, running around a boy on a mule,
throwing their arms in the air.

"What's going on?" Lauro said. He noticed the boy and the mule
were both spent. "What's the matter?" He knew what it was, the raids
had begun. "Quiet!" he yelled. Everyone looked at him. "Now tell me,
boy, did something happen? Take your time and tell me."

The boy looked at Lauro and knew he was a Kineño. He grabbed
the front of Lauro's shirt and through tears told him about the raid at
the Sauz Ranch. "They took everyone and put them in the store, but
harmed no one. They also took what they could carry and every one of

the horses we had—about fifty.''

''What's your name, chico?'' Lauro said.

''Jose Lopez. I'm the grandson of Francisco Lopez. Can I have a drink of water? I'm very thirsty.''

Lauro turned to one of the section gang. ''Get him some water, hurry. Now Jose, tell me how many were there and which way they headed.''

''There were eighty-two. I counted them when they made camp at Coyote Lake. Also, they had shiny new rifles.'' The man got there with the water and the boy drank all of it and asked for more.

''Go on. Tell me some more. Did they say they were coming here?'' the section boss asked.

''No, I didn't hear them, but where else could they go, Raymondville?'' Jose asked.

''Come with me, Jose. You folks get in the section house and barricade yourselves. And be sure you have plenty of food and water. Now go,'' Lauro said. He took the rope halter of the mule and led it toward Mr. Caesar's house across the tracks. '' Come on, Jose, let's get you something to eat.''

As they neared the main house and store, the boy remembered something. ''I'm not sure if he was the leader or not, but there was one bandit, who stood out more than the others. He was giving orders like a Patrón.''

''Would you recognize him again if you saw him?'' Lauro said.

''Si, señor. He would be easy to pick out of a group of men. He was a gringo, I think, and he had red hair and a scar that ran down the side of the face,'' the boy said.

Lauro stopped, turned toward the boy, and suddenly grabbed his shoulder. ''What did you say?''

The boy was shocked. ''You're hurting my shoulder. Let go.''

Lauro realized what he was doing and let go of the boy. ''I'm sorry, chico, but I must hear what you said again.''

''I said that the man would be easy to recognize. He just stood out with the red hair and the scar running down the side of his face. He was *muy macho*.''

Lauro stood there in a trance. ''Scarface. I might have known. And now after all these years he is so close.''

''I can't leave all these people alone,'' Lauro said. What if they are going to raid Raymondville, and not come here? There are too many men in town. The payroll—that's what he wants, and horses. No, he will come here. I just know it.

"Come boy, lets get you some food," Lauro said. He led the mule to the side of the house to the water trough.

Albert, who was African-American, stepped out on the porch and started ringing the dinner bell. He was the main house cook, and he and his wife Edna took care of the main house with the help of two Mexican women. There was also the ranch carpenter George Forbes and his wife. Lauro and Frank Martin and any other guests of the ranch ate and slept at the main house, but most had their own homes to go to. They just ate there. The Patróns and all Anglos ate and slept at the main house; the rest of the Mexican-Americans ate at the other camps and slept where they could. Still, the King Ranch always welcomed whoever wanted to eat and rest for a few days. That was why they had the separate camps.

Lauro made Jose clean up as best he could and went into the dining room. They sat next to Frank and noticed how Forbes and his wife didn't like it that the boy was eating at their table. "This is Jose Lopez," Lauro said. "He is from the Sauz Ranch, and just brought us some very bad news."

"What? What happened?" Forbe's wife said, almost rising from her chair. She was a big woman and not very pretty.

"Some Mexican bandits have been seen in the vicinity of the Sauz Ranch," Lauro said. He didn't tell the Forbes about the raid on the Sauz Headquarters. There was no need to panic everyone. "Frank and I talked with Mr. Caesar. He's going to send help from Brownsville just in case they come this way. The Rangers should be here by morning. There's nothing to worry about, but stay close to the house till this is over."

They all started talking at once, and passing the food around. Lauro and the boy didn't talk. Jose was in a hurry to get back to his parents at the Sauz Ranch. He looked at Lauro when he was full and signaled he wanted to talk to him away from everyone. Lauro had just finished, and they made their way to the front porch. It was a wide, long porch that ran all the way around the house. "What is it, Jose? What do you want to talk to me about?" Lauro said.

"I must go. I want to go home to my people. I did what my grandfather sent me to do, so I must go."

"But Jose, it's almost the middle of the night. You mustn't leave now. Wait till the morning, then go with the Rangers. They need your help."

"No, my people need me. Just tell the Rangers they are on the Sauz Ranch making camp at the Coyote Lake. They know where the lake is. What is your name, señor? You have been very kind."

"Lauro Cavazos, and I'm from San Perlita, where you are always welcome."

They moved toward Conejo, who was busy eating hay. The boy took the reins and leaped on the mule. "You know, someday I will work for you. Would you hire me?"

"Of course, I would. You are a brave boy. I will always remember you. Go with God."

Jose Lopez smiled and turned south toward the Sauz Ranch.

Lauro tried to sleep, but it was too hot and the humidity made it uncomfortable. He moved out to the porch and put his bedroll on the southeast side to stay awake in case of trouble. It was cooler with a light breeze from the southeast, and a half moon was rising.

Somewhere, a coyote was howling to its mate. Crickets were chirping. A horse stomped its foot and swished its tail to chase the flies away. Bull bats dove for something to eat. There were the night sounds, all in concert, and if something moved out there in the dark to change that sound, Lauro would know it. He laid down and looked at the beautiful moon and all the stars that were blinking and winking at him.

His thoughts were never far from Reina and he wondered if she might be looking at the moon that very night. Lauro's heart ached, because the next day he might die, and he would never see her again. He wasn't afraid of dying, only not being able to see her again, to hold her and feel her body close to his, to never kiss her lips or see her smile and hear her laugh. "Oh, my love, what happened to you? How could a love like ours die? How?" he whispered into the night.

He thought about Scarface coming. He knew he would come to the headquarters for the payroll. Lauro smiled, thinking how disappointed Scarface would be when he found out the payroll wasn't going to be at Norias. He had cleaned his rifle and pistol—he wanted nothing to go wrong. It was the showdown, and he would kill the outlaw or be killed himself. His thoughts returned to Reina and his mother. He wanted to introduce Reina to her, but that would never happen. He couldn't think about his loved ones. He had to concentrate on the job facing him.

19

NORIAS HEADQUARTERS—KING RANCH

The Raid

Finally, Lauro dozed lightly, awoke before dawn, and went into the kitchen. Albert, the cook, had put the coffee on the wood stove and started making breakfast. Lauro bathed underneath the water cistern where they had made a shower. He shaved, changed clothes, and went into the kitchen again. Frank was there drinking coffee and Lauro joined him.

"Buenos dias," Frank said.

"Buenos dias," Lauro answered. They didn't say much. They sipped their coffee and wondered what the day would bring.

Lauro glanced through the door that went into the kitchen. On the wall, he could see a calendar with a picture of a matador fighting a ferocious bull. The calendar read Saturday, August 7, 1915. Again, he wondered, what this day would signify in the history of the King Ranch.

"What pasture do you have the remuda in?" Lauro asked.

"The horse trap. It won't take long to round them up."

"Okay, let's go. The train should come from Brownsville about eight and we'll be ready." They both thanked Albert and went to the corrals to get their horses.

Lauro and Frank had the remuda in the corrals as the morning sun broke the horizon. Lauro was riding Lobo, and with the eye of an experienced horseman, he picked several good horses for the Rangers to ride. Frank helped, but he didn't know all the horses in the remuda. They just had to go by what Lauro liked to ride if he was riding them.

Albert came out on the porch and started ringing the bell.

"Stop ringing that thing," Frank yelled. "You want to let the bandits know where we are?"

"It doesn't make any difference, Frank. They know where we are, and how many guns are here," Lauro said. "Let's put some hay out for these caballos and then get some breakfast. Something tells me it's going to be a long day."

After breakfast, they walked over to the section house by the railroad and met with the foreman to see if they had barricaded the section house. They hadn't done one thing to defend themselves.

"Why haven't you done what we told you?" Lauro said. "You've got women and children in here. Put your gang to work."

The foreman, an Anglo, just looked at Lauro and frowned. "Listen, I know what I'm doing. If the bandits get here, we'll lock the doors and stay inside. They're strong enough to stand anything."

"You fool, those rotten doors won't take a hail of bullets coming at you. You better throw some of those mattresses on the doors and windows. This is no game, this is for real."

The foreman just looked at him and laughed. "You mind your own business, and we'll take care of ours."

Frank and Lauro looked at each other and shrugged. There it was again, two Tejanos don't tell a gringo what to do. "Okay, Mister. You call it, but don't blame me if they come rushing in here and hurt somebody." They walked back to the main house.

They sat on the porch and waited for a train whistle to announce their arrival, but none came. They smoked, talked, and nervously paced back and forth. Finally, Lauro called the ranch office again to see what happened to the help they were supposed to get. He didn't find Mr. Caesar but did get Nellie Jeff, the secretary. "Miss, is Mr. Caesar there?" Lauro said.

"No, he's not. Is this Lauro?"

"Yes ma'am. We're just wondering what time help is supposed to get here. We haven't seen hide nor hair of any."

"Well, we are kind of in a mess here ourselves. Coming into the office this morning J. B. Bell was found dead on the stairs. It was quite a shock to everyone. It was a heart attack. They found his pills at the bottom of the stairs. He must have been trying to get them and they fell from his hand."

Lauro was startled by the news that Bell was dead. "Yes, ma'am, but did Mr. Caesar say anything about help?"

"He told me if you called to tell you he was trying to get help down there. The Rangers should be there about eight o'clock this morning, and the Army is sending it's best troops. Are you saying they're not there yet? Why, it's almost twelve o'clock. I'll call down there right away and see what has happened."

"Thank you ma'am. I'll wait right here to hear from you, but please tell Mr. Caesar what has happened. Tell him to hurry."

"Yes, I'll send someone to find him. Good-bye." She hung up.

Lauro rolled another Bull Durham and shook his head. "Well, we better help ourselves," he said to Frank. "J. B. Bell is dead. They found him this morning. Heart attack."

The phone rang. It was Mr. Caesar. "Lauro, I'm sorry for the delay, but those idiots in Brownsville haven't been able to get going. The Rangers were scattered all over town, and the Army couldn't make up its mind how many men to send. It's a regular circus down there, but they said they would have a special train go out about two o'clock. I told them if they didn't and something happened to you all I'd personally come down there and whip every one of them.

"I'm having a hell of a time trying to get men. They won't go if I take Mexicans from the ranch to help. Why, I never heard of such a bunch of lame excuses in my life. They're all a bunch of yellow cowards. R. J. and the corrida are working cattle at Laureles in the Martillo country. They won't get there until tomorrow, even if they start out now, but I promise, boy, I'll get help as soon as possible."

"Yes sir, just as long as the Rangers and the Army get here before the bandidos do."

"Right. Hang on, we're coming. I have to go."

Lauro hung the receiver up and wondered if they would be alive the next day. They would if God willed it, and he said a silent prayer for all of them.

The special train didn't get there until after three-thirty and it was a circus like Mr. Caesar said. When the train slowed down and stopped, the people came out like flies on honey. They were completely disorganized. Bedrolls were thrown out the windows, people were climbing out of windows, and saddles, bridles, blankets, came flying out the same windows. Still, Lauro was glad to see them and among them his friend, Tom Tate.

"Hey Lauro, did you think we were not going to get here?" Tom hollered over all the noise. Tom was a hard man. It was rumored he had killed a few men in his lifetime. He was tall, slim, and burnt brown by the sun.

"Howdy Tom. Good to see you. Where did they pick you up? I thought you were farther west, scouting out around Red Gate."

"I was, but I had just arrived in Raymondville when I saw this train come into the station. I knew it was too early for the regular scheduled train. I figured there was something happening at the ranch." They shook hands. Tom and Lauro had worked together at Santa Gertrudis, then Tom was transferred to Norias to keep peace in the southern part of the ranch. He had done a good job, till now.

"Larry, I want you to meet these gentlemen." Some men had gathered close to where they were talking and listened to what Tom and Lauro were saying. "Gentlemen, I want you to meet Larry Cavazos, the best man on a horse I've ever seen; a man to ride the river with. Larry, this is Henry Hutchings, Adjutant General of Texas; Texas Ranger Captain, Henry Ransom; Captain J. M. Fox, Texas Rangers; and Captain George J. Head, U. S. Army."

"Appreciate you coming. We would have been in bad trouble if you hadn't. Captain Ransom, good to see you again," Lauro said. Ransom shook hands with Lauro.

"Lauro, what's the situation?" Ransom asked.

"We received word from a very brave boy who rode most of the night to warn us of bandits raiding the Sauz Ranch yesterday," Lauro said.

There was a murmur among the men who were listening.

Lauro continued. "He counted around eighty-two men, and they were camped at Coyote Lake. They'll hit us sometime today or tomorrow. We have to fortify this place and get ready for them."

"Eighty-two. That boy probably couldn't count. We got word that there were just a few," Captain Ransom said. "Well, it makes no difference if there are a hundred. We can handle a bunch of Mexicans. Hmm, Coyote Lake . . . They're probably still camped there, I'll take my men, and if you take the greater part of your troops, we can surprise them at the lake."

Captain Head agreed with him and turned to his corporal, who was a big Irishman. "Corporal, you and a squad of men stay here and protect this ranch. I will go with the rest of the men and will put ourselves under the command of the Texas Rangers. Those are my orders."

Captain Ransom turned to Lauro. "Now, young man, where are the horses we are to ride? Is that them in the corrals?"

"Yes sir, that's them. Frank and I tried to cut some that were the best of the lot. They're in the other corral."

"Good, that's a fine bunch, which one shall I pick?" Captain Ransom asked Lauro.

"Well, I would pick the bay. I haven't ridden him, but he looks like he has good stamina. He might be a little frisky."

Captain Ransom looked at Tom, who nodded his head. "Don't worry, Captain. If Lauro says he'll do, you can bet he knows what he's talking about. Lauro, how about picking one for the Adjutant General? He's not much of a horseman, but he wants to go. The rest of you men, pick your mounts."

The troopers and the Rangers made a slow entry into the corrals, two or three at a time. Lauro had picked a gentle sorrel for Henry Hutchings, who was an important man. Lauro thought he must have a lot of guts to go with this bunch to find Mexican bandits. He respected him for that.

All the Rangers were well-armed, with side arms and Winchester 30/40 Krag rifles in their saddleboots, *carne seca* to eat, and a ration of corn for their horses. They came for the long haul. The troopers were armed with Springfield rifles, and basic rations they always carried, but most of them preferred the *carne seca*. The Rangers knew what to expect. But the soldiers were new to the country. They weren't used to the brush and cactus. It was a new experience for them.

Lauro started for Lobo, who was saddled and ready to go. He had been waiting since morning. Lauro was just tightening the cinch when Captain Ransom rode up to him. "Lauro, I'm sorry, but you can't go with us. Someone has to stay here and coordinate things for us. You must be our go between—for us, the ranch and Fort Brown. If we get in trouble, you're the only one with sense enough to send for help. Also, you have women and children here. Someone has to look after them." Lauro started to protest, when he saw the look on the Ranger Captain's face. He wasn't going to change his mind. Scarface had escaped him, again.

"Alright. I'd give anything to go with you, but I understand. This ranch must be protected."

"Good boy. Tom's right, you'll do to ride the river with. When this is over maybe you will join us."

That was quite a compliment and Lauro knew it. "Thanks Captain, but you better get going. You have a long way to go and it's getting late."

Captain Ransom turned his horse and looked at his men and the troopers under his command. There was a silence, except for the familiar rubbing of leather on leather, the jingle of curb chains, the sneezing of a horse to clear its nostril, and a cough from a man here and there. Thirty-seven men ready to find and fight Mexican bandits who were breaking the laws of Texas.

The Ranger Captain raised his arm, signaling to the east. The whole bunch of horsemen moved as one. Dust flew everywhere. Lauro would have given anything to be with them, but he had his orders. He telephoned the Kingsville office to tell them that the Rangers and the Army had arrived and were on the trail of the bandits, and that he and Frank and a squad of soldiers were protecting the ranch headquarters. Nellie Jeff said she would pass the word to Mr. Caesar, who was still trying to find help among the good people of Kingsville. He would call Lauro later when he was ready.

Lauro looked around. All the people who were left at the ranch had come out and watched all the excitement. The soldiers had moved to the railroad tracks to take up positions on the embankment. The foreman of the section gang motioned his people to the section house. ''Come on. We'll go to the section house and take a siesta and wait for word from the Rangers.'' He heard a train whistle in the distance. It was the regular northbound that had departed from Brownsville. The special train that brought the Rangers had returned to Raymondville.

Lauro, Frank Martin, the ranch carpenter Forbes, his wife, Albert, the cook and his wife, and the two maids were all on the porch watching when the train began to slow down. It always took on water at the railroad tank by the tracks before leaving for the long haul to Kingsville. Lauro was surprised when he saw four men get off the train. They were all Anglo and were armed. He stepped out to find out who they were. It was five-thirty in the afternoon. ''Howdy. We're glad you came. How can I help you?'' Lauro said.

''Well, we're here to help you. Where are the Rangers? Don't tell me we missed them,'' one man said.

''Yes sir. They moved out about two hours ago. I'm Lauro Cavazos. I work for the ranch and I'm in charge. We're glad that you're here. We can use as many rifles as we can get.''

''I'm D. P. Gay, mounted Inspector for the U.S. Immigration Service; this is Joe Taylor, mounted Customs Inspector from San Benito; Marcus Hinds, mounted Customs Inspector; and Gordon Hill, Deputy Sheriff of Cameron County. We came to help save everyone from the Mexicans.''

Lauro sized him and the rest up real quickly. They were men whose job it was to stop the immigration of thousands upon thousands Mexicans coming into the country to earn a living for themselves and their families. These men were the reason everyone in south Texas hated the Immigration Officers. Most didn't even know how to speak Spanish, but had the law on their side. It was rumored that many Mexicans crossing the border were never heard from again. The ''wetbacks,'' as they were called, were defenseless. They were too poor to even own a gun, so if he or she gave the officers a hard time, they were never seen again.

These men were not invited by the Rangers or the U.S. Army to join their posse. They just came on their own to kill Mexicans. Still, Lauro needed them and every gun they could bring. Frank looked at Lauro. They knew that the strangers had missed the Rangers and the Army on purpose. They didn't want to really get into a battle with Mexicans who could shoot back. They just wanted to be able to say that they were there when it happened. Maybe the King Ranch would give them a reward for just being there.

''I'm taking over, boy. From here on out I'll give the orders,'' Gay said.

''Like hell, you will. You don't work for the King Ranch, and you weren't told by Caesar Kleberg to stay here and defend this place. You timed it just right so that you missed the posse. Mister Gay, you are going to take my orders or get the hell out of here.''

The Customs Inspectors were taken aback by this boy. ''You know the regular train has left. We're stuck here now. We couldn't leave if we wanted to.''

''That's right Mr. Gay, so you better make up your minds or join the section gang over there,'' Lauro said. ''Now, you are all welcome to come have supper if you decide to join us.'' Lauro and Frank turned and walked back to the main house. The Inspectors looked at each other and shrugged. They followed Lauro into the house.

The Corporal and his squad of seven army men came to the main house when Albert started ringing the dinner bell. They were talking and laughing, happy to be there instead of on horseback chasing a bunch of Mexican bandits. The rest of the people ate in silence. The two serving girls were kept busy by the soldiers, and Albert kept warning the girls to not flirt with the young soldiers.

Lauro looked at the Corporal and got his attention while they were all eating. "We'll have to set out night guards. You and your men will take the first watch. I'll take the second watch till morning. How much ammunition do you have?"

"About fifty rounds apiece," the Corporal said. "That's four hundred rounds in all."

"That's not enough. How about you, Mr. Gay? How many do you all have?"

Gay looked at the other Inspectors and shrugged. "I guess about sixty rounds apiece. What are you counting for? The bandidos aren't coming here. The Rangers will have them by now." All the Inspectors laughed. Frank and Lauro just looked at each other.

Lauro turned to Frank. "Where does Mr. Caesar keep the weapons and ammunition?"

"Upstairs in his office. He keeps it under lock and key, and he's got the key with him in Kingsville, just when we need them."

"We'll think of something," Lauro said. "Maybe we'll get lucky and won't need the rifles and ammunition."

They finished eating, and slowly began to leave the table one by one and go out to the porch. Some of the soldiers stayed behind to talk to the girls, and others joined the men outside to smoke. It was a beautiful day.

Lauro was on the porch rolling his cigarette, when he noticed dust devils slowly moving east to north. There was a bunch of riders coming toward the ranch. "Here come the Rangers back," Hinds said.

Everyone looked at the riders coming, there was silence.

"Hell boys, that's not the Rangers," Lauro said. "That's bandits. Get your rifles. Hurry." They took off like a covey of quail flushed from the brush. At approximately five hundred yards the riders were coming.

Lauro couldn't help but notice how beautiful a sight they made, with their sombreros moving in unison with their horses stride, their conches reflecting the sunlight off their saddles, and their rifles waving in the air. They yelled to encourage their compadres. Lauro and Frank ran to the railroad embankment. The rest of the men followed.

Lauro noticed that there weren't eighty men coming at them. He started to mention it to Frank when the bandits opened fire. The soldiers ducked when the angry zip of the bullets came close to them.

"God damn, what kind of rifles are they using? That's two-hundred-fifty yards at least," Gay said. He ducked from the bullets.

Lauro was looking for the rest of the comancheros, when he noticed the leader of the band of outlaws. He rode a white horse, yelling and firing as he came. He was like a wild man in front of the charge. His sombrero blew off and Lauro saw his red hair, like he had seen it in his dreams so many times. "Scarface Colorado!"

Lauro took aim and fired at one hundred yards. It was low. He hit the horse and killed him instantly. Scarface hit the ground running and headed for the section house. There was no fire coming from within. He dove for cover and just made it, as Lauro emptied his rifle at him. Lauro cursed. He had to take slower aim. Scarface could still move.

Frank yelled. "I'm hit. Oh God, I'm hit. I'm dying."

Two other troopers yelled for help. Lauro knew what had happened and he was ashamed for not thinking of it. Vallejo's words came to him —"*Pela el ojo.*" The bullets were coming from the south and west of them. They were trying to surround them.

"Help those men to the main house," Lauro said. "We'll cover for you. Move."

Frank could walk. One of the soldiers helped him; it took four men to move the wounded soldiers. The rest of the men set up a continuous fire while they moved away from the embankment to the main house. The bandits had altered their plans when Scarface's horse had been killed. They stopped the charge. If they had kept to it they would have overrun the defenders and killed them all. With their leader down, they didn't know what to do. They all got off their horses, and about ten bandidos had run to the section house. Others took cover behind a pile of cross ties, or behind the outhouse. Others took cover around the corrals. The lead was flying all over the place, from both the bandits and the defenders. It was a regular war, played out on a remote place on the King Ranch, a hundred miles from nowhere.

Men were being killed on that hot Saturday afternoon in south Texas, and no help was in sight for the small band of men protecting the brand for which they rode. They could have just ridden off and let the comancheros burn the Norias Headquarters. They were men—Anglo, Spanish, Mexican, and Black fighting for their lives. Lauro was fighting on his ancestor's land, the San Juan de Carricitos Land Grant. Protecting it from outsiders who were trying to take it away from him.

They took the three wounded men into the main house and built a barricade of rolled barbed wire and some heavy steel forms outside in the fence yard. The firing from both sides was heavy. Sweat ran into their eyes, spoiling their aim, and they were running out of ammunition.

Albert and Forbes were firing from the house. The five soldiers stayed with them after laying the wounded on beds in a room next to the dining room. Lauro and the rest of the troopers began laying a field of fire across the bare ground between them and the section house.

"Don't fire into the section house," Lauro shouted. The troopers were doing some good. Lauro's 30-30 sounded like a pop gun next to the Springfields' loud report. Bandits were falling dead or wounded all over the place. When Scarface signaled for them to take cover in there where he was, they rushed to the section house.

"Damn, Scar, I thought there was just supposed to be only a hand full of workers here," Vasquez shouted.

"There wasn't supposed to be this many people here. Wait a minute, you come here," Scar shouted at the section foreman. "Who are all those sons-of-bitches over there?"

The foreman put his hands up in surrender, pleading with the Mexican bandit. "Please, Mister, don't kill me. We just work for the railroad. We don't have any money. We're just poor working people."

"Shut up," Scar shouted, grabbing him by the front of the shirt. "Now tell me, who is that over there?"

"I don't know them all, but two of them are ranch cowboys and the others are soldiers from Fort Brown. One of the ranch hands is named Cavazos, the other is Frank Martin."

"Cavazos." Scar thought for a minute. "Cavazos, is he any kin to that bunch of Cavazos from San Perlita?"

All the railroad people were huddled in the far corner of the section house. "I don't know," the foreman said.

Scar looked around. "You." He pointed at the mother-in-law of the foreman, who happened to be Mexican. "Do you know him? Is he from San Perlita?"

"No, I don't," she said. "Why don't you go over and ask him?" Scar shot her dead before everyone's eyes.

"I think I will. Listen, I'll take two men and see if I can get around them. You cover us. I'll go around by the corrals. Keep shooting and keep your heads down. You, Vasquez, Jose, let's go."

They rushed out the back door heading for the corrals. Scar's hat hung on his neck, and he started running, moving low, keeping the section house between him and the defenders. There was one place where there was no cover and they were completely out in the open. Six strides and they were under the protection of the corrals.

Lauro saw the flash of the men moving toward the corrals, and just for a second he saw a flash of red. The 7 mm. Mausers ripped through the thin walls of the ranch house, striking George Forbes in the right lung; he went down immediately.

"George is hit!" someone yelled.

Lauro and the soldiers rushed to his side. Albert and one of the troopers picked him up and carried him into the back bedroom. They started to put him on the bed next to the wounded soldiers when more bullets came ripping through the thin walls, striking one of the wounded soldiers again. He moaned and rolled over onto the floor.

"Get everyone off the beds and on the floor," Lauro shouted. "You ladies get down with them. Albert, get those mattresses off the beds and throw them over the ladies. Hurry." Another volley came through the windows and doors just as the mattresses came off the beds. Mrs. Forbes and one of the maids worked to stop the wounded ones' bleeding. Forbes was in bad shape. He was bleeding internally and he was coughing up blood, but was still holding on.

Frank was moaning, holding his arm. Lauro knelt next to him. "How we doing, partner?"

"It hurts like hell. I think it's broken in two places. How's it going out there?"

"We're holding our own. A lot of those sons-of-bitches are in the section house. We could really do some good if we could fire at the house, but there's railroad folk in there. We might hit them. Just stay under the mattress. I'll come back in a little while."

"Lauro, you think we'll get out of here alive?" Frank asked.

"Yeah, we'll make it." Lauro patted him on the shoulder.

As Lauro rushed outside he could see the Corporal had the rest of his men pretty well under control. The firing was deafening and bullets were zipping into the defenders' barricade. He went around to the back of the main house and started toward the corrals. As he made it safely behind some bales of hay, he saw one of the bandits move for better cover. Lauro had left his rifle at the main house so he could move more freely. His Navy Colt was now in his hand and he shot Vasquez before he could reach cover.

"One down," he said. He moved to the crowding gate made of solid plank. He saw a flash of a weapon, and fired toward it. He heard a yell and the dropping of a body. "Two down," he said. A board splintered just above his head, he ducked and moved to a better position. There was a pause in the firing.

"Hey, amigo, who the hell are you?" Scar shouted from behind a gate. "You're a pretty good shot, you just killed two of my best men. Have we met before?"

"Yeah, we've met, Scar," Lauro said, with hatred in his voice. "We've met, in Brownsville a long time ago. Also when you tried to rob me in the desert."

"Oh, I remember now. You're that kid that ruined my plans of kidnapping Kleberg's daughter. You know, you're like a tick that gets in your britches. You know it's there, but you can't get rid of it."

Both men were moving through the pens, trying to get better position on the other. "You murdered my grandfather and stole his cattle. You're a no good son of a bitch, and you don't deserve to live in this world." He moved to another spot, remembering Vallejo's words, "*Pela el ojo.*"

"Well, the puppy has a sharp tongue. Your old man had the same bark, but he was no match for me." Scar moved again, trying to get behind Lauro.

"Yeah, well how about those men of yours he took out before you shot him in the back, and how about that little token he gave you to carry for the rest of your life? When the buzzards come for you after I kill you, they'll finally wipe that scar off your face." Enraged, Scar stood and fired, not sure of his aim, hitting just to the right of where Lauro had been.

"Close, Scar, but no cigar. Now, it's my turn." Lauro fired and splintered a board just above Scar, sending splinters into his face.

Scar yelled and moved to a different location. He was furious.

The firing had increased over by the railroad embankment. There were several horses in the corrals, but none had been hit. They were more valuable alive than dead. Scar moved into another pen, pushing the solid gate open a little at a time. He had lost sight of the boy. For the first time, Scar was afraid. Slowly, he peered around the gate, but all he saw was the horses moving around the pen. There was a water trough between two of the pens. Scar figured he knew where Lauro was. He waited for the boy to show his head just a little behind the water trough.

"Looking for me?"

Scar almost came out of his skin when he heard the voice behind him. The kid had used the horses to get behind him.

"Don't move. Put the gun in your holster. Don't turn around. That's it. Now you can stand up." Scar stood up with his arms down close to his weapon.

"Walk to the other side of the pen," said Lauro. Scar did what he was told. "Now, turn around slowly, but before you turn around put your arms up above your head. Scar slowly moved his arms above his head, turned, and there was the boy with a big Navy Colt pointing right at his stomach. Scar's breath came out in a rush. It was no boy that faced him, it was a man. He stood tall and lean, with his hat pulled over his eyes, the dust on his clothes, and the sweat on his shirt. He was a picture of his grandfather. Scar shook his head.

"Well, so we meet again. I always thought of you as a ghost. I could never kill you when I had you in my sights. You were just lucky."

Lauro looked at this outlaw, he was quite the hombre, with his Mexican clothes, all dirty, sweaty, his big sombrero hanging from his neck, and a week's growth of red beard on his face. A bandanna was wrapped around his head to keep sweat out of his eyes.

"So this is the famous Scarface, Colorado Red. I have wanted to face you and ask a few questions before we have our showdown." Scar was surprised.

"Well, the 'macho man' wants to have a show down." Scar laughed a little to himself. Good, let him talk and then I'll kill him, Scar thought.

"There's a few questions I've wanted to ask you," Lauro said.

"Okay, go ahead, but you better hurry. It sounds like my side is winning."

"Did Captain King have anything to do with the rustling of my grandfather's herd? Did he put you up to it?"

"No, it was Bell. He was behind it. Old man King never had anything to do with it. Bell thought the whole thing out. He knew that if your grandfather didn't get that herd to market, your family would lose the land your grandfather had put up for the loan. It would make Bell look good to the Captain. After all he is the one who thought up the deal. Besides, he got a hefty commission from the Kings for closing it."

"Well, I might have known," Lauro said. "How about the failed kidnapping in Brownsville? Was that his idea too?"

"Yeah. It would've made him really look good to have Klebergs daughter released through his negotiations, and make a nifty profit off the ransom. That Bell, he's a smart man."

"Not now. He's dead, died of a heart attack, yesterday, in the ranch office. He's burning in hell, Scar, just as you will."

Scar shrugged. "It happens to the best of people, even the rich, but you're wrong about me going to hell. Too many people have tried to send me there and failed. Are you going to try, hombre?"

Lauro had made sure that the sun was at his back. He cast a big shadow across the ground in the pen. "One more question."

"Sure, I know you don't want to die like your old man," Scar said. "Ask your questions, but can I put my arms down, they're getting tired?"

"No, to your question. Now here's mine, did Bell set this up too?"

"No, it was the Aleman, the German agent," Scar said.

"What are you talking about? What German agent? You better be telling the truth."

"Would I lie to you?" Scar said. "Yes, a real German agent paid for everything—the horses, the food, the drinks, the women, the rifles, the ammunition, everything."

"Why?"

"To keep the United States busy at home, to mind its own business. It's going to happen all up and down the Mexican border, from Texas to California. There's going to be an uprising. The Germans are going to give back the land to the people. I never believed them, but that's what they said." He nodded toward the outlaws. "They're a bunch of cut throats, but they want to believe in something. They think we're going to be rich. By the way, did the payroll get here?"

"No, I stopped it in Kingsville, just a waste of lives for your greed."

"Damn, you did it again. You messed up my plans again, but I'm going to put a stop to that today. Now, Bell did let me know when the payroll was supposed to have gotten here, but that's all. He didn't expect a cut."

"One more question," Lauro said.

"You're just full of questions, aren't you?" Scar asked. "Go ahead. You got the drop on me, what chance do I have?"

"Did you ever know Vallejo Garcia?"

"Yeah. He was my compadre a long time ago, but we had a misunderstanding over a woman. He loved her, and I got her drunk and raped her. Funny, he didn't like that, anyway he tried to kill me, but the boys ambushed him before he could get to me."

"Did you kill her?"

"Yeah. She resisted a little too much. I didn't like that. Too bad, she was a beautiful woman, the daughter of a big man in Mexico. She really must of loved him. He went crazy, killed three of my best men before they wounded him. I never knew where he disappeared to. He was the only man who could outdraw me. Did you know him?''

''Yeah. He's the one who taught me how to fast draw and shoot. I could beat him, but now I'm going to rid this world of vermin like you. Put your arms down and draw when you're ready.''

Scar lost all the blood from his face. He was shaken. This kid knew Vallejo Garcia. For the first time in his life, Scar felt fear. ''Now, wait a minute, you can't kill me in cold blood, it's not right.'' He slowly lowered his arms.

''I'm giving you a chance, bastardo, more of a chance than you gave to all the women and men you have killed. You're slime. You don't deserve the chance I'm giving you.'' Lauro put his pistola in his holster. ''Now draw.''

Scar looked around him. He was sweating profusely. He was hoping one of his men would come up behind this kid. No one came. It was just him and the kid. No, the man.

Lauro didn't think of anything but the job in front of him. ''Watch his eyes, you'll know just before he draws,'' Vallejo had taught him. ''Concentrate on nothing but his eyes, then when he moves, he will tell you with his eyes. Draw fast, smooth, and aim well.'' Lauro stood as still as a blue heron about to catch a mullet in the Laguna Madre.

That look came in Scar's eyes. He drew his pistol fast, but not fast enough. He felt a powerful hit in the chest before he had his Colt half way out of his holster. Scar knew he was shot.

The force of the bullet knocked Scar back against the wooden planks of the pen, and slammed him to the ground. His blood started flowing. Scar felt his chest, the wetness, he never thought that he could be beaten.

Lauro walked slowly up to Scar. He had shot him just a little to the right of the heart, just missed where he was aiming.

''Hey kid, you're good. I didn't even see you draw. You happy now? You killed me.''

''No, Scar, you killed yourself when you turned outlaw, when you killed my grandfather and Vallejo's woman and no telling how many more. You got justice served to you.''

''Boy, I hurt. I feel weak. Can you lift me up a little.'' Lauro reached down and lifted him up some. Scar reached behind him and drew his little derringer, but he was too weak to lift it and shoot. Lauro took the gun from his hand and threw it across the pen.

"Even when you're going to meet your God, you still want to kill. I hope you burn in hell, you bastard." Scar coughed and blood came out of his mouth.

"You're as much 'hombre' as your old man, *mu hombre.*" Scarface died.

Lauro didn't feel anything, not like he thought he would. He just turned to get back to the fight at the main house. There was heavy firing coming from the section house, but there were just a few rounds fired from the main house. Lauro made it back to the barricade.

"Where the hell you been?" Gay said. "How many rounds you got left? I'm running out of ammunition, so are the rest of the men. What do we do if they rush us?"

Lauro looked around the barricade. No one else had been hit. "Okay, keep your eye on those stairs." He picked up his rifle, under heavy fire from the bandits, and rushed up the stairs, ducked his shoulder and hit the door. It came off its hinges and fell inside. The bandidos were firing at the upstairs office, and the thin planking was no deterrent for the Mausers bullets. Lauro hugged the floor, crawled to the small closet and kicked at the door. The hinges finally broke. Inside he found a small arsenal, every type of shell, with rifles and pistols. Lauro started throwing ammunition out the window behind the barricade below. The ammo fell at the defenders' feet.

"Glory be, men. We're saved." They rushed to the ammo and passed it around to everyone. They started firing anew, and you could hear the smack of a bullet when it hit flesh.

Lauro jumped from the window into the waiting arms of some troopers. They patted him on the back. "Nice going. You saved our bacon. That was a brave thing to do. Thank you," the Corporal said.

"Sure, but keep firing. We're not out of this yet. I'll cover to your left. Watch they don't make a move to the corrals," Lauro said. The soldiers began laying a steady stream of fire with everyone else firing in between; it was a deadly field of fire. The sun began to go down.

An hour after darkness, the fire from the bandits stopped. There was an eerie silence, a blessed silence.

Lauro moved up and down the line of the defenders to see if anyone else had been hit. There were a few, but nothing serious. He went inside the house to see how they had fared. Then they began moving the wounded outside. They had better protection behind the barricade than the thin planking of the house.

Lauro knelt down where he could talk to Frank Martin. "How are you, pard?'' he said.

"I hurt like hell. How's it going out there? We going to survive this? Why don't those folks from Kingsville come? What's the matter with them? Why haven't we heard from Mr. Caesar? Damn, I hurt.''

"I don't know,'' Lauro said. "He's trying his best, I'm sure, but he's having a hard time getting volunteers.''

"They're a bunch of cowards, merchants and farmers. They have a yellow stripe down their backs. So do the people in Raymondville. Where's the help from them? And the Rangers, surely they must have figured that the bandits came here. Where the hell are they?'' Martin yelled. "We need a doctor, bad.''

"Mr. Lauro, I talked to Mr. Caesar on the phone,'' Albert said.

"You did?'' Lauro said. "Well, what did he say?''

"It was when you were gone to the corrals.'' He shook his head. "It was when the firing was heaviest, I thought I was a goner, but they never hit me. I told him we needed help now and he said that he had the men and horses and ammunition but they couldn't find anyone to drive the train. So I told him to just point the train in our direction and let her come on full speed, we need help.''

"That was a brave thing you did, Albert,'' Lauro said.

"Thank you. You know, it's funny, but Kingsville is a railroad division point and they can't find anyone to drive that train.'' Lauro just shook his head, not believing what he just heard.

"How's Forbes?'' Lauro said. He looked toward the women tending the wounded man.

"He's shot through the lung. I don't know if he's going to make it. I sure hope he does,'' Frank said.

"Well, you take it easy. We'll get out of this mess. We're holding our own. If we can hold out till dawn we'll be okay.'' Lauro moved down the line of defenders, giving them encouragement, talking to the Corporal, then finally settling down to smoke and try to figure out what to do. He was tired, and no matter how he tried to think, his thoughts always came back to Reina. He could be killed, never to see her again, and she would never know that his last thoughts were of her.

He longed to tell his grandmother that the debt had been paid in full, and that grandfather could lay in peace. He wanted to see his family, to tell them how much he loved them. He felt much gratitude toward Vallejo, and sorry for the man's loss. Now, he knew why he stayed to himself. And why he had that pain in his eyes.

Several hours passed. The actual fight had lasted two and a half hours, but it felt like an eternity. There were shell casings all over the ground, and the men were exhausted and scared.

"Corporal, how're your men?" Lauro said.

"We got two wounded, almost out of ammo, but other than that, okay."

"Why don't you all take the first watch? We'll take the second, if this lull lasts that long. My bunch is pretty tired."

The Corporal looked around and nodded in affirmative. "Okay, we'll keep our eyes open. You look beat. Get a few winks. I'll call you in a couple of hours."

"Don't forget to wake me if you need me. Mr. Gay, you all get some rest. It might be a long night. I'll call you when it's our turn to watch."

Gay looked at Lauro. "Yes sir," he said with respect in his voice. "We need a few hours of rest. You did a hell of a good job. If you hadn't gotten the ammunition, we would have been goners. Thanks." He stuck his hand out. Lauro looked at it for a second, then took it.

During the fight, he didn't think about finding something to drink, but now he was very thirsty. One of the maids brought a bucket of water to the troopers and another to Lauro and his group. She held the cup out to him with a look of awe on her face. "You were very brave, señor. I held my hand to my breast." She took Lauro's hand and put it to her heart, mostly on her breast. "I could hardly breathe when you went up the stairs while they shot at you. You were so brave."

Lauro was embarrassed, but the touch of her breast was warm and soft. "Thank you. Now you better give water to the other men. They fought, too." She smiled and returned to her duties. Lauro leaned against the wagon wheel that they had thrown against the barricade and pulled his hat over his eyes. He was thinking of Reina when he fell asleep.

It seemed it was just seconds when he felt a hand shaking him. "Riders coming!"

Lauro jumped up, grabbed his rifle and moved to the barricade. "Where do you hear the riders coming?"

"Over east of here. Could it be the Rangers?" the Corporal asked.

"I don't know. Wake the rest of the men. It's darker than hell. Get someone to cover behind us. They may have sent someone over there during the night. Tell them not to shoot until we know who it is for sure. How many shells have you got?"

"Not many. How about you?" the Corporal said.

"The same. Well, Corporal, it looks like this is it. Get the men ready."

They heard voices in the night. A normal voice could carry pretty far, but the southeast wind had picked up, and it was hard to make out whether it was the Rangers or bandits.

The little group of defenders waited for the uncertainty of life or death, once again. One more charge and they were done.

"Hello to the camp. Don't shoot it's the Rangers," a voice rang out from the night.

Suddenly, Lauro stood up straight. "It's Tom, don't shoot. I recognize that voice anywhere. It's the Rangers." Everyone let out a yell. They were saved, the danger had passed.

The men ran around the barricade, shouting and waving their hats. "Come on in. It's safe. Come on in. Boy, are we glad to see you guys. Where you been? You missed all the fun, if you hurry you might be able to catch some of the bandits going south." They yelled, shook hands and hit each other on the back, waving their hats, and laughing in relief.

The Rangers came at a gallop when they heard the cheering and laughing. "Damn, the bandits were here. No wonder we couldn't find them. They outsmarted us," Tom Tate said. "We were out on a wild goose chase. Well, I'll be damned."

The sun was beginning to break to a new day. Lauro walked away from the cheering group, to the edge of the corral facing the sun. He took off his hat. "Thank you, my Lord Jesus, the Holy Mother of God, Mary, for granting us this day. Thank you."

He walked on, jumped the fence of the corral, and walked toward the pen where he had left Scar's body. There he was, lying where he dropped. Lauro felt nothing.

Lobo's head came over the fence. Lauro went to him and rubbed his nose. "I see you made it, too. We'll go home soon." He walked over to a stack of hay, broke several bales for the horses in the pen, turned and put his arms around Lobo's neck. "Thank God we made it, old partner."

"Lauro, they want you over by the main house. The Captain wants to see you," the Corporal said.

They heard a train whistle coming down the track from Kingsville. "Well, I'll be damned. It's the train without an engineer. I guess we better rope it before it goes on by, clear to Brownsville.'' They both laughed and headed toward the main house.

The Rangers had gone over to the section house and seen the damage the bandits had done. The only casualty they had was the old woman killed by Scarface. It could have been worse, the defenders had not fired on the section house with the women and children there. They had refrained from firing unless they had a clear shot at a bandit.

Lauro and the Corporal got back to the main house just in time to hear the foreman of the section gang talking to the Captain of the Rangers. ''She smarted off at that son of a bitch and he killed her in cold blood. He didn't even blink an eye. He was red headed and had a scar that ran clear down to here.'' He pointed all the way from the top of his head to the bottom of his throat.

''That's Scarface, Colorado Red, the meanest outlaw on both sides of the border. We would sure love to get him,'' the Captain of the Rangers said.

''He's over in the corrals, waiting for you to pick him up,'' Lauro said.

''What do you mean, Larry,'' the Ranger Captain asked. ''Is he still there?''

''Yes sir, He's dead. I shot him.''

''Well, young man, you just did this country a great deed. We've tried to get him for years. He must of been the leader of this band of cut throats. That's why they didn't get you all. They were disorganized, their leader was dead. That's why they left during the night. They didn't even take their dead and wounded. From the looks of things, you men did a hell of a job. We're not even through counting the dead and wounded. You damn near wiped out the whole gang. The men are out there counting bodies now.''

They heard several shots—down the railroad tracks, out in the brush, and by the corrals. The Ranger Captain didn't ask what those shots were. He walked toward the train, which was slowing to a stop. Lauro caught him by the arm and turned him around. ''Aren't you going to stop that. They're killing the wounded.''

''No, I'm not. Did they give that lady a chance to live? Would they have given you a chance to live if you would have surrendered? Hell no. Besides, we have our own wounded to take care of. Mr. Forbes is in pretty bad shape. I don't know if he's going to make it.''

Lauro couldn't believe what he had heard. The Rangers were murdering them. No wonder the Mexican people feared and hated the

Texas Rangers.

When the shooting stopped, the Captain looked at Lauro. "This is hard country, Larry, you must know that. We have to go after the rest and we don't have time to mess with them. They're going to hang anyhow. By the way, there's a five thousand dollar reward for Scarface. If you go by the headquarters in Brownsville sometime next week, we'll give it to you." He turned and walked to the train. Another train whistle sounded down the track, this time coming from the south from Brownsville. It was getting crowded at that little spot in south Texas.

Lauro went to the tree where Frank Martin was holding his arm together. "How you doing, partner?" He knelt down by the wounded cowboy.

"Okay, as long as I don't move it. It hurts like hell. I don't know why. I haven't lost much blood, but I'm feeling weak. You think there's a doctor on those trains?"

"I hope so. You just hang on. I'll go find out," Lauro said as he headed toward the train.

People were pouring off the train. They were carrying all kinds of different rifles, shotguns, and pistols. It looked like a ragtag army, getting off the train. Horses were being unloaded, and everyone was yelling, laughing. It was like a three ring circus. Everyone wanting to get noticed. Of course, it was over and they were breathing easier, but they wanted to be counted as a Norias defender. That they had come was something in itself, even if they were hours late. The little band of defenders were the real heroes of the battle of the Norias Division of the King Ranch.

"Hey, look, there's someone coming out of the brush. Get him." They all raised their rifles.

"No, don't shoot, that's a kid, don't shoot," Lauro shouted and ran toward the stumbling boy. It was Jose Lopez, the boy from the Sauz Ranch who had warned them of the bandits.

"*Agua, agua, por favor, agua!*" he whispered through a parched throat.

"Get some water," Lauro said. The boy fell into his arms. It looked like he had been running for quite sometime. One of the soldiers had a canteen and handed it to the boy. He drank almost all of it. He smiled after a while. "Gracias. That was bueno."

"*Que paso,* chico. What happened? I thought you went home?"

"Si, señor, but then I came back to see what was going to happen. I hid over there behind the bales of hay over by the corrals. I saw you face the man with the scar. You were very brave and quick as lightning. Never have I seen anyone as quick as you. He didn't even clear his holster when you shot him. You were very brave, Patrón." Everyone saw Lauro in a new light. This was a fighting man, beware.

Mr. Caesar came running with the Captain of the Rangers. "Lauro, are you alright? Who's the boy?"

"I'm fine," Lauro said as they shook hands. "It's the boy from the Sauz Ranch. Give him some room. Let him breath." They all backed up.

"Alright, chico, tell us what happened."

"Well, after you killed the leader of the bandidos, I just got deeper in the hay. The bullets were flying everywhere. I stayed there until I felt my foot being jerked out by someone. It was them. I thought they were going to kill me. If I hadn't had my foot out of the hay, they would never have seen me. They were very mad. There were five or six of them, and they didn't know what to do. I heard them saying, 'Scarface is dead. Let's get out of here.' The men seemed to agree. They were going to kill me, but they said they might need me. They left and took me with them. They weren't sure how to get back to Mexico, they just headed south. They took some of the wounded with them, tied to the horses. They were in great pain. Every time the horse moved they moaned and cried. They couldn't rest. Only when one of the wounded died, then they would stop to bury him. They stopped five times. That was the only rest they got. While they were burying the fifth man, I ran away. I knew they would kill me. I ran fast. Where the brush was thick, I kept to the thickest part where a man on horseback couldn't go. I finally made it here. So here I am," Jose Lopez smiled.

"Well done, Jose. You were a foolish boy to return the first time, but a brave one. You were lucky the second time. Next time, listen to your elders, okay?" Lauro said.

"Si, señor, but someday I will work for you, okay?"

"Yes, maybe someday, Jose. Maybe someday."

"Jose, where did you last see the bandits?" Captain Ransom said.

"This side of Coyote Lake where the big motte of oak trees is. It's a good place to hunt armadillos. You know, where the sand is soft, that's where they buried their dead."

"Good boy. Take care of this boy Lauro. He's been a big help. Sergeant, get the Rangers ready to ride. Mr. Caesar, I hate to leave you with this mess, but we must leave immediately if we're going to catch them before they get to Mexico."

"Thank you for your help, Captain Ransom, but I think we can handle it from here," Caesar said. They shook hands.

"Thank you, sir. But it was Lauro's leadership that got them out of this mess. Everyone fought well."

"Lauro, I expect to see you in Brownsville next week. Good luck, everyone." The Captain mounted his King Ranch horse, and with the rest of the Rangers behind him, rode off after the raiders.

Mr. Caesar turned toward Lauro and the boy. "Well, you did do a hell of a job, Lauro. Thank you." He shook Lauro's hand and patted him on the shoulder.

"I'm afraid I broke your office door and the door to the storage room. We needed ammunition bad."

"Yeah, they would have gotten to us if Lauro hadn't broken into your office," Gay said.

"We were down to throwing stones, it was that bad," Hines said. "We never expected this many bandits. How many were there?"

"I don't know, but the bunch that came on the trains are gathering the bodies so we can bury them."

"Let's go see," Caesar Kleberg said. They made their way to the edge of the brush by the section house where they had decided to make one common grave. Tom Tate and other hands were roping the bodies by the feet and dragging them toward the grave that the section crew and others were digging.

Lauro and Jose headed toward the main house. Albert had made some coffee and *pan de campo.* The boy dug into the bread. Albert handed Lauro a cup of coffee. "Here, Mr. Lauro. You look like you need this."

"Thank you, Albert. I sure do. Is your wife alright?"

"She sure is—a little scared, but she's a strong woman. She'll make it fine."

"That's good. It takes strong women for this country. All the ladies were brave. Thank God they're safe."

Frank Martin and George Forbes were loaded on the Kingsville train. The wounded soldiers were put on the Brownsville train. Both trains had brought doctors, and the wounded were treated as best as they could be under the circumstances. Just before they loaded Frank, Lauro talked to him. They had looked at each other with respect. They shook hands, with a promise to stay in touch with each other. Lauro talked to Mrs. Forbes and wished them well.

He sat at the table on the front porch and drank his coffee, shaking a little. He thought of Reina. He never needed anyone as much as he needed her at that moment. He was alive and he thanked God for it.

He was brought back from his reverie by Jose Lopez pulling on his shirt sleeve. "Señor, señor. What are you thinking about? I must go."

"I'm sorry, chico. I was just thinking of something. You said it was time to go home?"

"Yes. Conejo has been tied up for two days over in the brush. I'm sure I'm going to be in trouble with my mother and father, but when I tell them what I saw, they will not be so angry."

"Okay, Jose. You better go. I don't think there's any bandits left within fifty miles of here, so you'll be safe. Go with God."

"Thank you, Patrón. I'll never forget that I saw Lauro Cavazos and the bandido Chieftain Scarface, mano a mano, to the end. Good-bye. Don't forget our deal. Okay?"

"Okay." Lauro smiled and held out his hand. They shook hands and Jose Lopez was gone.

Mr. Caesar came to the table and sat across from Lauro, taking his hat off and brushing the sweat from his brow. He called out to Albert to bring him some coffee. "Lauro, you did a hell of a job here. I want you to continue working here. I need good men. I'll put you as foreman in a few years. What do you say?"

"I thank you, Mr. Caesar, but I have to go see my folks in San Perlita and think about it. I'll let you know."

"Okay. Take your time visiting your folks. Take all the time you want, the job will still be open when you get back.

"Now," Caesar said, "this is what we have found out from one of the wounded bandits before he died. There were eighty-two when they started out from Mexico. They were going to make trouble up and down the border. Scarface, or Colorado Red, was their leader and they were being paid and outfitted by a German agent. He brought them new Mausers and paid for everything. He just wanted them to rob, burn, and kill as many Texans as possible and take all the loot. There were some ridiculous tales about giving the land back to the Mexican people. What did they think we were going to do, just sit back and let it happen? We showed them, or rather, you showed them." Caesar Kleberg laughed. Lauro didn't think it was very funny.

Caesar continued. "There had been some kind of rumor up in Austin that Immigration had arrested a Mexican by the name of Basilio Ramos, alias P. R. Garcia. He had a paper on him. They called it *The*

Plan of San Diego, which called for an all out war between the United States and Germany. It would unite Germany with Mexico and Japan and give back lost lands to Mexico. It's hard to believe that Germany is behind all this. We ought to declare war on them, the sons-of-bitches. Well, they came to the wrong place to start. You all killed forty-three bandits and five more that the boy reported, and no telling how many died before going back into Mexico.''

"You mean twenty-three that we killed and wounded, twenty that the Rangers later executed. Isn't that right, Mr. Caesar?''

"Lauro, you know as well as I do those men came here to rob and kill everyone here. No telling how many more they have already killed and raped. The Rangers didn't have time for them. They had to catch the others. I don't like it either, but it's done. Do you think they would have left anyone alive here, including the women and children? Do you?''

Lauro knew that Caesar Kleberg was right. They would have killed every one. He and the rest would have to live with it.

The two trains pulled out for their home depots. Everyone had left—the railroad crew, and their families, the wounded, the volunteers from Kingsville and Brownsville, the soldiers that had done their duty bravely, and Mr. Gay and his law enforcement friends.

Tom Tate had gone with the Rangers, so there was no one except the Headquarters main house crew, Lauro, and Mr. Caesar. The leaves on the cottonwood trees rustled in the light wind.

"I better write my report to R. J. before I forget some of it. Will I see you at supper?'' Caesar said.

"I think I'll take a shower, then go to bed. I'm so tired I can hardly keep my eyes open,'' Lauro said. "I haven't had a bath in two days and I need to get the smell of death off me.''

Mr. Caesar watched Lauro walk to his pack, which was in one of the back rooms. "There goes a man who just a few days ago was a boy. I wish I had a son like that.'' He turned and started walking to the stairs of his office. There were holes all up and down those stairs. He shook his head. "I wonder how in the hell he made it up these stairs alive?'' Caesar just kept shaking his head as he reached his office.

Lauro took his shower and scrubbed with the strong homemade soap for a long time. He let the water run over his head. Finally feeling decent, he stepped out, dried himself, and put on clean clothes and walked to the kitchen. He felt he could eat. "Albert, my friend, do you have a steak lying around here somewhere? I'm hungry as a bear."

"Yes sir, Mr. Lauro. I'll have you fixed up in a minute." Albert made a juicy steak, potato and onions, beans, and *pan de campo*. Lauro drank water because he was still dehydrated. Albert came out with the can of molasses and set it down on the table; then he sat himself down across from Lauro.

Lauro knew he wanted to talk. "The ladies are washing your clothes. Well, what's left of them. You came awful close to getting shot, Mr. Lauro. You came awful close," he said. He shook his large head. "You know, I wasn't scared when we were fighting, but when it was over I just shook and shook, and I cried a bit. I'm not ashamed to say it. I was scared. It is sure good to be alive, isn't it, Mr. Lauro?"

"Yes, it sure is, Albert. It's a feeling that you get after you come through something like this. Everything tastes better. You see things more clearly, the air you breath smells sweeter, and you feel more alive than you ever have before. You did good out there. I'm proud to call you my friend," Lauro said. He stuck his hand out to the big paw that Albert offered. They shook hands.

"You know," Albert said. "That Mr. Gay with the Immigration Service and those other friends of his were talking to those reporters from the newspapers that came from all over. They sounded like they were the only ones who fought. They hardly mentioned you and Mr. Frank, who fought just as bravely as the next man. In fact, if you hadn't gone up the stairs to get the ammunition and killed the leader of the bandidos, we'd all be dead now. It sounded like Mr. Gay and his friends killed him themselves, and you and I weren't even here."

"I wouldn't make much of that, Albert. The men who count know the truth of the Battle of Norias, and that's all that matters. Many men will say they were here, but you and I know who is telling the truth and who is lying. I'm just glad to be alive.

"Albert, thanks for the meal. You saved my life. I mean . . . Well, you know what I mean." They both began laughing till tears came from their eyes. All the tension of the last two days came out of them.

"Thanks again. I'm going to sleep. Don't wake me unless the house is burning." He made his way to his bed, where he took off his clothes and fell asleep. Lauro slept all the rest of that afternoon till the next afternoon. He got up, ate supper and slept till morning.

Albert was making breakfast when he walked into the kitchen and got a cup of coffee. He felt rested but drugged by the long sleep. The coffee was good and hot, and he began to feel like a man again. After breakfast, Lauro went to the corrals to get Lobo and put his saddle on him. He looked at the place where Scar had fallen. He was gone, picked up and buried with the rest of his *companeros.*

Lauro was tying his bedroll and slicker to the back of his saddle when Mr. Caesar came out of the kitchen. "Where can I write to get hold of you?"

"You can write to me in San Perlita, just address it to The Laurel Ranch, they'll know where to reach me." They shook hands.

"Here." Mr. Caesar handed him an envelope with his pay.

"Thanks, Mr. Caesar. Guess this is it. You've been nothing but great. I appreciate it, thank you."

Albert came out with a package full of food. "Here, for the trip. I'll never forget you, Mr. Lauro, not as long as I live."

"Thank you, Albert." They embraced and shook hands. Lauro waved at the ladies who had came out on the porch to see him off.

He mounted Lobo and turned south. The morning was just starting to warm up. "It's going to be another hot south Texas day. Maybe we'll get a rain. I hope so," he said. He turned in the saddle and waved the last time.

Silva, one of the maids, turned to Albert's wife. "That is one good looking man. I hope he comes back. Do you think he will?"

"I don't know," she said. "There goes a man with a lot on his mind. He's got a lot of forgetting to do before he can do anything else."

20

HOME AGAIN

Lauro stopped to gaze at the Laurel Ranch. The place looked the same, with its white house, barns, and corrals. It was good to see the old place again. For a while he thought he never would see it again. The tall palm trees seemed to be beckoning for him to ride on in. It had taken two days for Lauro to get there. The sun was about to go down, and he imagined his mother getting supper ready. The girls had all gotten married in the last three years and moved away. He wished he could have seen them.

He had done a lot of thinking along the way. He had camped and enjoyed all the peace and quiet, the many sea birds, done some fishing, and just laid around.

Lauro didn't like killing. He was trying to figure out why men wanted to kill other men. He was taught to respect life, to believe that there was a God who had made the Commandments so man could live in peace and enjoy the fruits of his labor. He could raise children to carry on when he was gone, so that the legacy that was given to him by his father and his father before him wouldn't die. That legacy had to be protected at all costs. There were always men who wanted to take that away.

Lauro had killed in hate—hate for a man who had taken a part of that legacy away from him. He had taken away the true legacy, his grandfather's love. He had killed in self-defense, but still he had gone looking for Scarface, and he had found him. He hoped that God would forgive him.

There were some other things he thought about, but mostly of Reina. Güero had said that in time he would forget, but how much time is enough? He still loved her with all his heart. He couldn't figure out why she hadn't written. She just let their love go like it never meant anything to her, just a plaything she had tired of and threw away. He made up his mind that he would forget her. He had tried to write to her, but his letters were never answered, so it was time to move on. He was young, there would be others. Maybe there would be one who was for him. Like Güero had said.

He felt rested and glad to be home, he gave the signal—a mournful call that he was taught long ago by Vallejo. It was sad, but sounded beautiful to the cattleman. Family rushed out of the house, waving and whooping, running around and laughing. They knew it was Lauro. He was home. What a glorious day.

He rode into the yard and rushed into his mother's arms. "Mi hijo, mi hijo, you are safe." Tears ran down her cheeks. "Thanks to God, and the Holy Virgin Mary, thank God." She kissed him all over his face again and again and held him tight.

"Mama, it's so good to see you. Thank God you're all safe."

"Here woman, let a man welcome his son. You've had him long enough." He felt his father's arms around him. They were strong and he could feel the love behind each *"abrazo."* "My son, welcome home. Welcome."

Next was his brother, Esteban. "Welcome, brother."

"Welcome home. You've grown taller, mi hermano. You look good." They embraced again.

It was Vallejo's turn. They looked at each other, then threw their arms around each other in *abrazo* that only two compadres understood. Vallejo pulled back, looked at Lauro, and smiled. "We will talk later. Go with your family. They've waited a long time for this. Go."

Lauro smiled. "See you later. We will talk. Come let's all go into the house, Mama. What smells so good? Did you fix one of my favorites, *pollo frito?* I have eaten so much beef I feel I'm turning into a cow." They all went into the house, laughing, and talking, with Lauro's arms around his mother.

After supper, they sat at the table and talked. The first thing Lauro wanted to know was how his grandmother and Aunt Alicia were doing? She had written only yesterday, his mother said. She was worried about you. She had dreamed that you had gone through a big storm and you were in great danger. She wondered if we had heard from you. I was going to write to her tonight, but now you can go and show her that you are alive and well, thanks be to God. She reached out and held his hand. Lauro marveled at his grandmother's ability to know when one of the family was in danger.

"Let's go out on the porch and smoke," his father said. "I wish to talk to my sons." He stood up and left the table. She smiled and watched her men going out to the porch. How proud she was of all her men.

His father took out his favorite pipe and the rest lit their smokes. He looked at Lauro. "We heard there was a raid at Norias, that you were there and many were killed. If it doesn't bother you too much, please, tell us about it."

Lauro told them about the raid on Norias, everything except that Scarface had been the leader. "There were brave men on both sides. Among the bandits, there were brave men driven by their greed. Among the defenders, there were brave men in desperation to save their lives. I now know what it is to fight for your life. I know what it is to be driven to the very edge. It's something I never want to feel again," Lauro said. "I thought I would never see you again, but thanks be to God, He must have heard your prayers."

His father reached out and gave him an *abrazo,* "I'm proud of you," he said. "It was God's will that you be spared, and we thank him for that."

"There is something else, something I haven't mentioned, something that will mean everything to this family." They were looking at each other except Vallejo, who kept looking at Lauro.

"What is it my son, what is so important to this family?" his father asked.

"The leader of the bandits was Scarface Colorado. He'll never hurt this family again," Lauro said. His father choked on the smoke from his pipe, and started coughing. Steven rose from his chair. Vallejo grabbed Lauro's arms and held them with a grip of death.

"Are you sure?" he asked. "Are you sure?"

"Yes, Vallejo, I killed him," Lauro said, looking directly into his eyes. "And I told him that you were the one who taught me, just before he died."

Vallejo took Lauro in his arms. "Thank you compadre, thank you. You don't know how much that means to me." He turned away and walked into the darkness. No one followed. They left him to his own thoughts.

His father looked at his son. "Lauro, you killed Scarface?" he said in a whisper. "You killed him?"

"Yes, Father, *mano a mano*. I gave him a chance he never gave grandfather, and he knew who I was and that I was going to end his miserable life. He'll never hurt anyone again."

"Thank God. It was his destiny to die at the hands of a Cavazos. Now your grandfather can rest in peace, and we can go on with our lives. The wheel has made a complete circle. Thank you, my son. I must tell the families of the men who died with your grandfather. May they all rest in peace now." He left the porch and headed to the homes of the workers, who were just a little way from the main house.

Lauro looked at Esteban. His brother was looking at him in a new light, as if he had lifted a big burden off everyone's back. "Lauro, I know what you are going through. It must have cost you a lot to kill a man, but you did the right thing by ending his life. You have saved so many good people from going through what this family has gone through all these years. It was God's will."

"Thank you, Steven. I want to talk to Vallejo alone. Do you mind?" Lauro said.

"No, go ahead. I'll go help Papa tell the families of the cowboys we lost. May it never happen again."

He left and Lauro headed toward the corrals where he could see the red glare of Vallejo's cigarette. "Vallejo, may I talk to you?"

"Of course, my friend. There is no one I would rather talk to than you right now." He was smoking the last of the cigarette and threw the butt away. He looked at Lauro. "He told you, didn't he?"

"Yes. The son of a bitch told me how it all happened. He knew that you had gotten your revenge through me. You should have seen his face when I told him that you had taught me, may he burn in hell."

"I wish I could've been there, but you handled it just like I taught you. Praise to God, it's over." They embraced in the strongest of friendships.

The next morning, he told his mother he was going to see his grandmother in Brownsville. He said he might not be back for some time, and that he would write to tell them where he was. Vallejo understood, his father and Esteban understood, but his mother would never understand. He saddled Lobo, said his good-byes and headed toward Brownsville, Texas.

Lauro arrived in Brownsville, late that afternoon. The sun had almost disappeared on that old mission town.

He followed the railroad tracks till he came to the main office. His old friend Mr. Carter was just closing shop.

"Howdy, Mr. Carter, how have you been?" Lauro said.

"Why hello, Larry. Boy, it's good to see you. Everyone is talking about the battle at Norias and how you just about won it single handed. They're ready to elect you Sheriff. I say they couldn't find a more deserving person. How about it, will you take the job?"

Lauro looked at him, and shook his head. "No, but thanks anyway." He rode on to his grandmother's home.

She was waiting on the porch for him. Tia Alicia was there also. They were crying softly at the sight of him. They took him in their arms and held him, praising God for his safe return.

After supper, he and his grandmother went out on the porch to talk privately. He helped her into her favorite rocking chair. How beautiful she was. The lines in her face made her beauty more pronounced. The blue eyes and the strong carriage of her frail body. Lauro was so proud of her. She was the picture of the women who settled this country. All of the hardships they had to endure to be with their man and bear children who could carry on when they were gone. The droughts that were so prevalent in this Wild Horse Desert. During the hot summer, except for drinking, every drop of water was used to keep the horses alive. Without the horses, all would surely perish.

Then it would rain until everything was flooded. The cattle would bunch up on the high ground and stay there till they had grazed all of the grass. Then if they weren't moved they would starve to death. Many times, those women would have to go with their men to push the cattle to another spot where there was grass, sometimes having to swim their horses to get to the cattle.

There were hurricanes that came with their terrible winds, bringing tornadoes, and destroying everything in their paths. With the Indians, bandits, and the sickness, he wondered how these people had survived in the Wild Horse Desert.

There was a slight breeze blowing from the southeast of town. A lover was serenading his girl somewhere in the night. He had a clear voice that the evening breeze was carrying clear across town. The bull bats were already feeding on the night insects. They heard the rustling of the leaves of the tall palms. A child crying for its mother, and a carriage going somewhere on the cobble streets of the town.

His grandmother sighed. "How beautiful the night sounds are. They carry across this old town to let you know that all is well and that it's almost time to prepare for bed and sleep, perchance to dream, as Mr. Shakespeare would say.'' They both laughed. Lauro rolled a smoke but didn't light it. It was just something to do with his hands. His grandmother looked at him with tears in her eyes. ''Tell me about it. I know that you went through a most horrible time, but sometimes it helps to talk about it.''

''I want to tell you about the fight at Norias, but I don't know how you'll feel about it. It's so strange to be sitting next to you here, after what has happened to me over these past three years,'' Lauro said. ''I don't know where to start. I have so much to tell you.''

''Well, so why don't you start at the beginning?'' his grandmother said.

So Lauro did. From the beginning he told her of his meeting with the Karankawa Indian, Güero, the Kineños, the King Ranch, the Klebergs, Mrs. King, and Reina.

She could tell by the sound of his voice that his heart had been broken by the girl. She hated her for it.

He told her about the *Paso de los Muertos,* J. B. Bell, and that he didn't think that the Kings had anything to do with the death of her love.

She closed her eyes when Lauro mentioned him. He could tell she was close to tears. He paused for a moment, thinking.

''Go on,'' she whispered. ''Tell me the rest.''

''It was rough. I thought I might never see you or my family again, but God or something was watching over me, and I suspect it was a lot of prayers from you all.'' She smiled.

He looked at her and reached to hold her hand. ''Grandmother, I avenged grandfather's death. I killed Bill James. You remember that was the name of the outlaw they call Scarface, Colorado Red. I shot him dead, face to face, so that he'd know why he had to die for the killings so long ago. He will never hurt this family again, or any family ever. May he get his just reward from God.''

She closed her eyes and squeezed his hand. She cried softly for a long time, but finally the sobs began to subside. She took a lace handkerchief and blew her nose. She looked at Lauro. ''I'm sorry, hijo. All the hurt and hate have been in me for a long time. I think of what could have happened to you and I shudder to even think about it. I'll light some candles for the ones who died at the battle of Norias. We must learn to forgive our enemy as well as ourselves. You did the right thing. You were only protecting yourself and others. It was his choice.

He could have never made that raid, but he chose to try to kill and rob everyone. May God forgive me for saying this, but I'm glad he's dead. Now your grandfather's soul can rest and the souls of the good men who died with him. I can go to my grave knowing that they have been avenged.

"Now, help an old lady up the stairs to her room. Let me tell Alicia in my own way, please."

"Yes, Grandmother, if you think it's best. I know in grandfather's fight she lost the man she was supposed to have married." Lauro helped her up the stairs to her room.

She kissed him. "I know that you have to think this thing about the Kleberg girl out, and you have to mend a broken heart, which is not easy. It will take time, but we learn from our mistakes. Your love for her was doomed from the start. You deserve better than that. It's her loss, not yours. Will you still be here when I arise in the morning?"

"No, I don't think so. I want to be clear of Brownsville when the sun is breaking at first light. Don't ask me where I'm going. I have a lot to think about, a lot to forget. I just might go see my friends in Mexico. It's been a long time."

"Very well. Please write so we know everything is alright and you are well. Go with God, my Son." She kissed him one last time. He watched her go into her room and close the door.

The next morning he had already crossed the Rio Grande river at his favorite spot when the sun rose over the Wild Horse Desert. A sea of gold covered the San Juan de Carricitos Land Grant and the Laguna Madre. He looked back at the beautiful sight. He had a long way to go to reach Fort San Miguel and Teresa. Maybe she would help him forget. But for now waves of thoughts poured in an out of Lauro's mind as he rode the trail.

He tried to put Reina out of his mind by concentrating on the King Ranch, Kingsville, and the great State of Texas. It had been almost eighty years since the Alamo, San Jacinto, and the independence at Washington on the Brazos. First a republic and then a state, larger and more prosperous than many entire countries in the world. Built by pioneers—cattlemen, farmers, ranchers, developers, and entrepreneurs willing to risk it all, including their lives, for a chance at success. And success meant bigger, and better, and more wealth. Texas had become known all over the world as the hot spot, the breeding ground, the shining example of what man can do when given the freedom take the risk of that success. A freedom that was bought with blood.

But he couldn't help keep coming back to the thoughts about the Land Grants, and the Anglos who had the guns and the gold. And of course, the political influence. And even though the Mexican-Americans and those of Spanish blood were good enough to fight side by side for that freedom, now they weren't good enough to own the land and other resources, or to, heaven forbid, marry their daughters. God, how can life be fair? But of course, it isn't fair and He never said it would be. Only that we are able to handle it. Lauro was having a hard time handling it, but he'd been in other fights most of his life, and won, and this was another one he would have to win.

As he had always believed, we play the hand we are dealt as best we can. Every hand is a loser, and every hand a winner, depending on how we play the game. Some things were not meant to be. A life with Reina evidently was one of them. Either accept it now and forget it, or go on the rest of life living with heartache. How many times had he said to himself, *Que sera, sera*? This just was another time.

He would convince himself that Reina would always be happy, sweet lovable creature that she was, and always have the attention and love she desired. But somewhere in her heart there would forever be a spot of sadness for her first love, the cowboy from the Wild Horse Desert.

THE END

Don Lauro Cavazos in later years

BLOOD WILL TELL

In 1915, after the Norias battle, Lauro Cavazos rode into Mexico to find solace, to sort out his life, and to recover from his hurt. Two years later, in 1917, he returned to Texas, enlisted in the U.S. Army cavalry (field artillery), and was sent overseas to fight in World War I.

After the war he married Thomasa Quintanilla, went back to work at the King Ranch, and in 1926 was made foreman of the Santa Gertrudis Division where he remained until his death in 1958. Thomasa's family, the Quintanillas and the Alvarezes, descended from the original group hired by Captain King at the village of Cruillas, in Tamaulipas, Mexico.

The Kineños had great respect for Lauro and called him Don Lauro, the godfather. They took their problems to him, asked permission for marriage, relied on his decision to settle disputes, and in nearly everything in their lives they first would ask "Don Lauro" if it was all right.

Lauro Cavazos was a sixth generation Texan, descended from the original Jose Narciso Cavazos who received the land grant, the San Juan de Carricitos Land Grant, directly from the King of Spain.

Lauro and Thomasa had five children. The children are seventh generation Texans.

Their daughter, Sarita Cavazos Ochoa, taught school for forty years before her retirement.

Dr. Lauro F. Cavazos, Jr., was president of Texas Tech University and was appointed Secretary of Education in the presidential cabinets of Presidents Reagan and Bush.

Richard E. Cavazos followed a military career and was a Four Star General in the United States Army. Thirty six years after the Norias raid and battle, Richard, then a Second Lieutenant, defended a hill in Korea where he was awarded his first Distinguished Service Cross (D.S.C.) for bravery.

Joseph A. Cavazos is a retired executive from Sears and Roebuck and Co.

Bobby Cavazos is the author of this book. Bobby went to Texas Tech University in Lubbock, Texas, and was selected All American for his success as a running back for the football team. His professional career in the NFL with the Chicago Cardinals was cut short by an injury and he returned to Texas Tech to complete his R.O.T.C. program. He became an officer in the U. S. military, and after serving his time, he returned to the King Ranch, where he was made foremen of the Laureles Division. His experiences with his father, Lauro, and as foreman himself, provided him with in depth knowledge of the King Ranch operation, its history, and the basis for the writing of this book.

Epilogue Two

HISTORICAL FACT AND FICTION

In 1915 German agents were hiring bandits for raids in Texas, New Mexico and California to draw attention away from the war in Europe. They promised to give back to Mexico the land that was lost to the United States. The raid on the Norias Division of the King Ranch, caused by these German agents, was real.

Scarface Colorado was fiction, but he signifies all that was evil in those days. Scarface was necessary to tell the real story of what happened and how the defenders felt. They were scared. Why defend a little spot in the middle of the Wild Horse Desert? It wasn't theirs. Only Lauro had a real claim to the San Juan de Carricitos Land Grant, and it now belonged to the King ranch. They all could have died there. They received no reward from the King Ranch, much less a thank you.

Lauro Cavazos shot the leader's horse and then the leader himself. That stopped the charge. The little band of defenders would have been overrun. Lauro did save the whole outfit by going up the stairs, under heavy fire, and getting the ammunition. No one else would go. He also recognized Tom Tate's voice and kept the Rangers from getting shot when they were returning that dark morning after the fight.

Lauro's family has always served this country when called upon, just as when he was called upon to defend his ancestors' land at the Norias Division Headquarters.

The woman killed by the Mexican bandits was killed just the way it is described. The second leader of the bandits killed her after he took over.

The African-American, Albert, fought as bravely as any man there. He was Lauro's friend.

Jose Lopez, the boy on the mule who warned them about the bandits, did work for Lauro later at the Santa Gertrudis Division and was one of the best cowboys they had.

The Texas Rangers were there, doing their duty. The problem was, they went the wrong way and missed the main battle. The soldiers from the 12th Cavalry from Harlingen, Texas, fought bravely.

There never was any conclusion about the rumor that the Rangers shot the wounded Mexicans. Lauro never talked about it.

J. B. Bell is purely a fictitious character, representing the big political bosses of those days who profited off the Mexican people.

The failed kidnapping in Brownsville, the mortgage on the San Juan de Carricitos Land Grant and the rustling of the cattle are fiction. However the economic hardships of the 1800's due to Mexico's demands for trading only with Mexico and not letting settlers in Texas trade with Louisiana, Arkansas and the southeastern part of the United states was one of the main causes of the Texas Revolution.

The sinking of the steamboat in the Rio Grande with many titles to Spanish Land Grants allowed the Bourland-

Miller commission in the 1850's to invalidate many land grants.

The relocation of the village to Texas from Mexico by Captain King is true. There is some necessary literary license used in crafting the language of the participants.

The Karankawa Indian tribe was real. They were there before the Spaniards came and were the very first owners of the Wild Horse Desert. The chief was fiction, but included to make the point about the original ownership. The tribe no longer exists.

La Chista, the cow outfit's cook; Güero Mendietta, the Caporal; and Martin Mendietta, Jr., the Segundo, were all real people and dearly loved by the author. I thank them for teaching me how to be a real vaquero. Also I want to thank them for some of the happiest days of my life.

Adios! I'll see you down the road!

Bobby

Glossary

Alemán - German
Agua - water
Bandoleros - leather straps to carry extra ammunition
Bastard and bastardo - bastard
Cama - bed
Camino de los bueys - road of the oxen
Canelo - cinnamon
Carne guisada - stewed meat
Carne seca - dried meat
Chico - boy
Chile petins - a very hot little pepper
Chivarras - chaps
Cuchillo - large, long knife
Cicatriz - scar
Cocina - kitchen
Colorado - red
Come te fue? - How did it go?
Como amancistes - Good morning
Con salud - Good health to you
Conejo - rabbit
Caporal - boss of the cowboys - cow boss
Corrida - cow outfit, cowboy crew (Texican)
Cuidado - "look out" or be careful
Esta el Coronel? - Is the colonel here?
Frontera - border
Ganado - livestock
Granhero - thorny brush
Grito - to shout - scream out
Güero - blond or blonde
Gusto - with pleasure
Hermano - brother
Hijo - son
Hombre - man
Huevos rancheros - eggs with hot sauce
Jaccal - hut
Jefe - leader, chief
Joven - young man
Kineños - King Ranch men
La Perla - the pearl
Laurel - bay tree
Lindo muchacho - handsome young man
Los Olmos Creek - The Elm Creek

Glossary

Mano-a-mano - (slang) man to man
Mariposa - butterfly
Mescal - liquor made of maguey plant
Mi amor, mi vida, mi corazon -My love, my life, my heart
Mi compadre - my friend
Mi padre - my father
Mojados - slang for workers who cross border
Monte - thick brush
Muy bien, hay cafe? - Very well, is there coffee?
Pajaro - bird
Paloma - dove
Pan de campo - flat round bread
Pan dulce - sweet bread, a cookie
Paso de los muertos - river "crossing of the dead"
Patrón - boss
Payaso - clown
Pela el ojo - look with caution (Tex-Mex, Texican)
Pistoleros - gunmen
Pollo frito - fried chicken
Por nada, senor - It was nothing, sir
Primos - cousins
Puta - whore
Que paso? - What happened?
Que paso, chico? - What happened, boy?
Reina - queen
Remuda - herd of horses
Remudeo - horse herder
Resaca - overflow lake, holds water
Rincon - corner
San Perlita - town name
Segundo - second in command
Si, como no - Yes, of course
Tia - aunt
Tienda - store
Tortillas de harena - flour tortillas
Tu solo tu - you alone, only you
Vallejo - person/family name
Vamanos, brutos - Let's go, brutes
Vaquero - cowboy
Venado - deer
Viejo - old